Praise for

MYSTERIOUS SKIN

"What Mr. Heim seems to want to do here is inhabit the mysterious skin of the anti-heroic and artlessly perverse. He does this less to flout convention and more because he seems hungry to explore extreme forms of experience." —*New York Times*

"The ending left me with tears in my eyes—which is about the highest praise I can make of a novel."   —*Philadelphia Inquirer*

"He creates scenes of genuine beauty, . . . and handles his complicated characters and delicate subject matter with calm assurance."   —*Publishers Weekly*

"Heim's real achievement is his artful blend of Dennis Cooper-like 'bad boy' fiction and the coming-of-age/coming-out story."
—*10 Percent*

"[A] quietly affecting first novel . . . *Mysterious Skin* impresses."
—*Swing*

"Perfectly capturing the essence of the 80s, Heim will take you back ten years and jolt your mind into today, all at the same time."   —*Pitch Weekly*

"This book explores new frontiers of sexuality in unexpected areas—like western Kansas. Insightful and beautifully written."   —William S. Burroughs, writer, painter, recording artist

"Eerie, precise, emotionally complex, quietly charismatic, and full of grace, *Mysterious Skin* is one of the most accomplished and mysteriously pleasurable first novels I've read in years."
—Dennis Cooper, author of *Try* and *Frisk*

"With uncommon poetry and clarity, Scott Heim paints a devastating portrait of a new Lost Generation. *Mysterious Skin* will haunt and enrage you. I am awestruck by Heim's courage. Read this book."   —Connie May Fowler, author of *Sugar Cage* and *River of Hidden Dreams*

MYSTERIOUS SKIN

A NOVEL

SCOTT HEIM

HarperPerennial
A Division of HarperCollins*Publishers*

Grateful acknowledgment is made for permission to reprint lyrics from the song "Here by Chance" by Breathless, words by Dominic Appleton, © 1989.

A hardcover edition of this book was published in 1995 by HarperCollins Publishers.

HarperCollins books may be purchased for educational, business, or sales promotional use. For information, please write: Special Markets Department, HarperCollins Publishers, Inc., 10 East 53rd Street, New York, NY 10022.

First HarperPerennial edition published 1996.

Designed by Nancy Singer

The Library of Congress has catalogued the hardcover edition as follows:

Heim, Scott.
    Mysterious skin : a novel / Scott Heim. — 1st ed.
    292 p. ; 21 cm.
    ISBN 0-06-017175-8
    1. Young men—Kansas—Fiction. 2. Sexually abused children—Kansas—Fiction. 3. Kansas—Fiction. I. Title.
PS3558.E4527M87   1995
813'.54—dc20   95-140969

ISBN 0-06-092686-4 (pbk.)

97 98 99 00 ❖/RRD 10 9 8 7 6 5 4 3

for Tamyra Heim
and for Jamie Reisch
before, during, after

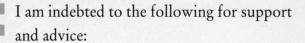

I am indebted to the following for support and advice:

Carolyn Doty, Louise Quayle, and Robert Jones; Jill Bauerle, Darren Brown, Michael Burkin, Eryk Casemiro, Dennis Cooper, Pamela Erwin, Donna Goertz, Marion Heim, Tamyra Heim, Anthony Knight, Eamonn Maguire, Denise Marcil, Kirk McDonald, Perry McMahon, Anne-Marie O'Farrell, Mike Peterson, Jamie Reisch, Scott Savaiano, and Helen Schulman.

part one

B L U E

1981, 1983, 1987

one

BRIAN LACKEY

The summer I was eight years old, five hours disappeared from my life. I can't explain. I remember this: first, sitting on the bench during my Little League team's 7 P.M. game, and second, waking in the crawl space of my house near midnight. Whatever happened during that empty expanse of time remains a blur.

When I came to, I opened my eyes to darkness. I sat with my legs pushed to my chest, my arms wrapped around them, my head sandwiched between my knees. My hands were clasped so tightly they hurt. I unfolded slowly, like a butterfly from its cocoon.

I brushed a sleeve over my glasses, and my eyes adjusted. To my right, I saw diagonal slits of light from a small door. Zillions of dust motes fluttered through the rays. The light stretched ribbons across a cement floor to illuminate my sneaker's rubber toe. The room around me seemed to shrink, cramped with shadows, its ceiling less than three feet tall. A network of rusty pipes lined a paint-spattered wall. Cobwebs clogged their upper corners.

My thoughts clarified. I was sitting in the crawl space of our house, that murky crevice beneath the porch. I wore my Little League uniform and cap, my Rawlings glove on my left hand. My stomach ached. The skin on both wrists was rubbed raw. When I breathed, I felt flakes of dried blood inside my nose.

Noises drifted through the house above me. I recognized the lull of my sister's voice as she sang along to the radio. "Deborah," I yelled. The music's volume lowered. I heard a doorknob twisting; feet clomping down stairs. The crawl space door slid open.

I squinted at the sudden light that spilled from the adjoining basement. Warm air blew against my skin; with it, the familiar, sobering smell of home. Deborah leaned her head into the square, her hair haloed and silvery. "Nice place to hide, Brian," she joked. Then she grimaced and cupped her hand over her nose. "You're bleeding."

I told her to get our mother. She was still at work, Deborah said. Our father, however, lay sleeping in the upstairs bedroom. "I don't want him," I said. My throat throbbed when I spoke, as if I'd been screaming instead of breathing. Deborah reached farther into the crawl space and gripped my shoulders, shimmying me through the door, pulling me back into the world.

Upstairs, I walked from room to room, switching on lights with my baseball glove's damp leather thumb. The storm outside hammered against the house. I sat on the living room floor with Deborah and watched her lose at solitaire again and again. After she had finished close to twenty games, I heard our mother's car in the driveway as she arrived home from her graveyard shift. Deborah swept the cards under the sofa. She held the door open. A blast of rain rushed in, and my mother followed.

The badges on my mother's uniform glittered under the lights. Her hair dripped rain onto the carpet. I could smell her combination of leather and sweat and smoke, the smell of the prison in Hutchinson where she worked. "Why are you two still awake?" she asked. Her mouth's oval widened.

She stared at me as if I wasn't her child, as if some boy with vaguely aberrant features had been deposited on her living room floor. "Brian?"

My mother took great care to clean me. She sprinkled expensive, jasmine-scented bath oil into a tub of hot water and directed my feet and legs into it. She scrubbed a soapy sponge over my face, delicately fingering the dried blood from each nostril. At eight, I normally would never have allowed my mother to bathe me, but that night I didn't say no. I didn't say much at all, only giving feeble answers to her questions. Did I get hurt on the baseball field? Maybe, I said. Did one of the other moms whose sons played Little League in Hutchinson drive me home? I think so, I answered.

"I told your father baseball was a stupid idea," she said. She kissed my eyelids shut. I pinched my nose; took a deep breath. She guided my head under the level of sudsy water.

The following evening I told my parents I wanted to quit Little League. My mother directed a told-you-so smile at my father. "It's for the better," she said. "It's obvious he got hit in the head with a baseball or something. Those coaches in Hutchinson don't care if the kids on their teams get hurt. They just need to cash their weekly checks."

But my father marshaled the conversation, demanding a reason. In addition to his accounting job, he volunteered as part-time assistant coach for Little River's high school football and basketball teams. I knew he wanted me to star on the sports fields, but I couldn't fulfill his wish. "I'm the youngest kid on the team," I said, "and I'm the worst. And no one likes me." I expected him to yell, but instead he stared into my eyes until I looked away.

My father strode from the room. He returned dressed in one of his favorite outfits: black coaching shorts and a LITTLE

RIVER REDSKINS T-shirt, the mascot Indian preparing to toss a bloodstained tomahawk at a victim. "I'm leaving," he said. Hutchinson had recently constructed a new softball complex on the city's west end, and my father planned to drive there alone, "Since no one else in this family seems to care about the ball games anymore."

After he left, my mother stood at the window until his pickup became a black speck. She turned to Deborah and me. "Well, good for him. Now we can make potato soup for dinner." My father hated potato soup. "Why don't you two head up to the roof," my mother said, "and let me get started."

Our house sat on a small hill, designating our roof as the highest vantage point in town. It offered a view of Little River and its surrounding fields, cemetery, and ponds. The roof served as my father's sanctuary. He would escape there after fights with my mother, leaning a ladder against the house and lazing in a chair he had nailed to the space beside the chimney where the roof leveled off. The chair's pink cushions leaked fleecy stuffing, and decorative gold tacks trailed up its wooden arms. The chair was scarred with what appeared to be a century's worth of cat scratches, water stains, and scorched cavities from cigarette burns. I would hear my father above me during his countless insomniac nights, his shoe soles scraping against the shingles. My father's presence on the roof should have been a comfort, a balm against my fear of the dark. But it wasn't. When his rage became too much to handle, my father would swear and stomp his boot, the booming filling my room and paralyzing me. I felt as though he were watching me through wood and nails and plaster, an obstinate god cataloging my every move.

Deborah and I frequented the roof for other reasons. On that night, like most nights that summer, we carried two things there: a pair of binoculars and a board game. Our favorite was Clue. We unfolded it on the chair seat and sat cross-legged on the shingles. On the box cover, the six "suspects" relaxed before a ritzy fireplace. Deborah always picked the elegant Miss Scarlet. I alternated between Professor Plum and crotchety Miss Peacock. The candlestick was absent from the group of weapons, so I'd replaced it with a toothpick I'd plucked from the garbage, its surface pocked with my father's teeth marks.

As usual, Deborah clobbered me. She announced her verdict in a voice that echoed over Little River's homes: "Colonel Mustard, in the study, with the wrench."

On the other side of town, the lofty spotlights that circled the ball park flickered on. Little River's adult softball teams—"rinky-dinks" my father called them, and he refused to watch such amateurs—competed there three nights a week. It seemed as though half the population of Kansas belonged to some sort of ball team that summer. Between our turns at Clue, Deborah and I grabbed the binoculars and focused on the field. We watched the players' bodies as they jogged through the green quarter-circle of the outfield. We kept track of the score by zooming in on the electronic scoreboard at the left-field fence.

A cottonwood tree towered beside our house. The wind blew seeds loose from its inferno of branches as we solved our murders. By summer's core, the green pods were splitting, and white cotton tufts butterflied through the air to fall on the roof, the game board, our heads. We knelt beside the chair and waited for our mother to call us to dinner. Dusk swept its inks across the sky, and she finally stuck her head from the kitchen window and hollered, "Potatoes!"

"We get to eat without him," Deborah said. We left the roof, ran into the kitchen, and began to eat, the potato soup our conspiracy. My mother had thickened the soup with crumbled chunks of homemade zwieback, and as I spooned them into my mouth I stared at my father's empty chair. It loomed larger than the other three. I imagined he had swallowed an invisibility pill; we couldn't see him, but we could *feel* his presence.

That night, I did something I'd never done before: I wet the bed. The next morning, I rose with my skin drenched, partly in sweat from the summer heat, and partly from the urine that soaked the sheet. My father stepped into the room, spiced from his morning cologne, decked out in the corduroy suit he wore to the office. I felt the muscles cramping in my chest. "You're nearly nine goddamn years old," he yelled. "And Pampers doesn't make diapers in your size." My mother blamed it on confused hormones, allergies from a new detergent, even something as simple as downing too much potato soup or too many glasses of water.

Not long after that, I began fainting without warning. "The blackouts," Deborah and I called them. They would come unpredictably, at erratic intervals, over the rest of my childhood and adolescence—as often as once a week, as few as once a year. My eyes would roll into my head, and I would drop like a shot deer. I felt emptied, as though my stomach and lungs and heart had been sucked from my body's midsection. When the school year arrived again, my classmates believed I faked the blackouts. They invented nicknames to refer to those times my senses clicked off and I fell to the classroom floor. Nutcase, they called me. Fake-fuck. Liar, Liar, Pants on Fire.

That summer, the summer of '81, the blackouts were both frequent and severe. My mother took me to Dr. Kaufman, the most expensive and revered of Little River's trio of doctors. His office sat on the top floor of an historic hotel, our town's most famous building and, at five stories, its tallest. His waiting room smelled like disinfectant and bandages; the smell made me woozy. "The doctor will be ready shortly," the receptionist told my mother. I lounged beside a potted fern, skimmed through women's magazines, and silently prayed I didn't have a disease.

Dr. Kaufman wore a bow tie, a tweed cap, and a white robe. He ushered me into his office and propped me on his table. I held my breath when the stethoscope's tip grazed my chest. "Like an ice cube, isn't it?" he said.

Dr. Kaufman questioned me about the fainting spells, and he furnished my mother with a checklist of possible food allergies. "Do you honestly think his problems stem from food?" my mother asked. She guessed that my first "spell" must have happened during that final Little League game. "Someone could have knocked Brian with a bat," she told the doctor. "A mild concussion, maybe?"

The doctor nodded. Perhaps that explained why I didn't remember who had driven me home or what had happened during that five-hour void. "Call me if something like this happens again," he said. When he touched the back of my neck, his fingers felt chillier than the stethoscope.

Two things defined my father's life: food and sports. Since I had disappointed him by quitting baseball, I decided to share in his passion for eating. I fixed hot dogs, bowls of popcorn, and lemon-lime gelatin, grapes buoyed beneath the molded surface like infant jellyfish. I climbed the ladder to the roof and served him. We ate together in silence.

One afternoon, as usual, the paperboy dropped the *Hutchinson News* on our doorstep. My father stopped my mother from slicing potatoes. "We'll eat out tonight," he said. He pointed to a quarter-page feature in the paper where an eaterie called McGillicuddy's advertised four hamburgers for a dollar. My father made enough money to treat us to dinner at Hutchinson's priciest restaurant, but he never did.

McGillicuddy's walls displayed photographs of fifties movie stars. The salad bar was built into the interior of a genuine fifties convertible, its dark purplish red the identical color of the sliced beets that filled one of the salad bowls. We ordered our burgers and stuffed ourselves. When my father looked at me, I pretended to be enjoying the most sumptuous feast ever prepared. He smiled as he chewed, nearly intoxicated by good food at an inexpensive price. Our waitress sported penciled-on eyebrows, drawn into her forehead's center. Her name tag said MARJEAN and I'M HERE TO MAKE YOUR MEAL AN EXPERIENCE.

Deborah couldn't finish her burger, so my father wolfed it down. Outside the restaurant, a fire from Hutchinson's dump lazily corkscrewed its smoke in the distance. In the parking lot, a young couple danced the two-step. The woman's dress sashayed around their ankles. My mother watched them, the edge of her water glass poised against her bottom lip.

On the drive home, my father hummed along to AM radio. We passed immense stretches of milo and corn, meadows overgrown with sunflowers, and wheat fields where combines rested like sentries waiting for the upcoming harvest. We passed bankrupt gas stations and fruit stands selling tomatoes, cucumbers, and rhubarb stalks. Deborah and I stared through our respective windows, barriered from their world by the dark vinyl seats.

Midway between Hutchinson and Little River, my father braked and muttered, "Shit almighty." A huge turtle lumbered along the stretch of asphalt ahead of us, painstakingly making its way toward a pond at the edge of a field where alfalfa plants stretched their purple blooms. The turtle was a snapper, its legs as thick as sausages. My father bounded from the car. He opened the trunk and pulled out a gunnysack filled with tools. From the backseat, Deborah and I heard the clang as he dumped hammers and screwdrivers and wrenches into the trunk.

My mother got out to help. The angle of her body displayed her discontent as she walked toward him, hands on her hips. She bent down. The turtle hissed at them, its ancient jaws clapping shut. My father stepped on its marbled back, slid the gunnysack's mouth beneath its body, and booted it in. "Meat," he said. He carried the sack to the trunk, arms held stiff in front of him.

Deborah nudged me and rolled her eyes. She started to say something, but my father poked his head into our backseat window. "Tomorrow night, your mother will make turtle steaks."

I skipped upstairs early that night, because I feared what might happen. I busied myself by scrubbing an old toothbrush over a lemon-colored urine stain on last night's bedsheet. As I was pulling pajamas from my dresser, my father tapped his usual one-two-three on my bedroom door, just as I'd expected. "Brian," he said, "I need help in the backyard."

I rewadded the pj's into the drawer and followed my father. He was dressed in jeans and tennis shoes. He clutched a knife, which glinted under the back porch light. He walked to the car, lifted the trunk, and hoisted the gunnysack into the air, the shape inside writhing and quivering against the burlap.

Earlier that spring, my father had demonstrated the proper way to gut catfish and bass. Now I would learn more. He dumped the hissing turtle onto the grass. "Step on its back," he said. I obeyed. I lifted my head and stared at my room's windows. Up there, I could see the blemished pattern of my ceiling's tiles, part of the wallpaper, and a frantic moth, its powdery wings beating against the globe of my bedroom light.

"Hold it down," my father said. "Put more pressure on it." I looked to the grass. The turtle's head stretched forward. My foot's weight forced it from its shell. My father gripped the knife in his fist, its blade inching toward the neck's craggy skin. The turtle couldn't move. For some reason, I hadn't minded when he'd filleted the fish, but now my strength fizzled. "Step down harder, Brian." The knife slid across the neck, and I saw a sliver of my face reflected in the blade. A gush of blood washed over it. "Dammit, stomp harder." The turtle was still snapping, its head nearly severed. My father sawed farther into its flesh. I couldn't stand. My body weakened, and my foot lifted from the shell.

With the sudden release of pressure, the turtle's blood splashed the toe of my sneaker and my father's jeans. Its jaw closed over the meat of my father's hand, its sharp edge razoring his skin. He yelled. He made one last cut, collected the head in his wounded hand, and stared at me. At that moment, the face wasn't precisely his. It resembled colorless taffy someone had stretched, then bunched back together. He dropped the turtle's head, and it bounced twice on the grass.

My father lifted his arm. I knew he was going to hit me. Before I felt his hand, I passed out, crumpling like a dropped puppet.

I awoke minutes later, sprawled in a living room chair. My father stood over me, smiling, offering me chocolate milk in my favorite cup, the one with a map of Niagara Falls that my parents had saved from their honeymoon. When I finished, my father took the cup from me. "You're better now," he said. "Nothing's the matter with *my* boy." He thumbed a brown trickle of milk from my chin.

The following day my mother cooked turtle steaks. On my plate, the cut of meat resembled a gray island, floating in its river of gravy. "Mmmm," my father said, savoring his first bite. "Brian helped carve these babies," he announced to my mother and Deborah.

The softball complex in Hutchinson sponsored a world-class men's slow-pitch tournament that summer, and my father didn't miss a moment. On Saturday, he finished the remainder of the leftover turtle in the form of a gristly stew my mother had filled with pearl onions and baby carrots. "Sunday school tomorrow morning," he told Deborah and me. He chugged away in his pickup.

My mother sprayed air freshener to immolate the kitchen's meaty smell. "There now, he's all gone." While she sliced potatoes, Deborah and I changed into our pajamas. I turned on the TV.

By the time we finished dinner, that night's comedies and news had ended. A late movie began on channel ten. The plot involved a teenage boy who hid behind a house's walls to spy on the typical American family who lived there. I kept dozing off, secure within the huge fur throw pillow, waking to catch fragments of the movie.

I opened my eyes. Deborah was smacking the side of the TV with her fist. "Haven't even had the thing a year," my mother said, "and it already needs repair." Staticky fuzz displayed itself across the screen, leaking blue beams through the room. The sound was fine—"Let's get out of here," a character screamed—but the picture was faulty.

A car honked from outside. "Someone's pulling in the driveway," my mother said. "His ball games must have ended early."

She opened the door, and a man stepped into the house. He looked about twenty-five. He wore cowboy boots and a threadbare, sleeveless gray sweatshirt. A pinch of snuff bulged behind his bottom lip, and he periodically spit into a plastic cup. "Christ, Margaret," he said to my mother.

"You've got to see this thing I've been following, all the way from the outskirts of Hutchinson."

"You're tanked," my mother said. She spun to face Deborah and me. The TV began whispering and buzzing, and the screen cast shadows over our four faces. Its blue reflected in the man's eyes, something familiar in its color. "Kids," my mother said, "this is Philip Hayes. He works with me at the prison."

"Brian," he said. "Deborah." He knew our names, which surprised me. His hands shook, and the booze on his breath saturated the air of the room. "Come outside." He was speaking to all of us now.

I put my glasses back on, then grabbed my sneakers by the laces and stepped into them. Philip Hayes hustled outside, and we followed him out. The night grew curiously quiet, lacking the regular sonata of crickets and cicadas. The silence made me edgy. Deborah and I passed Philip's Ford pickup, which sat like a dinosaur in our driveway, its humongous wheels jacked up. He had left its door open. "This way," he said. "Around to the north of the house."

He led us to the hillside, the side that faced away from Little River toward the field where my father raised watermelons. "Look there." He pointed to the sky, but the three of us had already seen it: hovering in the night air above our field, a group of soft blue lights.

I stepped forward. My mother gripped my shoulder. "What is it?" she asked. Philip shook his head.

I made out the form of a plane or spaceship. It issued a low hum, like the barely audible drone of machines. It looked like two shallow silver bowls, welded mouth-to-mouth into an oval shape. Lights circled the ship's middle, and they radiated cones of blue. A small rectangular hatchway protruded from the oval's bottom. It shot forth a brighter, almost white spotlight that meandered across the field below and illuminated rows of plants. The spotlight lingered, then retraced its paths, as if searching for some sign of life among the melons. The ship moved through the sky as leisurely as a cloud in a breeze. We stood at the north face of the house, not speaking. When I looked at Deborah, the silvery blue glowed against her face. It gave my own skin a bluish tone that sparkled on the toes of my sneakers, where a crust of turtle blood remained.

"While I was driving out of Hutchinson I saw it flying around," Philip said. He wiped his palm on his sweatshirt and spit snuff onto the grass. "It was going faster then. That white beam kept searching over a field of cattle. I followed it and followed it, and it went right over the sign that says LITTLE RIVER: FIVE MILES. I thought I'd better show this to someone so they won't think I'm nuts."

"It's one of those UFOs," my mother said. The blue lights seemed to intensify, and the humming got louder. My mother lifted her hand from my shoulder and shaded her eyes.

The spaceship began to move farther away, beyond our field, past the town's edge. Its spotlight crowned the tops of trees, giving a white corona to the oak and cottonwood leaves. We craned our necks toward the heavens as we stood on the hill, the two-story house behind us like a portrait's massive frame. I wondered how we looked to whoever or whatever manned the ship. Maybe the ship's inhabitants thought we were a family: Deborah and I were the kids who shared our mother's blond hair; this tall, dark-haired Philip Hayes was our father.

Soon the line of trees blocked the UFO. Its glare remained briefly, then disappeared. "Christ," Philip said. Spit. "I almost thought I was crazy."

"I wonder if anyone else saw it," Deborah said. She still watched the treetops, as if the ship would suddenly come zooming back.

We trudged toward the house, Philip following. As we entered the living room, the television gradually sizzled to life, its picture becoming clear again. In the movie, a policeman drew his gun and blasted the criminal teenager in the chest. An ambulance's wail blended into tinkling, plaintive piano music. "I'll make coffee," my mother told Philip. "He should be back soon." At first I wasn't certain who she meant. I fell onto the fur pillow, and Deborah sat on the floor.

Philip Hayes joined my mother in the kitchen. I heard her open the cabinet, the silverware drawer, the refrigerator. "What do you think—" I started.

"Shhh," Deborah said. In the television's glow, her eyes resembled the jewels of blue lights that orbited the spaceship. *Blue*, I thought.

The screen displayed the movie's closing credits. I lazed back into the softness of the pillow and closed my eyes. As I drifted toward sleep my mind focused on two things, a pair of the summer's images I'd never forget. I saw the cramped room of the crawl space, directly below where Deborah and I were sitting. And then, equal in power and mystery, I saw the UFO, still out there somewhere, levitating the earth.

two

NEIL MCCORMICK

Our new neighbors were losers. They loved spying on us. After sunset, a woman loitered in the street with binoculars. Two men sometimes idled their car along the curb or in the driveway, shining headlights into our living room. Mom and I tolerated it at first. We had just moved across Hutchinson, the fourth time in as many years, to a house on Monroe Street.

One night, less than a week after we'd settled, we heard a honk from outside. Mom upped the TV's volume and drew the blind on the bay window. High beams illuminated her from head to belly like spotlights on a go-go dancer.

"It's that El Camino again," she said. "Only assholes drive those. Well, I'll give them what they want." She began stripping. Her clothes piled on the floor like a miniature tepee. Shorts, blouse, pink underwear. When she finished, she pranced and discoed through the rooms, a dance I'd grown accustomed to. Her skin shone, as white and solid as frozen milk. She resembled a living version of the Venus statue I'd seen in Hutchinson's Carey Park, minus the scratches and misspelled graffiti.

She blew the spies a kiss, then shook her fist. "Screw you." We both giggled. The car sped away, and she dressed.

Later, I curled beside her on the makeshift couch we'd

constructed with red throw pillows. She ran her hand through my hair like a warm brush. We switched channels until we found a horror film. Mom finished her bottle and turned the volume down; we listened to the thunder in the distance. The portable fan blew a few hairs loose from her scarf, and they tumbled across her shoulders. She fell asleep first.

I was almost nine years old, and the new house was half-mine, half-hers. The summer of '81 was just beginning. She snored, her breath heavy and velour against my ear. The movie ended, and a picture flashed on the television: a test-pattern drawing of an angry Cherokee in headdress, numbers and symbols floating above him. Mom stirred in her half-sleep. Her bottom lip grazed my eye. "I'm dreaming about my Neil," she whispered.

During that first week in June, thunderstorms ripped through central Kansas. Podunk towns flooded, dried up, reflooded. One evening, the father-son weatherman team on channel twelve interrupted Mom's favorite sitcom to identify where tornadoes had been spotted. Hutchinson's warning sirens started screaming, and Mom and I rushed next door to take shelter in our new neighbor lady's fruit cellar. A single light bulb dangled on a cord from the ceiling. Peaches and tomatoes floated in Mason jars like the unborn puppies I'd seen in the science lab at school. "This place smells like a fucking sewer," I said. Mom nodded, but Mrs. Something-or-Other appeared as if she'd swallowed chili peppers.

The storm passed. We puddle jumped home. Mom telephoned her current boyfriend, Alfred. He chugged over to pick her up, and they left me in front of the TV. "No work tomorrow, so we're going barhopping," she said. She jabbed my ribs. "Be back in half past a monkey's ass."

An hour later, another branch of the same storm revisited Hutchinson. The sirens echoed through the street. The top corner of the TV screen displayed a sketchy funnel and the word *WARNING*. "Three's Company"'s innuendoed dialogue was replaced by a newsman's monotone. "The National Weather Service has issued a tornado warning for Reno County. Take shelter immediately. Keep clear of windows. If you are in a vehicle, pull to the side of the road, get out, and lie facedown in the ditch. . . ." I'd heard it all before, but for the first time I didn't have Mom to guide me.

I considered running next door again, then decided on Mom's room. Through the window's glass, nuggets of hail mixed with the spattering rain. Car headlights blurred into narrow white trails. The wind almost drowned the siren's noise. I crawled beneath Mom's bed and cupped my palms over my ears. It was dark under there, but I found a lacy negligee and a stack of magazines I hadn't previously seen. Sandwiched between the *House and Garden*s and *Cosmo*s was a ragged copy of *Playgirl*.

I'd riffled through porno magazines at school—a kid used to sneak them from his dad's closet and dole them out at recess. We would draw beards and eye patches on the naked women, then fold them into paper submarines and 747s. But the *Playgirl* was different; I didn't want to deface these models. All of them were males. I slid myself from under the bed, pulled the chain on the lamp, and returned to my hiding place. I skimmed the pages. Sullen-looking men lounged on plush sofas, beside swimming pools, amid a barn's scattered hay.

I focused on "Edward Cunningham"'s series of pictures: he nibbled a strawberry, poured champagne, relaxed in a Jacuzzi, toweled off. He had tanned skin, feathered hair, and, like almost all the other men, a mustache. Edward's was the shade of my "goldenrod" crayon in the Crayola box. The camera had caught the gleamy water beads on his shoulder and the trail of hair below his belly button. I slipped a hand into my Fruit-of-the-Looms.

"Edward" made me forget the storm. When I finished, I realized the sirens had ended. I carefully replaced the magazine exactly as I'd found it. Had the lower corner been dog-eared five minutes earlier? I tiptoed back to bed. Mom and Alfred returned at 3 A.M., and I held my breath, waiting, until certain they'd fallen asleep.

Alfred announced over a plate of sunny-side-ups that a cyclone had touched down three miles from Monroe Street. He drove Mom and me to view the minor damage. The storm had hit hardest in Yoder, a tiny Amish community we sometimes visited to buy sourdough bread or cinnamon rolls. Bearded farmers drove their horse-and-buggies on roads strewn with litter. Mom pointed first to a dead collie sprawled in a ditch, then to a shingle that had speared through a telephone pole. Tree limbs had avalanched onto a block's worth of roofs. "Boring," I said.

We headed back into Hutchinson. "Last night an A-bomb could have hit and I wouldn't have known it," Mom said. She swigged her can of Olympia and pressed it against my forearm.

Alfred stopped at Quik-Trip for another six-pack, then beelined across town to the Hutchinson Chamber of Commerce. He had told Mom how Little League might help keep me out of her hair for the summer months. They escorted me inside. A circle of rowdy kids lingered under a giant American flag, waiting to scribble their names on lists for the summer's baseball teams.

I leaned across a table lined with clipboards. On each page, two columns were labeled NAME and AGE. I had to choose from the Junior Division's twenty-two different teams. "Pick the one that'll win you the trophy," Mom told me. She was shitfaced drunk. A puny kid, his ear sprouting the wire from a hearing aid, pointed at her short pink skirt. If I'd been alone with him, I would have crushed the hearing device in my fist.

I chose the Hutchinson Pizza Palace Panthers. One, because their uniforms were snazzy—a crudely drawn cat leaping from a blue and white pepperoni pie. Two, because I thought the sponsors might treat the team to free pizzas after games. "Your coach's name is Mr. Heider," the balding man behind the sign-up booth said. "He's only been coaching a year, but he's got an enviable record already."

The man handed me a folded baseball jersey and matching pants. The number ninety-nine was emblazoned on the jersey's back. "I have to drag that old Polaroid from the closet," Mom said. She knelt, nearly falling at the feet of the circle of kids, and focused a make-believe camera. "Smile, baby."

Practice started one week later at a teeny baseball diamond even dwarves would feel stifled on. The fence behind home plate displayed tatters and gouges. The infield's mud hadn't yet dried, and a musky odor of rain choked the air. Horseflies buzzed around my head.

Coach Heider lined us up. He wore a white T-shirt, blue sweatpants, an A's cap. I noticed the bushy sand-colored mustache that curled at his lips' corners. I'd been thumbing through Mom's *Playgirl* almost daily, and I'd started to daydream those mustached and bearded cowboys, lifeguards, and construction workers clutching me, their whiskers scratching my face.

I had told Mom I wanted to look tough, so she had darted to the local Salvation Army store and United Methodist Thrift for wristbands and a used pair of rubber cleats. She also bought the black sunblock most major leaguers smeared below their eyes. I wore the bands, the cleats, and the sunblock to that first practice. My teammates watched me as if I might unsheathe a knife.

Coach squinted at the new troupe of Panthers, searching for defects. His gaze paused on me. Desire sledgehammered my body, a sensation I still wasn't sure I had a name for. If I saw Coach now, say across a crowded bar, that feeling would translate to something like "I want to fuck him." Back then, I wasn't sure what to do with my emotion. It felt like a gift I had to open in front of a crowd.

He told us to announce our names. We obeyed, and he repeated them, scribbling in a score book. "Bailey, Thieszen, McCormick, Varney . . ." He spoke with a German accent. "Lackey, Ensminger . . ." When he rolled his *r*'s on "Porter," my teammates silently mouthed the same name. I was younger than most of them, which made me want to try harder. I wanted to impress Coach Heider.

The players hit ten baseballs each. Coach stood at the pitcher's mound, poised like one of the gilded figures I'd noticed on trophies in the Chamber of Commerce hall. He cocked back his arm and pitched. Most kids hit ground balls that barely left the infield or, worse yet, struck out. I'd never seen many of them before, but I could tell they were poor excuses for players. Coach must have mirrored my feelings. "Come on." Disgust cracked his voice. "Concentrate, watch the ball, swing like you mean it."

My turn. I gritted my teeth and tried to form a synthesis of a few major league idols. I.e., I'd seen the Reds' Joe Morgan twitching his right arm before taking a swing, pistoning his elbow as if pumping blood into his biceps. I mimicked the gesture. Coach Heider grinned. His first pitch lobbed toward me, and I smacked a line drive to left field.

After practice, Coach shepherded us into the dugout and began a pep talk from the center of our huddle. He summarized his initial reactions. I might as well brag. It appeared I'd be the team's star player. My fielding was as topnotch as my hitting, so Coach positioned me shortstop. "And McCormick, I think we'll bat you cleanup. We need the home runs." He said the word as if it had three syllables. When he leaned over to pat my shoulder, I noticed a cluster of moles like spatters of chocolate on his neck.

A man walked toward the team carrying an expensive-looking camera. Coach lined us in two rows beside the dugout, and I got the privilege of standing in back, next to him. "This is for our records," the photographer said. "Say cheese. No, say yogurt." The numbskulls on the team laughed, and he snapped the picture.

"Refreshments served," Coach said. The fifteen Panthers fractured the posed configuration and rushed toward his station wagon, most running faster than they had all day. Coach opened the back door to a cooler filled with cans of flavored sodas. I fished around its icy pond and came up with a peach Nehi.

The parents began arriving after the two hours had finished. Mom drove Alfred's pickup to the ball diamond. She had started a job at an IGA grocery store on Thirtieth Street, and she'd bought an extra house key for me. She strung it onto a thin silver chain and slipped it over my neck. "Now, let me meet that coach of yours."

Coach jogged toward us. He held a baseball in one palm. He took off his cap and brushed it over the sweat on his forehead. His hair was blond and thinning.

"Mr. Heider, I'm Neil's mother." They shook hands. "I have a full-time job and don't know that many other moms. I was wondering if there might be a system where another Little League mom could drive my son home after games. We live on Monroe Street."

"No problem," Coach said. He looked down at me, then

scrutinized Mom, as if decoding her eyes' primal secrets. "I do this sort of thing all the time." He pointed toward his car. "That's what station wagons are for. Any time Neil needs a ride, he's got it."

I imagined sitting in the front seat, his leg brushing mine as his foot touched the accelerator. "That's some ball-player you've got," Coach Heider told Mom.

"He's mine, and I love him." She held my hand as if it were money.

Coach lobbed me the baseball. "Here's the one you nearly whacked over the fence." A grass stain on its leather resembled a screaming face. "It's yours to keep, your trophy." He touched his thumb to the black line of sunblock on my cheek. He glanced at his thumb, winked at me, then looked back to Mom.

The arms of our backyard's apricot tree drooped with wormy fruit. Three swings and a slippery slide stood under the tree. I never used them. The poles were striped pink and grayish white like candy canes, and 6411 North Monroe's previous tenants had painted clown faces on the plastic swing seats. Sparrow shit peppered the slide. Years later, Mom would ask a neighbor to tear the whole set down, and I'd realize I never did slide or swing on the thing.

As it turned out, Mom got more use from the set than me. The night of that first practice, I heard her and Alfred. His voice kept slurring things like "Jesus Priest" and "Christ above." After a while, I figured out his words weren't coming from Mom's bedroom but were creeping into my open window from the backyard.

I knuckled the crust from my eyes, crawled from bed, and peered out. The violet bug light crystallized everything in its somber, rheumy glow. Something that looked like a bat whirled figure eights above the tree. An empty bottle of

Beefeater gin sat beside Mom's portable eight-track tape player in the grass beside the porch. I could hear Freddy Fender's voice crooning the melody of "Wasted Days and Wasted Nights."

Alfred slumped in the center swing's seat. Mom hovered over him. His shirt was pulled to his neck; his pants, to his ankles. Her hands bustled in his lap. Alfred's cowboy hat had fallen off, and hair curled from his head in wisps, as lacy as the silk that covers an ear of corn. His body swayed back and forth, lazy and gin-seduced. His bare feet smashed apricots into the lawn. "Christ," he said again, drawing out the vowel in unison with the eight-track tune's schmaltzy crescendo.

Mom's head lowered to Alfred's crotch. When it lifted again, I could see his dick. It looked huge. I only remembered two, maybe three, of the guys from Mom's magazine having dicks that big. Alfred reached down, circled two fingers around its base, pushed her head back toward it. The bug light zapped, its purple flash ending the life of a mosquito, a grasshopper, something.

Mom blew Alfred. Someone among our cast of neighbors was no doubt spying on them, too. I watched it all and wondered the things I've come to realize, if those personal experience stories in all the porno magazines I read are true, are common things for a kid to wonder in this situation. How would it feel to have my dick in someone's mouth? To have someone's in mine?

I focused on Alfred's features. His jaw clenched. His eyes opened and closed. He talked ceaselessly during their sex—"Yes, Ellen," "Oh God that feels good. . . ." Looking back, it paralyzed me to hear him, but it wasn't long after that I became a sucker for blabbermouths in bed. I would learn to relish an older guy telling me exactly how I made him feel, precisely what he wanted to do to me.

After five minutes, Alfred hoisted Mom up, pulled off her blouse. Her nipples purpled under the bug light's blaze. She stumbled as he led her toward the slippery slide. He positioned her with a leg on each side, then pushed her onto it. I thought of Boris Karloff as Frankenstein's monster on the slanted doctor's table, jagged bolts of electricity jetting above his head.

Alfred fucked Mom on the slide. I imagined myself in Mom's position, my favorite "Edward Cunningham" straddling me. I unzipped. "That feels amazing," Alfred murmured.

Alfred pushed himself into her. Faster, harder, the usual. The slide buckled under Mom's ass on an especially deep thrust. She gasped. Double pause. They both laughed, and Mom touched a finger to her lips. The zapper jolted another bug.

The season's first game pitted the Panthers against a group of kids from Pretty Prairie. They had won the league championship the previous year. Still, we stomped them, 13 to 5. My first time at bat, I didn't concentrate. I looped a pop fly to the third baseman. But later I smacked a double and a triple, the latter with bases loaded. I slid into third base just for the thrill of staining the pants' knees with mud. From the bleachers, the row of moms and dads erupted into applause. None of them knew me. I fantasized them wishing I was their son instead of one of the talentless fuckups they were raising.

The game ended on a double play. A Pretty Prairie kid slid into second base, where a Panther crouched with ball in glove. An umpire barked, "Yer outta there." The crowd went wild. From the dugout, Coach Heider paraded his score book in the air and grinned.

After the win, the losers jogged toward the pitcher's

mound, then lined up to shake hands. This was a ritual after every Little League game: to display sportsmanship, each team congratulated the other. The Pretty Prairiers looked on the verge of tears. "Good game," each kid chanted as he touched a stranger's palm. We were supposed to repeat the same two words, but I stayed silent. This pissed off my opponents more than if I'd shrieked "Fuck you." I glared into their faces; squeezed their hands as if they were sponges.

Coach Heider watched me, still smiling.

Coach telephoned the Saturday after game number one. He told Mom the team would celebrate the victory by meeting at the Flag Theater on Main Street for Sunday matinee. If she would consent, he would pick me up in the station wagon tomorrow at noon. "Certainly," Mom slurred. She buttoned her IGA apron for the late shift.

He arrived at our house wearing his usual T-shirt, but jeans in place of sweatpants. His station wagon smelled mossy and artificial, a scent that pulsed from a tree-shaped air freshener hanging from his rearview. On the drive across town, he asked what theater candy I liked best. I listed Hot Tamales, black licorice, those pastel-coated almonds that looked like the eggs of some curious bird. Mom always griped that the almonds were beyond her price range. Not Coach. "Yes," he said, his voice flustered and boyish. "I could eat ten boxes of those."

When we reached the Flag, none of my teammates was waiting. The lobby was empty, save for twin girls who held hands with a furious-looking granny. Coach didn't say anything about the rest of the team, and I didn't ask. It surprised me that he would lie to Mom, but more than that, it excited me.

Coach stepped to the ticket booth. The scheduled

movie, some imitation Disney clunker, didn't interest me. I only liked the more violent sort of animation. I took a chance and asked if he wanted to drive over to the Fox. I knew they were showing the R-rated *Terror Train*. Even then, I was a sucker for horror flicks. Coach looked uncertain, but I shrugged. "Mom doesn't care."

Off we went. *Terror Train* featured a killer who struck during a masquerade party. I relished his skill in twisting the mask off each new victim's head and slipping it over his own to fool the next victim. Coach watched me during the entire movie, but I pretended not to notice. I munched two boxfuls of pastel almonds. I clapped when the murderer beheaded one partygoer, and Coach smiled. He seemed to be giving close examination to my every reaction, short-handing mental notes.

The Fox Theater's painted walls showed señoritas danc-ing the salsa and fringed matadors flapping scarlet sheets at bulls. Chandeliers hung from a three-stories-high ceiling. Burgundy curtains shrouded the screen, slowly brushing back as the film started. During the action, Coach tilted his head, as if spirits were flouncing among the chandeliers, but when I looked over, his gaze remained fixed on me. By the movie's finale, his head rested against the back of his seat. "You missed the last part," I said. The heroine on screen sobbed pathetically. "The killer finally bit the dust."

His hand cupped my shoulder. "Let's head home. I'd bet money you're hungry."

"Sort of." I walked up the aisle and kicked a bucket, scattering popcorn kernels across the carpet. "Pizza, maybe."

"There's a take-out place called Rocco's just down the street from my house," Coach said. "They use fresh mush-rooms instead of canned. They make zucchini pizza, which I've yet to try. Plus, their slices of pepperoni are bigger than this belt buckle." He pointed to a brass horse-head-inside-of-circle between his stomach and crotch. "So, if your mom didn't set a curfew, maybe we can watch cartoons and pig out and set up some strategies for next week's game." I nodded, curious about Coach's house.

We stepped toward the station wagon. The afternoon sky had darkened, the air thickening as another storm swirled into Hutchinson. The clouds looked like marshmallows dunked in grape juice. Heat lightning flashed in the distance.

Coach lived alone in a small house off Main Street, near the Kansas State Fairgrounds. Once a year, Hutchinson hosted the State Fair, our city's major tourist attraction. Catty-corner from Coach's porch, a billboard displayed the forthcoming September's entertainers. The names on the sign proved typical for the fair: The Statler Brothers, Eddie Rabbitt, magician Doug Henning. "'September twenty-sixth, Tanya Tucker,'" I read. "That's my ninth birthday."

Coach unlocked his front door and swung it open. I noticed two baseball bats in the umbrella stand. Directly in front of me, in his living room, were a giant-screen TV, a VCR, an Atari with game cartridges strewn around it. Some of my favorite games dotted the floor: Phoenix, Frogger, Donkey Kong, Joust.

"I'll order the pizza," Coach said. "Do whatever you want. Turn that thing on if you feel like it. Frogger's my favorite. How does pepperoni and mushroom sound?"

I nodded. He disappeared into the kitchen, the slatted half-doors swinging behind him like the doors in movie saloons. I heard him lift the telephone from its receiver. I glanced around the room. Three blue beanbag chairs lined one wall. Coach had thumbtacked an Aquaman poster above a leopard print couch. The end table was scattered with Disneyland brochures and a hardback called *Coaching*

Young Children. Other books, albums, and videotapes lined the bookshelf. I flicked the switches to the TV and Atari. *Bleep*, said the screen.

Coach returned and set the game panel for two-player mode. "Positive your mom won't be expecting you?"

"She'll stay pretty late at the store," I said, "and then probably go out with Alfred."

He raised one eyebrow and began pressing the joystick's button. "My guess is you spend a lot of time by yourself." On screen, his frog vaulted a ravenous electronic alligator.

"It's no big deal. I kind of like it. School's out for the summer. I watch TV or ride my bike. We have some weird neighbors, so I pedal around and spy on them."

"I'm alone a lot too. When I'm not coaching, I stay here. I mostly just like some good friends to be with now and then. Good friends like you." The screen's colors strobed against his blue eyes. He didn't blink. His frog drowned, and he handed me the joystick. "So, where did you learn to play baseball like that?"

"I taught myself." I could guess the next question, so I continued. "He's dead. I never knew him." I turned my head from his face to the television.

Coach won both games. In the middle of the third, the pizza arrived; he shut off the Atari and spread the open Rocco's box before us like a treasure map. "Wait here."

He jogged to the kitchen and returned carrying a Nikon camera in one hand, two cans of peach Nehi in the other. He gave me the pop. "I remembered you like this stuff." He watched each bite I took, each mouthful I chewed. After I'd finished my second piece, Coach opened a door to his stereo cabinet. He fetched a small microphone and plugged it into his receiver.

"This might seem weird at first," Coach said. "I want to do a little experiment with you." He handed me the microphone. "Just start talking as you normally would. I need to record my team's voices, especially my good players. And something else, too. Take a couple of big slugs of that pop. Don't rush it, there's no hurry. When you think you're about to burp, tell me and I'll record it." He fingernailed a switch on the camera flash, and a high-pitched squeal filled the room.

I swallowed a breath, uncertain what Coach was doing but having fun nonetheless. I had snagged his attention. "I'm ready," I said. I belched three times over the next five minutes, and he taped them all.

I spilled some peach Nehi on the carpet. Its fizzy puddle looked like battery acid, and I tried in vain to wipe it up. "Shit." When Coach heard me say that, he grinned. "Good," he said. "Keep that up. Say 'shit' again. Say 'goddamn.' And burp a few more times." I obeyed. I even said "fuck" once. That seemed to impress him. He knelt down and hugged me, my face even with his stomach. I could feel curly hairs through his shirt, the miraculous breath swelling inside him. He brushed his chin against the top of my head.

"I like you," he said.

Coach stood again. The tape continued recording. In between my giggles and cuss words and burps, he snapped photographs. For most of them, he instructed me to look up at him and smile. I stuck out my tongue in one picture. He fingered its pink tip—I tasted the salt of his skin—and clicked the shutter. For another photo, he made me push the microphone between my lips and close my eyes. "Oh, Neil, that's perfect." *Click.*

I couldn't sleep. Alfred and Mom were fucking in the next room. I tiptoed to the bathroom, locked the door, stretched out in the tub. The porcelain stung, as frosty as a glacier. I slipped my underwear to my ankles, grabbed my

dick, and lifted my forearm to my lips, feverishly kissing my
skin as if it were someone else's mouth. Thunder rumbled
from outside, and Mom's bedsprings squeaked. The sink's
faucet dripped every fifth second. I squeezed my eyes shut,
but this time I didn't picture the men from Mom's magazine. Someone else stood over me. He dropped his camera
and bent down, unbuttoning and unzipping, his face moving toward mine. I heard Alfred mumble an incomprehensi-
ble sentence. I mouthed the word "Coach," tonguing furi-
ously at my arm, grating my front teeth against the skin.

When I woke, my mother's knuckles were drumming the
bathroom door. "Are you alive in there or what?" I pulled
my underwear up, covered the purplish mark on my arm,
and stumbled out.

The second of July, 1981. Mom had been appointed to
work a double shift at the IGA. "I feel like a slave, there's got
to be something better," she said. She hugged me, her arms
wrapping around my body, her fingers aligning with my
ribs. I thought of the way Coach had hugged me and wished
Mom were him. "I know you're going to beat their asses
tonight. I predict four home runs." Mom kissed me between
the "four" and the "home runs."

I thanked her. At 7 P.M., the baseball diamond would feature the Panthers versus Hutchinson Taco Hut, who'd lost
every game for the past two years.

"Coach will drive you home, I guess." Mom hand-fanned
her face and skipped toward the door. "I love you, love you,
love you, and don't you forget it." The screen crashed
behind her. I waved with my baseball glove as she started
the engine.

Mom hadn't been gone ten minutes when Coach's car
idled in our driveway. The game wasn't scheduled for
another three hours. When I slid into the station wagon, I

planted my glove on the seat between us. "I'm glad you're early," I said. "It'd be great if I could try those other game cartridges."

Coach parked the wagon in his garage. I followed him toward the house. "Home is where the heart is," he said. He reached toward a shelf piled with five or six photo albums. He pulled one down, handed it to me. "I got the pictures developed."

I fell into a beanbag. The first twenty or so pages showed other boys I didn't know. Some wore baseball uniforms. One series displayed a shirtless red-headed kid, pizza sauce smudged across his chin, playing the game Battleship. I couldn't help staring at one blurry print, shot in extreme close-up, where the boy seemed to be nibbling the big toe of someone's—probably Coach's—bare foot. The kid's freckled face looked confused, as if he'd just been bludgeoned.

On the following page I saw myself, holding the microphone. I bent closer to examine. My hair needed combing. My skin was pale, and my pupils gleamed red. I looked haunted. I'd appeared this way to Coach as he'd stared down at me. I flipped through the next few pages, discovering more photos of me in the album than all the photos taken during my entire life. In one shot, my eyes had closed. "I look pretty stupid here."

"No, you're perfect," Coach said. "Your expression—like you're having a really great dream." He sat in the beanbag beside me and fit his palm over my knee. He had bitten his nails, and one finger's cuticle grinned a dried crescent of blood. "I think I like you better than those others in that book. You're definitely a better ballplayer." The hand on my knee tightened. It seemed faultless, the hand of someone amazing, superior, invincible. "Neil, I've been thinking about you a lot this week."

My face heated up. I squirmed from the beanbag, not wanting him to see it. "I'm hungry."

Coach stood and moved toward the kitchen. I followed. "Another pizza?" he asked. He opened a cupboard. "Or maybe you see something you like in here?"

He'd stocked his kitchen with bags of candy, fudge cookies, Jiffy Pop popcorn, Tang, boxes of pudding. I spied a Breakfast Sampler Pack, miniature boxes of ten different cereal brands packaged together. "Mom never buys those things," I said, pointing. "She says they're a big waste of money."

"Let's eat, then," he said.

I chose sugar Corn Pops. Coach, Cocoa Krispies. He pulled milk from his refrigerator and two spoons from another drawer. He positioned his fingers at each end of his box and faultlessly ripped it open. I tried to emulate, but when I tore, the box exploded. The cereal spilled across the checkerboard tiles. "Shit," I said. Gold nuggets lay at our feet, their sugar coatings gleaming in the kitchen light. I started to apologize, but Coach shushed me. He held his box over his head. He tipped it. Cocoa Krispies rained down. I watched as he opened the Froot Loops, the Alpha-Bits, the horrible-tasting Special K we wouldn't have eaten anyway. He spilled them all.

The cereal scattered the floor. In the moment that followed, everything around me clarified. I stared at Coach, every detail of him, this grown man's body standing before me. The kitchen's light sharpened the thin blond hairs that curled from his shirt collar. The darker shade of his mustache. His sideburns, clipped level with his earlobes. The small copper-colored sunbursts that ringed each black pupil. And, inside that black, a reflection of my face.

Coach's hand reached for me. It clamped the back of my

neck. I closed my eyes and felt him guiding me, regulating my actions, pushing me toward the floor. I fell to my knees, and he fell with me. "Here we go," he said. I opened my eyes, and he was leaning over my body. Hundreds of cereal bits were strewn around us like debris from a catastrophe. My nostrils bristled with a perfume of sugar. He moved closer, and I smelled his breath, the clean scent of his Panthers T-shirt, the coconutty residue of his shampoo.

He massaged my neck. "When I really, really like someone, there's a way I show them how I feel." He gently pushed my shoulders until I lay flat on the floor. He rested his head against my heart. I shifted under him, and pieces of cereal crunched beneath my ass. Snap, crackle, pop.

I knew what was happening. Half of me realized it wasn't right. The other half wanted it to happen. Coach hugged me, his fingers soothing and caressing, tracing and retracing the paths and angles of my shoulders, my back, my ass. "Shhh," he said. "Angel." His nose touched mine, and his breaths moved into my mouth. "There's nothing wrong with kissing someone like this. Nothing. Don't let anyone tell you there's anything wrong with it."

He shut his mouth over mine, pushing his tongue between my lips, trailing the line of my front teeth, moving back to circle my own, smaller tongue. It felt as though his tongue were gorging my entire head, tasting and licking behind my eyes, tracing the blue lobes of my brain. Our teeth clicked together. His bottom lip curled over my jawline. My head was disappearing, he was swallowing me. I moaned and understood it was the right noise. Alfred and Mom made that sound at night.

Occasionally I'd open my eyes, catch a random image, then snap them back shut. The images shuffled in my head: his fingers, loosening his circle-and-horse-head belt buckle;

teardrops of green glass on the chandelier; his shirt's pouncing, drooling panther; silver fillings in the recess of his mouth.

He stretched on top of me. More snaps and crackles. My hand made a fist against the linoleum, and my palm burst pebbles of cereal. The tongue kept darting inside my head. Trails of his spit dripped down my throat. I swallowed.

His head lifted. "Shhh." He unzipped, and somehow managed to wriggle his jeans to his knees. His dick stiffened against my thigh. "Open your eyes and look at it," Coach said. I did. At that second I would have obeyed anything. His dick curved slightly upward, a milky drop leaking from its tip.

"Neil, I like you so much." His eyes resembled chunks of stained glass. He kissed me again, and one hand wandered up my leg, rubbing my crotch through my baseball pants. "That feels nice, right?" He squeezed, ironed, massaged. "Right?" Yes, it felt nice. I heard something that sounded like fabric ripping. He reached inside my baseball pants. He grabbed my dick, the sweat of his palm almost stinging me. I focused on a vein in his bicep. The vein twitched like a puppet's vulnerable string. My body tensed, canting against the support of his other arm, nearly nine years of anticipation clamping in each tendon and muscle. I couldn't hold it. I moaned again to let him know, and then he shuddered. His entire body shook. He quickly pushed himself up to kneel over me, and in that second I saw the full size of his dick, candy pink and unreal, as it arched over my chest. His sperm shot from the head and pooled its white dribbles across the ninety-nine on my jersey front. It shocked me a little, but I kept quiet. After a while, I put my palm over the puddle. The come felt warmer and stickier than I'd expected. Beneath it, my heartbeat steadied.

He lay back down. He wore an awkward, pained expression, and when he sighed into my face, I could almost taste the heat in the rushing air.

"You liked it," Coach said. He wasn't looking at me. "It's okay that you liked it, it will all be okay."

Minutes passed. I counted the number of my breaths before either of us spoke. I was on sixty-five before Coach said anything. What he said was, "Shhh," again, although I hadn't said a word. I started shivering, and Coach hugged me, covering as much of me as he could, as if my skin had burst into flame and his body were a blanket to snuff it. Only my mother had held me like that.

"That's how I feel about you," Coach said. "There's nothing wrong with showing it. People are afraid to show it, but you should know there's nothing wrong with expressing to someone how much you really like them, how much you're proud of them."

I looked at the floor's mess: two spoons, a pearly bead of his come, and cereal nuggets in all colors, as if a kaleidoscope had shattered. I swallowed. The taste of his tongue seared my mouth.

He zipped up. It happened, I told myself; it happened. And I had liked it. I heard dogs barking outside, a group of kids fighting in clipped sentences. "I'm telling," one bawled. Coach dropped a five-dollar bill on the floor beside me, then stepped over my body, a black smudge from my sunblock on his shirt front. He hunched over the sink and twisted the *H* knob. The water splashed his hands. "I'll clean the floor later." He smiled at me. "My number ninety-nine. Guess we should think about heading over to smear that Taco Hut team."

We demolished Taco Hut. Somewhere within those seven innings I smacked three RBIs, but I don't remember a moment. I saw his hands giving signals from the coach's box on the third base line, and I thought about our sex. Although it was difficult to understand it then, what I wanted was more. For the rest of my days I would want it. I would see sex everywhere, splinters shoved into each molecule of each space, saturating everything I saw and smelled and tasted and touched.

I could leap ahead and detail the afternoons I spent with Coach, the money he gave me, everything I learned from him. I could mention the summer's end, the beginning of third grade, the following June when the Chamber of Commerce assigned Coach another, older group of boys. Without a guide, I would quit baseball. Our paths would trail further and further away, and our relationship would end.

But he's still here, in a way I can't explain. Oftentimes I wonder where Coach lives, what he's doing, whether something like prison or lynch mobs or disease hasn't killed him. But looking back it doesn't matter. What matters is how, for the first time in my life, I felt as if I existed *for* something. When I think back, and I do that a lot, the majority of that summer fades. I barely remember the vacation Mom and I took to Abilene, or her breakup with Alfred. I almost forget the other boys on the team, even the others Coach lured to that house across from the fairgrounds marquee.

Sometimes it's all I think about: the times I spent with him. It's as if he and I were all that mattered. My best dreams feature him, no one else, the two of us suspended in his sugary-smelling rooms, alone, as if God had positioned a beam on central Kansas, and Coach and I had stepped haphazardly into its light.

three

BRIAN LACKEY

Summers, my father raised watermelons. By September, they matured into ripeness, the salmon pink of their flesh deepening to vermilion. Before the morning's temperature moved above eighty, my father tramped between the vines, knife in hand, and carried watermelons to the house. Our family ate so much of the fruit, our veins might have contained a concoction of blood and melon juice.

Little River lies nestled one mile off Highway 56, and every autumn my father set up a fruit stand to attract the profusion of cars that drove to and from the yearly Kansas State Fair, held twenty miles away in Hutchinson. He appointed Deborah and me to oversee the truckload of melons. "You sell the goods, you make the money," he'd say.

One summer—two years after the summer of our UFO—my father decided we could sell unchaperoned. On the fair's opening morning, he parked the pickup in the gravel shoulder where the Little River road met the highway. He lifted himself into the cab and repositioned the melons, scattering the common, striped kind among the black diamond and pint-sized sugar baby varieties. He handed us an old Roi-Tan cigar box in which one- and five-dollar bills were peppered with handfuls of change. He gave us the thumbs-up and turned to walk home.

Deborah and I perched at the end of the truck bed, watermelons bubbling around us in a pell-mell sea. I felt important, like a merchant opening shop. While she weighed each fruit on a rusty scale, I multiplied the number of pounds by six cents and Magic Markered the price on each rind.

Our first customers coasted toward us: an elderly couple and their three grandchildren. The red frames on the woman's sunglasses matched the color of her smudged lipstick. She seemed frazzled and desperate. "We're spending loads of money on all those silly games and rides at the fair," she explained, "so we might as well spend even more on your melons. Better for the little ones than cotton candy or funnel cake." She tested a fat one's ripeness by thumping her fingernail against it. Then she scratched its rind and checked the color. Deborah rolled her eyes. Our father had shown us the secret of telling if a melon was ready: a thin, curly filament wormed where the melon met the vine; when that turned brown, the fruit was ripe. We didn't relay our secret to the woman. We let her thump until she made her choice. Deborah weighed it. "Harold, give them two smackers," the woman said, and her husband paid us.

All summer, the sun had lightened my hair, and Deborah's had bleached to the color of chaff. By noon that day, my hair had dried out, and my skin was tingling. I knew I'd be sunburned by evening. "We forgot suntan lotion," I told Deborah.

She pressed her thumb against my shoulder. It left a white impression for half a second before the pink returned. "You'll look like a lobster," she said. I remembered the previous summer, when we had taken a trip to Kanopolis Reservoir and I had fallen asleep on the beach. Sunburns made me nauseated. If I got sick, my father wouldn't let me sell the next day.

Deborah's best friend, Breeze Campbell, bicycled to the highway and joined us. She hadn't brought suntan lotion, either. She suggested we eat. I found a knife behind the seat in my father's cobwebby pickup, the same knife he'd used to sever the turtle's head, two years before. I chose a watermelon, strummed the gauze of sand from its surface, and aimed for its "1.25" price. Stab. The melon split in jagged halves, and we dug our fingers into the meat to gobble it up.

I was always shy around Deborah's friends, but as we ate I grew bolder. I stood beside the pickup, stuffing fistfuls into my mouth, making certain they were watching me. I didn't swallow. Instead, I punched both my swollen cheeks simultaneously, juice and seeds exploding from my mouth across the pavement. Breeze laughed. She hopped from her seat on the scale and joined me, repeating my actions.

The three of us waited for cars to speed by, then "vomited" watermelons across the highway. After a while I got carried away. I selected melons from the pickup bed, lifting them above my head and dropping them. They burst on the asphalt, echoing identical *splotch* sounds across the fields. In minutes chunks of pink meat, scraps of rind, and slimy seeds littered a stretch of Highway 56. Flies hovered around the mess as if it were an animal's carcass.

Deborah stopped laughing. I turned and saw my father. He had showered, dressed, and slicked back his hair, undoubtedly planning to drive into Hutchinson for softball games. The sun shone off the oil in his hair. He pressed both palms against the sides of his shorts, the fingers splayed out stiff and trembling. Breeze cleared her throat and began walking her bicycle up the road.

I could never predict my father's reactions. He would comfort my mother one minute; slam the door in her face the next. On that day, my father didn't hit me. He looked toward the east, then the west, for cars. The horizons were clear. He stepped toward the debris and began tossing pink clots of melon into the ditch. When he came to a piece of rind, he held it up and examined the price Deborah had written. "Dollar eighty-five," he said. He pitched another mess of pink. He found another rind: "Two fifty. A big one, Brian."

When my father had finished, only a stain remained on the highway asphalt, a burst of juice shaped like a star with countless points. He shuffled to the pickup and leaned against its side. I watched his hands. A fly landed on the left one, wriggling its spindly legs. He shooed it away and knocked a knuckle on the Roi-Tan box. "I'll be back around seven tonight." He smiled at Deborah, his eyes blinking mechanically. "Your brother owes me twelve dollars and forty cents."

In the two years following the night my mother, Deborah, and I saw the UFO, I became obsessed with watching the skies. I began stretching on the roof on summer nights. I went there alone; Deborah had grown exhausted with playing board games, but I didn't mind. I memorized the moon's phases and various constellations, and searched through binoculars for any hint of abnormal light.

I scanned newspapers for flying saucer stories, and on occasion I'd discover some brief bit about eerie lights over a city or a curiously shaped craft pursuing an airplane. I fantasized myself as the world's first adolescent UFO researcher, clandestinely funded by the U.S. government to jet between countries, gleaning information. I borrowed books from the library; examined their sketches and rare spacecraft photographs.

Halloween approached. I'd wanted to dress as a spaceman, but my father balked at the costume's expense. "My paycheck will not be spent on this foolish holiday." I had to settle for the cheaper Satan. At October's close, I dressed in cranberry-red sweatpants, suspenders, and rubber galoshes. "I feel dumb," I told my mother.

Back then, Deborah and I attended church weekly. For Halloween, we had helped decorate an abandoned house three miles from town. Our Youth Ministry was sponsoring a Haunted Mansion to amuse kids after they'd finished that night's candy grabbing. My Satan getup made me feel gutsy for once—the kids that picked on me at school wouldn't recognize me, I thought—and I anticipated lurching from a dark corner to scare them.

I remember beginning the night in Little River Lutheran Church. Deborah and I searched for candles, and as I tiptoed past the pews, my tail bobbed behind me. I lumbered forward as devillike as possible, rehearsing for the night ahead. The stained-glass windows shimmered their faint blues and golds, and I kept imagining the hand of God would slide aside the steepled roof to pluck away my mask.

Deborah stood beneath the crucified Christ. Moonlight angled through the stained glass to illuminate the green warts she'd rubber-cemented to her face. She was dressed as a witch and had dyed her hair red for the evening. Its shade matched the painted blood that dripped from the Savior's wounds. "Your mask's almost sacrilegious," she said as I emerged from behind the altar with the candles. "How perfect." She'd stopped believing in God months ago. She claimed she only continued with church because it gave her a chance to stare at Lucas Black, the pastor's eighteen-year-old son.

My father honked from outside, where he and my mother waited in the pickup. When the four of us squeezed together in the seat, my parents looked uncomfortable beside each other. Deborah and I should be between them, I thought.

"I've got to be on the job in twenty-five minutes," my mother said. Her uniform was the color of rye bread. Her gold badge spelled out M. LACKEY. KANSAS STATE INDUSTRIAL REFORMATORY patches covered each shoulder.

"Got to drop these two off first," my father said. Our truck passed the YOU ARE LEAVING LITTLE RIVER, KANSAS! COME BACK AGAIN! sign. He turned onto the abandoned road that led to the Haunted Mansion.

I checked my mask in the side rearview and adjusted one crooked horn. My breath slivered from the slit in my fleshy maroon lips. I wore new wire-rim glasses beneath the mask, the ones Deborah swore made me look like an owl, the ones kids at school had already teased me about. To get a better look in the mirror, I cracked a window, and Deborah's hat fell off, her red hair flying back. "Close it," she said. Her mouth displayed a blackened front tooth.

The world sped past. Out there, the moon hovered above the flat horizon like a jewel surfacing in a black lake. Below it, shadowy farmhouses, silos, and haystacks scattered the fields. A German shepherd chased a rabbit through weeds. Fog began its nightly slide over Kansas, as thick as peaks of meringue.

My father coasted the truck toward the Haunted Mansion. The headlights shone off the house's murky windows. "I won't be home until four in the morning," my mother said. "They make me spend the entire night in that lookout tower as if I'm Rapunzel or something. Thank God I've got only one more month of this shift." She looked at her watch. "Your father has accounts to balance tomorrow. He'll be falling asleep early, so you need to ask someone's mom or dad or, better yet, Pastor Black to drive you home."

My mother kissed two fingers. She touched Deborah's forehead, then mine. "Don't be too loud when you come home," my father said. I hopped from the truck and walked toward the house, Deborah following.

The Haunted Mansion stood in a collar of trees. Rumors claimed a man had slaughtered his family there, years earlier. Little River high schoolers tried to prove bravery by parking in its driveway, most zooming away when no indoor light switched on or no forlorn ghost stared from a window. The house, two stories of gray wood, displayed a surface of loose boards and nails, a roof with shingles bleached to a light tan. Its windows had been cracked or shattered by falling limbs or vandals' rocks. It looked as flimsy as a matchstick cabin.

A sign on the porch read ARE YOU BRAVE ENOUGH? ADMISSION: $1.00. The letters were written in a "blood" our group had concocted with Karo syrup and food coloring. I sidestepped a welcome mat stained with a splash of the fake blood.

The front room had once been a kitchen. Two jack-o'-lanterns sat in the sink, faces grimacing as if they'd felt every jab and slice of the knives that had carved them. Rubber bats and tarantulas bounced from strings Deborah had tied to ceiling hooks. She hadn't bothered to sweep away the spider webs in the ceiling's corners. "Leave them. They add atmosphere," she had said, even though Breeze Campbell had stepped face first into one.

Leaf, Breeze's older brother, lurched through the rooms, spilling the counterfeit blood from a plastic milk jug on the floors and walls. He was fat and always wore a black stocking cap. His costume consisted of a bloodstained sheet, the stocking cap, and a knife unconvincingly wedged in his armpit. "All the adults took off," Leaf told Deborah, "except for my dad, and he's out back drinking." Mansion tours were scheduled to begin in fifteen minutes.

Pastor Black had advised us to keep the scares to a min-
imum. We hadn't obeyed his rule. Upstairs, in one bedroom,
Leaf and his friends had decorated the floor with knives,
saws, drills, and hammers. They'd cut a hole into a rectangular table, draped it with a sheet, and lined it with candles.
One of them planned to sit beneath the table and poke his
head through the hole. A saw's blade would rest against the
neck he'd stained with syrup and food coloring. When the
tours began, the boy's "dead" eyes would open, and his
mouth would spew blood.

Deborah pulled a compact from her purse. She touched
her earrings, gigantic lightning bolts she'd cut from foiled
cardboard. She checked her warts and teeth in the mirror.
Her face looked sculptured from pea soup. "The man who
lived in this house got up from dinner one evening and went
to the toolshed." She was practicing for her job as tour
guide. "When he came back, he led his wife and each of his
eight children one by one to the nine rooms of this house,
and then. . . ."

She looked through the door of the next room, where
Lucas Black was rearranging weapons. Lucas was acting the
role of the father-murderer. The Campbells and the other
older kids got the jobs of the slaughtered family. I was the
youngest in the group. "You can wander from room to
room," Lucas told me, pointing a screwdriver. "Try to scare
any kids who think they're brave."

That night, my shyness had smothered, and I was eager
to do the scaring. Two Halloweens ago, my father and I had
driven to Topeka; we had passed a roadside Haunted House
similar to our Youth Ministry's. My father stopped the truck.
"Let's try it." A bloody-mouthed polar bear and a mummy
had stood at the front door, beckoning people in. But I
chickened at the last minute, crying when the mummy's
clammy finger slimed across my face. "You'll never go any-

where with guts like that," my father had said. "This world's not all peaches and cream, son."

Deborah and I stomped upstairs. The red syrup lent the whole house a breakfasty smell. Someone had tied a plastic doll to the banister, her eyes driven through with the spears of scissors. Her dress was lifted to reveal her naked, dimpled butt. I covered it as I passed.

Light striped the master bedroom wall. Breeze's face lit up, her mascara and lipstick suddenly as obvious and as crude as smears of jam on a pancake. "A car's pulling in the driveway," she yelled. She ran to her hiding place.

Downstairs, a tape player clicked on. Horror movie soundtrack music lifted through the air, a droning bass punctuated by a high, screechy violin's staccato. I took my place in the smallest bedroom, grabbed a broom, and crouched in a musty corner. On the room's opposite side, in front of the window, Breeze hung from a noose. She looked dead, in spite of the hidden sling around her shoulders and the foot she propped against the window. I waved the broom at her, and she winked back. She adjusted the rope. The candlelight glowed a pair of pink Vs against her face.

Lucas Black whistled from downstairs. Three seconds of silence. Outside, car doors slammed.

I listened as Deborah assembled some kids. "We'll have tours every ten minutes," she said in her regular voice. Pause. Then, gravelly, "Greetings to all. I hope you're feeling brave. This house is haunted. The man who lived here was a cold-blooded murderer. One night he left the dinner table. . . ." I closed my eyes and imagined a bundled-up, chickenhearted row of kids, their gazes fixed on the witch tour guide.

The rubber mask made my ears feel as if tiny hands were squeezing them. Slowly, the assembly began climbing the stairs. "The youngest daughter was the first to go," Deborah hissed at the kids. "He brought her into this room, where he told her to open her mouth and close her eyes. She thought she was getting a nice mouthful of candy corn or cinnamon bears for dessert, but boy, was she wrong."

Downstairs, the horror film music crescendoed. Upstairs, a series of wails. The kids had stepped into the room where Marcy Hathaway lay sprawled across the floor, her face drenched with a caul of blood, a raw veal cutlet poised on her chest to simulate a sliced-off tongue.

The tour group returned to the hallway. As I squatted there, my heart drummed in my chest. My throat trapped each thin breath. At any second, tonight's kids would burst into the bedroom.

The door creaked open. Breeze rolled her eyes into her head and lolled her tongue. "Go on inside," Deborah told the kids, and they filed in. "He hung this daughter. Open your mouth and close your eyes. That's what he said to all of them. He listened to the snap of this girl's fifteen-year-old neck." The kids surrounded the body, fascinated. A little boy with plastic fangs began to cry.

I waited. They spun around, ready to explore the next roomful of carnage. Then I sprang from the corner. They screamed as I swung the broom at them, careful not to touch their heads. They sprinted through the door. I laughed, and Deborah gave me the thumbs-up.

The tours sped by, one every fifteen minutes. After a while, Deborah lost her interest. I selected one member from each group to pick on, usually a girl or boy in a top-notch costume. It disappointed me that none were Martians or robotic aliens, so I wound up picking a favorite in the kid dressed as the Shroud of Turin. He or she wore a black body suit and headpiece, gilded head to toe to resemble the pre-Resurrection Jesus. I gave the "Shroud" a jab of my broom and soft pinches from my glued-on devil's claws.

With the final tours, the crowd began to change. I had

recognized most kids from Sundays at Little River Lutheran, but now more unfamiliar faces drifted through the rooms. Most unrecognizables seemed older. "I think they're from Hutchinson," Breeze whispered. The door reopened, and her irises rolled back into her head.

A group of boys looked familiar to me. Six of them filed into the syrupy-smelling bedroom. They had ditched their tour guide. I watched them through the slits in my mask. One belched, his breath visible in the chilly air. He had a blond crew cut and a choker necklace made of minuscule white shells. Another wore overalls and a Reds baseball cap, his teeth gleaming with a row of braces. None of the boys had dressed in a costume.

I emerged from the shadow. Metal-mouth spun and started laughing. "Hey, it's Lucifer." The others turned and stared.

The boys surrounded me. I opened my mouth and choked out the word "boo." All six laughed. Even Breeze Campbell laughed. Her body shook from its noose.

Then the crew cut boy with the shell necklace leaned forward. His green eyes stared into mine.

In that moment, I remembered. I'd known these boys a couple of years previous, during the summer of the missing time and the UFO, the summer I'd started Little League in Hutchinson. I had practiced with them; had listened to them yelling things like "four eyes" and "pansy" and "the only place for you is the bench." Now, years later, this boy reached toward me, and the memories flooded back—how I hated baseball, how I never returned, even though my father had urged me on, had bragged of the game's benefits.

Crew cut pushed me against the wall. "Really, unbelievably, incredibly frightening," he said. His hand shot toward my Satan mask. He tore it from my head, tossing it to the floor.

I felt hairs rip from my scalp. I opened my eyes, and the world had slipped out of focus. My glasses had come off with my mask.

They were laughing, all of them. Breeze's giggle blistered the air, shrill and pestering, like a blue jay's screech above their tenors. She was showing off for them. I stepped toward their circle.

My right boot landed on the glasses. I heard the crack, felt them snap like potato chips. I bent to pick them up. Nothing but shards, as thin and sharp as the teeth in a monster's mouth. I swept the pieces aside and grabbed my mask.

The boys watched me run from the room. I had made a fool of myself, just as I'd done again and again, summers ago. I remembered standing in right field, dropping a pop fly, the older boys taunting me. I staggered downstairs, and my foot slipped on a bloody stair, my arm knocking over the doll and her scissor-gouged face. I passed the hallway, where Deborah and the others stood talking. Without glasses, I could hardly see them. Deborah's warty face was pressed against Lucas Black's chest, smudging it with green makeup. "What's wrong?" she asked.

I didn't answer. I still heard them upstairs, my old teammates. Their voices echoed bits of sentences: "the decapitated guy in the next room," "one lousy dollar," "waiting for us outside in the station wagon."

Deborah held out her hand. "What's the matter?"

I sped through the kitchen. It seemed as though the entire town were laughing now, and the noise echoed through the house. I slammed the screen door and ran across the porch, past the row of cars, into the trees.

Thirty minutes later, I sat with Deborah and Breeze in the Campbells' car, riding back into Little River. I stared out the window, the black night rushing past, my eyes glazing over. Something had happened to me when I left the Mansion, something I couldn't quite remember.

I recall bits and pieces. When I sprinted from the house, I saw the moon, orange, almost electric, stalled between feathery clouds like a helium balloon, ready to burst into a million splinters. Without glasses, the world melted from focus. The house and trees seemed under water. I leaned against a tree and felt its knobby trunk pressing into my skin like a column of bones.

I put the mask back on. Behind me, the pipe organ music swelled, softened, swelled again. Most of the kids had gone home. "Let's call it a night," an adult said. I kept walking, trying not to cry. My scalp tingled from where the hair had ripped out, and my face pounded from the kid's hand.

I remember passing the parked cars. Ahead, nothing but air so cold it snapped, and an arena of trees, the bordering saplings leading into towering, ancient cottonwoods and oaks. I wandered through them, their arms whispering and creaking in the wind. I looked up to their blurry branches, as lacy and fragile as spiderwebs.

Back at the house, Leaf roared, no doubt grabbing some kid's shoulder. A chorus of wails. "Hey, Brian," Deborah yelled. I was no longer part of that scene. I didn't stop walking. The Little League boys are in the past, I told myself. Forget them.

In the distance I heard a creek's murmur. I moved toward the sound, deeper into the trees. Thorns from bushes snagged my cape, oak leaves fell around me, and my galoshes oozed through mud puddles.

A stick cracked behind me. I remember it making that exact sound—*crack*.

Then I noticed how everything had altered to an unbelievable silence. The crickets, the creek, even the wind had ceased. The quiet made me think of that night on the side of our hill; how I had stood staring up at the sky, a little scared but curiously peaceful, even happy, as the spacecraft hovered its carousel of blue lights above us.

The final thing I remember: In the center of the quiet, another branch snapped. And I turned.

Blur.

four

WENDY PETERSON

Neil McCormick was a scruffy, moody stick of a boy. I developed a crush the same day I set eyes on him. It didn't take long to discover my crush was doomed: he was one of those queers.

The kids at Sherman Middle School realized this fact during an afternoon recess séance. It was September 1983; at twelve, I'd begun to slip into the antisocial skin I've never slipped out of. The trends my Hutchinson classmates followed seemed foolish: neon rubber bracelets, nicknames in iron-on lettering on T-shirt backs, or illegal lollipops made with tequila and an authentic, crystallized dead worm. But when some other sixth graders became interested in the occult, I joined them. "Finally," I told Mom, "they're into something cool." Groups of us traipsed through graveyards on dares. We bought Tarot decks; magazines devoted to telekinesis or out-of-body experiences. We gathered at recess, waiting for some small miracle to happen.

My mom claimed she was observing a change in me. For my upcoming birthday, I'd requested albums by bands whose names sounded especially disturbing or violent: The Dead Boys, Suicide, Throbbing Gristle. I longed for the world that existed beyond Hutchinson, Kansas. "You,

Wendy Peterson, are looking for trouble with a capital T," Mom had started to warn.

In my eyes, that trouble equalled Neil. I'd noticed him, but I doubted anyone else had. He always seemed to be alone. He was in fifth grade, not sixth, and he didn't participate in the daily half-hour soccer games—two disqualifications from what most everyone considered cool.

That afternoon, though, he fearlessly broke the séance circle. Two popular girls, Vicky and Rochelle, were attempting to summon a blond TV star from the dead. Sebastian So-and-so's BMW had recently crashed into a Hollywood brick wall, and my classmates were determined to disclose whatever heaven he now hovered through. "Aaahhhmmm," the girls moaned. Hands levitated in midair, attempting to catch this or that spiritual vibration.

When Neil interrupted, his sneakered foot stomped squarely on a Ouija board someone had brought. "Watch it, fucker," a séance attendee said.

"You shitheads know nothing about contacting ghosts," Neil said. "What you need is a professional." His voice sounded vaguely grandfatherlike, as if his brain were crowded with knowledge. Eyes opened, concentrations broke. Someone gasped.

A few tall boys' heads blocked my view. I tried to peek above their shoulders; saw a mop of thick black hair. A breeze blew it. To touch it would be like touching corduroy.

Neil picked up the valentine-shaped beige plastic disk from the Ouija board. It looked like a tiny, three-legged table, a gold pin poking through its center. Sun glinted off the pinpoint. Only moments before, Vicky and Rochelle had placed their polished fingernails on the disk to ask about the coming apocalypse.

"My father's a hypnotist," Neil said. He waved the disk in front of his face like a Smith & Wesson. "He's taught me all the tricks. I could show you shitheads a fucking thing or two." From Neil, all those *fuck*s and *shit*s were more than just throwaway cuss words. They adopted some special meaning.

Neil slipped off his shoes, sat on them, and pretzeled his legs into a configuration only someone that skinny could have managed. The crowd blocked the sun and shadowed Neil. The air felt chilly, and I wished I'd worn a jacket. From somewhere behind us, a teacher's whistle shrieked. Some classmates chanted a brainless song, its words confused by the wind.

"Who wants to be first?" Neil asked. He excited me to no end. Maybe he'd expose their infinite foolishness.

Vicky volunteered. "No way," Neil said. "Only a boy will work for the kind of hypnotizing I'm going to do." Vicky pouted, planted her tequila pop back on her tongue, and stood aside.

Neil pointed toward Robert P., a kid whose last initial stuck because two other sixth graders shared the same first name. Robert P. could speak Spanish and sometimes wore an eye patch. I'd heard him bragging about his first wet dream. Some girls thought him "debonair." Like most everyone else in school, he seemed stupid to me.

People made room, and my view improved. Under Neil's direction, Robert lay on his back. Random hands smoothed the grass, sweeping aside pebbles and sandburs, and someone's wadded-up windbreaker served as a pillow. Roly-poly bugs coiled into themselves. The more nervous kids stayed on the circle's outer edge, watching for teachers, unsure of what would happen.

Neil sat beside his volunteer. He said, "Everyone, to their knees." We obeyed. From where I knelt, I could see into Robert P.'s nostrils. His eyes were shut. His mouth had opened slightly, flaunting teeth that needed braces. I wished for a spot at the opposite side of the circle. Being near Neil McCormick would have satisfied me.

Neil touched his middle and index fingers to Robert P.'s temples. "Breathe deeply." The fingers rubbed and massaged. I would die, I thought, to be that volunteer. Neil's voice lowered: "In your mind, begin counting backward. Start at one hundred. One hundred, ninety-nine. Keep going, counting backward, slowly." Everyone else's mouths moved in synch. Could he hypnotize an entire crowd?

"Eighty, seventy-nine, seventy-eight . . ." His voice softened, nearly a whisper. My eyes darted from Robert P.'s face to the back of Neil's head. I was so close to him. "Sixty," pause, "nine . . ."

By the time Neil reached sixty-two, Robert P. looked zombieish. His chest moved with each breath, but all else remained motionless. I figured he was faking it, but wondered what Neil would make him do or say. I hoped for something humiliating, like a piss on Miss Timmons's shoes or a brick demolishing a school window.

A girl said "Wow," which Neil seemed to take as a signal. He crawled atop Robert P., straddling his stomach. Belt buckles clicked together. "Fifty," Neil said. Robert didn't move. Neil gripped his wrists; pinned his hands above his head. The circle of kids tightened. I could feel fingers against my skin, shoulders brushing mine. I didn't look at any of them. My gaze fixed on Robert and Neil, locked there as if I were stuck in a theater's front row, its screen sparkling with some beautiful film.

Neil's body flattened. He stretched out on Robert. The buckles clicked again.

Clouds crawled across the sun. For a few seconds, everything went dark. Another whistle blared. "Recess over," Miss Timmons screamed, but no one budged. We couldn't care less about the whistle. The silence grew, blooming like a fleecy gray flower. A little voice inside me kept counting: thirty-three, thirty-two.

Then it happened. The lower half of Neil's body began grinding into Robert's. I watched Neil's ass move against him. By that time in my life, I'd seen some R-rated movies, so I knew what fucking looked like. Only these were boys, and their clothes were on.

Neil positioned his face directly over his subject's. Robert's eyes opened. They blinked twice, as beady and inquisitive as a hen's. A thick line of drool spilled from Neil's mouth. It lingered there, glittered, then trailed between Robert's lips. Robert coughed, swallowed, coughed again. Neil continued drooling, and as he did, he moved his face closer to Robert's. At last their mouths touched.

Vicky screamed, and everyone jumped back. Kids shouted things like "gross" and "sick." They sprinted for Miss Timmons and the classroom, their sneaker colors blurring together. I stood and stared at the separated pair of boys. Robert P. wriggled on the grass like a rattlesnake smashed by a semi. A chocolatey blob stuck to his chin: dirt, suffused with Neil's spit.

One of Robert's buddies kicked Neil's ribs, then hustled away with the others. Neil didn't wince, accepting the kick as he might accept a handshake.

"Queer," Robert P. said, plus something in Spanish. He was crying. He kicked Neil, too, his foot connecting with the identical spot his friend had chosen. Then he ran for the school's glass doors.

Neil sprawled there a while, smiling, his arms spread as if he'd been crucified to the earth. He struggled to get up. He and I were alone on the playground. I wanted to touch his arm, his shoulder, his face. I offered my hand, and he took it.

"That was great," Neil said. He squeezed my fingers and shuffled toward the school.

Something important had happened, and I had witnessed it. And I had touched Neil McCormick. I waited until
he departed earshot. Then I pretended I was a character in a
movie. I said, "There's no turning back now." A small spit
bubble lay on the dirt at my feet like a toad's gleaming eye. I
bent down and popped it. If I could make Neil my friend, I
figured I wouldn't need anyone else.

The séances vanished. By the end of that week, the kids
who'd brought their Ouija boards and magic eight balls had
jumped back to four-square and soccer. I watched them and
wanted to scream. I longed to approach Neil again, this boy
I saw as my doorway from the boredom I wanted to escape.

That Friday, a team of bullies gathered on the soccer
field. They found Neil standing by a tree and cornered him.
"You're one of those queers," a kid named Alastair yelled.
Neil flew at him. A crowd formed, and I joined it. Arms and
legs darted and windmilled, and the ivory crescent of Neil's
fingernail sliced Alastair's chin. There were tears and a few
drops of blood, all of which turned out to be Alastair's. At
twelve, I'd seen more tornadoes than blood. Its red looked
magnificent and sacred, as if rubies had been shattered.

When the fight was history, Neil stood beside the same
oak. He wore a hot rod T-shirt, a real leather coat with zip-
pers like rows of teeth, and matching boots. Animals had
died for those clothes, I thought. He would be perfect holding a switchblade in one hand, and me in the other.

I took a deep breath, collected the gumption, and tiptoed over. I tilted my head heavenward to look cool. The sun
rebounded off the steel plates of Sherman Middle School to
reveal the roof's slant. It had been littered with toilet paper,
a yellow ball some vandal had sliced from its tether, and
random graffiti. GO STRAIGHT TO HELL was all someone could
think to spray paint. I stared at the jagged red letters and

kept walking. Around me, brown five-pointed leaves fell like the severed hands of babies. I moved through them. Neil heard the crunch, crunch and glanced up.

I leaned against another tree, feigning nonchalance. "You *are* a queer, aren't you?" I said the *Q*-word as if it were synonymous with *movie star* or *deity*. There was something wonderful about the word, something that set him apart from everyone else, something I wanted to identify with.

"Yeah," said Neil.

I felt as if I were falling in love. Not so much with him, though, as with the aura of him. It didn't matter that he was a year younger than me. It didn't matter, all the distaste I detected in teachers' voices when they called his name during recess. Neil McCormick, they barked, the fence is there for a reason, don't cross it. Neil McCormick, put down that stick. I had eavesdropped on Miss Timmons in her office, as she whispered to the school nurse how she dreaded getting the McCormick boy in her class next year. "He's simply evil," etcetera.

To me, "evil" didn't seem all that bad.

Neil's long hair frayed in the breeze, as shiny black as the lenses in the spectacles of the creepy blind girl who sat behind me on the morning bus. His eyebrows met ominously in his forehead's middle. Up close, I could smell him. The odor swelled, like something hot. If I weren't so eager to touch him again, I would have shrunk from it.

I breathed again, as if it were something I did once a day. "But you're a tough queer, right?"

"Yeah." He examined the blood smear on the back of his hand. He made certain I was watching, then licked it off.

In my room, I fantasized miniature movies starring Neil and me. My parents had okayed my staying up to watch *Bonnie and Clyde* on the late-late, and in my Neil hallucinations I assumed bloodred lipstick and a platinum bob that swirled in the wind, à la Faye Dunaway. I clung to his side. We wielded guns the size of our arms. We blew away bank tellers and other boring innocents, their blood spattering the air in slow-mo. Newspapers tumbleweeded through deserted streets. MCCORMICK AND PETERSON STRIKE AGAIN, their headlines read.

In these dreams, we never kissed. I was content to stand beside him. Nights, I fell asleep with clenched fists.

Weeks passed. Neil spent most recesses just standing there, feeling everyone else's fear. I wasn't afraid, but I couldn't approach him again. He was like the electric wire that separated my uncle's farm from the neighbors'. Touch it, Wendy, my little brother Kurt would say. It won't hurt. But I couldn't move toward it. Surely a sliver of blue electricity would jet from the wire and strike me dead. I felt the same way about Neil: I didn't dare go near him. Not yet.

Zelda Beringer, a girl who wore a headpiece attached to her braces and who wouldn't remain my friend much longer, teased me about Neil. "How in the world can you think a queer is cute? I mean, you can tell he's a freak. You can just tell." I advised Zelda that if she didn't shut up, I'd gouge out her eyes and force her to swallow them. The resulting look on her face wouldn't leave my mind for days.

For Columbus Day the cafeteria cooks served the school's favorite lunch. They fixed potato boats: a bologna slice fried until its edges curled, a scoop of mashed potatoes stuck in its center, watery cheese melted on top. They made home fries, and provided three squirt bottles of ketchup per table. For dessert, banana halves, rolled in a mucousy marriage of powdered gelatin and water.

Fifth graders sat on the cafeteria's opposite end, but that day I was blessed with a great view of Neil. He scooped the boat into one hand and devoured it in a single bite. If

I'd had binoculars, I could have watched his puffy lips in close-up.

I remember that day as near perfect, and not just because of potato boats. The yearly sex-ed filmstrips arrived. All afternoon, teachers glanced at clocks and avoided our gazes. We knew what was happening. We'd been through it before. Now we could view those films again, together in the room with the virgin fifth graders. "We're going to see cartoon tits and ass," Alastair said, the slightest hint of a scratch still on his chin.

Grade five lumbered in. Neil stood at the back of the line. For the first half of the process, the principal, Mr. Fili, separated boys from girls. The boys left, and Miss Timmons dimmed the lights. The room felt stifling, as if some killer had snuck in to poison our air with a noxious nerve gas. I rested my elbows on my desk; planted my chin on my fists.

Miss Timmons hesitated before reading the film's captions. "Sometimes, at this age, young men will want to touch certain places on a young lady's body." She bit her lip like the section of an orange.

When the filmstrip was over, Miss Timmons handed out free Kotex pads. Most girls popped theirs into purses or the back shadows of desk drawers. I examined mine. It resembled something I would hold over a campfire or take a chomp from.

After ten minutes, the boys returned. "Find a seat, men, somewhere on the floor," Mr. Fili told them. "This time, try to keep quiet. If you feel the urge to make some capricious outburst, please hold your breath. And no commentaries. This is serious stuff." When he said that, he scowled at Neil.

Neil moved toward me, as if following a dotted line to my desk. I swallowed hard. He sat, his knee touching my calf.

Part two of the birds-and-bees rigamarole was special: a film instead of filmstrip. Kids oohed and aahed when they heard the projector's buzzes and clicks. Perhaps this meant we would see real, live sex action.

Some fool of a filmmaker had dreamed up the idea that humor was the best way to teach sex. Tiny cartoon sperm wriggled and roller coastered toward a bulging, rouged egg. The egg licked its lips, as eager and lewd as an old whore. The music—*The 1812 Overture*—swelled, and the quickest and most virile sperm punctured the egg. "Bull's-eye!" the voice-over cackled.

Some kids clapped and cheered. "Shhh," said Miss Timmons.

Neil looked up at me. I swore I could smell bologna on him. A smear of ketchup had dried on his shirt front. He smiled, and I smiled back. He mouthed the words, "This is total bullshit," moving to lean against my legs. When he shifted, I felt his backbone move. No one was watching us.

On screen, drawings of a penis and the inside of a vagina flashed on and off. A couple of fifth graders giggled. Penis entered vagina, and white junk gushed forth like mist from a geyser. More giggles. Miss Timmons shhed again.

"Ridiculous," Neil whispered. "Not everyone fucks like that." Some kids heard him, glared and sneered. "Some people take it up the ass." One girl's face reddened, as if scratched.

As the credits rolled, Neil's hand rested on my sneaker, resulting in a goose bumpy feeling that lasted three tiny seconds. I wiggled my toes. Lights clicked on, and his hand moved away. "Let's go, fifth grade," Mr. Fili said.

"How fucked up," Neil said to me. He was speaking to no one else now. "Why don't they teach us something we don't already know?" Disappointment amended his face.

Neil waved as they filed out. Kids' heads turned to stare

at me, and I felt as though it were Neil and me versus everyone else. It was a good feeling. I let my classmates gawk
awhile, then shook my middle finger at them.

That evening, I upped the volume on the stereo to
drown out the TV my parents and brother were fixed in
front of. Even with the bedroom door closed, I could hear
televised trumpets blaring "America the Beautiful." A newscaster said, "Happy Columbus Day." I lifted the needle from
my Blondie album and started side one over again:
"Dreaming," my favorite song.

My geography book toppled off my bed. I was just
beginning to effectively imagine myself as a singer onstage,
a cluster of punks bouncing below me, when Mom rapped
at the door. "Can you hear in there?" she asked. "You'll
shake the house off its foundation. Anyway, you've got a
phone call. It's some boy."

I ran to the kitchen's extension. Mom had just finished
drying dishes, and her set of knives lined a black towel on
the table. By that time in the fall, it was starting to grow
dark by six o'clock, so the room looked like some kind of
torture dungeon. I left the light off.

The music on the phone's other end sounded cool. I listened for three, four, five seconds. "This is Wendy."

Someone stuttered a hello. Then, "You might not know
me. My name's Stephen Zepherelli."

My eyes widened. Everyone knew the notorious
Stephen Zepherelli. He attended class in the adjoining
building at school, one of the Learning Disabilities trio we
occasionally saw delivering messages to Mr. Fili or bending
over water faucets in the hall. The LDs, we called them.
Stephen Zepherelli was the most severe of the three LDs.
He wasn't retarded, but he was close. He drooled, and he
smelled like an old pond.

Then I realized the absurdity of him calling me. I'd heard Zepherelli's voice before, and this wasn't it. "Okay," I said. "Not funny. Someone's got to have at least half a brain to know how to dial a telephone. Who is this really?"

A laugh. The new-wave song paused, then began blasting a guitar solo. "Hey Wendy, this is Neil McCormick." I couldn't believe it. "I've called three Petersons in the phone book already, and I finally found the right one. What are you doing?"

I forgave Neil for the Zepherelli joke. "Nothing," I said. "As usual. How about that film today?"

We chatted for ten minutes about people we despised most at school. While Neil spoke, I handled the knives, arranging them on the table from longest to shortest. "I'd like to stab all those fools," I said, my back turned from the direction of the den and my parents. "Make it hurt. Stab them in the gut, then twist the knife real slow. I've read it really hurts that way. Or I'd cut their heads right off."

When I said that, Neil laughed. I pictured him throwing his head back, his mouth open, his teeth gleaming like an animal's.

By Halloween I stopped riding the bus home and began walking with Neil. His house was only four blocks from mine. Sometimes we carried each other's books. We tried alternate ways home. Once we even went the opposite direction, heading toward the prison on Hutchinson's east side. Neil stood at its gate, his shoelaces clotted with sandburs, breathing in the wistful smells of the rain-soaked hay and mud, the raked piles of leaves. "Kansas State Industrial Reformatory," he read. "Maybe I'll end up here someday." A guard watched us from the stone tower. We waved, but he didn't wave back.

Neil lived with his mother, and had no bratty brothers

or sisters to deal with. And his father wasn't a hypnotist at all. He was dead. "Killed in a war," Neil said. "He's nothing but a corpse now. I know him from one picture, and one picture only. He looks nothing like me, either. What should I care about the guy?"

Mrs. McCormick drank gin straight from the bottle. On the label, a bearded man was dressed in a plaid skirt. The first time I visited Neil's, his mom slid the bottle aside and took my hand in hers. "Hello, Wendy," she said. "It's not often I see a friend of Neil's. And such vibrant blond hair." Her own hair was as black as her son's. She had pinned it back with green pickle-shaped barrettes.

A bookshelf in Neil's house was piled with paperbacks with damaged or missing covers. Neil explained that his mother had a job at a grocery store, and her boss allowed her to keep whatever books the customers vandalized. Many concerned true kidnappings and murders. Mrs. McCormick saw me eyeing them. "You can borrow whatever you like," she told me. Soon I stopped reading about the tedious exploits of that ignoramus Nancy Drew. Within days I knew all there was to know about Charles Starkweather and Caril Ann Fugate, two teenage fugitives who blazed a trail of murder and mayhem across the Midwest a few decades ago. They weren't that much older than Neil and me. They even hailed from Nebraska, our border state. In two grainy mug shots, their grimaces couldn't have been more severe if their mouths had been clogged with thumbtacks. If I thought hard enough, Neil and I almost resembled them.

I had decided that '83 would be my last year as a trick-or-treater, and I wanted to dress as something special. I considered a gypsy, a freshly murdered corpse, an evil nun with a knife beneath her habit. Then I decided Neil and I should go as Charles and Caril. On Halloween night, I stared at the criminals' pictures and tried to change my looks.

Neil stretched out on his bed. "It's not working," he said. He tossed a baseball into the air, caught it. "No one will get it, so why bother?"

I wiped the lipstick on a Kleenex and watched him watching me in his bedroom mirror. When I peeled off the fake eyelash, my lid made a popping noise.

Mrs. McCormick dragged two spider costumes from her closet. She and a date, Neil claimed, had gone as "Daddy and Mommy Longlegs" to a party last year. "She lost that boyfriend around the same time," he said. "Sometimes she can't handle anything. But she's my mom."

We mascaraed circles around our eyes and thumbed black blobs across our mouths. Before we left the house, Neil gave me three yellow pills. "Swallow these." The box in his hand read DOZ-AWAY. I wasn't sure if that meant we'd grow sleepy or stay perky, but the box's cover pictured a pair of wide-awake eyes.

By that point I would have done anything Neil told me. I popped the pills in my mouth, swallowing without water.

Neil handed me the telephone beside his bed. He told me to call my parents and claim his mom would be escorting us. When I lied to Mom, it didn't feel so scandalous. "I'll take Kurt around the neighborhood without you, then," she said. "Call back when you want me to drive over and get you. Don't stay out too late, and remember what I told you about those perverts who prey on kids on Halloween." She laughed nervously. I thought of her stories of razor blades wedged into apples, stories that never ceased to thrill me.

Two hours came and went. We wandered around Hutchinson as spiders, our extra four legs bobbing at our sides. The rows of our eyes gleamed from our headpieces. The shadows we cast gave me the creeps, so we shied away from streetlights. Neil hissed when doors opened. One wrinkly lady touched my nose with a counterfeit black fingernail. She asked, "Aren't you two a little old for this?" Still, our shopping bags filled to the top. I stomped a Granny Smith into mush on the sidewalk. No hidden razor.

Neil traded his Bit-O-Honeys for anything I had with peanuts. "I'm allergic to nuts," I said. That was a lie, but I wanted to make him happy.

At Twenty-third and Adams, a group of seven kids walked toward us. I recognized the younger ones from school under their guises of pirate, fat lady, and something that resembled a beaver. "Hey, it's you-know-who from school," Neil said, and pointed to a green dragon in the crowd's center.

I couldn't tell who it was. "It's that retardo," Neil told me. He was right. Even under the tied-on snout and green pointy ears, I could make out Stephen Zepherelli.

"Hey," Neil said. Their heads turned. "Hey, snotnoses, where're your parents?"

The beaver-thing pointed west. "Back there," it said. The words garbled behind its fake buck teeth.

Zepherelli smiled. The dragon snout shifted on his face. He carried a plastic pumpkin, chock-full with candy. "Let's kidnap him," Neil said to me.

I'd witnessed Neil's damage to Robert P. and Alastair. Now, some dire section of my brain longed to find out what twisted things Neil could do to this nimrod, this Stephen Zepherelli. Neil checked the sidewalk for adults. When none materialized, he grabbed the kid's left hand. "He's supposed to come with us," Neil said to the rest of the trick-or-treaters. "His mom said so. She doesn't want him out too late."

Zepherelli whined at first, but Neil said we were leading him to a house that was giving away "enough candy for three thousand starving kids." Zepherelli didn't seem to mind the kidnapping after that. We stood on each side of him, gripped his scrawny wrists, and pulled him along. Mahogany-colored leaves spun around our rushing feet. "Slow down," he said at one point. We just moved faster. He stopped once to retrieve a handful of candy corn from his plastic pumpkin, and once to find a Zero candy bar. His painted-on dragon's teeth shone under street lamps, as white as piano keys.

We arrived at Neil's. "Is this the house with the candy?" Zepherelli asked. He rummaged through his pumpkin, making room.

"Good guess."

Neil's mom snoozed on the living room couch. Nearly every light in the house had been left on. Neil pushed Zepherelli toward me. "Hold this little bastard while I'm gone." He trotted from room to room, flicking switches. In seconds, darkness had lowered around us. Neil slid aside a record by a band called Bow Wow Wow and slipped another LP on the turntable. Scary sound effects drifted through the house at a volume soft enough to keep his mom sleeping. On the record, a cat hissed, chains rattled, crazed banshees wailed.

"Neat," Zepherelli said. His snout showed a smudge of white chocolate from the Zero. He nibbled the tip from a piece of candy corn.

I heard Neil pissing. I suddenly felt embarrassed, standing there with our victim. Neil returned, carrying a flashlight and a paper sack. He opened the latter. Inside were firecrackers and bottle rockets. "Left over from Fourth of July," Neil said. He winked. "Let's take him out behind the house."

The McCormick backyard consisted of overgrown weeds, an apricot tree, and a dilapidated slippery slide–swing set. Behind the swings was a cement-filled hole someone had once meant for a cellar. We walked toward it. The rotten apricot odor permeated the autumn air. Stars glittered in the sky. Down the block, kids yelled "trick or treat" from a doorstep.

Neil pushed Zepherelli toward the stretch of cement. "Lie on your back," he said.

The yellow pills had done something to me. My skin tingled like I'd taken a bath in ice. I was a hundred percent awake, and prepared for anything. I adjusted a loose arm and stood above the victim; Neil spilled the bag's contents onto the cement. "Bottle rockets," the dragon said, as if they were hundred-dollar bills. I could smell Zepherelli's breath, even over all those apricots.

Neil told him to shut up. He pulled off the dragon's snout. The string snapped against Zepherelli's face. "Ouch."

I watched as Neil took three bottle rockets and placed their wooden ends in Zepherelli's mouth. He pinched Zepherelli's lips shut. He moved briskly, as if he'd done it all a thousand times. Then he straddled the kid. I remembered that seance, Robert P.'s still face. Stephen Zepherelli's resembled it. It looked drugged, almost as if it really were hypnotized. It didn't register any emotion. Its cheeks had been smeared with green makeup. Its eyes were cold and blank, not unlike the peeled grapes we had passed around during the inane Haunted Hall setup at school that day. "These are the dead man's eyes," Miss Timmons had told us in her best Vincent Price voice.

"Keep these in your mouth," Neil instructed the LD boy. "Do what we say, or we'll kill you." I thought of Charles and Caril Ann. Neil's extra eyes caught the moonlight and sparkled.

From the effects record inside the house, a girl screamed, a monstrous voice laughed. Neil turned to me, smiling. "Matches are in the bottom of the sack," he said. "Hand them over."

I fished out a book of matches. The cover showed a beaming woman's face over a steamy piece of pie and the words "Eat at McGillicuddy's." I tossed the matches to Neil. "Be careful," I said. I tried not to sound scared. "Someone could see the fireworks." I still thought this was all a big joke.

"Tonight is just another holiday," Neil said. "No one's going to care." He lit the first match. The flame turned Zepherelli's face a weird orange. In the glow, the rockets jutted from his lips like sticks of spaghetti. His eyes were huge. He squirmed a little, and I sat on his legs. I felt as though we were offering a sacrifice to some special god.

Zepherelli didn't spit the rockets out. He made a noise that could have been "Don't" or "Stop."

Neil touched the match to the fuses. One, two, three. He shielded me with one of his real arms. We skittered back like crabs. I held my breath as tiny sputters of fire trailed up the fuses and entered the rockets. Zepherelli didn't budge. He was paralyzed. The bottle rockets zoomed from his head, made perfect arcs over the McCormick home, and exploded in feeble gold bursts.

The following silence seemed to last hours. I expected sirens to wail toward the house, but nothing happened. Finally, Neil and I snuck toward Zepherelli. "Shine the flashlight on him," Neil said.

The oval of light landed on our victim's face. For a second, I almost laughed. Zepherelli resembled the villain in a cartoon after the bomb goes off. The explosives' dust covered his dragon snout, his cheeks, his chin. His eyes had widened farther, and they darted here and there, as if he'd been blinded. We leaned in closer. Zepherelli licked his lips and winced. Then I saw what we'd done. It wasn't funny at all. His mouth was bleeding. Little red splinters stuck through Zepherelli's lips, jammed there from the wooden rocket sticks. Bubbles of blood dotted the lips.

The victim's eyes kept widening. I remembered thinking blood beautiful when Neil had punched Alastair. Now, from Zepherelli, it looked horrible, poisonous. I turned away.

Zepherelli made a mewling noise, softer than a kitten's. My heart felt like a hand curling into a fist. He whimpered again, and the fist clenched. "Neil," I said. "He's going to tattle on us. We're going to get it." I wondered if my parents would discover what we'd done. For the first time, I wanted to slap Neil.

A look spread across Neil's face, one I'd never seen there. He bit his bottom lip, and his eyes glassed over. Then he shook his head. The glassiness left his eyes. "No," he said. "He won't tell. There's things we can do." He spoke as if Zepherelli weren't lying beside us. "We'll get him on our side. Help me."

I didn't know what to do. I gripped the flashlight until my palm hurt. Neil wiped dust from Zepherelli's cheek. When their skins touched, Zepherelli trembled and sighed. Neil said, "Shhh," like a mother comforting a baby. His left hand remained on the kid's face. His right moved from Zepherelli's chest, down his stomach, and started untying the sweatpants dyed green for Halloween. He squirmed a finger inside, then his entire hand.

"When I was little," Neil said, "a man used to do this to me." He spoke toward the empty air, as if his words were the lines of a play he'd just memorized. He pulled the front of Zepherelli's pants down. The kid's dick stuck straight out. I swung the flashlight beam across it.

"Sometimes I wanted to tell everyone what was going on. Then he'd do this to me again, and I knew how badly he really wanted it. He did it to some other kids, but I knew they didn't matter as much to him, I was the only one whose photo he kept in his wallet. Every time he'd do it he'd roll up a five-dollar bill, brand-new so I could even hear it snap, and he'd slip it into the back pocket of my jeans or my baseball pants or whatever. It was like getting an allowance. I knew how much it meant to him, in a way, and after a while, it kept going further and further. There was no way I could tattle on him. I looked forward to it, for a while it was every week that summer, before the baseball games. It was great, he was waiting there, for me, like that was all he ever wanted."

Neil's voice sounded lower, older. It wasn't spouting nasty words or giggling between sentences. Then Neil shut up and leaned beside Zepherelli.

Neil buried his head in the kid's crotch. The dick disappeared in Neil's mouth. I watched the spider arms bob as Neil hovered over him. I slid back. The flashlight flipped from my hand. Its column of white illuminated the apricot tree's branches. Up there, a squirrel or something equally small and insignificant was scampering around. Already-dead fruit tumbled to the ground.

Stephen Zepherelli moaned. His breathing deepened. He didn't sound scared anymore.

The shadow of Neil's head lifted. "That feels nice, right?" The shadow moved back down, and I heard noises that sounded like a vampire sucking blood from a neck. I wanted to cry. I tried to fold myself into my dream of Charles and Caril Ann, those teenage fugitives. What would the blond murderess do in this situation, I wondered. Neil and I were nothing like them. I heard another chorus of "trick or treat"s, this time closer than before, maybe right there on the McCormicks' doorstep. I thought of Neil's mom, sleeping through it all. Where had she been when the man from Neil's past had put his mouth on her son like this?

I lay on my back until the noises stopped. Neil retied Zepherelli's sweat bottoms and handed him the dragon snout. "It's okay."

When Zepherelli stood, his eyes had resumed their normal luster. He was drooling. A comma-shaped trickle of blood had dried on his mouth. I got up, carefully pulled a splinter from his upper lip, and dabbed the blood with my black sleeve.

Neil patted the kid's butt like a coach. "I'll walk him home," Neil said. He smiled at me, but he was looking over my shoulder, not at my face.

We tiptoed through the McCormick house. In Neil's bedroom, I could see his tousled sheets, his schoolbooks, his baseball trophies. The scary record had ended, but the needle was stuck on the final groove. "Scratch, scratch, scratch," Zepherelli said. I faked a laugh.

Neil's mother was still sleeping. She snored louder than my father. I shone the flashlight on the bookshelves above her, making out titles like *Monsters and Madmen, Ghoulish and Ghastly, All the Worst Ways to Die*. Only days ago, I'd wanted to read those. Now I didn't care.

"I know the direction home," Stephen Zepherelli told Neil. He seemed anxious to lead the way. "I can show you where to go."

We left the house. The cool air smelled like mosquito repellent, barbecue sauce, harmless little fires. When the air hit my face, I ripped my headpiece off. A single beady spider's eye fell to the sidewalk. I bent to get it. In the weak street light, that eye stared back at me. I saw my reflection in its black glass. Instead of picking it up, I stood and ground it beneath my shoe.

"See you later, Stephen," I said. It was the first time I'd said his name, and my voice cracked on the word. "And you too, Neil. Tomorrow."

And I knew I would see him tomorrow, and the next day, and the day after that. Neil had shown a part of himself I knew he'd shown no one else. I reckoned I had asked for it. Now I was bound to him.

Neil led Zepherelli down the block. I watched them shuffle through the dead leaves, moving farther away, until the shadows swallowed them up.

five

DEBORAH LACKEY

My brother spent most of his time alone, and sometimes I wondered if my mother and I were his only friends. No one accompanied Brian on his walks home from school. He never went to parties or special school functions like the homecoming dance or Christmas formal. When he *did* venture from the house, it was to attend the latest program at the Hutchinson Cosmosphere, a conglomerated space museum and planetarium, which I found boring. Still, I often joined him, driving him into Hutchinson to see whatever space film happened to be showing.

Although I never mentioned it, I felt sorry for Brian. One night, I'd picked up the telephone to hear teenagers giggling. "Is The Nightmare home?" one voice mocked. "Zit patrol," another said. "We make house calls." Laughter, click, a dial tone.

Brian still performed his nightly practice of trudging to the roof. I'd given that up long ago, and by then my father had stopped as well, preferring instead to drive away in his truck after fights. Even the ragged rooftop chair was gone. But night after night, about an hour after sunset, Brian would climb the ladder, binoculars bouncing from the strap around his neck.

I wouldn't be around to watch his ritual much longer.

I'd graduated, and Christmas 1987 marked my final week in Kansas. The night before the holiday, I sat in front of the antique mirror at my bedroom window and decided to procrastinate packing. I looked outside. The crisp combination of the moon and the back porch's light allowed the normally obscure surroundings of our house to slide into focus. A group of rabbits, their fur thickened to adapt to winter, scampered around the evergreen trees that flanked our driveway.

For the first time, I wondered if I would miss Kansas. After eighteen years in Little River, I'd grown to despise it. My friend Breeze still lived in town, but she was already preoccupied with her husband and son. My other friends had all left for college, but chances were they'd return. I was certain of one thing: I didn't want to stay here all my life.

I heard Brian above me, stomping to the roof. I remained at the window. In seconds his shadow cast its freakish proportion across our lawn. I could tell he was wearing his down coat, mittens, a stocking cap peaked with a fluffy ball, even the bulky earphones that pounded out his favorite spacey computerized music. This was Brian's private time, his brand of monasticism, and watching him filled me with both embarrassment and guilt, as if I were viewing him in the shower. He lay on his back on the pebbled shingles, one leg crossed over the other, lazily twirling a foot in the air.

Then his shadow lifted the binoculars to his face. Instead of spying on Little River, he lifted his head and peered toward the moon and stars. He scanned the night sky for something, some inviting slant to his life, excitement he couldn't get in the house below.

I missed him already.

Before bedtime, Brian left the roof and reentered the house, where the rest of us were waiting. According to ritual, my family spent Christmas Eve by gathering in the living room to open one gift each. Brian slumped next to me at the base of the tree, his stocking cap still on. My mother sat in one half of the love seat, hunched over, her face close to ours, not wanting to miss a single detail. Across the room, my father leaned back in the rocker, pulling handfuls of popcorn from a silver bowl. The Christmas lights flashed from the window that overlooked Little River. From our hill, we could see the entire town, lit in reds and blues and greens like the cobbled surface of a fruitcake.

As with every year, my father went first. I chose a gift for him, avoiding the package that said TO GEORGE FROM M, trying to decide between gifts from Brian and me: the tackle box, the Old Spice aftershave, or the key chain. I settled on the key chain and handed it over. He ripped the paper in one motion and dropped it to the carpet. "NFL," he said, thumbing the gold emblem. "That's neat." He only used words like that at times like these.

"I'm next," Brian said. He selected a package. "From your sis," he read. Smiling penguins ice-skated across the wrapping paper, treble clefs and quarter notes trailing from their beaks. Inside was a hardback book, the type of gift that appeared most on the lists he'd slipped into my mother's purse and under my bedroom door. He held the book for my parents to see: *Loch Ness: New Theories Explained.*

"That's just what he needs," my father said. He squinted toward the tree, to other obvious book-shaped gifts. "Let me guess. Those are Bermuda Triangle, UFOs, and Bigfoot." He reached for the Loch Ness book, skimmed to the center's photo spread, and tossed it back to Brian. "A load of bunk," he said.

My mother received a bottle of White Shoulders perfume from Brian and me. She tipped the bottle against her thumb and streaked a drop beneath each earlobe.

My gift was last. I tried to conceal a blush as I unwrapped a boxful of bras from my mother. "Whoa-ho-ho," my father said.

"You can always use new underthings," my mother said. The lights flickered emerald green against her face. "No matter where you're living, Little River or San Francisco." Brian watched my reaction. I smiled at him, and he looked away.

That night I woke to hear my parents screaming downstairs. Whenever this happened, I usually sandwiched my head with pillows. But that night their bickering amplified. When my father yelled "Fuck you" and my mother fired "Fuck you" back, I knew they meant business.

I opened my door and padded into the hallway. There was Brian, listening at the top of the stairs. They had woken him, too. He put a finger to his lips when he saw me.

"Sick of everything in this life . . ." It was my mother, and it sounded as if she'd been crying. The radio mingled with her voice, a tinny chorus of children singing the first verse to "O Holy Night."

My father cleared his throat. "Then why don't you just end it all."

"Why don't you just go to hell."

"I wouldn't want to be anywhere you're going to end up."

I held my breath. I knew Brian was doing the same. The electric heater in his room made a hollow click, the sound of a knuckle, cracking.

Stomping feet, a drawer opening, and the clink of kitchen utensils floated toward us from downstairs. I heard the crash of knives and forks and spoons dumped onto linoleum tiles. This was my mother's method of expressing her rage: the kitchen was *her* territory, and she could just as soon serve my father meals with the silverware as stab him in the throat. Once, after a fight at dinner, we'd seen her fling a plate at the wall as if it were a Frisbee. The scratch was still there.

They continued shouting. But this time, their words had a finality that made it clear they had wearied of fighting, that twenty years of it was enough. Looking back I think it didn't matter that the following morning was Christmas. Somehow my parents must have known that Brian and I sat at the top of the stairs, listening. I believe they wanted us to understand that it was over.

"Fuck you," my father said again, and then he was off. He tore through the house, the door slamming behind him. He revved the pickup's engine once, twice. He sped from the driveway, tires skidding in icy puddles.

Silence. I imagined my mother standing in the kitchen, silverware strewn around her feet. Amid that quiet, my mother blew her nose. For some reason, I found that hilarious. Brian looked at me, and we both clamped hands across our mouths to keep from snickering.

My mother blew her nose again, and the sound trumpeted toward the second floor. This time, Brian's laughter burst from his mouth, resonating in the air like a shook tambourine. He sprinted down the stairs, taking them three at a time. I heard him trace our father's path through the house, out the front door. *He'll freeze out there,* I thought. He was still laughing when the door slammed behind him.

I tiptoed down. I didn't want to see my mother's tear-streaked face, but I figured I should help her clean the mess. "Are you okay?" I asked. She wasn't in the kitchen. I stepped into the living room: toppled chair, overturned lamp, cinnamony-smelling potpourri spilling from a chipped bowl. A slice of pumpkin pie lay smashed in the floor's center, leaking a dollop of whipped cream like a teardrop. The fire in the hearth had fizzled out, but the Christmas tree's lights still blinked, casting rainbows over the wadded remnants of wrapping paper.

I turned and saw my mother. She shuffled toward the window, unaware of my presence. She bumped her shin on the fallen rocking chair. "Owee-owee," she said, and I remembered her speaking that way when Brian and I were kids, when we'd come to her with scratches or cuts. She continued to fumble forward, her arms held out as if offering something to the dark. It horrified me to see her like this: she had always held reign over these rooms, and was now suddenly blinded and clumsy within them. When she reached the window, she brushed aside the curtain. "You'll catch pneumonia," she yelled to Brian. Her breath misted the glass.

I slid into a pair of boots and walked outside. Snow fell in orderly specks, dusting the evergreens. Somewhere, far away, a sparrow was shrieking. I followed the footprints. Brian, dressed in his pj's and gym socks, stood on the hillside, facing the field. In the distance, the taillights from my father's truck became smaller and smaller, two minuscule rubies dissolving into black. I wondered if he had used his new key chain to start his engine on this, the night he had finally left.

When the lights on my father's truck were completely gone, I waved toward his unknown destination. "That's that," I said. The words seemed awkward and inconsiderate, and I immediately wished I could take them back. But Brian hadn't heard me. He lifted his head and stared at the sky. He had stood just like that years before, on the night we'd seen the blue lights in the air above our field. Now, nothing resided there but the snowfall, a mass of white that blanketed any trace of moon and stars.

Head still raised, my brother began to dance. He

swiveled his hips and stomped his stocking feet, arms reaching out, fingers scratching the air. He was smiling, sheer bliss spelled out on his face.

Behind us, my mother opened the window. "Pneumonia," she repeated. I knew she was leaning her head outside, snow sequining her hair and her face, the face no longer lined with concern about the man who'd left us. She was only thinking of the two people who really mattered, her kids.

I didn't turn around. Instead, I joined Brian in his dance. I was eighteen, and in three days I would be abandoning Kansas for San Francisco, perhaps leaving forever. I didn't care how foolish I looked. I lifted my arms and twisted my feet in the snow's thick carpet. The snow began coming faster, shattered bits of gemstones zigzagging through the air. It was a celebration. Brian and I danced on the side of the hill, almost as if dancing on my father's grave, as the torn pieces of sky tumbled around us like confetti.

six

NEIL MCCORMICK

Once I stole a bicycle. It was as simple as swiping a gingerbread man from our kitchen's beehive-shaped cookie jar. But the thrill I got from the bike was more profound. I searched the evening street for snooping pedestrians, lifted my leg over the seat, and pedaled down the block. The icy breeze stung my face. I ended up on Seventeenth Street, at Wendy's house. "My new set of wheels," I told her when she opened her front door. I'd grown too tall for my old bike years ago.

Her mouth formed a precise O. She said, "That's a White Bicycle," as if each word took an exclamation point. Then her amazement faded, and she got the same idea as me. "Let's find the spray paint."

The bicycle metamorphosed from white to black. I furthered its makeover by covering the handlebars and back wheel guards with stickers that Wendy had taken from her favorite punk bands' LPs. On one, Charles Manson's eyes peered out. I stuck it on the seat.

I laughed just considering the scandal. One year before, the Hutchinson community had started a program called the "White Bicycles." Volunteers had bought ten white Fujis, then placed them at various spots around the city. Residents could ride whenever the need arose—when their legs tired, when they were tipsy, when a knife-wielding attacker chased them, whatever. The rider parked the bike for the next person.

I considered the program a big joke, but it didn't concern me until the day I committed my crime. That morning's Hutchinson newspaper headline had announced the one-year anniversary of the White Bicycles. In a gigantic photo, teenagers stood grinning beside the bikes, their hands on the seats. I recognized so-and-so and his girlfriend from school. They were just the sort of people I hated—the kind who regarded life as a hunky-dory trip in a helium balloon.

"Tonight I get the last laugh," I said. The spray paint sizzled from its can. The balls of my fingers had turned as black as olives, and I jabbed them into Wendy's ribs.

Wendy borrowed her little brother's Schwinn. The night was cold, lacerated by wind, so we donned scarves and stocking caps and raced toward Monroe Street. On the way there, we passed a stretch of road construction. A chunky female traffic cop waved an orange, diamond-shaped sign at us. "Slow down, goddammit, slow down!" Wendy hated being lectured as much as I did. She lifted her fist from her handlebars and shook it at the cop.

We parked in my garage. Mom had left the porch light on for me. Tiny icicles hung from our roof's edge, gleaming like fangs. Inside, Mom was sliding a tuna-noodle casserole into the oven. She had crumbled barbecue potato chips across the top layer of noodles. It was her third week off booze, and she'd been concocting new dishes every night. Wendy rubbed Mom's shoulder. "Smells delicious, Mom," she lied.

Mom kissed her cheek. "Weatherman says tonight will be the first snowfall," she said. "It might be a white Christmas. You can stay for casserole, Wendy." We hadn't dined with a guest since Mom's last boyfriend.

I turned on the stereo. The annoying deejay began introducing the next song in his top-forty countdown, so I quickly switched it off. TV was better. On screen, a "Gilligan's Island" rerun played in black and white. The girls wanted something from Gilligan. Ginger fluttered her eyelids and massaged his neck while Maryanne displayed a just-baked coconut cream pie. Nonexistent humans giggled and guffawed on the laugh track. Wendy asked me how much I'd take to screw the Skipper. "A hundred," I said. The Professor? "He's not bad. Fifty."

When I said that word, Wendy looked at me and arched an eyebrow. For weeks we'd been discussing the easiest ways to make money, namely prostitution. I'd been reading about the concept for years in my stash of porno magazines. Wendy called me obsessed. I'd even written my freshman term paper on the topic. I'd given it the predictable title "World's Oldest Profession," but I was content with my B minus. During my research, I'd found a dusty hardback in Hutchinson's library that listed cities where older men pay hustlers top dollar for a fuck, a blow job, whatever.

Recently I'd discovered hustling even went on in Hutchinson. Christopher Ortega, a not-bad-looking kid in Wendy's sophomore class, claimed he did it on the side. He lingered around the playgrounds of our city's Carey Park on weekends, thumbs in pockets, watching as lonely middleagers circled the roadway. "Fifty bucks is my charge," Christopher had said, and I believed him for the simple fact that he hadn't lied to us about these sorts of things before— i.e., he supplied us a bag of pot when I didn't believe he sold drugs, and once, when I accused him of faking being a queer, he'd rammed his tongue into my mouth on the spot.

"I've been thinking about hanging out in the park," I told Wendy. It was the third time I'd mentioned it that week.

Wendy leaned to peek into the kitchen, then turned back

to me. "I'd rather see you make a buck some other way." A wave of fishy odor floated into the living room. Wendy pinched her nose and continued in an altered voice. "But fucking's perpetually on your mind anyway, so you might as well get paid for it."

I watched the woman on the TV commercial choose the less-expensive detergent over the most popular brand. "Old guys will pay anything to get off with someone else. Anything different than their own hands," I said. "It's that feeling of a young guy's skin touching theirs. Think of it as a service. They could get something from me, and I could get something from them."

"True." Pause. "But be careful. I know that sounds dumb, but even Hutchinson has its freaks. You're only fifteen. You could trick with the wrong guy. I'd find pieces of you scattered everywhere."

"You've been reading too many books," I said. I could sense Wendy's eyes drilling into my face, so I looked down. Paint smudges blackened my sweater sleeve. "Besides, it's not that I haven't done it already. For a little money, I mean."

She'd known this was coming. "Coach?" she said. She was the only one I'd told about what happened that summer. I'd confessed everything to her, again and again. Wendy could practically hear Coach's voice herself, could smell his breath, could feel the texture of his skin.

She repeated the word, this time without the question mark. "Coach."

The stolen bike propelled me from poverty to affluence. The following Saturday afternoon, I slipped on an extra pair of socks, downed a plateful of leftover casserole, yelled good-bye to Mom as she headed to work, and rode toward Carey Park. The idea of money for sex thrilled me like nothing before.

A thin layer of ice sheeted the pair of ponds that flanked the park. The golf course and basketball courts were empty. I lowered the stocking cap around my ears.

The johns didn't take long to spot. Four or five different men drove back and forth, around and around, circling the park in outdated cars. The guy in the Toyota Corolla and the guy in the Impala—it was almost identical to Mom's car, its color a shade darker—tapped their brakes when they passed my bicycle. I trudged alongside the park road, pretending not to notice. But I did notice. The idea of their wanting to pay for me rendered me breathless, thrilled, delirious, flustered. . . . I glanced into their windows, searching for any scrap of attractiveness, any absorbing or aberrant facial feature that might lead to me enjoying the actual sex.

I lapped Carey Park for thirty minutes, then stopped the bike at a playground. I tried to remember everything Christopher had told me. "Look innocent, yet old enough to be legal." "Empty the emotion from your face." "Smile crooked-mouthed; you look cuter."

I walked toward the brightly painted circus animals, the ones hooked to concrete blocks by heavy springs. I sat on an elephant, and the cold metal stung my ass. I watched clouds curl through the sky, and in seconds the Corolla parked. I squinted at the driver; saw his dark curly hair and mustache. A finger poked from a crack in the passenger seat window and motioned me over.

Bingo.

Already I'd scored. I wasn't sure what to say, so I opted for the direct. "You've got cash?"

"I've paid fifty before, and I'll go no higher," he said. I must have looked like a pro. I nodded and opened the car door.

He said his name was Charlie. He'd been married, divorced, and had married again. Three kids—a boy and two girls. "I'm in Hutchinson on business," he said in a gruff monotone, "and my business is marketing snack foods." I took a good whiff of his car, and it smelled like those orange cheese crackers with the peanut butter filling. He must have predicted my thoughts, because he offered me a package. I grabbed it and chowed down, then looked Charlie over. He wore a green suit, a name tag, a Santa Claus tie. His hands fidgeted at his face, the fingers returning again and again to touch his chin, as if it might crumble. I slid closer to him, and he patted my knee and massaged it. He shifted into drive and watched the road like the eye of a needle.

"Cops patrol this place," Charlie said. "Even when it's freezing outside, they've got brains enough to know what's up." His hands were shaking. "Let's get a room somewhere."

That "somewhere" was the Sunflower Inn. Room 102's welcome mat spelled *hospitality* with two *l*s. The bed was comfortable, but the room was creepy. An orange bedspread showed a fist-sized black stain; the TV hadn't been dusted in what seemed decades. A draft from the window sucked the corner of an orange curtain in and out of the room like a massive lung.

I unlaced my shoes. "Go slow," Charlie said, "we've got all hour." I thought, one hour equals sixty minutes. Sixty divided into fifty equals about eighty-five cents per minute. I couldn't help grinning at that, which Charlie no doubt took to mean sensual pleasure. He started massaging my back.

He set the pace. I hardly touched him until he unzipped my pants and wormed three fingers inside. Then I pinched at his nipples, tickled the hair over his belly, rubbed his crotch through his slacks. *I'm good at this*, I thought. He pushed me onto the bed. He knelt beside me and shoved his head in my lap, his head bobbing and zigzagging as if filled with fizz. His tongue darted around my balls. It felt as flat and cold as a Popsicle.

I naturally thought of Coach. Charlie paled in comparison. That summer was six years past. I'd fucked around with a few guys since, but they'd been in my age group, hadn't enraptured me much. I traced the outline of Charlie's ribs and wondered where Coach was now. I knew he'd moved from Hutchinson. At school, I'd heard a grapevine story about someone's parents being suspicious, causing Coach to quit Little League. At that precise moment, he might have been lying on a bed in some other state with another kid like me. For all I knew, he could have been dead. That idea seemed incredibly romantic. If I'd been alone and high, my imagination would have roamed—me dressed in black, lumbering toward Coach's open coffin, a tear on my cheek, to center a single white lily on his motionless and impeccable chest. . . . Charlie's grunt made my fantasy evaporate.

While Coach's fingers had "caressed" me, Charlie's merely "touched." My mind drifted, and Charlie stopped blowing me. He lifted his head and stared at my dick. "Come on, kid, you're losing your hard-on." I apologized. His head plunged back in.

Charlie sucked, and I fidgeted on the bed. My watch's minute hand moved from nine to ten to eleven. Coach's mouth had felt so much warmer than this. He had massaged the backs of my legs, his entire hands fitting over the muscles in my thighs. My dick and both balls could disappear into his mouth, and I would feel the clamp of his lips around my entire sex, trails of saliva streaming to the knees I'd scuffed from sliding into home plate.

"I'm ready," I told Charlie. He didn't pull away. I said it again. This time, I shuddered. He sucked harder, scraping his teeth over the head of my dick. In those seconds, I couldn't tell pleasure from pain. I tried to extricate myself, but he cupped his hands over my ass's curves. I came, and he swallowed.

Charlie stood and cleared his throat. "I know what your expression's saying," he said. "That wasn't safe. But this is Kansas, not some city full of disease. And you're just a kid." It was the first time I'd heard a man say that, but it wouldn't be the last.

I lay back, already wanting to leave.

Charlie tiptoed to the bathroom and fastened the lock. He started whistling "Strangers in the Night." I felt like slugging him, taping his mouth shut, anything. Water needled from the showerhead, and I leaped from the bed. I dressed, then ransacked his suitcase. His clothes were nicely folded. Every sock was white. I uncovered packages of snack crackers, bubble gum, plastic trash cans full of candy, and chewable wax "lips." I found Vitamin Cs, magnesium tablets, and aspirin. I grabbed my coat and filled its pockets.

During the drive back to the park, we barely said a word. He stopped beside my bike. "Maybe I'll see you sometime." He didn't look at me. His eyes focused on the kid's toy that hung by a string from the rearview mirror. It was a stuffed bear, the expression on its face vaguely tragic, an expression I'd seen on kids on milk cartons. Its red shirt read DADDY.

He handed me two twenties and a ten. "Thanks," I said. "It was nice."

The temperature was dropping, so I dashed home. Mom had left a note: "Early Shift Tomorrow." In the living room, she lay napping in a chair, the alarm clock at her elbow. For some reason, I wanted to hear her voice. The house was too quiet. I almost woke her, then decided against it. I shuffled to the bathroom and shelved the vitamins. The dusty mirror showed me as always: same bushy eyebrows, same square jaw, same zit on the same neck I needed to smear with alcohol. I walked out; locked myself in my room. My algebra homework remained on the bed, where I'd tossed it. The candy and the money fit perfectly in the bottom dresser drawer, next to the bag of pot I'd bought from Christopher. I wedged one of the twenties into my wallet, pocketed the weed and the trash can candy, then picked up the phone. Wendy answered. When I opened my mouth to speak, I tasted peanut butter. "You'll never guess what I finally did."

I met Wendy on her porch. She had screwed a glowing taillight into the back end of her brother's bike, and I spotted her from two blocks away. She stood in the light's flashing red, waiting for me, bundled in her coat and scarf. She looked beautiful. "It's freezing," she yelled as I skidded to a halt. "And you're conning me into following you to your new whorehouse."

We rode toward Carey. I wanted to write a schedule on the park bathroom walls, to "fill the johns in on their new merchandise," as I'd told Wendy. I'd already been thinking about what fifty dollars a week could bring—more drugs for Wendy and me, a new pair of high-tops, even a real tree this coming Christmas in place of the artificial one Mom kept in our neighbor's cellar.

I stuck a pair of Charlie's wax lips over my own. When we stopped at the tracks for an oncoming train, Wendy leaned toward me and kissed them.

In the pitch black, the park was downright creepy. I propped my bike against a tree, and Wendy let hers fall to the ground. We pussyfooted toward the men's bathroom. It was unlocked, and she switched on the light.

In magenta crayon, I drew an erupting volcano, then wrote: "Saturday afternoons, from 2 until 3. Ready to please." That sounded stupid, so I x'ed out the last three words and wrote "Young and willing." Under it, in green, I scribbled a dollar sign. In less than twenty-four hours, I thought, I've become a hustler.

"Let's head home," Wendy said, "before frostbite sets in."

I stopped her. "Wait. I want to show you something." I unzipped. Wendy looked at me as if I were crazy. I pointed to my dick, to the bruises from that afternoon, already purple from the teeth marks Charlie left on my skin. "Look what the guy did to me," I said. "No brains whatsoever in the blow job department."

"Put that back in your pants, exhibitionist." She stomped out, lecturing. "From now on, don't let anyone do that to you. Your prick is not a candy cane. Next time somebody might chomp the whole thing off. You should start carrying Mace or a switchblade. At least charge them extra if they do that to you."

"I didn't realize it was hurting until it was over." I bit a chunk from the wax lips and handed the rest to her. "Here. An early Merry Christmas." The cold knifed my skin. I zipped back up.

We biked another half mile west. Our bodies hurtled through the dark. My eyes teared up, blurring the city lights that zoomed past us in stark, rhinestoney streams. After a while, the wind numbed me completely. I wiggled my fingers, barely feeling the gloves. I thought of the twenty-dollar bill in my wallet.

We sped past the entrance road to the Riviera Drive-In Theater. It had been closed since summer, but a feeble light still illuminated the marquee. Random letters were stuck there, and someone had rearranged them to spell HES COMING SOON. Wendy and I abandoned our bikes. We climbed the fence and walked forward, through the labyrinth of speaker poles. The projection booth's paint was chipping. Ahead of us, the rectangular drive-in screen resembled a gigantic white envelope. It obliterated part of the sky, the open door to an empty world.

We stopped in the lot's center. It was nearly midnight. The silence snuck up on us. I listened carefully for a siren, a dog's bark, or a car horn, but I heard nothing. I remember thinking, It should be snowing now, and then, as if I'd punched a button marked MIRACLES, the sky lit up, speckled with thousands of moving flakes.

I felt I had to speak to prove this was happening. "It's snowing."

I took Wendy's hand. Snowflakes clung to our coats. "I wish they were showing a movie right now," she whispered. "A film about our lives, everything that's happened so far. And we would be the only ones standing here, just you and me."

With her free hand, she unhooked a speaker from its pole. She twiddled the dials and lifted it to her ear. "Listen. I hear something. It's the voice of God." She laughed, and I leaned to where she held the speaker, the side of my head brushing against its chilly ridges. The snow began tumbling faster in sharp diagonal darts. I closed my eyes and listened. Wendy gripped my fingers tighter. After a while, I heard a whispering from deep within the speaker. It could have been something as explainable as Wendy playing a joke, or our gloves bristling together, or the wind that gusted the flakes around us. But I wanted the noise to be something else. "Yes," I told her, "I hear him." The rest of the world had frozen, and Wendy and I were all that remained. I brushed snow from her face. "I hear him."

part two

GRAY

Summer 1991

seven

BRIAN LACKEY

The summer air seemed ready to burst into flame. I finished mowing the grass and stretched in the rubber-ribbed lawn chair. Ten feet away, my mother stood with her head tilted, her sunglasses reflecting two white specks of sun, and aimed her gun at a pyramid of 7-UP bottles. *Bang-bang-bang*. Only a green shard remained from the top bottle, but her other shots had missed. "I'll flunk my accuracy test tomorrow," she said.

"Keep practicing," I said. I was dressed in sandals and shorts, my bare knees smudged with grass stains. I sipped orange juice through a straw. I had basted my chest with suntan oil that smelled like toasted coconut.

The newspaper and mail had arrived early that morning: a telephone bill, a postcard from Deborah showing Haight Street under a tie-dyed sky, and a membership notice from the National Rifle Association for my mother. The other letters came from colleges in Indiana, Arizona, and a Kansas Christian school called Bethany that had no doubt gotten my name from some church function I'd participated in years ago. "Congratulations Christian Graduate," the envelope said. I dumped the letters on the grass unread. I'd already decided to stay close to home for two years and attend the community college in Hutchinson.

My mother reloaded and aimed again. The bullets missed, missed, and missed, whizzing down the hill on the house's north side. She gingerly placed her .38 on the grass. Watching my usually serious mother at target practice made me want to laugh. I wondered what the town's busybodies thought, whether avenues of women were standing on their porches, squinting toward our house. Maybe a write-up would appear in the weekly paper, something like "Shots Heard on North Side of Town." Since my father and Deborah had left, I reasoned that Little River regarded my mother and I as weirdos: the forever solemn, gun-toting divorcee and her acned, bookworm son.

My mother rubbed the gun against her thigh, slipping it into an imaginary holster. "Get dressed," she said. "It's time to go food shopping, and I need the company." In the month since I'd finished high school, this had become our Saturday routine: a trek to Hutchinson to buy the week's groceries, then stop for chocolate-and-vanilla-swirl ice cream cones on the way home. We were both free for the day—me from my occasional lawn-mowing jobs, and my mother from the prison.

Inside, I bounded the stairs to my room. I kicked aside paperbacks, plucked a shirt from a pile of clothes, and slipped it over my oily shoulders. Downstairs, I grabbed the newspaper and followed my mother out the door.

The heat rose in visible waves from the highway. My mother drove forward. She flipped a switch, and cool air filled the Toyota's front seat. I withdrew my mother's country-western cassette from the car stereo slot, retired it to the glove compartment, and replaced it with a tape by Kraftwerk. My mother protested but began tapping her fingers on the steering wheel. The band's robotic voices droned lyrics about romancing a machine. I "sang" along, then unrolled

the *Hutchinson News* and scanned the headlines: COMMIS-
SIONER INDICTED ON RAPE CHARGE; FLOOD WARNING FOR RENO
COUNTY.

Neither story interested me, so I turned the page. What
I saw took a few seconds to register. The individual letters *U*
and *F* and *O* were stamped across the top of the paper. On
the page's left side, someone had penciled an amateurish
drawing of a spaceship.

I'd seen similar drawings in hundreds of books, but I
never expected an everyday newspaper to run a story about
UFOs. "Listen to this," I said to my mother. I announced the
headline. "NBC to Broadcast Local Woman's Extraterrestrial Story."

The car swarmed with a gunpowder smell that
emanated from my mother's skin. She looked at the newspaper in my lap and nodded, pressing me to read on.

I skimmed the article's first half. "This woman from
Inman," I said. "She doesn't live that far away. Her name's
Avalyn Friesen. This says she's been abducted by aliens at
various times during her life. It all came out under hypnosis. Some TV show is doing a special on alien visitations
this coming Friday night, and she's among the people
they're featuring."

I believed the woman's story, and my mother knew it.
She and I had discussed UFOs countless times. Before my
parents split up, these discussions had acted as a bond: my
father hadn't accompanied us when we witnessed the UFO
hovering over our watermelon field, so talking about the
incident was our way of shutting him out. My mother knew
I still read magazines and books, still watched TV shows
about unexplained spacecraft and close encounters.

"I feel sorry for her," I said. "People in her town will
think she's a freak." I stared at the thumb-size picture of

Avalyn. She had chubby, rouged cheeks and a close-mouthed smile that looked like a tiny bow tie. She wore oversize, rhinestone-framed glasses. She resembled a widow, struggling against the pull of tears. She didn't seem the sort who'd fabricate an outlandish story for attention.

According to the caption, Avalyn had drawn the UFO herself. She shaped it like a gray football with legs and antennas. I could remember the spectacle of *our* UFO as if I'd sighted it only yesterday. During the first week of school after that summer, I had drawn a similar spacecraft on poster board, its lights shooting beams of energy in blue crayon. I was in third grade then. I remember standing for show-and-tell, displaying my handmade poster, and relating my UFO sighting to my classmates. They had laughed until I fell back into my seat. On my walk home from school that day, a group of kids wrenched the poster from me. They stomped and spat on the drawing until all that remained were tattered bits in a puddle of mud.

The grocery was located two blocks from the Cosmosphere. When we got to the store, I usually loitered in the parking lot, squinting at the Cosmosphere's marquee to check for any upcoming shows or special announcements. But now I'd found something more important, more *real* than the shows I watched from month to month on that domed screen.

I followed my mother through the store's aisles, carrying the newspaper in front of my face, sidestepping other shoppers. I kept staring at Avalyn's photo. For years I'd wanted to actually meet someone who confessed to an alien encounter. I didn't know anyone beyond my mother and sister who claimed to have even seen a UFO; now, twenty miles from my own home, a woman had been abducted and taken aboard a ship from some other world. Even through the photograph's grainy ink, I could tell she knew something remarkable, something ethereal and profound. Beauty resided in that knowledge. I wanted it. Perhaps Avalyn Friesen was in Hutchinson at this moment, maybe even shopping at this very store. Carts wheeled past me, and I looked up from the photo for any scrap of resemblance. While my mother bagged radishes and cucumbers, I noticed the profile of a woman weighing zucchini: similar nose, same hair pulled into a bun. I moved to stare into her face. The woman turned away. It wasn't Avalyn.

I waited for my mother to finish, then stepped out the sliding glass doors. A plane of heat replaced the store's cool air. I knelt before the newspaper machines—Hutchinson, Kansas City, Wichita. No headlines about Avalyn, but I guessed that a story might be lurking somewhere within those pages. I took a chance on Wichita. I plugged two quarters into the machine, pulled out two papers instead of one, and returned to the Toyota.

On page C-12, in the "People and Places" section, I found it. The story in the Wichita *Eagle-Beacon* mirrored the one I'd read in the *News,* complete with the innocuous spacecraft drawing. But this piece contained specific additions. Avalyn had drawn one of her abductors. The alien was short with droopy arms and an enormous, hairless head shaped like a lightbulb. It had tiny pinpricks for a nose. Its ears were question marks. Its mouth thinned to a slit, a mere line scissored into its face. But the wildest aspect of Avalyn's alien was its eyes. She had blackened them in, huge almond-shaped pools embedded in its face. The drawing was crude, almost childlike. I tried to imagine coming face-to-face with this being, this thing that had touched Avalyn's skin.

Beneath the pair of columns was something else the

first article had omitted. A psychologist who specialized in treating alien abductees had provided a list of signs and signals that indicated possible interaction with aliens.

HAVE ALIENS CONTACTED YOU?

Wondering about the possibility of a past alien encounter? Ren Bloomfield, psychologist and self-professed "spiritual counselor," lists six signs that could indicate a "close encounter" in his third and most recent book, *Stolen Time*. According to Bloomfield, some signals to look for are:

1. Any amount of stolen time; missing hours or even days you can't account for.

2. Recurring, overwhelming nightmares—especially those of flying saucers or extraterrestrials, or of being examined by these aliens on an observation table.

3. The occurrence of unexplained bruises, sores, nosebleeds, or small puncture wounds.

4. Constant foreboding feelings, paranoia, and sensations of being watched.

5. Fear of the dark or of being outside alone.

6. Unexplained, continued interest in movies, books, or trivia about unidentified flying objects—sometimes to the point of obsession.

If you have experienced more than one of these phenomena, chances are you're not alone. Memories of a close encounter may lie buried within your subconscious mind.

Item number one, regarding the stolen time, reminded me of the night I woke in the crawl space. Sometimes, even now, serious concentration could bring back the air of that room, the smell of my nose's bewildering blood. Ren Bloomfield had mentioned nosebleeds in item number three. And I remembered times in my life when the dark had petrified me, times I'd felt paranoid, times I'd had strange dreams. Finally, the list's last item was an understatement in my case. Ever since the day I'd seen my UFO, I'd been fascinated, searching everywhere for scraps about extraterrestrial life. *Chances are you're not alone,* the article said. The urge to speak to Avalyn overwhelmed me. I wanted to discover all the knowledge she'd been unwillingly given.

My mother tapped on the passenger's side window. I jerked my head from the article and saw her standing in the parking lot. A chubby kid stood beside her in an ink-smudged apron, his arms laden with grocery sacks. "Open the trunk," my mother yelled. I folded the paper in my lap and pulled the latch.

"Let's get ice cream," she said as I started the car. When I didn't answer, she stared at me. I pointed to the newspaper on the dashboard, and she picked it up.

"Oh, her again," she said. She began the article, her finger guiding from word to word, and while she read I coasted through the Snow Palace drive-thru and ordered the regular.

I steered home with one hand; held the ice cream cone with the other. My mother polished off the article. "So," she said, "I guess we'll be spending Friday night in front of the TV." A half-brown, half-white ice cream smear covered her upper lip.

During the week, I searched the papers for updates on Avalyn. I watched TV for commercials about the upcoming UFO special. Before bed, I read books from my bookcase's top shelf. Some were yellowed large-print paperbacks my mother had bought from book fairs or kids' mail-order clubs when I was younger. Their covers showed drawings of lanternlike spaceships, more cartoon than reality. Some included blurry black-and-white photographs of objects that resembled Frisbees, hubcaps, beanies, and, in one case, a newfangled telephone. The stories in these books only concerned UFO sightings; none told details of alien encounters. It was as if the abductions were something intimate and secret, relegated only to books geared toward adults.

On that hot Friday afternoon, my mother suggested we go fishing—something we hadn't done since my father lived with us. "An angling excursion," she called it, and I agreed. I brought along a skimpy paperback, *Searching the Skies*. Its final sentence made a poor attempt at scaring preteen readers: "Will you or your family be the next to make contact with a craft from another world?" I lobbed the book into the backseat. "Stupid," I said.

My mother steered onto a sandy, tree-framed road that led to a field of grazing cattle. A family named the Erwins owned the land. Years before, Mr. Erwin had told my father he could fish in the pond whenever he wanted. My mother wasn't certain the welcome still extended to her, more than three years after the divorce. "What's the worst that could happen?" she asked. "You and me, hauled into jail for trespassing."

We sidled through weeds, carrying our poles toward a pond shaped like a mirror-image Oklahoma. Fish bones and plastic six-pack rings littered the bank. Wind winnowed through maples and oaks that circled the water's edge, the sound like distant applause. It served as percussion for the bawling cows in the distance. I mooed back at them. My mother sighed and plucked a bass lure from the tackle box. It was the same box that Deborah and I had bought my father for Christmas years ago, the same he had abandoned.

She held the lure toward the sunlight. It looked like a beetle coated with purple feathers, and my mother squinted at it as if it might suddenly spring to life. "There's nothing like the taste of grilled widemouth bass," she said. Crescents of sweat had already formed on her blouse.

"I predict there will be no widemouth bass in this pond," I told her. "Perch, catfish, carp maybe"—I guided a wriggling night crawler onto my hook—"but no bass."

I cast my line. I breathed in, and the confectionery air filled my nose. Kansas always smells great when summer has kicked into gear—damp, almost flowery, as if an exotic tea is brewing in each cloud. My mother and I sat on buckets of white plastic, the buckets we hoped would carry loads of fat fish by the day's close. She chewed gum that smelled like apples. When I asked her for a piece, she tongued her fingers and wiped on her jeans. She bit her own gum wad in half, rolled it into a green ball, and dropped it into my open mouth.

My bobber floated in the center of the Erwins' pond, and I examined it for the slightest movement, any ripple of water. Nothing. Beside me, my mother reeled in slowly, remembering what she could about the proper way to snag a bass. She hummed a melody I seemed to remember from some faraway time. Aisles of cattails rose from the incline behind her. Above her head, bobwhites overpopulated the oaks. A single meadowlark stared down from a tree limb, its black V a banner across its yellow chest.

Watching the pond's surface made me queasy. The water was the sort where some faceless and neglected kid might drown, only to be dredged up years later. I waited ten minutes; when no fish nibbled, I lost patience. I reeled in and reached for the coffee can my mother had filled with worms and mud clods. That morning, she had stepped to the shade beside the back porch. She had stabbed her shovel into the ground, drawing out triangles of black earth. *"Voilà,"* she said. She pinched night crawlers from the mud and dropped them into the can.

I baited my hook with another cashewlike worm. The hook tore it in half, and it wriggled in the dirt, blindly searching out some earthly haven where it could perish in peace. I stared, humming, my mind drifting elsewhere. *Avalyn*, I thought. Her TV show was scheduled to air at nine o'clock that night. I couldn't imagine how it would dramatize her UFO abduction. I planned to record it with the VCR my mother had bought last Christmas, to watch the program over and over. I wondered if Avalyn had fished in ponds around this area. Perhaps she had ponds of her own, centered in the fields that surrounded her farmhouse, the fields where they'd beamed their spotlights before whisking her into their ship.

My mother stood from her bucket. Her pole bent slightly, and I knew she had a nibble. She said "Shhh," and I held my breath. The sun's rays continued their heavy massage, and the wind paused. My mother reeled in slowly, teasing her fish, and in that silent space of time I realized how alone we were. Quite possibly there was no one within a mile radius, only us. I thought about the UFOs, the alien spacecraft that could suddenly stall over the barren fields. I thought of how, even in broad daylight, we could be taken, and of the utter simplicity of our abduction—how the aliens could beam us up just as they'd done to Avalyn. No one would see it, no one would suspect a thing.

The fish slipped away. My mother pulled her line from the water and frowned. "Must not have been a bass." She sat back down, opened the tackle box, and began rummaging through the mess of lures and weights and hooks.

My thoughts moved to another abduction story, one I'd read about in books. In October 1973, two men, Charlie

Hickson and Calvin Parker, were fishing near the town of Pascagoula, Mississippi, when a UFO landed near the lake. I always remembered this story—first, because it had happened almost exactly one year after I was born, and second, because the description of the craft—platelike, with blinking blue lights—resembled my own UFO. As I scrutinized my motionless bobber, I rattled on to my mother about this case as if she were my student. "The aliens were as short as dwarves," I said. "When they came toward them, one of the guys fainted. But the other stayed awake, and unlike most people he remembered everything. They examined him on a silver table. There was a weird contraption, like a moving eye on the end of a rod. It gave his body a series of X rays."

My mother played along with my lecture: "Then what happened?"

"Nobody believed either of them," I said. "Even when they passed lie detector tests." I wondered if Avalyn had taken such a test. I wanted to ask her a million questions.

"What would you do," I asked my mother, "if a UFO came zooming over those trees right now and sucked us into it?"

Her mouth twisted into the half-smile of a disbelieving judge. "I'm not sure. When we saw that one before, all I wanted to do was stare. It was so odd, like a Ferris wheel floating through the sky. I'm sure there was some explanation." The half-smile evened out, and I knew she was playing along. "But now, if one tried to take you away, I'd probably run for my gun. I'd blast them all between the eyes before they could harm you."

"I doubt you'd have the chance. They'd be quick." I paused. Sunlight needled through the trees, stinging my eyes. "Besides, they'd stun you or something. You wouldn't know what hit you, and you wouldn't remember it afterward."

My mother rummaged through the tackle box. When she pulled her hand out, it held a green can of mosquito spray. She doused her forearms with it and threw the can to me.

I sprayed my neck, arms, chest, and legs, then asked, "What do you think about the fact I've been obsessed with UFOs and stuff like that all my life? Do you think that's odd?"

She didn't answer, so I continued. "That article about Avalyn Friesen. It's made me think. There's a specialist on the UFO abduction thing. He conducts hypnotic regressions of these abducted people. Anyway, he says that an unnatural preoccupation with UFOs may mean you've had some sort of past contact."

"If you had gone to some other planet, surely you'd know something about that—" My mother stopped and stood again. The bucket tipped from behind her, somersaulting toward the water's edge. "Bite, Brian," she said. "A bite." My bobber was shaking back and forth, its red and white now a pink blur. I gripped the handle of my pole. Whatever was under the pond paused, then took the bait, endeavoring to speed away with the worm. The bobber shot downward, purling the water, and I tugged at my pole, keeping the line tight as I reeled in.

By eight o'clock, the sun had slid beneath the row of oaks. The shadow spilled across our faces like an enormous veil. "Are we done?" my mother asked. She didn't wait for an answer. "Then let's leave." She had snagged three perch, which she had tossed back, and one catfish, which she kept. I had caught a pair of keepable catfish. The second had a flat and loamy gray head as large as the ball of my foot.

We walked to the car. I sat and sandwiched our catch between my feet. My mother drove through the Erwins' pasture, the foul-smelling water sloshing at each bump and splashing the seat's burgundy vinyl. I thought of afternoons long past, when my family had chugged home in my father's pickup from a day of fishing. I remembered Deborah and me lounging in the back of the cab, choosing our favorites from the fish that curled against one another in the bucket's brackish water. My father, the experienced angler, had caught them all. He would gut and filet them. My mother would cook, and the whole family would eat.

I hopped from the car and opened the gate to the Erwins' pasture. The Toyota trudged past it, onto the sandy road. Behind us, under the trees, a cow mooed, as if saying good-bye. I shut the gate, ending our day of trespassing, and returned to the car. "I had fun today," I said, and replaced my feet beside the bucket. I meant it. My mother smiled, and I knew this was how the next two months, the remainder of my summer, would fall into shape. Only my mother and I, occupying our days with whatever spontaneous urge pleased us. In the mirror beside my window, the sun melted into Kansas, and the sky made an amazing change from pink to blue.

I ditched the bucket on the back porch. A catfish tail cut the murky water, droplets pearling my shirt. In the twilight, the three fish gleamed like intestines, and I covered the bucket's top with a towel I'd used for sunbathing.

Inside, my mother chopped tomatoes, cucumbers, and lettuce for sandwiches. The TV was already on. "Coming up next on 'World of Mystery,'" a voice said, "our investigators probe the terrifying world of UFO abductions. Is the phenomena just mass hysteria, or is it something ALL TOO REAL? And after that, on the ten o'clock news . . ." I grabbed the VCR's remote control, punched the record and pause buttons, and waited.

My mother handed me a plate and took her seat beside

me. She had changed into terry cloth shorts. A spray of thin blue veins branched up the side of her leg. Trapped among the veins, the red dot of a mosquito bite.

"It's on," she said, and the program started. The show's producers obviously favored style over substance. Eerie synthesizer music comprised the soundtrack, which I loved; the visuals, however, were corny. The first person interviewed, an elderly man from Michigan, claimed a spacecraft had kidnapped him when he was a boy. As his shaky voice narrated, the screen displayed a soft-focus "interior" of a "UFO": a silver table, an array of lights, and a tray laden with misshapen surgical instruments. "They stuck the damned probe into my stomach," the man's voice said. On screen, a blurry hand, which I figured was a kid's in a wrinkly gray glove, reached for an object shaped like a small silver wishbone. The hand guided it toward a belly button.

Four others were interviewed: a young married couple, a sculptor who decorated his house with life-size replicas of the beings who'd examined him, and a Polish woman who'd been abducted not long after her immigration. The latter woman's eyes teared when she told of the "horrible, unspeakable acts" the aliens had performed on her. "Get to Avalyn," I said to the TV. "There's only fifteen minutes left."

After a stretch of commercials, the show resumed. The camera panned across a flat, sunlit field, obviously Kansas, where a woman played with a polka-dotted mutt. "It's her," I said. Avalyn tossed a ball, and the dog retrieved it. "She looks exactly the same as her picture."

"She's sort of homely," my mother said. "She seems sad, as if no one's ever loved her."

According to the lead-in, Avalyn Friesen lived on the outskirts of the farming community of Inman, Kansas. She'd never married, and her brother and mother were both deceased. She shared a small log cabin with her father, and she worked as a secretary at the local grain company. She was thirty-two. The everyday details of her life ended there. "But there is something special about Avalyn, something beyond ordinary experience," the narrator said. "For as long as she can remember, strange things have happened to her, things she cannot explain."

The camera centered on Avalyn in a rocking chair. Sunlight angled through a window behind her, illuminating a fourth of her face. I could see a corner of her house; hard-back books lined a shelf behind her, and a posse of stuffed animals scattered an end table. She sipped from a coffee mug and began to speak.

"I was always scared whenever I watched movies about UFOs," Avalyn said. "Even *E.T.* horrified me. I wasn't sure why. And one day I saw this book in the grocery store by Ren Bloomfield. In it, he talked about people who've had experiences with missing time, pieces of their lives they can't account for. I'd had so many of those. I contacted Ren, and the rest, I guess, is history."

During the next part of Avalyn's story, the camera alternated between its gaze on Avalyn's face and another soft-focus re-creation of her tale. The music swelled, keyboards tinkling a high melody.

"Ren flew to Wichita to meet me. He wound up conducting our first hypnotic regression session. Surprisingly, the stuff just started pouring out of me. Over the next months, I wound up remembering the more-than-twenty times I've been abducted."

I could feel my mother watching me. Outside the window behind the TV, the night sky deepened its smooth, starless black.

"The first time it happened, I was six years old. This was back in 1964 or so. I'd gone on a picnic with my twin brother and my grandparents in Coffeyville. It was getting dark, and I remember Grandpa driving down a dirt road. There was this blinding light behind us that got brighter and brighter." Bluish white beams strobed across the television square, and I thought about our own UFO, so long ago. The TV framed my mother's face with that familiar blue.

"Teddy and I turned around in the backseat to see where all that bright was coming from. Suddenly the car swerved off to the ditch and Grandpa made this sound like 'huh?' like he had no control over it. The light surrounded the car, a whole ocean of it. It was jewellike and unlike the regular lights you'd see in a regular house. Well the next thing I *remembered*, at least for the next twenty-three years or so, was my grandparents driving back into the driveway, and my parents waiting there for us, saying where have you been, you're three hours late, you could have at least called.

"So under hypnosis I found this out: the aliens only chose me to examine. My grandparents and my brother Teddy stayed in the car, unmoving, their eyes closed like they were asleep or frozen in some sort of suspended animation, as Ren calls it. But I floated right up out of the backseat and into the mouth of this disc-shaped ship."

The synthesizer music swirled, and a pink-dressed girl appeared on screen, an actress in the role of the young Avalyn. The girl bit her lip. Her eyes darted back and forth, and her pigtails shot behind her head like a pair of blond horns. The girl screeched. "Creepy," my mother said.

"Under hypnosis," Avalyn continued, "I remembered lying on a table, all silvery white and smooth like Formica. A group of aliens surrounded me. They carried little silvery boxes, out of which they pulled thin tubes and instruments, like things a dentist would use. They were bald with huge marshmallowy heads and tiny arms that appeared as if they didn't have an ounce of muscle in them. The fingers were cold and didn't feel human at all. But the worst things about them were their eyes: big black diamonds is the closest description I can give, only instead of hard like diamonds they were all jellylike and liquidy."

"Yes," I said, answering her, as if she were speaking only to me.

Avalyn's interview ended there. The narrator reappeared to describe how many victims of abduction, Avalyn included, were often "tracked"—aliens inserted devices into a person's brain, nose, stomach, foot, wherever, making it easier to locate the person later. "Humans become guinea pigs," the narrator said, "with the extraterrestrials coming back for them at various times in their lives, conducting ongoing experiments. One might think that the person is free after the first abduction. But that isn't always the case in this world, the 'World of Mystery.'" A hasty summary followed. The camera zoomed in on a spaceship, moving closer and closer to its rays of white, until the entire screen drowned in light.

Before falling asleep, I thought about how repercussions from a single incident had shaped Avalyn Friesen's entire life. And the more I considered Avalyn, the more I considered my own life. The idea of abduction made perfect sense. It had first happened on a night more than one decade past: I had opened my eyes to find myself curled in a dark corner of the crawl space, five hours erased from my mind. And if the theory of aliens "tracking" humans was true, I reasoned I was a victim of that as well. My nose had been bleeding that night because of the tracking device the extraterrestrials had jammed deep into my brain. Two years later they had returned to find me again, on that Halloween night when I'd blacked out in the woods beside the haunted house. I was almost nineteen now. Was the tracking device still embedded in my brain like a tiny silver tumor? What other times, I wondered, had I been abducted? Were there other encounters so deeply buried in my mind I hadn't the slightest memory? And would the aliens reappear to find me again?

I waited until the following Sunday to tell my mother my theory. We were returning from Hutchinson, after the grocery shopping and ice cream. The Fourth of July was approaching, and merchants had fashioned fireworks stands on the roadsides, multicolored banners and signs flapping in the breeze.

I began by discussing stories I'd read about other UFO abductees, and I gave my voice as matter-of-fact a tone as I could muster. Then I spoke of myself. "The fact is," I said, "that we still don't know, we've never known, what happened to me when I was little. But that was so close in time to the night we saw the UFO. I'm wondering now, no, I'm certain, that those two nights are connected somehow. Connected also, maybe, to my blackout on the Halloween night a couple years after that." I paused. "And watching that show about Avalyn made me realize how similar my story is to hers."

My mother nodded hesitantly. I wiped ice cream from my mouth and continued. "Don't you think it might be true? I mean the whole alien bit?"

We passed another fireworks stand. Two separate families gathered around it, leaning over the colored boxes. "Maybe," my mother said. She spoke slowly, as if *maybe* were a foreign word she wasn't certain how to pronounce. "Maybe." She gripped the steering wheel, veins visible on her wrist.

I started to speak again, but she cut me off. "Some memories," she said, "take time to clarify."

I knew then that my mother had at least opened her mind to the possibility that my theory was true. I knew she would support whatever move I made next. She would stay beside me until I solved it. Even if to solve meant to lose another block of time, to slip into the unknown world where I was certain they'd taken me before.

In a cabinet drawer at home, I found a package of stationery and envelopes my father had given my mother years ago. Lilacs and daisies garlanded each page. The stationery seemed like something Avalyn would cherish. I made sure the pen's ink wouldn't smudge; that my handwriting remained steady. Then I carefully wrote "Avalyn Friesen, Rural Route #2, Inman KS" on an envelope. I found her zip code in the telephone book.

I selected a piece of the paper. I wouldn't leave anything out—I wanted Avalyn to know about the crawl space, our UFO sighting that same summer, the strange blackout on that later Halloween. I wanted to confess everything to her.

"Dear Avalyn," I wrote. "You don't know me, but. . . ." In my mind, a spacey voice finished the sentence. *You will*, it said.

eight

ERIC PRESTON

Neil McCormick was turning me into a criminal, and I loved it. Our new hobby: thrift store theft. In the month since graduation, we'd generated a wealth of secondhand books, housewares, and enough clothes for an army. School was over forever; crime seemed the only thing left to do.

Our favorite target was the United Methodist Thrift on First Street. On that particular Friday in June, I eyed a barely worn pair of combat boots, but I wasn't about to pay the twenty-dollar price. Neil distracted the clerk by complimenting her bleached flip, which even a two-year-old could have guessed was a wig. He also bullshitted about central Kansas's recent rain and hailstorms. "I've begun to worry about flooding," I heard the woman say. He had her in his spell. I shuffled toward the back of the store, removed the boots from the rack, and kicked off my ragged high-tops.

One important shoplifting rule I'd learned from Neil was to simultaneously buy something else to erase all suspicion. I watched him drop a rubber snake on the clerk's counter. "Ninety-nine cents," she said. While he dug through his pockets for change, I saw my chance. I concentrated on the clerk's face and telepathically transmitted *Center all your attention on the cash register*. It worked, and I moseyed out the door. "Stop back in, boys," the clerk yelled.

Neil and I got into his gas-guzzling Impala and tore from the parking lot to begin our daily cruise around the city. I'd only lived in Hutchinson four months, but I already knew enough to hate the place. How else could I feel about a city bordered by the following attractions: to the west, a meat-packing plant; the north, a boring space museum; the east, a maximum security prison; and the south, "The World's Longest Grain Elevator"? In Modesto, I'd had a scattering of friends who shared the same interests in music and were queer like me. Here, I only had Neil.

I spat on a finger to shine the boots. I untucked my shirt, revealing the wadded-up gloves and the belt I also stole. "I could get arrested," I said.

"Stealing's the least of my evils." His voice was thick with pride. I'd become a thief with him, but I knew I could never hustle. The idea of taking money from men for sex unnerved me; in addition, I didn't have the looks, the irresistibility I knew Neil used to every advantage.

"If you're free tonight," Neil said, "you can come to the ballpark with me." Neil worked Friday nights and weekends as announcer and scorekeeper for tournaments at another of Hutchinson's lamebrained attractions, Sun Center. KANSAS'S LARGEST HAVEN FOR SOFTBALL FUN, its glitzy signs screamed. I hated that place. On the previous weekend, I'd joined him in his press box. We got high, and I pierced his earlobe with a safety pin and a fistful of ice cubes. We practically ruptured our stomachs laughing at all the morons.

"I'll think about it," I said, which meant yes.

Neil's elbow jutted from his open window, the full weight of the sun's rays slamming into his skin. It was only June, but he had begun to turn as dark as milk chocolate. A fitting simile, since that was a staple of his diet. While he drove, Neil tore the foil from another half-melted Hershey's.

He bit a corner off. He held the bar toward my face: its shape was the spitting image of my new home state.

I pointed to the center of the chocolate Kansas. "Here we are, stuck in the middle of hell."

"But not for long," he said. "In my case, anyway." Soon, in August, Neil would be moving, leaving the Midwest for New York. Now, he was biding his time, coasting until his life would begin again. He would abandon me in Hutchinson's dust.

Neil turned onto a shady avenue, his car winding its way toward my grandparents' trailer park. When we got there, I spied Grandma and Grandpa in the yard, pruning a bush with flowers like red-skinned fists. "The grannies are home," I said. "Let's go to your house."

Neil made a U. He smiled at me and took a last bite from the chocolate bar. The look on his face suggested he'd never tasted anything so perfect.

After my parents' accident, I'd moved from Modesto to Hutchinson to live with my grandparents. I spent my first day in Kansas in my new school's vice principal's office, filling out forms, enrolling in classes that paralleled the ones I'd taken in California. American government, senior English, advanced art—everything seemed unnecessary. I scribbled my name on countless papers. On each page, someone had thoughtfully blacked out the spaces designated for parents' signatures. "All done." I handed a secretary the finished forms. Her eyes, which darted from my clothes to my expertly applied eyeliner to the dyed spikes of my haircut, couldn't fathom how to feel sorry for such a freak. I trudged to the hall, dreading every moment.

There he stood: Neil, jamming books into his locker. His looks were faultless. He had lips so pouty they might have been swollen; brown eyes; brows that met in his forehead's center. His angular nose, chin, and cheekbones seemed sculpted by an ecstatic, mescaline-fueled god. His hair was the color of onyx. Everyone else seemed to be avoiding him. When he saw me watching, he smirked. That smirk delivered me from hopelessness.

Later that week I learned his name; I also heard the word *fag* used in the same breath. We shared two classes. During discussion in American government, I stared at him instead of the Bill of Rights notes that Mr. Stein scribbled across the blackboard. After school, Neil would rush to his Impala, as if fleeing a burning building. He was sometimes accompanied by a shady-eyed kid named Christopher. They'd drive off, oblivious of me, and I'd walk home. Those first few nights, I fell asleep imagining what he looked like naked.

It didn't take long to discover that being a queer in a Kansas high school was a world of difference from being one in California. I learned to proceed with caution. After two weeks, I spied Neil hanging out with this "Christopher" in the park on the south side of town, a place I'd heard through various grapevines was notorious as queer cruising ground. He wore sunglasses and a cantaloupe-colored windbreaker. As I later wrote in my journal, Neil would have "averted my eyes from an uncapped grenade." I assumed that a young guy in Carey Park was strange, because I'd only seen the over-forty crowd there.

I'll never forget the smug expression on Neil's face as I drove by in my grandparents' powder blue Gremlin. It was as though Neil knew he'd wind up sleeping with me.

Neil waved, and I blushed. I sped home.

The next day, he turned toward me in American government. He briefly appeared as if he would spit or swear. Then he grinned. He pointed to my exam; held up his. We'd both gotten D pluses.

"You forgot to answer the *Brown* v. *Board of Education* question," I said. I injected my voice with all the cockiness I could muster. "At least I wrote *something* down."

"You stare at me a lot," he said. "I'm Neil."

"I know."

His bangs fell in his eyes, and he angled his head to shake them away. "Is your mother aware of where you were yesterday?"

"My mother's dead," I said.

He didn't flinch. I liked that.

"That's why I'm here," I said. "I would have moved eventually anyway. Sooner or later they would have kicked me out of school. My friends and I started some fires, did some vandalism."

That was a slight exaggeration, but Neil seemed impressed. He told me I had guts for dressing like I did at such a backward high school. On that particular day, I was packed into tight black jeans. The usual cross dangled from my neck. My T-shirt, massacred with rips, featured Christ's stigmataed hand reaching from a thunderhead toward an amazed crowd. Neil touched JC's dripping nail hole. He winked. A girl in a cheerleader's uniform rolled her eyes, as if she'd seen this process a billion times before.

Neil and I skipped last hour. We headed for the parking lot, where Christopher was waiting. "See you later," Neil yelled to him, not bothering to introduce us. He showed me his Impala, and I crawled in. Although it was a chilly March day, we bought tutti-frutti ices from the 7-Eleven. We whizzed toward my grandparents' house, which by that time I was calling my house as well.

No one was around. I shut the door to my room, and Neil stood there, staring heavenward. What could have been so engaging about a mobile home's waterstained ceiling? Curious, I looked up too, and that's when he pinned me against the wall. He kissed me. His mouth was extra cold and wet, as if his tongue were a chunk of pink ice. We took all of ten minutes to get our clothes off.

It's not the actual sex I remember best. It's what he said to me after we'd finished. Neil toweled off, slipped his underwear back on, and sat at my bed's edge. He asked when I would turn nineteen, and I answered December. Then he looked away, smiling. "That makes you younger than me," he said. "What a novelty."

As it turned out, "novelty" wasn't a bad word to describe our sex. We only fooled around a couple of times after that, but I soon discovered that Neil's major focus was older men—preferably, ones with cash. Strangely though, he didn't discard me; since his pal Wendy had moved to New York, he claimed, he only had Christopher and his mom to hang out with. "But Chris has *serious* problems," he explained, "and my mom's not around much."

What the hell, I thought: I didn't have friends, either.

The air in Neil's neighborhood smelled like hamburgers and split hot dogs, like lighter fluid and barbecue sauce. It was an odor of permanence and familial bliss. After he parked the Impala, we jumped out and ran for his front door, if only to get away from that smell and into somewhere familiar and cool.

Neil's mom was at work. She had left the windows open, the door unlocked. "What this means," he announced, "is we can watch porno on the VCR." I followed him to his room. On the wall, a framed photo showed Wendy, the best friend I'd yet to meet. The sides of her head were shaved, the rest matted into worm-slender dreadlocks and pulled back into a ponytail. She'd autographed the photo's bottom like a movie star. Beneath her was Neil's nightstand, littered with small hills of pennies, a dead violet-winged butterfly, and two trophies he won in Little League years ago. MOST RBIS, SUMMER 1981, the gold plaque on one of them read. A towel was wadded on the floor. It reeked of sex, and I wondered if the dried sperm on its surface was Neil's or the memento of some middle-aged trick he'd brought to this very room. I didn't have the nerve to ask.

Neil reached under his bed's mattress and retrieved a key. He unlocked his bottom dresser drawer, his back blocking it. He closed the drawer and turned. He held a videotape in one hand, a bag of pot in the other. We shuffled to the front room.

The movie, an old one, starred men with mustaches and an abundance of body hair. There was substantial fucking, but not a condom in sight. Neil and I sat at opposite ends of his sofa, not touching ourselves or each other. "Here's my number one scene," he said. A beefy ranch owner entered a barn, only to find a young ranch hand bound and gagged, pleading for mercy. The ranch owner untied, caressed, then seduced him. Their sex gradually transformed from tender to ferocious. At one point, the pale skin on the young guy's ass grew streaked with red welts. The film ended with ranch owner once again holding ranch hand in his glistening, tanned arms.

After the credits, I poured two glasses of lemonade from a pitcher in Neil's refrigerator. His mother had left a cherry-colored lipstick trace on the pitcher's rim. The air conditioner's cool wasn't enough, and Neil plugged the cord from a portable fan into a socket. My hair whipped back, and I smelled the black dye job from the previous day. The smell was identical to the antiseptic odor of the Modesto Funeral Home. I made a mental note to wash my hair again before I joined Neil at Sun Center.

Neil ejected the tape and inserted a horror film called *Suspiria*. "I've seen this one hundreds of times. It's great, but if I fall asleep it's your job to wake me. I have to be at work by six."

I sat at an angle that offered a view of his face. In the opening segment, a hairy hand repeatedly stabbed a woman's chest; the camera closed in on her heart as the knife torpedoed it. The hand tugged a noose around the woman's throat; tossed her through stained glass. Neil stared at the screen. His expression was identical to the one he'd worn during *Rawhide*.

"Defenestration," I said. "'The act of throwing someone through a window.'" I knew a lot of words like that.

Neil stretched out, his foot brushing my hand. I wondered what he would do if I said, "I want to move to New York, too." If I said, "I'm falling into uncontrollable love with you." Save it for your journal, I told myself.

We got stoned, and half an hour passed. More murders and mayhem. I glanced back at Neil and discovered he'd fallen asleep. A feeble red vein branched across his eyelid. Behind it, his eyeballs darted and wobbled, surveying the details of a dream I doubted would feature me. I concentrated, attempting to psychically drive a message into Neil's brain: *Hi. Although I've known you nearly four months, a large chunk of your life remains as strange and enigmatic as one of those unidentified people the authorities found in that circus fire I recently read about, their faces burned beyond recognition. The mystery that surrounds you only makes me love you more. Oh well, what can I do?* I leaned over Neil's ear, wanting to kiss it, but instead whispering against the skin, "Sweet dreams."

In the film, an hysterical woman crawled through an open window, only to drop headfirst into a roomful of twisted barbed wire. *That's precisely how I feel right now,* I thought. When her screams grew too loud, I muted the volume and watched him sleep.

•   •   •

I arrived at Sun Center to find Neil positioned in his press box. He wore white, his shirt wounded with gray sweat stains. On a table in front of him were pencils, a score pad, and a microphone, its mouthpiece covered with a red foam ball that made it look obscene. He listened to a portable stereo playing music from a tape I'd made him, one I'd labeled "Depressing Shit." Genuine pain racked the singer's voice. *"Ooh, you're still standing in my shadow."*

"Hello, hello," Neil said. He revealed a bottle he'd been concealing beneath his chair. Vodka. I wondered if his mom would notice it missing, or if she would care. "Now shut that door behind you before someone spies this."

I sat beside him. From the press box vantage point, I could see nearly all of Sun Center. There was the gleaming white of the powdered chalk, its straight lines trailing to first and third base, its batter's box rectangles and on-deck circles. The dugouts, each tagged with a sign displaying the team's name, each with a mammoth orange cooler filled with water. The rubber of home plate and the pitcher's mound, the base paths scarred by players' cleats; the out-field that shone with a green so vibrant I wished I could view it on acid.

The night's opening game was about to start. The teams took their places on the diamond. The players' wives and friends sat on the bleachers, most drinking from beer cans, shoving burgers or hot dogs into their mouths.

Neil took a swig from the vodka bottle, then clicked on the microphone. He lowered his voice to sound "official," "professional," or some other adjective he assigned to his expected job performance. I, however, could see right through it: he thought it all a big joke. "Welcome to Sun Center," he said. Some softball-adoring morons glanced up at us, and I scooted my seat back so I wouldn't be seen. Neil continued. "The first game of the Men's Class C Divisional Tournament features First National Bank, out of McPherson, against Auto-Electric, from Hutchinson."

The umpire, a man wearing a light blue shirt over his beer gut, turned and gave the okay signal. "Play ball," said Neil.

The first inning dragged by. In seconds I was bored. Neil and I passed the bottle between us, waiting for something hilarious to happen. "Watch this." He clicked the mike. "Ward is the batter, with Knackstedt on deck," he said, giving extra emphasis on the *K* in the latter name.

A man in the bleachers' top row shot up from his seat. He was the typical softball moron, dressed in his straw hat, his yellow-framed sunglasses, his black socks with jogging shoes. He turned, glaring at Neil. "It's Nock-Shtitt," the man pronounced. He shook a noisemaker at us, one he'd brought in case his chosen team won the game. Neil gave the okay sign, and the man sat back down.

Nock-Shtitt flied out to left field. End of inning. I felt like saying, He couldn't hit worth shtitt, but just as I opened my mouth, Neil's mike clicked again. "No runs, no hits, no errors," he said. "After one full inning of play, the score is First National Bank zero, Auto-Electric zero." He reached for the keyboard to the electronic scoring device and punched a button. I looked toward the left field fence; on the scoreboard, the inning changed from one to two.

While I sipped from the bottle, Neil pointed out men he thought handsome. During game number two, he said, "Look at that one," indicating the third baseman. "Oh, baby." At first I thought he was kidding. The guy had huge sideburns, a toast-colored mustache, and a bald spot the circumference of a hubcap. "I'd have him for *free*," Neil said.

A player hit a foul ball. I watched it loop over the fence, bounce into the parking lot, and disappear beneath a Jeep.

"Please bring all foul balls to the press box," Neil said into the mike.

Seconds later, there was a knock on the door behind us. "Enter." The door opened, and a boy stepped into the box, his hair cropped short, sweatbands cuffing his wrists. He presented the grass-stained ball to Neil, cupping it in both hands like something sacred. "My daddy hit this," he said.

Neil reached into a box beside the scoreboard buttons. Inside were wrapped pieces of bubble gum and some shiny dimes. "What do you prefer, little man?" I'd never seen Neil around a kid before. He'd seemed the type who would ignore or torture them, but that wasn't the case. He shifted his eyes from the game and scrubbed at the boy's hair. "Will it be the money or the bubbles?" The boy shuffled forward to get a better look at his choices, and Neil patted his shoulder. "I'll decide for you," he said. He held out three dimes and five pieces of gum. The boy took them, the smile practically cracking his tiny face, and scampered out.

"When kids do well, you've got to reward them." Neil looked back to the game. "Jesus, look at that catcher's ass."

The second game was ending, and Neil and I were drunk. His fingers drummed the vodka bottle in time to the music. I wanted to kiss him, but that part of our relationship was over. In the sky, a low-flying plane trailed a banner that advertised something, its letters unreadable in the waning light.

On the drive home, I could only think about Neil. If what I felt was love, it had happened unexpectedly, like a slap from a stranger or a hailstorm of cherries from a cloudless sky. We're supposed to be just friends, I told myself. He likes only older men. I stepped on the Gremlin's accelerator, figuring the best thing to do was get home and write some really fucked-up, drunken lines of poetry in my journal. I was contemplating moronic possible poem titles—"Raining Tears of Blood"; "The Bottomless Pit Called Me"—when I zoomed through a red light. I didn't see the pickup. I slammed into its back end.

I sat there, dazed. I took a breath, paused, breathed again. I carefully rearranged my thoughts. A picture of my mom and dad took shape in my mind, and I forced it back into some far, neglected corner. *I'm alive,* I thought. *They weren't so lucky.*

The pickup was illegally parked alongside Fourth Street, in front of an apartment complex. In the apartment's lot, partygoers whooped it up, speakers blaring an old Led Zeppelin tune at top volume. I picked out the words "woman," "baby," and "shake that thing." I waited, but the music didn't cease. No one came cussing or flailing out. Gradually, the fact dawned on me that I'd hit the windshield. The glass had spiderwebbed.

I felt an ache in my forehead, like a hot scalpel along my right eyebrow. I guessed no one had witnessed the wreck, because I sat for minutes without anyone approaching. Fingers of steam plumed from the new bend in the car's hood. I thought of Neil, less than a mile away in his press box, as drunk as me but unscathed.

I touched my head, swiped away some blood. The sight of it made me strangely happy. I shifted into reverse. When I tried to move, the Gremlin's wreckage caught a little on the pickup's back end. "I am so fucking *wasted,*" a partygoer's voice declared over the Led Zeppelin. I waited for the guitar solo to crescendo, then revved the engine. The car separated from the pickup. I steered back onto Fourth and headed home.

The next afternoon, I woke and realized it was true: without warning, I'd fallen in love with Neil McCormick. It

was a doomed, impulsive, and criminal sort of love. I felt
the vicious effects of both vodka and accident, and in the
mirror I saw the purplish black crescent beneath my eye. It
would turn purpler and blacker. I touched a peroxide-
soaked cotton ball to the eyelid, and the sting made me
flinch. "I'm the ugliest son of a bitch on earth," I said in my
best Clint Eastwood.

It was raining outside. Soggy leaves fell everywhere,
clinging to my bedroom window, their greens already sunburned to yellows. I telephoned Neil, hoping the sudden
storm had temporarily postponed Sun Center's tournaments. He picked up; drowsily answered, "Yeah?"

"I take it they canceled the games," I said.

"Praise the lord." On his end of the line, his mother was
singing along to a TV jingle.

I asked if he wanted to hang out. He coughed and said,
"I don't feel too hot. I think I'll sleep most of the day. Call
me later." *Click.*

Grandma waddled around the kitchen, grilling cheese
sandwiches. She had skewered black olives on each finger
like ten miniature hats, and she periodically bit them off.
She spooned a kidney-size wad of butter onto a plate and
dipped a slice of bread. "Yummy," I said. My head was ready
to implode.

She regarded my eye, one olived finger on her chin.
"You've been hurt."

"Um, yeah." I figured as little as my grandparents used
the Gremlin, they wouldn't notice the damage. I let my
tongue spew forth the lie. "Last night, I was so tired, while
visiting Neil, I stumbled down the steps leading to his Sun
Center press box. Nothing else was hurt, but oddly enough I
landed face first on one of the steps. . . ." Grandma wrapped
three ice cubes in a paper towel and held it to my eye. When
I used to have headaches, my mom would do the same thing.

After lunch, I went back to sleep. I didn't wake until the early evening, crawling from bed into a graceless and disarranged world. I waited for it to arrange itself again, then found my journal.

A Saturday night, and I'd spent the entire day at home. I wrote the word BORED across the top of a page. Then I wrote LONESOME, decorating each letter with art deco swirls. "Better get used to it," I said aloud. "He won't be here forever."

Seven o'clock, eight. The rain stopped, but it was still cloudy. I watched the claustrophobic trailer park from my window. The neighbor family, replete with mom and dad, obviously couldn't wait for Independence Day. They touched cigarettes to firecrackers, tossing them toward the street. Their two children applauded as Roman candles spat pebbles of red and blue over their trailer. I picked at the dinner plate Grandpa had brought to my room, forking the cornbread, hominy, and butternut squash into a colorless mash.

When my grandparents retired to the TV room, I ran a wet comb through my hair, took another gander at my eye, and said, "What the hell." The mobile home's door slammed behind me. The neighbor family turned their heads to look, and I strutted toward the car.

I drove the familiar route, imagining how Hutchinson would look on fire. The Impala wasn't parked in Neil's drive, but I tried anyway, ringing Neil's doorbell one, two, three times. No answer. I prepared to jam my finger into the bell a fourth time when I noticed the note, written on a small grocery list that bore the logo of the store where his mom worked, attached to the screen with electrician's tape. The note's edges harbored thumbprints of milk chocolate. He hadn't addressed it to either his mom or me. It read: "G—At Sun Center. There all night due to rain delays. Meet me @ 10ish. You won't regret it.—N."

G? I thought. And "won't regret" what? My answer wasn't hard to figure. "He's hustling again," I whispered.

The sky was almost dark, the sun leaving an umber residue across the bank of clouds to the west. Below them, Sun Center's stadium lights glowed in a silvery nimbus which, if I hadn't hated the place so much, I might have found beautiful. I returned to the wounded Gremlin and hightailed it over there.

By the time I arrived, the rain had begun again. Under the ballpark's lights, it looked like billions of needles. No games were in session. The bleachers had emptied, save for a few random fools under umbrellas. The players huddled in dugouts. On each diamond, ground crews layered the infields with shimmering tarpaulin, skittering from base to base to secure its blue corners.

The rain drenched me, plastering my hair to my head, and I smelled the black dye again. I took the stairs that led to Neil's press box three at a time, half-knowing what I'd find. Then I stood on tiptoe to peer into his window. I saw Neil's shiny black hair, the top of his ear, his closed eyes. He sat in his scorer's chair. Mmmm, his voice said, the sound as lazy and as one-step-shy-of-genuine as the noises the actors in his porn films made. Then another head—G's, I assumed— entered the square frame of the window: this one nearly bald, a neck so sunburned it looked smeared with scarlet paint. I couldn't see the face. The head kissed Neil, then moved down, out of the frame. I heard an audible slurp. Neil's eyes opened, his gaze locked on wherever the head had maneuvered itself.

Below, between the diamonds, a softball player cowered beneath an umbrella. As I moved away from the window, the player stared up at me. "Are the games called off or aren't they?" he asked through the pounding rain. I shrugged and walked back to the stairs. I could hear muffled car doors slamming, people yelling good-byes. None of them knew that nearby an eighteen-year-old boy was receiving a blow job from another in a long list of johns. I wondered about the sunburned man's age; how much he'd negotiated to pay. Mud bubbles splattered the boots Neil had helped me shoplift, and I deliberately stomped through puddles until I reached the car.

Before I left, I squinted back at the shadow of Neil's press box. *I won't deny I love you, but you're basically an asshole.* I doubted he'd receive the message.

I couldn't stomach the trailer park, so I detoured toward North Monroe. I needed to hurt him somehow, to raze and weaken him, or, as I suddenly longed to scribble down as the line of a poem, "to scissor through the starched gristle of his heart." Looking back, all that seems senseless—I'd known all along Neil was a hustler, understood I had no hold on him. But to know it was happening was one thing. To see it was another.

I ran through the rain to Neil's front door and tore away his note. I reread it, wadded it, aimed for a puddle and pitched it. When I tried the door, it was unlocked.

The house reeked from Neil's mom's cooking, in this case a dish she'd obviously sprinkled with too much cumin. In the kitchen corner's trash can, charred onions and beans rested beside a recipe card marked MULLIGATAWNY. I hurried through the hall and opened Neil's bedroom door.

The place appeared virtually the same as the day before; Neil's sheet twisted into a new configuration, and he'd spilled some pot across his night stand. Yet things seemed different. I danced around the room, toppling stacks of tapes, kicking pillows, shoes, letters from Wendy. I pushed the lamp from the table. It knocked against the floor with the vacant clunk I imagined a decapitated head would make when striking pavement. I ruined his meticulous stacks of pennies. I closed my fist around a baseball trophy, the points and ridges from the tiny gold figurine's face cutting into my palm. "Most RBIs, Summer 1981," I screamed, my voice raising with each syllable, and on the "eighty-ONE!" I flung the trophy at the wall. It didn't break. I ran toward it as if it might scurry off, then threw it again. No luck.

The key, I thought.

It was still under the mattress. It burned its forbidden shape into my hand, catching a ray from the streetlights outside Neil's window. It turned easily in the dresser drawer's lock.

The drawer's contents were divided into two sections. On the left were wads of bills—I noticed tens and twenties among the fives and ones—plus pills, acid tabs, a bag of pot. The right side contained a thick stack of things. *Rawhide* rode the top of the mountain. I brushed aside some random pieces of paper, skimming through an unintelligible letter from Christopher Ortega and a torn Panthers baseball line-up, the name "McCormick" fourth from top. Finally, I pulled out what looked to be an enviable collection of porno books and magazines.

Neil's magazines were beyond belief. I couldn't venture a guess where he'd gotten them. Most boasted glossy, hard-core photo spreads of rough-looking men. I recognized one guy as the ranch hand from the movie; once again, he was being dominated by a mustached muscleman. The others had similar appearances. But these pictorials of older guys sucking and fucking were tame compared to the magazines at the bottom of Neil's stack. In one, the photos were so amateurish they seemed taken during a tornado. Bracelets and cummerbunds of leather secured a young boy to a wall. In the magazine below it, a grinning, obese man paired up with a different boy, this one sporting closely cut blond hair and freckles. On the cover, under the title of "Free Range

Chicken," the handcuffed preteen knelt before the man. The kid's jeans bunched at his ankles. I turned the pages, skimming the photos, and saw an arm with an anchor tattoo wrapped around the kid's body; an erect adult dick pressing against the kid's obviously terrified face; a close-up of two stubby thumbs as they meticulously separated the kid's ass like the seam of an overripe peach.

I replaced the stuff as I'd found it. I picked up the trophy again, threw it, watched it fall to the floor and bounce. I wanted to open my mouth and scream. I needed a soundtrack for my rage. There was a tape in Neil's stereo, so I turned up the volume and pressed play.

I scattered more pennies, gave more kicks to the pillow, and then stopped. Slowly, the things I heard came into strange, acute focus. I had expected Neil's tape to be some earsplitting, rhythm-heavy band with just the right brand of self-possessed and mournful lyrics to match my mood. But the tape wasn't playing music at all. Two people spoke in voices I didn't recognize, the voices of a man and a little boy. The boy giggled, and weird buzzes and blips echoed in the background like noises from a cartoon. *This one's going to be a good one*, the boy said. Pause. Then I heard a burp, an extended hiccup at once obscene and undeniably cute. It was the burp, I thought, of a prince in the guise of a toad, of an angel on the outs in Heaven.

That was a bi-i-i-ig motherfucking burp, the older voice on the tape said. *Go ahead, into the microphone. Say it.*

The child took a deep breath. *That was a big motherfucking burp.* The kid giggled again, and the adult joined him. In the midst of their laughter, I heard another high-pitched bleep, and I recognized the noise as the sound effect from a video game I'd played years ago. Pac-Man, I thought. No, Frogger. There was a recorded rustling and a bump, as if an arm had brushed the microphone, and at that second I remembered Neil, just yesterday, leaning over his mike at Sun Center, the mouthpiece padded with red foam.

I knew the identity of the child on the tape. It was in the warped vowel of the boy's *fuck*, the lilt of his giggle. I loved that voice. Whether then or now, I would know it, and I would love it.

The tape's voices paused again, and within that silence I heard someone moving in the house. My first thought was, burglar; my next, more realistic, was, Neil. I leaped up, clicked the stereo off, and took the tape out. Written on its label was NEIL M.—JULY 81. It wasn't Neil's handwriting. I shuffled to the dresser drawer, slammed it, and returned the key to its precise hiding place.

"Neil?" someone asked, and a shadow entered the room. It was his mom. "Whatever's going on in here, I have to ask you to keep it down a little, because—" She stopped, seeing I wasn't her son.

"Oh," she said. "Oh."

I put my hands in my pockets, then took them out again. Mrs. McCormick bit her bottom lip. Her face was shiny and apologetic. "I thought you were Neil," she said. "But that's okay." She surveyed the room's damage, then glanced at my hands, perhaps checking if I was armed.

"There was a fight," I said. I took the trophy from the floor and replaced it on the table. "I went slightly crazy, I guess. Now it's time to clean up." I reached toward the penny avalanche. "The ball games are still going out there. Neil's great at that job, you know." I sat on the bed and began stacking the pennies, one after the other, rebuilding the gleaming copper tower on the night stand.

Mrs. McCormick found some letters I'd scattered and put them on Neil's dresser. A photograph fell from one, and Wendy's face smiled out, two fingers raised in peace. Neil's mom saw the picture and watched it, her eyebrows raised. Her movements were labored and effusive, as if she'd just crawled from a sea of bourbon.

"I need to fall asleep," I said. "I'm so tired." I wasn't, really. Somewhere outside the house, a cricket chirped. "Kansas is horrible. All it does is rain here. School is over at last. Do you think my hair color is too severe? Neil won't give me an honest answer." These words meant nothing to either of us. I had to say it. "Oh, yeah, I'm in love with him."

Neil's mom didn't look away from the floor. I sat on the bed, and she sat beside me. She inhaled sharply three times, and for a moment I believed she would cry. What did she know about the voices on the tape? What did she know about Neil's current whereabouts?

"Why are you telling me this," she said. "I'm his mom."

"My parents used to claim the word *love* was useless, that people say it too often."

Mrs. McCormick hadn't heard me. "You think I'm drunk." Something sour and oily covered her voice. "You think I'm drunk, but I'm not. I'm perfectly sober." In the darkness, she had her son's precise features: his full lips, his jagged bangs.

Outside, a car sped past, its radio wailing a song from before I was born. I watched the dresser drawer as if it might fly open. "My parents are dead," I said. Neil's mom lay back on the bed and patted the space next to her, a signal she wanted me to join her. The thought of doing that terrified me. "I have to go," I said, or perhaps I thought I said it. I stared at the figurine on Neil's trophy, its repulsive grin beneath the gold cap. And then I left. Neil's mom didn't see me to the door.

At home, I took my journal outside and sat in the damp garden grass. The trailer park gave off an eerie glow, as if it were the chosen setting for an upcoming miracle. Mosquitoes buzzed the air. Dead earthworms scattered the sidewalk like veins. "I'm in love more than ever with Neil," I wrote. "My heart feels like a cartoon valentine card that some bratty kid's balled in his fist until it's become nothing but a ragged wad of paper, then thrown into churning, chopping depths of the trash compactor. If only he liked guys his age and not over-thirty-five men with more hair on their chests than heads. Where's the razor when I need it?"

I read what I'd just scribbled down. It all seemed so pathetic, I could do nothing but cross it out, blacking over everything with the pen. I kept picturing that look on Neil's face, his satisfied smile as the john's head moved toward his crotch.

The wind shifted, rattling the trailer's frail walls. Perhaps I should try writing another poem, I thought. I wanted to create something profound, something generations of people would read, nod, whisper, *I know exactly what he felt*. "That's ridiculous," I said. "Shit." The words caught in my throat. I reopened the journal, squinted at the mess of ink, and tried to remember what I'd written.

nine

BRIAN LACKEY

The dreams began two days after Avalyn's appearance on "World of Mystery." Generic at first, they harbored images of rubbery-armed spacemen with blue-gray skin and penetrating eyes that seemed equivalent to the Hollywood depictions I'd seen on TV. These aliens petrified me nonetheless.

After the second dream, I telephoned my mother at work and told her how the memories had revealed themselves. She returned home that evening holding a spiral notebook decorated with an elaborate bow. "To record them in," she said. "Whatever's inside your head, let it come out." I drew a crescent moon and stars on the notebook's cover; beside that, a spaceship whizzing past a chunky cloud.

I kept the journal at bedside, and during the following week I logged what I could from each alien scenario, sometimes sketching a face or hand or beam of light. In my half-sleep, I'd misspell words or stop midsentence. A typical entry:

6/29/91—
I get out of a station wagon, my little league uniform is on—I stand in the middle of a yard—crows are flying (indecipherable) getting darker. My hand is crammed into the baseball

*glove my father bought when (indecipherable)—in the trees a
blue light, the color at the bottoms of swimming pools, I walk
closer but it seems I'm running toward it then I see the
spaceship and a light shoots out, the light tugging me
forward—like a giant hand—the blue light (indecipherable)—
really scared, and the hand starts to m (word trails into
scribble off edge of page).*

The dream log aided my memory. But something else
bolstered my ability to remember, something apart from the
dreams, something I couldn't explain to my mother. I began
recalling other bits and pieces about my first abduction,
images beyond those that took shape during sleep. I would
be watching TV, eating lunch, or sunbathing on the side of
the hill, when out of nowhere a scene would surface in my
head. For instance, I suddenly remembered this: that
halfway through my final Little League game, it had begun
to rain. The rain became a downpour, and the umpire had
officially canceled the game midinning. My teammates had
abandoned me in the dugout, running hand in hand with
parents to their family cars.

Had that been the moment I'd initially been taken? Had
the aliens witnessed me through the net of clouds as I'd lingered, alone, on the baseball field? I wasn't yet certain. I had
no idea why I remembered these pieces now. The more I
remembered, the more alone I felt, as though some devious
secret were just now being revealed, as if for ten years I'd
been the butt of an enormous joke. Yet I knew the information that tangled like wire inside my head was all-important,
clues that moved toward some destination.

July commenced with a telephone call from Avalyn
Friesen. Her voice sounded angelic, just as it had on the TV
program I'd rewound to watch at least twenty times by then.
She said she had received my letter—"my first and only

piece of fan mail," she called it—and wanted to meet me.
"You said you think you've had similar experiences," Avalyn
said. "Well, Mr. Brian Lackey, your eagerness is usually the
first step toward coming to grips with the truth." She
paused, and a dog yapped from somewhere on her end of
the line. "I just hope you're ready."

We talked for nearly an hour. I informed Avalyn of additional details beyond those I'd written in my letter. I mentioned my recent series of dreams, and she told me she'd
been through a similar pattern. "Your memories are ready
to make themselves known to you," she said.

We scheduled our meeting for July third, Avalyn's day
off from her job as secretary at Inman's grain elevator. I
dialed a couple of numbers to cancel my lawn-mowing
appointments. Then I called the prison in Hutchinson. A
receptionist directed the call to lookout tower number five,
where my mother no doubt sat staring over the prison yard,
her .38 in her side holster. She picked up, and I asked if I
could borrow the car.

"I'll find another ride to work that day," she said. "This
is something you have to do."

On July third I dressed in my best khaki pants, a short-
sleeved blue oxford, and a pair of oversize loafers I'd confis-
cated from a box of clothes my father had never returned to
fetch. I slicked back my hair and touched a pair of zits with
dabs of my mother's flesh-colored makeup. I didn't look half
bad.

The stretch of highway from Little River was one I'd
passed hundreds of times, but on that afternoon it seemed
utterly new. Midway between Little River and Hutchinson, I
slowed for the turnoff toward Inman and glanced at the
inside cover of my dream log. There, I'd jotted instructions
for reaching Avalyn's: "Go six miles east. Right after the sign

advertising Kansas Beef, look for driveway with the blue mailbox. . . ."

The Friesen farm sat a quarter mile off the main road. Holstein cattle grazed in overgrown stretches of pasture. A lane of flesh-colored sand trailed toward the house, flanked by trees that appeared centuries old. The trees folded over themselves like clasped fingers, squirrels and birds darting between the branches. I drove under them, parked at the side of a boxy log cabin, and rechecked my reflection in the side mirror.

I've never excelled at meeting people, but meeting Avalyn seemed inevitable. My nervousness was nowhere near as uncontrollable as I'd feared. I passed rows of zinnias beside the gravel path; before I reached the door, she opened it. When I saw her, I felt tingly, the way I imagined I'd feel glimpsing a celebrity. Avalyn wore silver teardrop earrings, a white housedress, and no shoes. Her hair gleamed, pulled into an oily bun that sat like a cinnamon roll on her head. "Brian," she said, and it sounded more like *Brine*. She offered her hand, and I took it. The hand felt soft and feverish, as if I were holding a hummingbird. I released it, and she brought her fingers to her chest. "It's good to meet you," she said.

Avalyn introduced me to her father, an ancient-looking man who slurped from a coffee mug. Beneath his red cap, his face was grooved with wrinkles. He had thick, tanned biceps that shone from his shirtsleeves. One arm revealed a tattoo, an eagle bearing a scroll that read LIBERTY. He smiled, tightened a strap of his overalls, then coughed and cleared his throat. "Avalyn and I are all that are left in this family." He spoke so slowly, cobwebs could have formed between his words.

Avalyn's father opened the refrigerator's top compartment, unwrapped a green Popsicle, and gestured toward the back door with it. "I've got work to do in the field," he said. He took off his hat. Hair fluttered from his head as if startled.

After Mr. Friesen had gone, Avalyn led me toward a rocking chair, and I sat. I surveyed the simple room—the TV, a dusty wood-burning stove, a rolltop desk, her collection of stuffed animals. The wall displayed various pictures of an older woman, assumedly the late Mrs. Friesen, and a chubby young man with a crew cut who resembled a platypus in military garb. Avalyn saw me staring. She shrugged, stepped into the adjoining kitchen, and returned with a plate of Saltines and a bright red sardine tin. "I haven't eaten lunch," she said. She unsheathed the tin with three twists of the tiny key, then placed chunks of sardines on the crackers. They were the kind doused with mustard, and yellow blobs spilled onto the plate. "Help me with these," Avalyn said. I bit down, cupping my hand to catch the crumbs.

I began. "I videotaped your TV show. I've watched it over and over."

"It wasn't bad," she said. "A little showy for my tastes, and they left out some things I told them, but they managed to get across the right idea."

"You were playing with a dog."

"That's Patches," Avalyn said. She swiped the back of her hand across her lip's mustard smudge. "He's an outside dog. He follows Daddy into the fields to look after the cows." She got up and padded back to the kitchen. She reached into a cracked pitcher, pulling out two sticks of incense. "Which do you prefer, frangipani or sandalwood?"

Before I could answer, Avalyn touched a match to the tips of two sticks. She jammed the incense into the dirt of a potted plant in the kitchen window. Curlicues of smoke lifted around her head. "Let me give you a tour of my little home," she said. "And I can show you around the farm if you want. And we'll talk."

Her father's bedroom was empty save for a small dresser and a double bed. The bed seemed to separate into two distinct hemispheres; the first had a rumpled pillow, the blanket's corner pulled away to reveal the sheet underneath. The bed's second half was immaculate, unwrinkled. The room smelled like an elderly spinster's perfume. Avalyn switched off the light. "And now, my bedroom," she said.

She opened the door. Her room looked like a teenager's: posters and triangular college banners covered the walls, and clothes, books, albums, and tapes scattered the floor. The room was messier than my own. "I cleaned," she said, "just for you." She laughed.

Avalyn flopped on the bed. Her housedress lifted, revealing her thigh, as white as porcelain. I turned away and focused on the wall's largest poster, where four scraggly-haired men in makeup stood on silver podiums. They pouted and scowled dramatically. "That's my all-time favorite band," Avalyn said. "They went by the name of Kiss. Are you old enough to remember?"

"Vaguely," I said. "I don't know if I've heard their music." I sat on the floor, next to an album by that very band. "I mostly listen to electronic stuff, music no one else listens to."

"I went through the same rebellion in high school," Avalyn said. "But I've always liked the glitter rock, the heavy metal. Kids around here just listen to country-western twang and not much else. Things never much change." She gestured toward the Kiss poster. "What a group they were," she said. "So theatrical. You could get lost in them. The band members were each a specific character, hence the makeup. Every day was Halloween. They were the lover, the vampire, the kitty cat, and the spaceman. Guess which member I loved the most." I scrutinized the spacey-looking-one's out-fit: shiny boots with spiked heels, metal plates crossing his chest and crotch, starbursts of silver makeup around his eyes.

Avalyn leaned over and took the Kiss album between her fingers. She slid the record from the sleeve, lowered it onto her turntable, and clicked the stereo switch. A guitar riff filled the room. "Yes." She lay back on her bed, directing her voice toward the ceiling. I looked there; saw glittery speckles in the dimpled surface.

"As you've no doubt figured out by now," Avalyn said, "there's a reason for everything. Something as simple as me, in my teens, being attracted to the guy in the band that dressed and acted like a spaceman. Or me, throughout my life, reading all these books . . ." She pointed to a bookcase, and I noticed several titles from my own room's shelves. "These are clues. For me, memories were buried there. The aliens don't want us to remember, but we're stronger than that. For you and I, nearly everything we do stems from our abduction experiences. You know what I mean, don't you?"

I nodded. "I think so."

"There's so many of us. Not all of us realize it. Yet we have a drive to know what's happened. What they've done to us."

On the record, the guitar solo started, and the singer howled in ecstasy. Avalyn sat up and tugged at sections of her dress to fan herself. "From what you've told me on the phone, I know you're at a difficult position. I was there a few years ago. Things are starting to come back to you, and you're curious. You want to know what's going on."

"You're exactly right," I said. Her hand had fallen to the bed's edge, motionless. I wanted to hold it. "Something hap-pened to me that summer, that night I told you about. And maybe, later, on that Halloween night. I know it."

The music ended. In that empty groove of vinyl between the two songs by Avalyn's favorite band, I heard sounds from outside: barn swallows twittering, cicadas humming. Somewhere, far away, a round of firecrackers popped and snapped.

"There may be even more to it," Avalyn told me. "Instances you don't yet know about. Brian, it's odd. People like you and me are in this for the duration of our lives. The first time they take us, we are tagged. They track us, and they come again and again. We're part of their experiments.

"Let me show you something," she said. "Here's one thing they left out of that foolish 'World of Mystery.'" She lifted the frilly edge of her housedress, her white thigh cold and shocking against the dark bedspread. "Lean closer," she said, her words coming in perfect synch with Kiss's pounding bass.

Avalyn thumbed a V-shaped scar on her thigh's upper region. I felt a blush spread across my face as she traced it back and forth. "You can touch it," she said, and the blush grew warmer. In the dim light, her eyes were the color of outdated pennies, the ones I used to collect in hopes of making a fortune. She reached out to take my hand, guiding it toward the scar. I touched it, then withdrew.

She sighed, and I could smell the sardines on her breath. "When the aliens returned me to my grandparents' car that first time, my leg was bleeding. We got home, and I remember my parents being furious, with the whole 'what the hell happened to Avvie's leg' and so on. But none of us knew anything about it, not even me. The cut didn't even hurt.

"Through Ren's hypnosis, I discovered that was where they'd put their tracking device. They've known where to find me, all these years, because they inserted something into my skin. It's floating in here, somewhere, just as much a part of my blood as the food I eat and the water I drink. It's filling them in on everything I do. I wouldn't be surprised if they're up there watching us right now, taking notes." She waited for my reaction, her eyebrow raised as if she knew what I'd say. Her finger returned to the scar. She caressed it as she might caress a pet salamander.

"I think they tracked me too," I said. "I might have told you this in my letter, but when my sister found me in the crawl space, my nose was bleeding. They must have put something there."

"Aha." Avalyn nodded. "The old nose trick. Some have scars on the leg or the arm. But others, like you, get it right up the nose, where the scar can't be seen." She moved closer to my face, peering into my nostrils, as though she might spy their miniature machinery. "Now we need to figure out how they've used you. It's doubtful they would shove something into your brain without coming back to experiment further."

"I think they tried to take me again that same summer," I said. "When my mother and sister and I saw the ship over our house. All my life I've connected that night with the crawl space night. Only now am I starting to understand why."

Avalyn lifted the needle from the record. She stared me right in the eye, letting me speak. It was the first time someone beyond my mother and sister had listened like this. I wanted to saturate the room with the complete story of my life.

"I want to tell my mother what I'm slowly beginning to discover," I said. "I need her to believe me."

"It's not easy for those who aren't like us. Remember that. But if you ever need someone, I'm here. And I know what it's like." Avalyn pushed herself from the bed and shuffled toward the door. I followed her lead. "As for me," she said, "my father doesn't believe a word I say. He refuses to support me. I pay for the trips to New York with my own cash, and Inman Grain isn't exactly the world's best-paying employer. Hypnosis sessions cost money, but I'm willing to pay, if only for the temporary peace of mind until they abduct me again."

Avalyn walked to the front room. She reached above the screen door, plucked a pair of clip-on sunglasses from a nail, and put the dark lenses over her own rhinestoned frames. She opened the door. The July heat tidal-waved into our bodies, and we stepped out. Avalyn's father had dropped his Popsicle in the space of grass beside the front porch. It looked like a lemon-lime knife, melting in the sun. Somewhere in the distance, more fireworks exploded, echoes crackling across the dry fields.

"This sun could kill me," Avalyn said. "You now, with your towhead, undoubtedly tan at the drop of a hat. But feel this." Once again, she took my hand and guided it toward her flesh. This time, she scrubbed my fingers over her shoulder, as if trying to erase an indelible smudge. "This skin is as soft, as cold, and as white as skin's ever going to get."

"Then let's find shade somewhere," I said.

Avalyn led me to a mulberry tree. Earlobe-size berries hung from the leaves, ranging in color from white (under-ripe) to red (halfway there) to a deep purplish black (fully ripe). The blacks polka-dotted the ground around the tree, staining Avalyn's bare feet. "The red ones are my favorites," she said. "They're sour." She pinched some from the tree; dropped them into my hand.

Two birches stood beside the mulberry tree; an island of grass stretched at one's trunk. The tree's bark was scabrous and mottled and mushroom colored, the color of an extraterrestrial. Nearby, a scattering of bees swirled in the air between two bushes: one bulged with yellow roses; the other, with pink. The heavy smell lingered in the air. Avalyn and I sat in the grass simultaneously; on our way to the ground, the frames of our glasses clicked together. I shrank back, but Avalyn laughed.

Avalyn lamented that she hadn't fixed a picnic lunch. "I'm always hungry." She leaned against the tree, strands of hair loosening from her bun. The teardrop earrings glittered from her lobes. She parted her legs a little, exposing the scar. It curled like a worm against the white thigh. I remembered when I used to attend church; the booklets with photographs of stigmata and other miraculous hieroglyphics on human bodies. Avalyn's scar was like that— remarkable, holy, a mystery imprinted on her skin that only she and I could unravel.

The afternoon droned on. Avalyn loved to talk. She told me about her mother's death from cancer, her brother's death that same year in a car accident. "It's been four years now," she said. "And Daddy still hasn't gotten over it."

Avalyn cut her history short and asked more about me. "I want details you haven't told me yet," she said. I related what I knew about my father, the life I was no longer part of. I told about Deborah, now in San Francisco; how she planned to return home for the holidays. I filled her in on my mother's recent promotion at the prison, about my nervousness concerning the upcoming autumn and my first year at college.

Avalyn listened to everything. Still, the words we spoke about our lives and families seemed conspicuous substitutes for what we truly wanted to say. Avalyn and I kept swinging back to the matter at hand: the experience of our abductions, the bond and the link from the majority of people who walked the earth around us.

Avalyn suggested that hypnosis would be the best way

to discover the truth. "But specialists in regression for UFO abductees are expensive. And they're mighty hard to come by in Kansas."

"We have money," I said. I stared at the purplish smudges on her foot soles. "We've always had it, even since my father left. But I doubt that my mother is ready to send me to a hypnotist."

"I'm not saying you'll only remember through hypnosis," Avalyn said. "It sounds to me as if you're on your way already. Keep logging the dreams you talked about. They act as clues. Be your own detective. If you see a place in a dream, hear a name, whatever, be sure you seek it out. Soon you'll have the answers you need."

By five o'clock the breeze began picking up. Wind gusts carried the odor of distant fireworks, the dangerous musk of gunpowder that often stained my mother's hands. "It smells as though the world is burning," Avalyn said. Through the crisscrossing nets of branches above us, an airplane trailed across the blue air, sparkling like tinsel, scarring the sky with its vapor. The people on board had no idea that Avalyn and I sat thousands of feet below in the grass. They had no idea what had happened to us.

I didn't want to leave, but I had recently started helping my mother with cooking—I fixed dinner on alternating nights—and I needed to arrive home before her. I told Avalyn I planned to bake a Cornish hen with stuffing. She Mmmmed and rubbed her stomach.

We walked back to the house. "It would be a good thing to meet your mother," Avalyn said, and I agreed. She smoothed wrinkles from her dress. "We could all go to the Cosmosphere together." I hadn't told Avalyn about my obsession with the space center. She just knew.

Inside, the frangipani and sandalwood replaced the firecracker smell. I poured myself a glass of water; Avalyn went to her bedroom for "some gifts," as she called them. She returned with a handful of pamphlets. "These were published underground," she said. "They are hard to get, unavailable in bookstores." I scanned the titles: "What Our Government Isn't Telling Us," "Were You Abducted?," and, my favorite, "The Wild World of UFOs."

I thanked her. Avalyn smiled, exhibiting shrimp-colored gums. She handed me another book, a copy of Ren Bloomfield's *Stolen Time*. I'd already read it, but I didn't tell her. "One of the people studied in chapter five is based on me," she said. "They used a pseudonym—I'm 'Georgia Frye.' How silly. Anyway, you can have that copy. I autographed it for you."

Inside the front cover, Avalyn's writing appeared beneath the title and author's name. *To Brian. To know you're not alone. We have to stick together. Love, "Georgia Frye," i.e. Avalyn*. Below her signature, she'd drawn a series of tiny valentines.

The dreams continued. The shell was cracking; pieces were showing through. I filled page after page, scribbling additional revelations in the log. I even dreamed about that Halloween night, years ago. Far from elaborate, the dream featured me in the hokey Satan costume, peering up at a blue cone of light in the sky. Simple as it was, I understood it as necessary information.

I telephoned Avalyn nearly every day. One afternoon, two weeks after our visit, I was rereading a pamphlet when I found myself thinking about Little League. I could remember that first baseball practice—how nervous I felt, my clumsiness at holding the glove and the bat, the row of teammates that had gawked as if I were a cripple.

I closed my eyes and saw myself as an eight-year-old. Another kid held my hand, leading me forward. Both of us

wore Panthers uniforms. It was crazy—I could somehow
feel the boy's damp palm, could smell the freshly mown
grass, could hear the thunder that boomed from the storm
around us. The boy directed me into an open door, and we
stood in a room diffused with blue light. Was it the interior
of the UFO? I couldn't quite tell, but as we stepped into the
light I saw that someone else stood there, someone taller
than the two of us. The person's presence commanded us
like a king's. I looked up at the tall figure—and then, the
daydream ended. No matter how desperately I pushed it,
nothing else materialized across my screen of memory.

My mother was napping, so I dialed Avalyn's number.
She must have been at Inman Grain, because no one
answered. Still, I couldn't let this new recollection rest.
Something Avalyn had told me kept repeating in my head:
her insistence that my dreams were clues, that I should seek
out the necessary information. "Be your own detective,"
she'd said. And now I knew that the aliens had kidnapped
someone else besides me, another boy on my Little League
team. I asked myself if this boy might still be around, still
living in Hutchinson. And I wondered what, if anything, this
boy had managed to remember.

It was essential, I thought, to determine the names of
the kids who'd played on my baseball team that June. Most
had lived in Hutchinson; they hadn't been boys from my
school. Perhaps there were records somewhere. I remembered the Hutchinson Chamber of Commerce, the building
on the city's west side where my father had taken me at that
summer's outset. Surely they had files, documentation that
could lead me toward the boy I'd dreamed about.

I did something out of character and decided to take the
car into Hutchinson without asking my mother's permission. I found a shirt in the pile of dirty laundry, tugged it
over my head, and bounded down the steps. I scrawled a

note—"URGENT. BE BACK SOON"—and stuck it to the refrigerator door with a magnet shaped like a celery stalk. Then I rummaged through my mother's purse; the car keys, a lipstick, nickels and dimes, and a few bullets toppled to the floor. Without cleaning the mess, I grabbed the keys, ran outside, and hopped into the Toyota. I turned the key in the ignition, praying it wouldn't rouse my mother.

The roads into Hutchinson needed repair, but I took them at seventy miles per hour anyway. I sped past fields of corn and wheat; overgrown meadows intersected by branches of Cow Creek and the Little Arkansas River; pastures where cattle hunched under trees to avoid the heat. Oat and sorghum silos gleamed in the sun, and farmers I'd never met waved as I passed. Leftover fireworks debris had been strewn through the ditches. When I passed the turnoff toward Inman, I thought of Avalyn.

The Chamber of Commerce stood tall and shining in the center of a series of buildings, a buckle on the belt of the street. A few people milled around inside. I entered the main hall and opened the first office door. A dark-haired receptionist sat at her desk, nibbling on beef jerky, one hand typing fiercely at a manual typewriter. She turned to me, asked the standard "May I help you," and listened as I fabricated a foolish story. I was researching a college baseball player who'd played for Hutchinson Little League teams ten summers ago. "This guy's going to be the next big thing," I said. "I'm doing a story on him for the community college paper."

Luckily, the receptionist believed my hogwash. She explained that they kept no records of the summer's teams. "What we do have, however, are old photographs." She indicated the floor by shuffling her fingers. "In the basement hallway, chronologically by year, are photographs of all the League squads since we began sponsoring the program over twenty years ago. Makes the walls rather unsightly, if you ask me." She stopped gesturing downward, took another bite of the beef jerky, and turned back to her typewriter. "You might be able to find things easier if you know the name of the team you want."

"Panthers," I said, and descended the stairs to enter the empty basement, its fluorescent lights buzzing. Framed glossy photos covered the hall walls. I could vaguely remember our first team practice, that initial week after my father had signed me to the Panthers' list. I had made certain my uniform was in place, then lined up with the others as a photographer had snapped our picture. I thought it strange that for all these years, my photo had been nailed to the wall, here in this building, without my knowledge.

"Nineteen eighty-seven, eighty-six, eighty-five . . ." I wandered the hall, sliding back in time, until I arrived at 1981. That year's team photographs were grouped together, twenty-two in all. The navy and white pizzas on our uniforms' fronts divulged my team. I stood eye-level to the picture. I scanned faces, not really seeing them, until I came to mine. There—me, kneeling on one knee in the front row center. I rested my gloved hand on my other knee, faking a smile. My hair was blonder than I remembered, my face flushed and sheened with sweat.

I looked away from the photo and made sure I was alone in the basement. And then, for the first time in my life, I committed a crime. I reached up, delicately maneuvered the frame from its nail, and pulled the photo from the wall.

Upstairs, I wedged the photo inside the waistband of my shorts, then untucked my shirt to conceal it. I scurried through the Chamber of Commerce, my steps punctuated by the chattering of the receptionist's typewriter. I made it.

When I got back to the car, I sat for a second, breathing. I felt as though I'd just done something unspeakable, like a bank heist or a gun blast between someone's eyes.

I slid the photograph out, and the smiling faces stared back at me. I focused again on the eight-year-old me. I glossed over the front row, and once again, folds of memory layered in my head: here was a kid I remembered as our pitcher, his arm gunning forward to strike me out during practice; another kid, one of a pair of twins, whom I remembered spraining his ankle during the Panthers' opening game; and another, the weaselly-looking boy at the end of the row, was the one, I suddenly knew, who'd broken my glasses and laughed at me, that Halloween night when the aliens had returned for me.

But none of the boys in the front row was the kid in my dream.

When I switched and began scrutinizing the top row, I found him. He stood there, his jaw clenched, a line of black sunblock below his eyes like warpaint. He wore jersey number ninety-nine. His face looked savage, the face of a kid who'd been raised in the jungle by wolves or apes.

I didn't bother looking at the others. I knew those were the eyes that had looked into mine; the hands that had led me into the blue room. The kid stood next to the end of the top row, his arm brushing the arm of the Panthers' coach.

Something about the coach stopped me. Strangely, I couldn't remember anything about him. For years I had recalled things about baseball practices, those agonizing first games I'd trudged through before quitting. But I had erased this coach. Still, something about him looked familiar, as if he'd starred in an outdated movie I'd seen through my half-sleep, years ago. In the photograph, he towered above everyone else, smiling broadly, the expression almost noble, brimming with pride for his team. His teeth shone unnaturally white beneath the broad curve of his mustache. He was the only person in the picture who gave me as intense a response as the boy from my dream, and I wondered if this coach had somehow played a part in the abduction as well. Perhaps he had been there, just as Avalyn's grandparents and brother had been there when the aliens had kidnapped her on that long-past afternoon.

My heart was thrumming. I had taken one step, perhaps one giant leap, closer to discovering an answer. "What next?" I said aloud. Curiously, I felt queasy, as if I were being watched by someone or something that wanted to harm me. I glanced at the side and dashboard rearviews, then rolled the window down and squinted up at the sky.

7/21/91—

A dream about the kid from the ball team—we're together in the blue room again. This time, we're on opposite sides of the room, I'm just watching as the tall alien figure glides over to him, slowly stretching him out on the silver table. The alien's fingers are a sickly gray, the color of fish scales, and they're shaped like frankfurters, they're touching my teammate's arms, his chest, his face—when the fingers get to the kid's mouth they linger there, caressing the skin of his lips, and then the kid's lips move—they mouth the words "here we go" and I know the kid is speaking to me, he's looking at me, and then he smiles and the alien's fingers penetrate that smile, they slip between the lips, reaching into the boy's mouth—I'm watching this all, I'm horrified but I can't move. And then the boy's clothes are in a pile on the floor. I look up at the blue light that floods everywhere, waterfalls of blue, and I know the boy's hand is reaching for me, the alien's hand is reaching for me, but I won't look at them, I only look at the light, because the light is blinding me, and I want to be blinded.

7/29/91—

I stand in the middle of trees, I'm wearing the Satan costume—the Haunted Mansion is behind me, it's that Halloween night again—and this time when the stick cracks I turn and see the alien—its skin is gray and rubbery, it has unbelievably long arms—its hairless head and those huge black eyes—it resembles a joke sculpture made from marshmallows or bubble gum wads. It shuffles toward me, almost gliding as if its feet are wheels—and then its arm comes reaching out, stretching and stretching toward me—it twists off my mask and its fingers touch my face—I feel the fingers land there like heavy bugs, one-two-three-four. And then it takes me in its arms, it lifts me up to hold me like it's in love with me, and then the most surprising thing, the alien's teensy slitted mouth opens and it speaks. It says Brian you don't remember me do you, but I sure remember you—it says I sure liked you Brian, I always hoped I would see you again, I always wanted you to come back to the team.

Sleep came fitfully, disturbed by the aliens' black eyes and their disembodied blue-gray fingers. Some nights I barely slept at all. After dinner my stomach ached, sharp pangs shooting through my body, as if sea creatures rested inside, prodding and flexing their pincers. The pain and the insomnia reminded me of certain UFO cases, and I returned to the books that contained passages about a couple named Barney and Betty Hill. I read how Barney, plagued with ulcers and sleeping disorders for years, had finally opted for hypnosis, only to discover that he and his wife had been abducted during a drive through the White Mountains of New Hampshire in 1961. The Hills knew something I, too, would soon know.

One night, around 2 A.M., I was preparing for bed when the telephone rang. My mother was sleeping, and the house had been still for hours. The ringing cut through the silence with a clamor I've always associated with sadness or bad news. The noise made me think of the night the hospital had phoned to notify us of my uncle's fatal stroke. It made me think of times when my father would call, those random nights after he'd left, to scream at my mother in a drunken rage.

Before the third ring, I picked up the receiver and whispered hello. It was Avalyn. I thought she might be calling to cancel the upcoming dinner I'd planned at my house, but that wasn't the case. She sounded flustered. "Something's happened," she said. "I'm a little jittery. I want you here with me."

I didn't question her. But I knew, for the second time in as many weeks, I would borrow the car without my mother's approval. She hadn't minded when I snuck to the Chamber of Commerce; I'd told her about the dream and that I'd seen the photo, but she didn't yet know I'd stolen it. I doubted, however, that my mother would okay my leaving at two o'clock to drive to Inman. But it couldn't wait. After Avalyn said good-bye, I listened to the swollen hush at the other end of the line and knew I had to go.

The car radio's station played nonstop romantic favorites. Faceless singers crooned about finding love, losing it, and finding it again. "Just look at it out there," the deejay said between songs. "It's the perfect night for making love."

The road linking the highway to the Friesen cabin was spooky after dark. Thin tentacles of moonlight stretched through the overhead dome of trees, accentuating some shadows, deepening others. The area was as gloomy as the roads that twisted through the White Mountains or that fishing pond in Pascagoula. The Toyota coasted forward, and I eased it into the space where I'd parked before. A single light shone from Avalyn's bedroom window.

Once again, Avalyn met me at the door. She wore a similar white dress, this one even frillier than the last, its pearl buttons gleaming like a row of cataracted eyes. "Thanks for coming," she said. At the sound of her voice, Patches trotted forth from the darkness, his tail feathering behind him. I bent down, and he licked my face.

Avalyn stepped onto the porch and shut the door. "Follow me," she said.

We walked out into the night, Patches lagging behind. Toward the north, heat lightning blinked on and off from a wall of clouds, luminescing distant acres of wheat. Leaves rattled in the wind, but everything else seemed uncomfortably quiet. There were no cicadas, no crickets, no random bullfrog making its lewd croak. "The silence," I said, and I realized I was whispering. Avalyn and I were tiptoeing as well, as though we'd become spies, and this trek to her pasture was our secret mission. I suddenly wanted to tell Avalyn about the dreams I'd had since our last phone conversation, about the shards of memory that concerned my Little League teammate. But the worry lines across Avalyn's brow stopped me from speaking. I knew she meant business. Whatever she needed to show me, it had to be something significant and indismissable, something potentially threatening.

After we'd walked a few hundred feet, we reached the pasture's edge and its stretch of barbed wire fence. I turned. The Friesen log cabin sat behind us in the shadows. The single bedroom light still burned, but the rest of the windows were sheeted with black. Avalyn's father slept inside. He was separate from us because the dreams he dreamed were safe and warm, the dreams of a regular human, of the unblemished.

Avalyn leaned to touch the fence. Several of its barbs were wrapped with balls of red and black hair, furry twists where cattle had scratched their hides against the sharp points. She tugged one hair ball away and slipped it into the pocket of her dress. "For good luck," she said, smiling.

The smile faded. Avalyn's touch on the fence became a grip. "You first." She stepped on the second line of the wire, then pulled another upward to make a gaping barbed wire mouth. I crawled through it. I made another "mouth" for her; she grunted as she shimmied through. Patches flattened himself on the ground, shrugging his body under.

We stood inside the field. I breathed the sweet smell of alfalfa, the manure and the dewy, freshly turned earth. And, underneath that pungency, the faint odor of roses, the yellows and pinks from the bush where we'd lazed only days before. Avalyn gave me a soft shove. "Keep walking," she said. "It's a couple hundred feet forward, over by that tree." I squinted toward her finger's point; saw the outline of a small evergreen.

More lightning in the distance. We headed for the tree. As we approached, I made out the shape of a cow, standing still beside the evergreen's webby fronds. Its stomach's curves expanded and contracted on each breath. The cow suddenly mooed, a drawn, haunting bawl aimed toward us, frightening me a little. We got closer, and at the cow's feet I saw another form. It lay in the grass beside the tree trunk. In the dark, it looked like a pile of discarded clothing. Patches galloped ahead. He stopped when he reached the reclining form, nosing and sniffing it. "Patches, get back," Avalyn said, and she skipped closer to shoo him away.

I bent level with Avalyn. The cow stood over us, breathing heavily, her warm air fluttering my hair. I was sweating, and Avalyn's dress stuck to my skin like a tongue against dry ice. I could feel the heat emanating from her body to blend with mine. "Here he is," Avalyn said.

The form on the ground was a young calf; the adult cow,

I presumed, was his mother, standing guard beside him. The moonlight made the calf look silky, cocooning it in a faint glow. I could see its hide's pattern, black spots against white, and the tiny coarse hairs on its face. I touched its ears, the curved cartilage like rubber cups. I touched its fragile eyelashes, the pad of its nose. Instead of damp and velvety, the nose was dry and stiff. The calf was dead. When I understood this, I looked at the full of its body. There was a gash in the calf's neck, a smile wedged into its flesh. Most of the animal's form was unharmed, but under its stomach was another cut, this one an immense gouge between its back legs. The calf's genitals had been severed.

The cow softly lowed again, a sound not unlike the noise a human mother in mourning would make. "This has happened before," Avalyn said. "Farmers around here have been finding mutilated cattle for years now. Happens all across Kansas. I told 'World of Mystery' about it, but they edited it out. And my father still denies the truth, even though he himself found two of our holsteins dead on the same night last autumn. He insists it's a bunch of maniacs or Satan worshipers that drive around chopping up cows. Ha ha." She touched the calf's throat, tracing the incision's border with her finger. "What kind of maniac cuts with this precision?"

Avalyn lifted her hand from the calf, and it landed on my own hand. "Feel this," she said. Together, we reached toward the wound in the calf's underside. I ran my fingers over it, feeling a meaty organ, a mass of guts that coiled around my fingers like cooked onions. "This is what's left," Avalyn said. "They take the sex organs away, the udders and the slits on the females, the you-know-whats on the males, even their anuses. The aliens experiment on cows, because animals can't complain, they can't voice themselves like humans."

Something was building from deep inside my throat, something rising toward my mouth that could have been vomit or a scream but felt sickeningly like a fist, a fist slowly opening. Avalyn continued, her voice muted and far away, as if spoken from behind a mask: "Us, on the other hand, they can't kill. But we have to live with the memory of what they do. And really, it's what they do to us that's worse."

She still held my hand, pressing it into the wound. "Notice anything else strange? I'll answer for you. There's no blood. They took that, too."

Avalyn was right. The calf's throat had been cut, and it had been bizarrely eviscerated. But the grass wasn't glistening with its blood. I knew the aliens had taken it, necessary fluid for more of their enigmatic experiments. I moved closer to the calf, shuffling my knees forward in the grass, and as I did I drew my hand from Avalyn's. With no reason, no reason at all, I pried my fingers under one of the exposed organs, probing deeper inside the wound. The innards were bloodless, but still as damp and sloppy as sponges. They closed around my wrist, accommodating my hand. I moved farther inside the body, searching for any remaining drops of blood.

Within minutes I was up to my elbow. I closed my eyes, and at that moment the clouds across my mind broke. Something like this, I knew, had happened before.

In my head I saw him just as he'd appeared in dreams: the boy, my Little League teammate, crouching beside me. *Open your eyes*, he said. *Here we go.* He whispered in my ear. *It's okay, he likes it, he'll give you money. It feels nice. It's fun isn't it, tell him you think it's fun.* I heard him speaking to me, but I couldn't comprehend his words, tangled chunks of sentences that meant nothing to me. He told me to open my eyes, to see what was happening, but I wouldn't do it. I was eight years old again, and I wouldn't open my eyes.

Like before, the boy was nothing more than a vision. This time, however, I wasn't certain how to control the dream; it seemed far removed from the usual security of sleep and the sheltering knowledge that I would soon wake up.

I was up to my elbow. *It feels nice,* the boy's voice said.

I lost hold of the fact I wasn't alone, must have briefly forgotten Avalyn and Patches and the cow beside me, because I started crying. I tried to hold it, but the sob broke like glass in my throat. Avalyn held me, her arm around me as shocking as icy water. I leaned into her and cried, cried because, at that moment, I considered the possibility that everything I'd recently accepted as fact was wrong—my new beliefs about my buried memories, the aliens and their series of abductions, these perfect explanations for my problems. What if all of it, each particle of this new truth, were false? What then?

The animal's mother mooed, and the silence closed around us. We sat there, no one in the world but Avalyn and me. I tried to persuade myself they were watching us, hidden away in some cubbyhole of the heavens, analyzing our every move with their infinite black eyes, waiting for the upcoming day when they would once again touch us with their mushroomy skin.

Avalyn pulled me closer. After a while, she took her hair from its bun; it cascaded across her face like a black veil. The hair smelled extravagant and secret, the smell of a rare flower that only bloomed at night. Avalyn rested her head against my shoulder, and I breathed that scent.

Minutes passed. I tried to erase the picture of the boy from my mind, because I knew that whatever had happened then—whatever I'd done, the unspeakable thing he'd wanted me to open my eyes and see—was beyond anything I could handle. I stopped crying and pressed into Avalyn. "It was the aliens," I said. My arm grew numb, still inside the calf. "It was, wasn't it."

"Yes," Avalyn said. "And it's okay. As hard as it is to believe, it's going to be okay." Her right hand gripped my shoulder, and then, gradually, her left hand snaked into the wound. I felt the warm slide of her skin as her fingers reached, reached slowly up, searching higher into the calf's carcass until her fingers stopped to intertwine with mine.

ten

NEIL MCCORMICK

New York beckoned, two weeks away. Both Mom and Eric avoided the topic, choosing instead to speak about the twenty-cents-an-hour raise offered by the grocery store (Mom) or the grandparents' latest dessert concoction (Eric). Neither wanted me to leave. Mom did everything she could to keep me at home; Eric went so far as to buy me drugs with the weekly allowance from his grannies.

Whenever opportunity knocked, I tricked, usually on nights Mom was working. I had saved enough to survive a while in the city, and Wendy promised I wouldn't pay rent until I could manage. But Kansas sex began boring me. As my departure date neared, I spent evenings watching horror films on the VCR with Eric. On the Wednesday during *Nail Gun Massacre*, he fell asleep, his head on my lap. I wanted to be elsewhere. "Sleep tight," I said. I kissed Eric's knuckle, something I wouldn't have done had he been awake.

The Impala stalled at traffic lights. It was on its last legs, but at least the stereo worked. I blasted the volume on a song's whirlpooling guitar feedback, rolled the window down, and burned rubber. A cluster of kids gawked from their spot on the corner of Eleventh and Main. I recognized them from school: their drugged faces, their short-on-

top/long-in-back haircuts, their clothes advertising heavy
metal bands. They conformed to a past I'd soon forget. I
yelled "Fuck you" out the window and thanked god I wouldn't
live in Hutchinson much longer.

I headed toward the far east end of Seventeenth. For a
Wednesday night, Rudy's was busy. Cars crowded the curb
and parking lot. I eased into an empty space, stepped on the
emergency brake, wedged my hand into my back pocket. A
folded envelope housed the acid tabs I'd bought that morning from Christopher. He'd written "Lead My Thoughts Unto
Sensation" across the envelope's front. I selected a square of
paper that showed a tiny sailboat and dropped it under my
tongue. It fit there perfectly, like the final piece of a jigsaw
puzzle. "Mmmm," I said to no one in particular. I sat in the
car until the tape ended, then switched off the ignition.

The bar had no sign, just a yellowed piece of paper on
the door, its name inked in capital letters. When I set foot
inside, everyone turned to stare. I remembered a dumb saying from childhood: "Take a picture, it lasts longer." Then I
said that exact thing. In seconds, a tubby bald man grabbed
my shoulder. He had shifty shark eyes and a wounded trout
mouth. He wore a studded leather bracelet and a Rudy's
T-shirt: white logo across pink triangle. "Let's see an ID."

I handed it over. "Shit, you know I've been here before."
Fatso tried his damnedest to detect the ID as counterfeit. No
such luck.

Rudy's, the only queer bar in Hutchinson, always
seemed caught in an extremely twisted time warp. I'd read
somewhere once how trends and practices of the east and
west coasts usually took three years to catch on in the
Midwest. If that were true, Rudy's lagged a decade behind.
On that night, for instance, a late seventies tune pulsed from
the jukebox. "I wanna disco with you all, night, long," the
singer wailed.

Another thing: the customers were perfect. Most were men I wanted, men I found myself picturing before I dozed off at night. They looked nothing like the guys that starred in the current pornos Eric and I saw on display at video stores, those poofs with blow-dried hair, shaved chests, glistening and steroided muscles. The guys at Rudy's sported facial hair, beer guts, and expressions that weren't practiced in front of home mirrors. Not everyone was attractive, but they were *real*. In the couple of weeks since I'd discovered the place, I'd already met several of them, had gone home with three, had even accepted fifty bucks from one.

On that particular Wednesday, most guys stood around in plaid flannel shirts and jeans. At the bar, the rips in the knees of their denims formed a straight line that resembled a row of singing mouths. For fun, I counted mustaches; divided the number by the total people there. Seventy-nine percent.

The air smelled like a mixture of smoke, spilled beer, the cedar chips that littered the floor, and a musky cologne that had probably been all the rage in New York one decade previous. Walking through that air felt like breaststroking through a murky lake. I ordered a Bud and reflashed the ID to the bartender. On the TV above the bar, a St. Louis Cardinal cracked a single over the shortstop's head. In a water-stained poster on the wall, collies and Saint Bernards were involved in what looked like a pretty interesting game of poker. I snuck to a corner, holding the beer bottle like a magic lantern.

The jukebox light cast a liquidy pink over my face. I hovered in front of it, searching its selections for anything I might want to hear. Ever since I was a kid, Mom had craved a jukebox. She'd point to the TV screen when a game show host unveiled one. "When we win the lottery, we'll dance around the house to *that*."

Dancing with Mom was my earliest memory. I must have been three or four years old. We had been in the kitchen, the radio blaring. She had grabbed my hands and lifted me, standing my bare feet on her own, larger, sandaled feet. She had led me, stomping and twirling through the room, holding on all the while, moving me with her. There, in Rudy's, I could still sense the rhythm of her movements, could still smell her perfume. Mom, who danced whenever she drank. Mom, who wanted to plug a jukebox into the living room socket. I wondered how difficult it would be to unplug the jukebox and carry it out the door.

I surveyed the crowd again. I recognized some faces; the guy at the end of the bar was one I'd slept with last week. Robin. Since I'd last seen him, he'd shaved his beard into a goatee. He wore the same ripped-sleeve flannel shirt and too-tight Wranglers.

Robin chatted with a guy who could have been his brother. The familiar way they watched each other and the casual positioning on their barstools told me they were just friends, not the night's bed partners. Guy number two wasn't bad-looking. I thought I'd seen him before at Sun Center. He noticed me staring, raised an eyebrow to Robin. His mouth formed the words, "You know him?" They looked over. Robin nodded his head. I slid through the cedar chips toward them, and the entire crowd rubbernecked.

"Robin," I said. I acknowledged his pal by a jerk of my head. "Who's this, Friar Tuck?" That was ridiculous, but I knew they'd love it.

Bingo. Both laughed, their heads thrown back. "Whatever," the unfamiliar one said. "You can call me that if you want."

"We rob from the rich and steal from the poor," Robin said. He looked at Friar, apparently amused by the way he was gawking at me. "Are you rich, or are you poor?"

I remembered the Robin Hood tale, the one Mom read to me at bedtime, eons ago. "Very poor," I said.

"Then we'll have to give you something," Friar said. They laughed again. I had to gnaw my lip to keep from rolling my eyes.

Robin plucked a pretzel from a basket on the bar and crunched it in half. "Neil here's new in town," he told Friar. "His dad's an actor out in Hollywood, and his mom's an international stewardess. They're only in Hutchinson briefly." I barely remembered telling him those drunken lies.

"An actor," Friar said. He turned to me. "What's he starred in that I might have seen?"

I hadn't anticipated this. Lying's best when it's spontaneous, so. . . . "He's starring in an upcoming film called *Blood Mania*. Plot: tainted meat supply infects already-weirdo family. They go nuts, cannibalizing all who near the vicinity of their spooky, off-the-beaten-track farmhouse. The end. Mom and I are flying to France for its premiere next month." I swigged the beer.

"Wow." Friar winked. "Are you planning on starring in movies? You could do it. You look a little like, oh, who's that cute star?" He sipped from a snifter of a thick and chocolatey-colored liquid in which two ice crescents tinkled like bells. I'd seen Mom drinking something similar, only she often decorated her glass with a mini umbrella she'd saved from a date with someone whose name I'd forgotten.

The jukebox blasted a country-western song from years back. Once, after the Panthers had won a Little League game, that same song had played as moms and dads celebrated in the parking lot with barbecued hot dogs and a cooler of beer. The space of pavement became a hoedown beneath the buzzing ballpark lights. My teammates and I watched, stunned, as the parents square-danced and sang along. I remember rushing for Coach. "Drive me away from this," I'd said. "Now." He took me to his house, not mine.

Robin hummed the chorus off key. "Work's been hectic since I last saw you," he said. I couldn't recall any specifics about his life. I vaguely remembered a brown-paneled studio apartment on the city's south side, next to the railroad tracks. I must have been really stoned that night.

I clunked my empty bottle on the bar between their elbows. "Need another?" Friar asked. He was already reaching for his wallet, a gesture I'd grown familiar with in men his age.

After three beers, I'd heard enough bits and pieces about Robin to remember he was a lawyer, owned a poodle named Ralph, had celebrated his thirty-ninth on the night before we'd screwed. Friar was his "business associate," in from Wichita for the night. "You guys should get to know each other better," Robin said, his eyes darting between our faces. I loved that sort of blatancy.

The acid was beginning to affect me, and I closed my fist, pressing my fingers into the ball of my palm. The heavy pulse in my hand thrummed against the weaker pulse in my fingertips, blood eddying beneath the flesh. My skin felt elastic. Right then I wanted to knead it against someone else to get that amazing sensation of two skins pulsing together, that pliability and friction. I held out my hand and placed it squarely against Friar Tuck's cheek. He smiled. His muscles tensed, and I felt the line of his gums, the ridge of each individual tooth.

"I need to take a piss," he said, but the words were a code for something entirely different.

Friar clomped to the bathroom, looking over his shoulder once, twice. "He wants you," I heard Robin whisper beside me, but the voice seemed fathoms away, as if coming from a secret cavern beneath the bar's floor. "Go get him," the voice said. Friar paused before he opened the bathroom door. I followed his path.

A ring-nosed bull had been drawn in the center of the bathroom door. I shut and locked the door behind us. At that instant, the remainder of the acid soothed into me, and my body felt delicate, glistening, a figurine on a shelf. "Hey," I said, and I smiled. Tuck repeated the word and the smile. I said it again, because I knew it was the stupidest possible thing I could say, and he'd love that. This time I reached up to touch his hair. "Heeeyyy." The word lingered in the air, not really my voice at all. It sounded like it had blown in on a wind.

The faucet dripped. The water in the toilet bowl glowed sapphire blue, a wad of TP blooming in its center like an immaculate lily. I looked up; saw a crown-shaped gray stain on the ceiling.

The meat of my forearm met his. Hundreds of his hairs brushed against me, tickling like insect legs. "My little actor," he said. That did it. I shoved him against the wall, slapped a hand on his butt and kept it there. I stood tiptoe and maneuvered my chin into his open mouth.

He raised his arms above his head and crossed his wrists. I was in control. I held him pinioned, my hand a clamp over his wrists, pushing him against the cold tiles as if the wall were a barrier I had to break with his body. He kissed at my ear, still sore from when Eric had pierced it. I moved away. He struggled a little, and I pushed harder, immobilizing him. "You're one strong kid," he said. "I bet you could do some damage." I nodded, but inside I was thinking *shit:* what he said hit the bull's-eye, but the way he said it wasn't right, his voice high and tinny. I remembered something Christopher Ortega had said once about a guy he'd screwed: *Looks like Tarzan, sounds like Jane.* Friar started to speak again. I crammed my tongue between his teeth, stretching it far into his mouth to shut him up.

My free hand tore at his shirt. It seemed as though I were moving in fast motion, and he in slow. His ivory shirt buttons popped open to reveal his chest. There, the tattoo of a whale skimmed across waves, a geyser of water shooting from the top of its head. I bent and bit it. He made a sound like "yeah." He wriggled so his nipple met my mouth. I took it between my teeth and nibbled, grinding my teeth on its tough gristle.

I wasn't hard—typical when I'm tripping—and I nudged his leg away when he tried to maneuver it up my thigh. I thought how this wasn't sex, really, just another experience. Yet it was what I wanted: the heavy contact, the two bodies shoving and slamming together, the stuff that could be proved the next day by bruises. I also wanted the thrill of knowing I made him happy. I wanted him to return to Wichita and tell his buddies about it. "Guess what, I made it with an eighteen-year-old tonight."

I stopped biting his nipple and returned to his mouth, sucking his bottom lip as if extracting poison. This was something I excelled at, something I'd learned long ago. Friar tried to say a few words, but they garbled without the use of the lip.

In ten minutes I'd ascended over him. I could take him like a vampire. The words "at mercy" flashed on and off in my head, and I wanted to do something neither of us would forget: scratch my initials into his shoulder, plunge my dick into his ass without a condom, bite the lobe from his ear. He knew nothing about me, nothing but a first name, four measly letters that could have been another lie. He didn't know a single truth about my life. He didn't even know my face, a face that wouldn't be the same tomorrow, in the mundane light of day.

I jerked my tongue from his mouth, leaned my head

against his shoulder, and in that second I saw myself, a flash of tanned skin in the bathroom mirror. His body blocked mine, and my head hovered above his back like a swollen trophy. I realized he was naked, although I couldn't remember stripping him. For some reason, that struck me as uproarious. I smiled at my face. The reflected expression didn't seem anywhere near a smile. It must have been the acid.

By the time I left the bathroom, the digital numbers on the bar's clock read one-thirty. Saliva from Friar's kisses covered my ear, which felt like a steamed mussel when I touched it. I heard him behind me, clearing his throat, zipping up. I slammed the door. Two men stood there, waiting. One applauded as I walked past. I didn't turn around for Friar's standard handshake or telephone number. "Whoa," I heard Robin say. The bar's perspectives were a hundred percent off-kilter. I stepped forward, leaving a trail in the cedar chips, and galloped out the door.

I did that out of boredom, I thought. *New York will be better.* I took Main at fifty miles per hour. On the other side of the windshield, everything kaleidoscoped; streetlights slid together into white ribbons.

I stopped at the Quik-Trip and pumped five gallons into the gas tank. I wandered inside the store, pretended shopping, and managed to steal two boxes of Hot Tamales from under the clerk's nose. Even that didn't seem as exciting as it once had.

The Impala sputtered to life. I tore at the candy box, popped a handful of Tamales in my mouth, then shut off the stereo and listened as the motor's rattle echoed through Main Street. I figured there would be some freaks prowling Main, drunken kids in the parking lot of Burger Chef. There was no one.

Carey Park had emptied as well. "No luck tonight." I didn't care; since I'd discovered Rudy's, hustling the park was a thing of the past. Now the place seemed like an old carnival I'd once visited, its memories shrouded like spirits. The car coasted past a sign bragging Hutchinson's history, its words still obliterated by the FUCK AUTHORITY and NO FUTURE graffiti Wendy and I had sprayed there years ago.

The moon looked like the tip of a fingernail. My headlights branched across crowds of skeletal oaks, cutting arcs in the humid and honeylike air. I eased the Impala into a gravel path that led to a playground. I switched dims to brights. They illuminated a swing set, two slippery slides, a rickety merry-go-round. For a second, I feared the acid would trick me, and I'd hallucinate the phantoms of murdered children. I got out and shook the thought from my head. The lights fell across the edge of a tiny jungle gym. I couldn't believe my body had ever been small enough to fit inside its silver squares.

I shuffled through the Impala's high beams toward the bathroom shed. The door wasn't locked, and surprisingly, the lightbulbs hadn't been smashed by vandals. I tugged at the dangling wire. Click-click. The walls had recently been painted orange, but when I squinted I could still see the ghost of my handwriting from months previous. I'd actually scribbled "FOR A GOOD TIME:" above the terms.

Back to the car. I lifted the neck of my shirt and buried my face inside it, smelling a sour fusion of breath and sweat and come. I left the park, running a red light, overwhelmed by the urge to speed home and ease into the world's hottest bath.

By the time I reached Monroe Street, I remembered that Thursdays were Mom's early mornings at work. I imagined Mom as I'd seen her so often whenever I came home late: snoozing on the couch, one arm fallen to the side, her fingers touching the carpet, her mouth open slightly, eyes trembling behind the lids as they surveyed the details of another dream.

I didn't want to wake her, so I drove toward Eric's trailer park. My mouth hurt, its soft parts throbbing, as if its layers of skin had been tweezered away. "*Blood Mania* wins Grand Jury prize at Cannes," I spat out. "Best Actor Richard McCormick dedicates his award to his only son, Neil, whom he claims will follow in his footsteps and then some."

A dog howled in the distance. I slid into Eric's curb. He was home, because the Gremlin was there, its front fender still crushed from his "little accident." I closed my eyes and tried to imagine the scene inside the house. This time, I pictured his grandpa and grandma, snug under their patchwork quilt in their brass bed, their spectacles or dentures or whatever else placed carefully on the nightstand beside them. Across the hall, Eric slept on half his futon. His face set into its permanently depressed frown. His heroes stared down from his walls' posters.

Next I drove to the Petersons'. I could hear their air conditioner whirring, and they'd left their lawn sprinkler on. Inside were Wendy's little brother Kurt; her mom and dad. In the year since she'd moved, I hadn't set foot in there. No doubt her room was empty, its rug tattooed with burns from candles we'd dropped during sleep overs, its walls pocked from times we'd tacked up posters of favorite new-wave bands. Once, years ago, we'd written our initials on the wallpaper of purple irises. In one corner, near the floor, we etched "WJP" and "NSM" with the rusty point of a carpet knife. We had taken turns holding the knife, me spelling her letters, Wendy spelling mine. I wanted to break into the Peterson house, sneak to her room, and check to see if the initials remained.

I thought about the three houses, three distinct worlds

where I'd lived my life. The lawn sprinkler circled back to shower the Impala's grill. It made little crunching sounds, as if dwarf hands were scrabbling to get in from under the car. It was oddly soothing. Eventually, my thoughts of Eric and Wendy and Mom merged to form a path that led toward one other place, one other person. I was coming down from the acid. I had no memory of starting the car again, or of driving back toward the side streets off Main. But by the time my thoughts clarified, I was there, idling in front of the house where Coach once lived.

I sat staring at the door and shuttered windows. I half expected Coach to come running out, his arms held open as if created solely to fit around my body. My Neil, he would say. He had moved from Hutchinson years ago. The house had since been painted, regaraged, reroofed. Yet I still could smell him there, could hear him breathing. *This is where it started*, I thought.

And then I heard sharp wails coming from the house: a baby, crying. I saw a light in one room's window. It clicked back off, and another room's light clicked on.

As I watched the window, I realized the sound emanated from Coach's old bedroom. I imagined a young mother in a lacy nightgown, calming her infant in that same perfect square of world where Coach had stretched beside me in bed. In there, he would hold me for hours, my head on his massive chest as I balanced my ear against him, listening for his heartbeat.

After some time, the wailing subsided. Maybe, I thought, the mother would speak to her baby. Maybe she would start to sing, a secret and peaceful song to lull her child back to sleep. I closed my eyes and clutched the steering wheel, leaning my forehead against it, listening.

eleven

BRIAN LACKEY

On the night of Avalyn's scheduled visit, I helped my mother cook my favorite dinner: Caesar salad, asparagus, and pork chops surrounded by a moat of au gratin potatoes. I opened the stove's door to peek. "You'll ruin the food," my mother said. Her apron showed a large fish preparing to devour a small fish, who in turn prepared to eat an even smaller one. She hadn't worn it since the days of my father.

I went upstairs to wait for Avalyn. Under the bed, my eight-year-old eyes gazed out of the Little League photograph from the Chamber of Commerce. Only Avalyn knew I'd stolen it. By now my mother resided in a different realm, apart from Avalyn and I, beyond the boundaries of our experiences as UFO abductees.

It was the beginning of August, and my dream log was half full. In my sleep I still saw aliens, and I tried to forget the doubt that had entered my mind on the night I'd viewed Avalyn's mutilated calf. I held firm to the belief that my dreams were all clues, pieces of my hidden past now revealing themselves. It was as though my brain had little rooms inside it, and I were entering a room that had been padlocked for years, the key sparkling in my fist.

I'd grown bored with skimming through the borrowed

pamphlets, so I bided my time staring at the boy at the end of the photograph's top row. I truly believed he provided my most effortless way toward a solution, that he would reenter my dreams to tell me his name, where he lived, what he'd retained from our concurrent abduction and any similar experiences he'd since had. I needed him.

The presence of the coach still bothered me: his squared shoulders, his broad, sandy mustache, and the coyotelike gaze that speared through the picture as if he knew he'd be locking eyes with me, thousands of days in the future. Whenever I looked at the picture, I'd press my hand against the coach's form to block him out. This queasiness was just another enigma I couldn't solve. I hoped my teammate, whenever I would meet him, could explain it.

"Come down here," my mother yelled from the bottom of the stairs. If I joined her, I could count on her to avoid the UFO subject, pushing it out of conversation to discuss instead my "upcoming college life" or "future career in the real world." I wanted no part of that. I made certain my bedroom door was locked tight. I pretended I couldn't hear her over the din of synthesizers and computerized drums. After a while, she walked away.

Avalyn arrived ten minutes early. When I heard her car in the driveway, I leaped downstairs. She stood at the door, holding six yellow carnations. She wore a dress, her wrists ornamented with silver bracelets, her face rouged and eye shadowed. She'd taken her hair from its usual bun, and it meandered down her back in a dark ponytail. I let her in, holding out my hand to shake. She waved my hand aside and hugged me instead.

"Avalyn," I said, "this is my mother." For a second I thought she would hug my mother too. Instead, she gave her the carnations. My mother took them as she might take a wriggling child.

It was the first time I'd invited a guest for dinner, so leading Avalyn from room to room seemed the apt thing to do. She lingered over my mother's plants, caressing individual leaves and fronds with the tenderness a nurse might administer to a burn patient. "Someone's watered this little guy too much," she said. She arched a plucked eyebrow at the stack of gun manuals and NRA magazines on the couch.

Avalyn followed me to the kitchen and sat at the table. I put the carnations in a mayonnaise jar, filled it with water, and sat beside her. My knee brushed her leg. I thought first of her scar, and then of the way she had touched me that night in her field as I cried.

"Brian tells me you're a fan of this Cosmosphere place as well," my mother told Avalyn. "I don't think he's missed any of their programs since the place opened."

"I haven't either," Avalyn said. "As I told him over the phone the other night, it's a miracle we never bumped into each other there." She unfolded the napkin I'd arranged beside her plate. "My favorite show was the one on unusual weather. I also loved the shows on volcanoes and roller coasters. The one on the history of railroads in America, on the other hand: boring." My mother brought the food to the table, and Avalyn continued to explain how that particular night's program concerned the history of flight. "I've a feeling Brian and I will enjoy this one."

We ate. The conversation lagged, my mother and Avalyn its only participants. My mother seemed to be testing our guest, unraveling her layers to get at some kernel of truth, and I didn't like it. "I'd enjoy hearing more about the whole process of hypnosis," she said. "Since Brian is so interested in it, after all."

Avalyn began relating stories I'd already heard. My mother hadn't said much after she'd seen Avalyn's feature on "World of Mystery." But there, at the dinner table, in front of the flesh-and-blood Avalyn, my mother wore the look of a hardened skeptic. She even clucked her tongue at one point.

"Now I'd like to ask you a question," Avalyn said. "Brian tells me you were there when he sighted his first UFO, the one he remembers. It's not uncommon for those who've seen one to see another." She wriggled her fingers beside the frame of her glasses to indicate the flutter of memory. "Do you have any other sightings inside your head?"

"No," my mother said. "I barely remember the one he's told you about." She paused and pressed her knife into what remained of her pork chop. "But I'm eager to find out what's behind his suspicions about his missing time."

"Oh, I'm convinced that Brian's suspicions are true," Avalyn said. "There's no question in my mind; *something's* happened to him." My mother stared at Avalyn with the exact eyes I'd seen her center on the 7-UP bottles beside the house, the gun in her hand.

"No question in my mind at all," Avalyn repeated.

My mother gripped the steering wheel, her eyes locked on the road. Avalyn lounged in the passenger's seat as if it were the world's coziest chair. I leaned forward from the back, my head inhabiting the uneasy air between them. Hutchinson's skyline loomed closer, and Avalyn pointed toward the structure of white plaster in the distance. "The famous mile-long grain elevator," she said.

We reached our destination as dusk was frosting the trees and rows of homes. The breeze smelled of honeysuckle and highway tar. The Cosmosphere building, a mammoth chocolate-colored octagon, sat near the community college. I scanned our surroundings. I was familiar with the college's buildings and sidewalks and lawns, but the place now carried a growing sense of dread: I'd no doubt spend the next two years of my life here, studying toward a degree I still wasn't certain of.

Yellow flyers had been pasted to each of the parking lot's light poles. I read one as we walked toward the building. They pictured a pigtailed little girl named Abigail Hofmeier. She had been missing since July twenty-first. "Please Help Us Find Our Baby," her parents had written at the bottom. My mother, reading over my shoulder, said, "That's heartbreaking."

The three of us entered the sliding glass doors. Touristy-looking people shuffled through the lobby and the adjoining gift shop. The next show was scheduled in fifteen minutes, so Avalyn and I browsed through the absurd souvenirs we'd seen hundreds of times already. My mother took her seat on a bench and waited.

Posters of planets covered the gift shop's walls, as well as astrological charts and informative lists about U.S. astronauts. Rocket mobiles and kites dangled from the ceiling, twirling in a counterclockwise ballet. Compasses, various key chains and pencils, miniature robots, and space-laser water guns crowded the shelves. One box was filled with dehydrated squares of food that resembled sections of brick. IDENTICAL TO THE HAM-AND-EGGS BREAKFAST EATEN IN SPACE BY ASTRONAUT ALAN SHEPARD! read a package's glittery letters. Avalyn examined a dehydrated meat loaf, then kneeled to a shelf containing make-it-yourself model kits. In one, kids ages eight to eighteen could construct a model unidentified flying object. "They don't know what they're messing with," she said.

We walked back to the lobby, where a maroon-coated man ushered people through the door. "Time to take our seats," my mother said. We paid for our tickets and filed into a long hall leading to the Cosmosphere's domed auditorium. The ceiling was blank and white. The room smelled synthetic, almost sugary, as I half-remembered the interior of the blue room in my dream had smelled.

The auditorium filled in a matter of minutes. An older couple with identical shag haircuts sat on Avalyn's left. The woman's eyes were dazed and slightly unhinged, eyes that may have just seen her own house burn to the ground. She, like everyone else, watched the ceiling, waiting for the show to start.

Lights dimmed, and I heard music that sounded like the electronic tape we'd listened to in the car. What had been a white dome above us became a replica of the night sky. From the corner of my eye, I could see the couple beside us shift in their seats. Their identical digital watches gave off twin green auras. Gradually, on the "sky" above, pinpricks of twinkling light flickered on, one by one. This opening sky simulation was always my favorite part of the Cosmosphere trips—it reminded me of the past, when I'd climb to our roof at home and watch as the night's stars gradually appeared, stars so familiar I almost possessed them. Avalyn must have sensed my excitement, because she whispered in my ear, identifying constellations. "Cassiopeia," she said. "Ursa Major, with Leo right beside it."

The moody music ceased, and the feature film began. The announcer's voice was enthusiastic and sexless, its timbre like a game show host's. "Welcome one and all to 'The Boundless Blue: The History of Flight in America,'" he/she said.

The film, which proved to be nothing special, traced the discoveries of the Wright Brothers all the way to current developments in air and space. Nothing concerning extraterrestrial life materialized. At one point, my mother squeezed my right hand. Then, slowly, Avalyn took my left. I wondered if either of them knew where my other hand was.

I pretended to be uncomfortable in the seat and fidgeted, clasping my hands in my lap to empty them.

On the way home, we saw fires on the horizon, farmers burning skeletal stalks of corn after harvest. The orange glow at the sky's edge made the world seem ready to crack open, and I watched until the fire fizzled to nothing more than a sparkle in the distance. By the time we arrived in Little River, sleepiness had filtered through my limbs. Avalyn helped me out of the Toyota and looked toward her pickup. "Don't leave yet," I said. "I need to finish the tour of the house. There are two important places you haven't seen."

My mother clicked the TV on, brushed aside her magazines, and sat on the couch to watch a weatherman trace the meanderings of a tropical storm in the Atlantic. Her mouth pinched into a pout. I walked to the basement door, switched on the light, and led Avalyn down.

At the bottom of the stairs, I stood on tiptoe, reaching to move the crawl space door aside. Once I had needed a chair; now I was tall enough to stretch my head into the opening as Deborah had done a decade ago. "Here's where my sister found me," I told Avalyn. She nodded, already familiar with the story.

I looked inside. The room appeared exactly as it had years before, the dust a little thicker, the cobwebs tangled and dense on the cement walls. *Here is where I chose to hide,* I thought. *Here is where I went to get away from them.*

"Now, the top floor," I said. "You still haven't seen my room in all its splendor."

My mother didn't look as we passed her. I trudged up the steps, opened the door to my room, and stepped inside. When Avalyn followed me in, I remembered what she'd said when I'd first visited her. "I cleaned just for you," I mim-icked, sweeping my hand over the books and tapes and clothes I'd ever-so-slightly tidied that morning.

Avalyn stood in the room's center. I couldn't remember anyone beyond my immediate family being there before. She surveyed my bookcase from top to bottom shelf, finger-ing titles, hmming or aahing occasionally. She ran her hand along the knobs of wood on my bedpost, then faced the wall. "I didn't like that film," she said, indicating my *Capricorn One* poster. She turned to *Angry Red Planet*. "And that, I never saw."

I stretched out on one end of my bed; Avalyn took the other. "Your mother doesn't care much for me," she said. "We are very different people. She thinks I'm stealing you away, I can tell."

"I don't think that's true." I forced a smile, as if it were no big deal.

"I had a boyfriend in high school once," Avalyn said. The sentence came out of nowhere, scaring me a little. "I wasn't so fat then. On our second date he brought me home late, and while I was getting out of the car my father appeared from the darkness, clamped his hand on the boy's arm, and told him if it happened again he'd personally blow his head clean off. So much for my love life."

From where I sat, I could see out the open window. Wasps dipped and spun from their muddy roof nest, threat-ening to fly inside. Down the hill, random lights in Little River's kitchens and porches and rec rooms flickered on and off. The ballpark's lights created a halo over the entire town. I remembered times when Deborah and I watched the play-ers running bases, catching fly balls, sliding into home. I wondered if the boy from Little League still played ball somewhere; if he lived close enough to contact.

I reached under my bed for the framed photograph.

"This is what I need to show you." Avalyn scanned the fifteen Little Leaguers to find me; when she saw my face, she tapped her finger against the glass. "Oh, don't look at him," I said, and I swaddled her finger with my hand to guide it toward the top row. "Here he is: the one from sleep."

Avalyn stared at him, glanced up at me, and stared at him again. "So he's your man. Yes, he could well be one of us." Minutes passed without a word, and I wondered what she'd say next. Then, without warning, Avalyn lifted the framed picture and slammed it, hard, against her knee. The glass splintered. She brought it down again, the frame's corner striking the spot where the tracking device's scar curled across her skin. Glass shards tumbled onto my mattress and fell to the floor.

"What—" I began. "Why?"

"Shush." Avalyn brushed the glass away with her hand, unconcerned with cuts. She extracted the photograph from its frame, shook off excess splinters and glass dust, and held it to her face. "Oh, Brian," she said. "It's just as I thought."

She handed me the eight-by-ten, back side facing up. Printed there, in blue ink across the white, was a list of names:

(Top row, l to r): C. Bailey, M. Wright, O. Schrag, M. Varney, D. Porter, J. Ensminger, G. Hodgson, N. McCormick, Coach J. Heider. (Bottom row, l to r): V. Martin, J. Thieszen, B. Lackey, B. Connery, E. Ellison, T. Ellison, S. Berg.

Our names. My name, "B. Lackey." And the kid's name. "I can't believe this," I said. "I should have thought of this." I didn't care about the others; my mind had speedily linked the boy at the end of the top row with "N. McCormick." I said the name aloud; said it again. It was the one the aliens kept secure in their confidential files, the one they'd logged alongside "B. Lackey."

"And now we have to find him," Avalyn said, reading my mind.

She reached into her dress pocket. "By the way, I almost forgot." She centered something in my open palm. It was the hair ball from that night on her farm, the red and white and black fur she'd pulled from the barbed wire fence. "I wanted you to have this," she said. "Whether it's the little calf's fur or not, it's proof that he was alive, that he was a living, breathing thing before they came for him." Avalyn closed my fingers into a fist around the hair ball and moved closer to me. "We always need proof. To remember something's happened."

She began unbuttoning her dress then, fiddling with one after the other until she'd reached her waistline and the dress had bunched around her stomach. She wore a T-shirt underneath, a shirt that had once been black but had faded to a dark gray. The front sported a cracked and flaky iron-on transfer of her favorite band, their caricatured faces pouting and snarling.

"Kiss," I said, and before the word had fallen from my lips she pressed against me, leaning into my body, my head twisting against the pillow. She muttered something like, "I thought you'd never ask," and as she spoke she jammed her mouth against mine. Our teeth clacked together. She thrust her tongue inside my open mouth, and somehow I recognized it, as if her tongue had dwelled there before, long ago. But I didn't know how to kiss back. I kept my mouth as still as possible, waiting for her to stop.

She pulled away and winced. "Ouch." The muscle of her palm had snagged on a stray glass shard. I leaned toward her to examine it, but she pushed me back, untucking my shirt to maneuver her hand inside. She touched my chest, feeling the tiny blond hairs around my belly button, moving up to tickle the scattering of hair between my ribs. Her hand leaked a residue of blood, and it left a dark red grin beneath my right nipple. Her finger erased the smudge; flicked the nipple. "I really want to make you feel good, Brian." When she said my name, my face went hot.

Avalyn slid the shirt from her shoulders. Her body's top half exposed, she lay down on me, her head on my chest, her breasts brushing my stomach. Something was horrifying about it: Avalyn, cowering against me, suddenly pitiful in the way her weight bunched together, the white flesh folding into itself, the skin terraced and scalloped and ridged. But even more horrifying was the body she lay upon: my scrawny arms, the uneven tan from the days I'd spent mowing lawns, the zits in a scarlet constellation on my chest.

I tried to concentrate on something else—the new name I'd learned, the upcoming days that would be filled in pursuit of N. McCormick—but, as desperately as I tried, I couldn't detach myself from what was happening. I was hard. Avalyn snaked her bleeding hand into my jeans, not bothering to unbuckle or unzip.

Before she even touched me, I realized what would happen. It was as if I'd known this for years, that I knew the secret to the reason I'd never approached anything remotely resembling sex: it would take me back to something I didn't want, a memory that had hovered for years, hidden, in my head. Her hand clamped around me, one finger gingerly tracing a line up my penis, stopping at the tip. I felt as though a part of me were vanishing. I felt the same trapped feeling I'd felt only days before, that night in her pasture.

"I can't," I said. "Don't."

"Brian," Avalyn said, and although her lips moved, I heard another voice entirely.

It will feel good, the voice said. The kid's voice. Yes, the voice of N. McCormick.

Open your eyes, it will feel good.

Something was spinning. My head had become a confused Ferris wheel, winding and twirling out of control. I had cried in Avalyn's pasture, but I would not cry again. Out the window, the wasps still buzzed and dipped from their nest, peering in at us with their rainbowy eyes. *B. Lackey,* they murmured. *N. McCormick.* I gripped Avalyn's wrist and pulled her arm from my jeans.

She went limp. "I'm sorry." This time, the voice was hers, not the kid's. I wanted to tell her no, don't be sorry, it's not you, it's me. But I couldn't speak. She rose from the bed, wriggling into the arms of her dress. I could see the red trickle forming a line from her palm to her wrist. One of the wasps had flown into the open window; it twirled in intoxicated circles against the ceiling. "I'm so sorry," Avalyn said.

After Avalyn left, I waited forty minutes. Then I called her from the downstairs telephone. I began by thanking her for discovering the names on the photograph's flip side; gradually, I led into my apology for the evening's uncomfortable culmination. "Forget about what happened just now. There's something in this head, something they did to me. I can't shake it."

"I understand," Avalyn said. In the front room, my mother lounged on the couch, the TV's light fireflying across her face, her head cocked as if straining to hear me. "And don't worry, you'll get over this. It just takes time."

After I hung up, I joined my mother. It had been years since we'd had an honest-to-goodness fight, but I could still remember the precise curl of her lip, her jawline's rigid architecture as she had scolded and yelled. That look was identical to the shape her features took now.

She held the remote control at eye level, switched off the set, and stared me down. "You need to explain something to me," she said. I thought of Avalyn, her top half exposed, lying across my bed, her hand inside my pants. Did my mother know? Then my mother's voice raised into a question. She almost screamed. "Why are you shutting me out of your life?"

She was angrier than I'd anticipated. "She understands things," I said. "You don't."

My mother mocked me. "'She understands things.' That's just it, Brian. I *want* to understand things. But it's hard. Soon you'll be in school, you'll be so preoccupied. I want this time to be ours. You're shutting me out." She was yelling, her voice a hammer, nailing me in place. The remote control leaped from her hand. I watched it bounce under the coffee table, resting at last beside the folded entertainment section of yesterday's newspaper. ACTOR DIES AT 32, a headline read.

My mother continued. "It's not that I don't want to believe you. I watched that silly program with you, I bought you the notebook to record your dreams in. But you're not foolish. I mean, think about it." Although she wasn't saying it directly, I knew she meant this: *the idea of you, Brian Lackey, being abducted by a UFO and examined by space aliens, is completely preposterous.* If she had said those words, something inside me would have ignited.

"I just want more time with you," my mother said. "Time that isn't spent talking about what the interior of that damned ship looked like, how you think their fingers felt when they reached out and grabbed you. Please. I know you need to sort those things out." Her expression melted slightly. "We should have brought this up earlier. If you want to see someone for help on this, really, there's nothing wrong with it, they even offer it free at the prison. A lot of people I know—"

In all honesty, the idea of psychiatric help for what I truly believed had happened to me didn't make me all that angry. At the time, however, a tantrum seemed the proper response. I allowed my eyes to widen, to reach cartoon proportions. There was nothing near me to grab and throw, so I simply stomped from the room. She didn't follow. I strode outside, toward the car, and as I walked I remembered the night my father had left—how Deborah and I had listened from the staircase as he had stormed through the house, slammed the door, and departed our lives forever.

I drove and drove. I was nothing like my father; I would eventually return. But at the time, I wanted to be alone, wanted to plan my next move. The car careened down dirt roads, tires spinning. I crossed rickety bridges; the steel ribs of cattle guards that sent wicked vibrations through my body. I drove past acres of stubbled cornstalks. My headlights revealed a shadowy scarecrow, hunched and emaciated on his cross. Ahead, Hutchinson's feeble lights beckoned.

Open your eyes, it will feel good. I had to know what that meant.

When I got to Hutchinson, I crisscrossed random streets. The majority of the city was safe behind closed doors. I puttered here and there for nearly two hours, pausing before each individual house. I scrutinized mailboxes, searching out his name. "McCormick," I said, hopeful. "Come on, just one McCormick."

By three o'clock, I'd found one McLean, one McCracken, and two McAllisters, but not a single McCormick. Soon it would be morning. My mother would be worried. I looked at my glazed eyes in the mirror, made a U-turn in the center of the street, and headed home.

twelve

ERIC PRESTON

The morning of Neil's scheduled move to New York began like any other. It was a day of stalled air conditioners and rapidly melting ice cubes, a day when the sky was so cloudless and gorged with sun it granted no one the privilege of shade. I had a stomachache and a fever blister the size of a dime. The latter didn't bother me; I wasn't expecting a good-bye kiss anyway.

I waited until noon to dial his number. Mrs. McCormick answered. "Hello, Eric," she said. "The weather is exceptional, and I don't have to work. The sleepyhead's still in bed. Let's make his final day in the breadbasket of America a memorable one."

My grandparents had been awake for hours. They crouched in the garden, dressed in matching aprons and sun bonnets. Grandma touched her yellow rubber gloves to the vegetables she'd cook for me on the next night I was home and hungry. Grandpa fiddled with marigolds and pansies he'd planted inside tires, the worn Michelins strewn about the lawn that added to the ramshackle antiquality of the mobile home. The temperature gauge on the porch—a rusting tin hobo, pulling down his dungarees to display a thermometer—pushed its red level toward ninety degrees.

I sat beside them. Grandpa handed me a crisp twenty-dollar bill. When he asked where I was headed, I explained how my "good friend" was leaving town that night, said I'd be back before dark, and hurried to the Gremlin. Grandma warned that the day's pollen count had surged to an uncomfortably high level. She pinched at the feverish air, and Grandpa waved. Good-bye, good-bye, see you later.

During the drive toward Monroe, I paid close attention to my surroundings. On one lawn down the block, a gathering of children played in their bathing suits, screaming and giggling through a game of sprinkler tag. Three blocks later, a man hunched in a ditch and tried to coax something from a culvert. Kids sat on car hoods, their radios blaring heavy metal. Hutchinson was no different from before. But today, Neil would leave forever. I was stuck, an off-color thread weaved into the city's bland fabric.

Neil stood at his garage door, beside his mom. They grinned suspiciously. Mrs. McCormick wore a green dress printed with daisies. Neil wore jeans and the usual white shirt. He was the taller of the two. Her hair, a little longer than his, was the same thick and heavy black, only streaked here and there with gray.

I slammed the car door. "Not so fast," Neil said.

"We're in the mood for a little trip," his mom said. She held licorice whips, curled around her fist like a red-and-black lasso, and a fold-out Kansas road map. A paper sack sat at her feet. "The Impala's been acting up," she continued. "I fear it's the transmission. I'm willing to give you gas money if you're willing to chauffeur us"—she placed her palms on the Gremlin's scarred hood as if to spiritually heal it—"in this little gal."

"No problem," I said. "Where to?"

Mrs. McCormick unfolded the map and smoothed it on the hood. She traced a line from Hutchinson to Great Bend, a city nearly an hour's distance northwest. Then her finger curled toward a pastel green square on the map. I squinted at the green and read the words, "Cheyenne Bottoms Nature Conservatory."

"We'll spend the day there," she said. She picked up the paper sack, and I heard the sound of bottles clunking together. "Wine and cheese. And if it's okay by you, when the time comes we'll see Neil off to the airport."

Their minds set, I couldn't argue. Neil took the passenger seat, and his mom clambered into the back. "Cramped," she said. Her eyes met mine in the rearview. "But I'm not complaining!"

I left town via Plum Street, out of Reno County and into McPherson, turning onto Highway 56 and its sign for yet another county, Rice. The band of asphalt stretched before us, shimmering and curved like a water moccasin. August's sun scorched the flat fields, and we saw three different ditches burned black by grass fires. Grain silos disrupted the smooth tedium of the land, their silver cylinders reflecting nothing but blue sky. It seemed that Rice County had emptied of people. In one pasture, a group of palominos lazed beneath a single tree, so exhausted they didn't bother looking up when Neil reached across my arm and blared the horn. We filed past the array of towns—Windom, Little River, Mitchell, Lyons, Chase, Ellinwood—all the while nearing Great Bend. As much as I wanted to hate Kansas and its smothering heat, it dawned on me that the state was almost beautiful, almost like home.

Neil's mom consulted her map, filling us in on historic landmarks and population numbers. She scanned the sketch of Kansas from top to bottom, announcing noteworthy town names: "Protection. Nicodemus. Medicine Lodge." She pointed to Holcomb, home of the murdered family in that famous book. She pointed to Abilene, Emporia, Dodge City. She showed us the tiny Herkimer, where an ex-boyfriend had lived. "What a waste. Driving that far just to be wooed by that shit-for-brains."

Neil nodded as she spoke. He chewed the same gum he gave for foul balls at Sun Center, blowing bubbles as wide as his face.

Billboards announced Great Bend's restaurants. The Black Angus, Smith's Smorgasbord ("Down Home Cookin' at Rock Bottom Billin'"), Jim-Bob's, and Country Kitchen ("Free 72 oz. Steak if Eaten in One Sitting"). Neil's mom leaned into the front seat. "Who's hungry? Let's get something in our systems before the wine and cheese and the trek through nature."

We decided on the Kreem Kup. Its sign sported a towering ice cream cone that twinkled and glittered in white neon even in the blistering daylight. Mrs. McCormick led the way, the licorice still in her hand. The twenty-or-so customers stared as we stepped inside, some literally leaning from their vinyl booths, their heads craning toward us. The waitress scurried away from a frying cage of onion rings and took position at the counter cash register. Neil ordered for us.

"You're not from around here, right?" the waitress asked.

"We're exchange students from a small carrot farming community in Iceland," Neil said, scratching unabashedly at his crotch. He indicated his mom with a nod. "She's our geography teacher, who joined us to write a book about the flora and fauna of Kansas." Neil's lies were amazing.

"Is that right." The waitress handed us a plastic placard displaying the number twenty-nine. I grabbed it and slid into a booth, across from Neil and his mom. On the café's opposite side, a group of teenage boys watched us. They were all ugly. Their eyes gave close scrutiny to my haircut, my eyeliner, Neil's earring, my clothes, my fever blister, and

Mrs. McCormick's breasts. I heard a drawling voice spout the word "homosexuals," almost cheering it, as if it were the final word in a national anthem.

I mouthed "white trash." Neil's mom winked at me. "They're just jealous," she said. Neil stuck his chin in the air. He was relishing the moment, having grown accustomed. I feared he would spit or throw ice at them.

The waitress brought the food and plucked the twenty-nine card from our table. Cocktail toothpicks skewered each bun like teeny, festive swords. Mrs. McCormick's pork tenderloin leaked a puddle of grease, tomato slices and wilted lettuce leaves beside it. "This should hit the spot," she said.

Under the table, my foot brushed Neil's ankle. He moved his leg and looked out the window.

We were half finished before the assholes at the neighboring table mustered enough courage to approach. One of them accepted some sort of dare and walked toward our booth. His front tooth was chipped. He wore a studded leather armband, black cowboy boots, ripped jeans, and a T-shirt showing an intricate drawing by some German "artist" who'd been popular with kids in art class at school. In the drawing, stairs spiralled and wound around and between and across each other, creating an optical illusion. The scene was the exact opposite of Kansas's elementary landscapes.

The lamebrain crossed his arms, biceps flexing. He cleared his throat, and I knew something wounding and sarcastic would spew forth. "We could tell you weren't from around here." His chipped tooth resembled a minuscule guillotine, suspended from his puffy upper gum. "And we just wanted you to know"—pause—"this is an AIDS-free zone."

My mouth opened. I wanted to bludgeon him, but

instead attempted to send him an especially damaging tele-pathic message. *Drop dead, shithead* was all I could generate.

Mrs. McCormick fared better. She looked him straight in the eye. "You are an evil little man," she said.

It was Neil's turn. "Fuck off," he told the kid. Then he leaned across the table, in full view of the entire café, and placed his tongue between my still-parted lips. He was only doing it for the effect, but I closed my eyes, forgetting the context for a split second, letting the restaurant's humdrum atmosphere melt around me, cherishing the tongue that hadn't been inside my mouth in months.

"Fucking faggots," the kid said, and headed back to his buddies.

I remembered how, before sex, Neil would crunch cup-fuls of ice; the chill that emanated from his tongue as it searched my mouth. There, in the Kreem Kup, his tongue tasted just the same, felt just as cold. I wanted him to thrust it past my teeth, down my throat, to choke me.

"Let's leave," Mrs. McCormick said. She dropped the remainder of her sandwich, and we scurried off. As we passed the jerks' table, two legs arched out to trip us. Neil breathed in deep and belched at them, and I remembered the little boy's voice on the tape I'd heard in his room. I still hadn't asked him about that.

Without turning to the café's windows, I could feel their eyes on us. "*That* was horrific," Neil's mom said. She crawled into the Gremlin and started laughing. "And greasy, too. We'll not come to the Kreem Kup again."

On to Cheyenne Bottoms. I pulled into a gas station, its green brontosaurus logo painted on a cement wall. Mrs. McCormick leaned from the back window and asked direc-tions. "Two blocks that way, make a right, then two more blocks, watch for the sign," the attendant said. He fanned his arms back and forth like windshield wipers.

We followed his instructions. I piloted the car onto a road that twisted away from Great Bend's city limits. We moved farther from everything. Two signs advertised the nature conservatory, one in the right ditch, one in the left, simple black CHEYENNE BOTTOMS block letters against white. The left sign had been tampered with, and the words now read HEY TOM.

When we reached the place, the world seemed to open up and level out. Cheyenne Bottoms was a five-mile-by-five-mile stretch of marshland, a scene that seemed more typical of, say, Louisiana than Kansas. Its air was heavier, smokier. There were few trees; in their places stood tall, rustling grasses and ferns, azure reeds and bracken. Banks of cattails swayed in the breeze, poking from shallow ponds and mud hills. Everything looked scrubbed with bleach. "Amazing," I said. We left the city behind, going deeper into this new realm.

Birds ran everywhere, their matchstick legs skittering across mud the color of peanut shells. Killdeer mingled about, thrilled, guests at an amazing party. Their forked footprints left zigzagging patterns on the mud. A cream-colored egret stood alone, looking forlorn. "Look there," Neil's mom said, indicating a glassy pond where wood ducks swam in figure eights. The scene looked unreal, almost comical. I half expected a crocodile's jaw to pop forth and devour the birds.

Neil peered into the rearview, then over his shoulder. "There's no one around for miles," he said. "We're alone."

I parked the car in the road, in a spot I estimated as the exact center of Cheyenne Bottoms. The heat slammed down. Neil and I got out, and a mosquito lighted on my forearm. It left an apostrophe of blood beneath my hand.

Neil's mom wriggled free from the backseat, the sack snug in her fist. She arranged the wine and cheese on the car hood. She pulled out three chocolate bars as well, all the while staring, mesmerized, at a flowering shrub nearby. The blooms grew close to the earth, thick white-petaled knobs surrounding red centers that stretched forward like the bells of trumpets. A few bees hovered there. Neil walked over and plucked a flower from the bush, then brought it back and tucked it behind his mom's ear.

A bullfrog began croaking. Neil tugged at his shirt—one he'd stolen from United Methodist Thrift—and tossed it through the open front seat window. He gulped his wine and sat on the hood, beside the block of cheddar. "Aaaaaaah," he said, arms stiff in front of him. At the sound of his voice, the frog silenced.

I removed my shirt as well to expose my white skin. Mrs. McCormick donned sunglasses and slipped from her dress, revealing a tight bikini. We joined Neil, our legs stretched on the hood, our backs and heads against the windshield. Neil rested between us, where he belonged. For him, New York was eight hours away.

The three of us ate and drank, eventually abandoning the cheese, but continuing to sip the wine. We stared out at the marshes, listening to crickets, the hissing of dried grasses, the various bird whistles and quacks and trills that somehow managed to harmonize in the steamy air. I kept hoping to see a kingfisher or some equally provocative bird, but none showed up. "Neil has a birthday coming," his mom said, languidly slurring her words as if easing into a dream. "The first time in nineteen years I won't be there to celebrate."

"We're celebrating now," he said.

She patted his knee, then leaned across to pat mine. "We are, aren't we."

Nearly an hour passed in silence. I found it strange how

there was so much to see, to hear, even smell. Cheyenne Bottoms, the land of slow motion. Occasionally a flock of geese flew over the car, caterwauling and honking, and Neil's arm shot up to follow their path across the sky. The sun devoured any cloud that tried to materialize. The chunks of cheese were practically steaming; Neil gave them a barefooted kick, and they bounced into the sod, a banquet for ants. I looked at his mom to see her reaction. She was sleeping. The flower had fallen from her ear. Her face and shoulders had already lobstered. I retrieved my shirt from the car and covered her sunburn with it.

Neil poured the wine's remnants into his cup and swigged it. "My bladder's about to burst," he announced. He jogged to a ditch, his feet audibly sloshing, and stepped into the reeds. I listened to his zipper unzipping, the patter of his piss as it hit the mud. Overhead, more geese soared in a group so thick they briefly obliterated the sun.

"Eric," Neil said. "Come here." I rolled my body off the hood, careful not to wake his mom.

I headed toward the reeds, grasshoppers catapulting every which way. One dive-bombed toward Neil's back, and I saw him standing there, jeans bunched at his knees. He turned. He gripped his balls and his dick in one hand, displaying himself to me. The other hand scratched idly around the ridge of his pubic hair. "Do me a favor. Take a look." I bent down, dropping to my knees on the spongy earth. I remembered assuming the same position once, in Neil's bedroom, under different circumstances. But he wasn't hard now. "I'm bleeding," he said. He sounded like an innocent kid. "What's wrong with me?"

I shooed away the hand that wouldn't stop scratching. Scattered across the flesh of Neil's crotch, almost hidden within his hair's black curls, were tiny dots of blood from his fingernails' abrasions. And interspersed with the blood were black specks, like little peppercorns, imbedded in his skin. I recognized them immediately as crab lice. I pinched one away. In the sun's slant, I could see the thing's whisker-like legs wriggling against my finger. "Gross." I tossed it and stared up at Neil, his soft dick and its parasites even with my mouth. He had no idea. The reeds around his head rustled softly, haloes of gnats darting between their towers. "You've got crabs," I spat out.

His eyes widened. He smiled, the pained, divided smile a person would make while being tattooed. "Oh." I wanted to slug him, to preach to him about hustling, about having sex here and there with this guy and that without knowing anything about the consequences. And then my thoughts of Neil's sex life led to other thoughts, all my surfacing fears of herpes and syphilis and AIDS, and before I could muzzle myself I opened my mouth and said something I should have simply tried to send through brain waves. I said, "You'd better be playing safe."

Neil stared down at me: beautiful, exquisite, a bronze statue I wanted to worship. "I stay in control," he said.

At the sound of Neil's voice, the reeds beside us shuddered, and something lifted in the air, its wings flapping sluggishly. Neil and I glanced up, breathless, and saw a great bird, a heron, its narrow banana-colored bill cutting across the sun, its crested head jutting forward, its neck bowing and dipping, its webbed feet drawing into its body as it ascended. For a brief moment it loomed directly above us. It cast us in its shadow, and I saw that its coat wasn't white, but sapphire blue, a color even I knew was rare for Kansas herons. It was the raw color of sky before the sun breaks. We watched it leaving. Neil hiked his pants, and we shuffled from the reeds, our eyes fixed on it. His mother still slept, unaware, on the car hood. The heron's wings coasted and waved, coasted and waved, as it moved farther away, as it flew northeast.

The direction of New York, I thought.

By the time we began seeing signs for Wichita International Airport, most of the day had burned away, the evening now a colorless husk. We had barely spoken since we'd turned onto the highway. I knew we each thought the same thing: what direction would our lives take now? The thought seemed wildly melodramatic, and I concentrated on the road, the wheat fields, the sandy driveways leading to farmhouse after farmhouse.

Neil's flight—one-way, not round-trip—was scheduled to leave at 7:30 P.M. sharp. He stood before the baggage desk, grinning. An attendant verified his ticket, punching keys on her computer. In the loading zone outside the sliding glass doors, the wounded Gremlin sat, a blue eyesore. I would have to hug Neil now. I knew if I so much as touched him, I would start bawling. Instead, I handed him the sack I'd carried from a Great Bend drugstore after we'd left Cheyenne Bottoms. I'd explained to Neil and his mom how "the grannies need aspirin." I'd lied. Inside was a box of lice killer, "pediculicide," the solution to annihilate his crabs. "A little going-away present," I whispered, and shoved it into his carry-on.

Mrs. McCormick leaned into Neil. She rubbed the tip of her nose against his chin, kissed his cheek, and rested her head on his shoulder. He watched the surrounding airport, his eyes darting among the horde of unfamiliar people, not focusing on me or his mom. "I love you," she said into his shoulder. Then—as if she knew—"Be careful."

Neil made a hip-swaying motion, his way of scratching without using his hands. He positioned his bag on the X-ray conveyor and stepped through the security sensor. I would have bet a month's worth of allowance on it beeping. It didn't. "Hooray," said his mom.

On the other side of an enormous plate glass rectangle, the 747 waited, scheduled to board in mere minutes. There was no sense in staying to watch. Neil raised a hand to us, and we turned away.

I figured if I were a true death rocker—if I honestly believed in my black clothes and dyed hair, in my fascination with skulls and crosses and dilapidated cemeteries, or in the melancholy and nihilistic lyrics that littered my favorite bands' songs—then this would be the point I'd hang myself. My parents were ten feet under. Neil might as well have been with them. I picked up my journal, scribbled a stick figure distended from a noose, and debated for ten minutes on a proper metaphor for what would lie ahead. I finally settled on "my future is a booby prize."

Two weeks to the day after Neil left, I vowed to stop moping in my room. The poems I'd been writing were nothing but whiny diatribes I'd surely blush at later. "Time for a change," I said. I waited for my grandparents to catch the senior center bus for their afternoon of bingo. Then I rummaged through some junk in the garage until I came up with the dog grooming kit they'd used years ago on their now-deceased poodle. I clicked the attachment I needed onto the clippers and took a deep breath. In the bathroom mirror, the hair fluttered off in fuzzy black clumps to reveal the shabby blond beneath. "Ouch." I looked as though I'd just escaped from a death camp. I'd dye it again later.

I drove around Hutchinson, windows down, relishing the slight breeze against my shorn head. I passed the fairgrounds, where carnies and commissioned KSIR prisoners mowed, cleaned, and set up rides and ticket booths for the imminent Kansas State Fair. It would be my first, but Neil would miss it. Across the street was the discount bakery where he and I had shoplifted fruit pies. In one window, left over from the recent holidays, were stale cakes lettered with HAPPY MOTHER'S DAY, FOR A FANTASTIC FATHER, etcetera.

At a traffic light, two heavy-metallers looked over from their car. "Skinhead," one of them barked. The word was so different from *faggot* or *freak*. I could get used to it.

I drove to North Monroe, anticipating Neil's mom's reaction to my hair, hopeful she would accompany me to thrift stores. A car sat in the ditch, a Toyota, the sun's glare ricocheting off its windshield. But the Impala was nowhere to be seen. I figured Mrs. McCormick was at work. I rang the doorbell anyway; heard the spooky echo from inside, like a child's voice calling across an empty canyon. I doubted she'd locked the door, but I didn't try opening it.

"You're probably having the time of your life," I said aloud to the nonexistent Neil. And then, telepathically: *Come back.*

There was no way I could steal from the United Methodist Thrift without Neil. I couldn't do a lot of things without him. I walked back to the car, and as I did I noticed someone watching me. A figure lounged in the Toyota's driver's seat, a blond kid whose eyes approached a bugging-out-of-his-head wideness. I recalled the stories Neil had told about his neighbors: how they were morons, how they had eavesdropped and spied on him and his mom since the day they'd moved in.

I started the car. In the mirror, I saw him getting out, stepping toward me. For a millisecond I panicked, half-remembering a story about a young drifter-murderer who crept up on victims in their cars, unsheathing his foot-long butcher knife, ripping it across their throats before they had the chance to scream. . . . No, this kid looked as harmless as a baby beagle.

He stood beside the Gremlin, contemplating me. His stare was benign, not the kind I was used to from strangers. Sweat stained his too-tight shirt, his glasses disorganized his face, and the zit above his lip looked ready to burst. Still, something about him was cute. "Are you N. McCormick?" he asked.

"N.?" I almost laughed. "Neil?" Then I did laugh. "No. I'm certainly not Neil McCormick. He doesn't live here anymore."

"So it's *Neil*," he said, then said the name again. He seemed briefly excited; in seconds, that excitement fizzled, altered, became something close to disappointment. "Doesn't live here. I've visited nearly all the McCormicks listed in the phone book, trying to find him. It's taken all week. I've spent too much money on gas."

That sounded illicit. I leaned out the car window, inspecting him head-to-toe. "Who are you, the FBI?"

"I used to know Neil," he said. "At least, I think I did. But weird things happened to us, he and I together, and I need him now. To help me remember." He blinked twice nervously, a gesture that made him seem close to tears. He was holding something, twisting and twirling it in his fingers. It was an unsightly ball of red and black hair, and it resembled a chunky mouse. He pocketed it. "Do you have any clue how I could get in touch with him?"

"Yes," I said. If he was interested, I could tell him a lot. And perhaps he could tell me something about Neil, could answer some of the million questions that had sprouted in my head during the past few months. I held out my hand. "I'm a friend of Neil's. Eric Preston."

He shook it. "Brian Lackey," he said.

We looked away, toward the McCormick house. Neither of us spoke for what seemed a very long time.

part three

WHITE

Autumn–Winter 1991

thirteen

BRIAN LACKEY

Amazing things were happening. Summer fizzled, depositing its remains in swirling piles of leaves, sap that trickled from trees, and skeletal tumbleweeds that bounced through our town's streets. The air smelled of ripening squash and melon. The nights became longer and cooler. I spent them lazing on my bed, my gaze directed out the window, watching migrating birds that scattered the sky. A family of possums took up residence in the trees beside our house. The cicadas buzzed their autumn lullabies; in the mornings, as I mowed my designated lawns for the final times that year, I'd find their crispy yellow shells fastened to trees, signposts, the frames of Little River's decks and porches.

Gradually, my alien dreams ceased. Other dreams replaced them, these more brief and unsophisticated, new crystal-clear scenarios into which the eight-year-old Neil McCormick sometimes figured. I abandoned my dream log beneath my bed.

A certain sentence rang through my sleep, one spoken by Neil McCormick, seven words that I first remembered on the night Avalyn had been inside my room. *Open your eyes, it will feel good.*

College began in September. I enrolled, bought books,

and studied. My mother surprised me by pulling into the driveway in a used Mustang she'd bargained from a lot in Hutchinson. The Toyota became my hand-me-down. I drove to school in the mornings and returned in the evenings, the routine falling into place.

Things went as expected; my courses, however, were easier than I'd predicted. And my psychology, calculus, meteorology, and English classes interested me less than did my growing friendship with Eric Preston. Since I'd met him, we'd been spending the steamy afternoons by frequenting the dollar-fifty matinees at the Flag Theater or listening to tapes in his room. I fibbed to my mother and claimed he was a friend from school I studied with. Initially I'd thought him strange, insisting we had nothing in common. But I realized that was wrong—I was no doubt just as strange. Besides, had I ever had a real friend before? Avalyn, perhaps, but she was thirteen years my senior. And as the days pitched forward, as my uncertainty about the UFOs and aliens grew, I wanted to divorce myself from my obsession with Avalyn. Although still preoccupied with the need to discover the solution to my missing time, I was no longer so certain the answer emanated from the spaceship I'd seen hovering over my house. The only thing I now knew was that somehow, Neil McCormick had my answer. And Eric Preston would lead me to him.

One night, not long after we'd met, Eric and I sat in his room and told each other about our lives. He outlined his childhood in Modesto, California, describing what he called "a completely normal life" until he started high school—when, he said, he "hung out with a wild crowd," began "committing little crimes and taking cheap drugs," and "came to the conclusion" he was gay. "A queer. A full-fledged fag." He watched me when he said that, waiting for my reaction.

"Doesn't bother me," I said.

Eric continued. "Ultimately, I was knocked senseless by my parents' car accident." At that point, his face thawed slightly. "So here I am, in Kansas, with my dead dad's parents." His eyes closed and opened in slow motion. "Reborn."

My turn. My childhood seemed tame when compared to his. I hadn't taken drugs, hadn't committed crimes, and was about as versed in sex as I was in sign language or acupuncture. So I made things brief, supplying little details: as a kid, I loved to capture grasshoppers and dragonflies in mayonnaise jars. Once my sister, Deborah, her friend Breeze, and I had tromped through an overgrown field to search for sandhill plums, only to be plagued with poison ivy the following day. My father never really liked me. In high school, I'd snagged second prize in a state-wide math contest. . . .

Ultimately I cast anchor on what I knew Eric wanted to hear: why I'd chosen to seek out Neil McCormick. I chronicled the central mystery of my life, my obsession. I explained why I thought something important, even profound, remained hidden in the empty cracks from my eight-year-old summer; that Halloween two years later. And I ended by telling him about my interest in Avalyn. I hesitated; although no longer certain the UFO belief was truth, at least I considered that story intriguing or out of the ordinary. So I told Eric about the slight possibility that Neil and I were the victims of an abduction.

Eric appeared amazed, but I felt relieved when he didn't laugh. He professed to be interested in unexplained phenomena as well, especially parapsychology. "I'm telepathic," he told me. "Well, slightly." He could prove it by a test: I would concentrate and close my eyes; he would transmit a message, just by staring at my head. I did as he instructed, but didn't hear any inner voice. "What message did you receive?" Eric asked.

I ventured a guess. "Um, the weather sure is nice today?"

He winced. "Oh, forget it."

Outside, cars drag raced through the trailer court's cul-de-sac. When the noise quieted, Eric asked further questions about the aliens. I mentioned the dreams I'd had; my recent inklings that something more lurked beneath them. When I finished, Eric promised to prepare Neil for our upcoming meeting by informing him about my UFO suspicions. "No, you don't have to do that," I said.

"Yes I do. I'll send him a letter."

"Hmm." I imagined Neil McCormick's fingers tearing at Eric's envelope, the same fingers I'd dreamed gripping mine. I saw him reading, pausing over the words about me, and then, as he gradually remembered, closing his eyes and smiling.

One morning, the telephone woke me, and minutes later my mother appeared in my bedroom doorway. "It's Avalyn," she said. I hadn't seen Avalyn since that night on my bed, the night of her failed attempt at whatever she was attempting. I'd only spoken to her twice that month. In many ways, I missed her. But an inner voice held me back, instructing to put my Avalyn visits on hiatus until I discovered more about Neil and our past together. "Tell her I'm asleep," I said.

My mother grabbed the upstairs extension. "I'm afraid he's still in bed. All that studying makes him sleepy." Something—possibly triumph—soured her voice. "Bye-bye."

Just as I began dozing off, the phone rang again. I knew it wouldn't be Avalyn, so I answered. It was Eric, asking if I wanted to "go hunt watermelons." That sounded odd. I hadn't eaten watermelon in years, due to the simple fact that they had overpopulated my childhood. After my father had left, the field beside our house had become just that: a field. It was no longer a venerated patch of land for growing that sticky-sweet fruit; no longer a place where my father spent summer and autumn hours planting, cultivating, and ultimately picking.

Still, when Eric asked, it piqued my interest. I brushed aside papers scribbled with notes for my upcoming psychology exam. "They won't be ripe anymore," I guaranteed. "It's nearly November." Then he told me we would go along as guests of Ellen McCormick. Neil's mother. The person closest to him, the woman I still hadn't met. "What time should I be there?" I asked.

Now that I had unlimited use of the Toyota, I could come and go as I pleased. I hedged telling my mother the truth, tapping a knuckle on my psychology book to indicate I planned to study at the library. My mother seemed to like Eric slightly more than she had Avalyn; nevertheless, the day after she met him, she'd referred to him as "weird" and "morose," claiming she believed he "carried some secret in all that depression." I didn't care what she thought; he was my friend. I stepped out the door, waving good-bye.

It was jacket-wearing weather, and the road from Little River to Hutchinson had changed color, everything now a dull, deerskin brown. When I pulled into the trailer court and knocked on the door, Eric's grandma answered. She and her husband gave me the same polite "hello" and "how are you" I'd grown accustomed to. Eric emerged from the hallway, dressed in black, fiddling with a limp, spotted banana peel. "Hey, man," he said. I followed him to his cramped bedroom, selected a tape by a band I'd never heard, and popped it into the stereo.

"We're meeting Neil's mom in an hour," Eric told me. "Don't be shocked, but I think we'll be trespassing through someone's pasture. Neil's mom found some field on the west side of town, and it's full of melons and pumpkins. She wants to make watermelon-rind pickles. She hopes the owners don't mind if she borrows some melons."

Eric's grandpa knocked and entered with a plate of brownies. I sat on the opposite end of Eric's futon, positioned the brownies between us, then asked, "Why'd she invite me? She doesn't even know me."

"Actually, it was my idea to invite you. When she called, I suggested it. She and I became friends, sort of, when Neil was still around. Strange, I guess." Eric licked the corner of a brownie, testing it, then took a bite. Clumps of hair poked in awkward, three-quarter-inch angles from his head, uncombed from last night's sleep, his haircut identical to a band member's on the poster behind him. "Honesty time. I sort of fell in love with Neil. Wasn't reciprocated, though. Hope that doesn't freak you out. Anyway, I think Neil's mom knows that. Could be she feels sorry for me. Could be she's like us, she doesn't really have anyone to hang out with. Especially now, with Neil in New York."

So that was it, I thought. Eric had fallen in love with Neil. "Is Neil—" I couldn't think of how to finish.

"Yes, he's a queer," Eric said. That sounded too harsh, a word I remembered hearing my father say, a scowl engraved into his face, whenever he described the women players on certain softball teams he drove into Hutchinson to watch. It dawned on me that my father, back when he lived with us, had always frequented tournaments at Sun Center, the same softball complex where, according to Eric, Neil had been employed as a scorekeeper.

"Do me a favor," I said. "Before we meet Mrs. McCormick, I'd love it if you could take me to Sun Center. To see where Neil worked."

Eric grinned, revealing something almost mean in the angle of his mouth. "Gotcha. I'll show you Sun Center. And then I'll show you where he *really* worked."

We left the bedroom. Eric handed the plate back to his grandpa. "These were scrumptious." He didn't bother informing his grandparents where we were going.

Sun Center had closed, the summer's tournaments finished. Eric stopped the car at the padlocked gate. Ahead of us, a sign read KANSAS'S LARGEST HAVEN FOR SOFTBALL FUN. He clucked his tongue at it. "Sorry. Looks like we can't get in." I surveyed the place. The only signs of life were some sparrows, a hunchbacked groundskeeper sprinklering brown plants, and two children who'd somehow managed to climb the fence and now seesawed in the complex's playground.

"See those press boxes above the bleachers?" I looked to where his finger pointed. "That's where Neil sat, hour after hour, blabbing on and on about this and that nonsense. You know, 'Preston the batter, Lackey on deck.' That sort of stuff." I tried to imagine Neil sitting there, his face behind the glass, watching every move the players made. All I could envision was the boy's face in the Little League photo. I saw Avalyn smashing that picture against her knee; next, the prepubescent Avalyn from "World of Mystery," her pigtails shooting behind her.

"We had sex up there once," Eric said. He paused and looked at me, the expression on his face now flushed and dithery, his eyes gone glassy. "Oh, sorry. I'm not trying to shock you. That stuff's over with anyway." He backed away from the gate and stomped the accelerator. Dust and dead leaves spun behind the car in a brown cyclone. The kids on the seesaw watched us leave, shaking their middle fingers.

Eric checked the dashboard clock. "This thing's fifteen minutes slow," he said, "so we should be meeting Neil's mom in about ten minutes. Enough time to show you Carey Park."

We drove east, then south. My parents had taken me to Carey Park once or twice, years back. I remembered playgrounds, softball diamonds, a golf course, a fishing pond, and a minizoo where ostriches, gazelles, and a dusty-bearded buffalo lazed under cottonwood trees. "The animals aren't there anymore," Eric said. "Losers from high school were poisoning them, so the city called it quits on the zoo."

The road twirled through the park. A ubiquitous, decaying odor pervaded the air, a smell like sun-poached fish on a riverbank. Leaves fell on the windshield, and the sky smeared with barn swallows and sparrows. On the right, more kids were swinging and seesawing. On the left, two men in white pants carried their clubs toward a dirt mound. This golf course needs mowing, I thought.

"Time for some information on Neil," Eric said. "He used to come here and get picked up by old men. Do you know what I'm talking about?" I shook my head. "Prostitution. Neil was a little whore; had been for quite a few years. He'd come out here whenever he needed money. The oldsters would get their rocks off and hand him a couple of twenties, boosting his ego somewhere into the stratosphere range."

The park sped past. "Wow," I said. I'd thought only women could work as prostitutes; thought it only happened in the largest cities. The idea of Neil-as-prostitute seemed like a feature from the sensational TV programs my mother adored. I imagined a newscaster's voice-over: "This teenage boy generates an ample amount of money for sex, and it all happens right here in the sleepy midwestern city of Hutchinson, Kansas." Eric was watching me; I wondered what reaction he expected. I couldn't think of anything to say. "Did you send him that letter?" I finally asked.

"Oh, the one about you?" He looked at the dashboard clock again and steered toward Carey Park's exit. "Indeed I did. Took me a week to finish. I doubt Neil will write back. But he knows who you are, knows you're going to meet him when he comes home."

The park's road intersected Reformatory Drive, and as we passed I could see KSIR and its four turrets. I noticed a shadow in the southwesternmost tower. The figure might have been my mother, standing guard over the grounds; although I couldn't be certain, I reached over and honked Eric's horn, then leaned out the window and waved my arms. It was something I did sometimes.

When we got to North Monroe, Mrs. McCormick was sitting on her front steps. "There she is," Eric said. Her hair fell across her face, the same color as Neil's in the photograph. She looked a little wild, dark, very pretty. I instantly liked her.

She trotted over to the car and squeezed into the backseat. Her hand reached forward, its fingernails painted pink, and I shook it. "Eric's told me about you," she said. "You're an old acquaintance of my Neil?"

"Sure am." Then: "Little League." Whatever Eric had said, I hoped he'd chosen to disregard the UFO story. Since she didn't look at me as if I were crazy, I assumed she didn't know about it.

As for what I knew about her, Eric had sketchily detailed her job at a grocery store, her sense of humor, the fact that she drank. Like my mother, she was a single woman with a teenaged son, but Mrs. McCormick seemed unrestrained, more independent and feisty than my austere, workaholic mother. The two of them wouldn't get along.

Ellen McCormick seemed especially friendly with Eric, almost acting as if they shared critical secrets, or as if he were her son instead of her son's friend. What did she know about him and Neil? And what about Neil's doings in Carey Park? Perhaps it didn't matter now. She leaned forward, her perfume oozing its nectar, her eyes scanning the ditches for identifying road markers. "Up here by this red barn, make a left," she directed. "Go a couple of miles. You'll pass some haystacks and a felled tree in the ditch." She offered us black licorice whips, pushing them into the front seat as if she'd magically retrieved them from the air. "From the same batch as the ones we ate at Cheyenne Bottoms," she told Eric. "I can't get rid of this candy now that Neil's gone." I took one, and it slid snakelike from her fingers.

Eric honked as he passed a hilly cemetery, its stone crosses and mausoleums outlined against the horizon. He drove farther into the boondocks. Hutchinson's city limits disappeared behind us. "Here it is," Mrs. McCormick said from the backseat; Eric steered into the ditch and stopped.

The watermelon field—a flat, sandy plot lacking trees— was separated from the road by a damaged barbed wire fence. A sign, wired to a fence post, spelled out TRESPASSERS WILL BE SHOT. We began trespassing regardless. I could tell the melons had seen better days: their leaves and vines had yellowed, with carcasses of fruit scattered here and there, exhibiting crimson wounds, ravaged to smithereens by raccoons.

We crawled over the fence. "My father taught me—" I said, then stopped myself. No, that was not what I wanted to say. "Um, I know how to tell if a melon's ripe. There's a little coil where the fruit meets the vine. It turns brown, and the melon's ready. I hate to say it, but these are rotten." I sounded like my professors at the college, and I suddenly wished I'd shut up.

Mrs. McCormick was unfazed. "I don't need the meat," she said. "Just the rinds. My neighbor lady taught me to make watermelon rind pickles. Ooh, they're good. I could get drunk on them. Now, let's get to picking."

I searched awhile. A scattering of pumpkins freckled the field's far end; since Halloween was approaching, I robbed the three with the most intriguing shapes and carried them back to the fence. Good melons were harder to find. Still, I discovered some whose curlicues were brown instead of black; these I ripped from the vines and placed beside the pumpkin trio.

Mrs. McCormick began whooping, her voice lilting in the air like a yodeler's. She had spied a raccoon. I glanced up and saw her hightailing through the watermelon patch. She chased the coon, gaining on it, her speed almost super-human. The stripes on the animal's tail bobbed through the dying vines, and twice she leaned to try and snatch the tail, her feet sliding in the loose sand. Eric laughed, one hand clasped over his mouth, his eyes darting from Mrs. McCormick to me to watch my reaction. Just before she could snag it, the raccoon reached the pasture's end and scurried under the barbed wire, secure at last. Mrs. McCormick raised her head, gave a final whoop, then turned back to us, exasperated.

Eric calmed down and began wandering around lazily, stirring up clouds of dust. Neil's mother returned to her pre-vious spot and continued foraging for healthy melons. After a while, she looked up from the space where she was crouching and mock-frowned. She pointed to Eric and aimed her voice at the sky. "What to do with this one? He doesn't want to work." Then her finger pointed at me. "But this one," she said, "is a keeper. This is the one my Neil will have to meet." I wasn't certain what she meant by that, but I liked the sound of it. She pushed a sugar baby melon with the flat of her hand, and it slowly rolled toward the fence, leaving a trail in the sand.

After the watermelon afternoon, the weather became explicitly autumn. Eric began wearing a series of bulky black sweaters, his pale skin turning paler. I told him the sweaters looked comfortable. The following evening, when I stopped by the mobile home after class, he presented me with a blue one. "No need to think I'm in love with you," he said. "I just wanted you to have this. A gift from a friend."

My mother was working overtime, so I invited Eric back to Little River. He fetched his tapes and a bottle of whiskey. I started to say, Don't let my mother see that, but that sounded inane. I started to say, I've never been drunk before, and that sounded even more inane. I finally said, "Let's go."

At home, my room was chilly, so I slipped the blue sweater over my head. "That's better." I chose a tape by a band called Breathless and blasted the volume. Eric uncapped the whiskey, took a drink, and delivered it to me. He began to search my closet, finding sheets of paper and a cigar box full of magic markers. Scribbled on the box, in my father's handwriting, was 6¢ PER POUND. He had written that years ago, when Deborah and I had sold watermelons during the Kansas State Fair.

We sat on the floor. I drank, trying not to wince. Eric took a large piece of paper and folded it into three sections. He explained a game he'd learned in art class: one person would draw a figure's head on the first third of paper, then make guidelines for the body into the top edge of the middle section and pass it to the next person. Artist number two would draw the body, leaving guidelines for legs and feet. A third artist finished the figure.

Eric handed me the folded paper. The head would be my assignment. "I know," he said. "Draw an alien."

I frowned. "Is it in the rules that you have to tell me what to draw?" I began sketching a lightbulb-shaped noggin to appease him. The alien's nostrils seemed bigger than the ones I remembered from my dreams. After I finished the enormous eyes and the mouth's miniature slit, I took two more swigs of booze. It felt hot going down, a giddy fusion of fire and water.

"Neil's lips have touched that exact bottle," Eric said.

His turn. *"I'm* not going to tell *you* what to draw," I said. I left him the pair of required lines so he could begin his body. He started in, taking twice as long as I had, nibbling his bottom lip in concentration. On the stereo, the band sounded especially melancholy. *"There you are with your idiot ideas,"* the singer sang. *"More or less as far-fetched as mine."*

When Eric had finished, he turned up the final third of paper. "Stupid me. I guess there's only two of us."

I thought for a second. "Let's pretend Neil's here," I said. "Do the feet the way you think he'd do them."

Eric drank. I drank. He chose a different magic marker, started to touch it to the paper, and stopped. "No," he said. He slid the paper across the floor to me. "You do it. Based on what you know about Neil, based on what you remember, start drawing."

Neil's appearance from the Chamber of Commerce photograph formed in my head, and I began from the lines Eric had traced on the paper's last third. I concentrated on any scrap of evidence I'd discovered about Neil until the drawing was finished. My head felt disordered, and I knew I was getting drunk. I centered the paper between Eric and me, and we unfolded it together.

First came my alien's head, a picture nearly identical to the one Avalyn had drawn for the Wichita newspaper, its eyes slightly lopsided and overwhelming its face. "That's good," Eric said. His torso, a detailed representation of a skeleton, held a blood-dripping scythe in hand, its finger bones splayed at angles, its hipbone shaped like a fat heart. And the skeleton's legs led into "Neil"'s—my—drawing of feet. Eric regarded it; said "and this is good, too." I'd sketched a bowlegged form with knobby knees. The legs wore clodhopper, cleated tennis shoes, the laces untied.

Next to the left foot were a baseball bat and a glove, the number ninety-nine written on its thumb. And next to the right foot, an oversized baseball. Across its surface, I'd written one word: COACH.

Eric tapped a finger against the baseball I'd drawn. "Coach," he read. "What's this?"

"I don't know," I said. I downed the remainder of the whiskey as if it were water. "I really don't know."

I didn't remember falling asleep, but I woke to the telephone ringing. I sat up from the floor, suddenly dizzy, my head pounding. I nudged Eric's knee. "I think I'm drunk," I said.

"I think you are too," he said. He staggered over to answer the phone.

"Wait. It could be Avalyn. I still don't know what to say. Just tell her I'm asleep or something. Tell her I'm not here."

Eric stepped into the hallway and positioned the telephone on my room's floor. He wrapped his hand around the receiver and paused, thinking. Then he picked it up. "Hello." I waited to hear what he said next. "Well, yes." He was stammering. "Just a second. I'll get him."

I mouthed, "Who is it?," slightly panicking, since the clock beside me said 11:45. Shouldn't my mother be home by now? I imagined her car in a crushed heap at the side of the road, her body lacerated by flying glass. I imagined a bullet from an inmate's gun hammering into her skull.

"It's some guy," Eric mouthed back. He kicked off his shoes, fluffed a pillow on my bed, and eased his head onto it.

I crawled across the room and grabbed the phone. "Hello."

Silence. The person on the other end swallowed, took a deep breath. "Brian," a voice said. "It's me." At first I didn't recognize the voice, and I stared at Eric as he began to drift into dreamland.

The voice repeated my name. This time, I couldn't mistake the caller. It was my father.

I hadn't seen my father in three years, since the Christmas of 1988 when he'd visited Deborah and me, when he'd tucked a twenty-dollar bill into each of our fists and perched in a corner to watch us open gifts. And he hadn't telephoned since last year's Christmas. He'd forgotten both my graduation and my recent nineteenth birthday. For some curious reason—the fact I was drunk, maybe, or Eric's companionship in the room—I felt uncommonly brave. I also felt angry. I wanted to scream at my father. I wanted to dig deep into the place where I kept all my feelings for him, all the pieces of dissatisfaction or rage or hatred, then stir them around, retrieve a fiery amalgamation, and throw them into his face. "What the fuck do you want?" I asked. That sentence almost hurt my mouth, as though it had been jimmied from my lips with an invisible blade, and when I said it Eric shot up from bed, his eyes widened toward me.

"Brian," my father said, almost scolding. My question had shocked him, too. Then his voice calmed and stationed itself. "I missed your birthday. You should get some—you know, some form of apology."

"I don't need anything from you," I said. I'd never spoken to my father like this. If I had mouthed off to him when I was little, he would have backhanded me. But now, woozy within this drunken fog, I had to do it. So much had happened since he'd last called, so many people and places and memories. My father had no connection with any of them. He knew nothing about me. I was no more his son than the boy that probably delivered his morning paper or the kid from the house next door in whatever city he now lived in.

"That's not true, son," my father said. "You know, I've

been meaning to visit you again, because we have so much catching up—"

"Like hell we do," I interrupted. Eric was standing now, head cocked in curiosity.

"Don't be angry with me. Please." My father had said *please* to me, and it made me sick. "Just talk to me, son. I want to know how you've been, what you've been up to."

I felt on the threshold of something. For years I had wanted to ask my father what he knew about my missing time, and now, our telephones connected, I wondered how I could gather together the words for the question. "You do, do you? Well, here's what *I* want to know." I could hear his breathing, lucid and steady, and for a moment I saw my father's chest rising and falling with each breath, his image absolutely clear, as if I'd only seen him yesterday.

"Something happened to me when I was little," I said. "Maybe you can tell me about it."

"What's going on?" he said. "What has your mother—"

"My mother isn't here. She has no part of this. Right now I just want to hear from you. I've been fucked-up inside my head for so long, dear father"—on that word, Eric put his fingers to his mouth—"and since the last time you called I've been trying hard to figure out why. Maybe you can help. Maybe you remember that night years ago, when I woke in the crawl space. I was bleeding, and I was dirty, and I smelled horrible, half-dead. Do you remember that? Or were you upstairs, too busy sleeping, not caring a fuck about me? Do you remember how she took me to the doctor, and all you cared about was the fact that I wanted to quit baseball? And do you remember all the times I passed out after that, all the times I pissed the bed, with you never questioning why, only screaming at me for it? Do you remember that Halloween night a few years later, when I passed out again, and I knew something else had happened, and all you did was shrug it off? Do you?" I stopped to take a breath. My voice had elevated, becoming something I no longer possessed. And the words kept coming: "Could be that someone did something to me, on both those nights. Could be that someone tried to kill me even, or did even worse than that." My sentences blurred together, and I wondered what he could understand of my ranting. "So what do you know, dear father? What do you have to tell me?"

There was another pause, this one lasting entirely too long. My chest hurt—no, not my chest, my *heart*—and as I waited I realized the preposterous idea of this conversation, and I knew he couldn't answer me.

"I don't know," my father said at last. He sounded exhausted. "There's nothing to say here. I can't help you, Brian."

I started to slam the phone down, but that seemed one step too far. I figured I at least needed to tell him good-bye. "Good-bye." I hung up before he could speak again.

My hand throbbed. I looked down at it. Somehow I had grabbed the drawing Eric and I had made; had crumpled it in my fist. I let go, and the paper swelled a little, its wrinkles loosening. I could see Eric's skeleton wrist. I could see a single, staring eye of my alien. I could see the *C* and the *O* from the word I'd written on Neil's baseball.

Eric lay back on the bed. He didn't ask questions. A brilliant blue light shone in the window behind his head, but without investigating I knew it was merely the porch light from one of Little River's homes. Only that, nothing more.

"It's just as I thought," I said. "He didn't do anything to me. It wasn't him. He had nothing to do with it." I stared at the telephone for what could have been hours. After a while, it seemed to crawl across the floor. I knew the hallucination was due to the darkness, to the bittersweet spell of the whiskey. I stretched my leg, rared back, and kicked the phone as hard as I could. It sailed through the hallway. A pure, almost miraculous second of silence passed before the telephone smashed against a door, the closed door to the room where my father had once slept.

fourteen

NEIL MCCORMICK

Life in New York didn't begin as planned: I suffered through a record-breaking four weeks—twenty-nine days, to be exact—without sex. "I always knew you had willpower," Wendy said. I didn't tell her that my abstinence wasn't due to willpower, but to the crabs, which kept returning. I'd already administered doses three and four of Eric's medicine from that day in Great Bend, a day that now seemed part of some other eon. Finally, with dose number five in mid-September, I'd decimated the crabs forever, free to do as I pleased.

I'd heard from various people how I could find sex anywhere in New York. Great, I thought, but I also remembered something Christopher Ortega had said months earlier, when I'd detailed my plans to relocate. "Don't have sex up there," he'd told me, as if I were spaceshipping to some distant and ominous planet. "Dangerous."

I figured sex couldn't be as dangerous as the street where Wendy—and now, where I, too—lived. The apartment sat on the fifth floor of a grungy building on Avenue B. As soon as the sun rose, unemployed women and men perched on the sidewalk and sipped from beer cans in brown paper sacks. Kids chased one another, dodging traffic, screaming sentences in Spanish. The neighborhood drug dealer prowled around, chanting his code words "bodybag, bodybag" to anyone who approached. Try as I might to sleep late, I couldn't, tossing and turning in the makeshift bed Wendy had set up in one of the three rooms, the street's seismic chatter squeezing into my ears until I woke.

On the evening after I knew the crabs had gone, I wandered through the West Village. New York's streets made it seem I'd been dropped into some tricky labyrinth. Corner groceries sold autumn flowers in bundles, a concept completely unfathomable in Kansas. Men traipsed outside clothing stores and drugstores, thrusting flyers into the faces of passersby: "Big sale tonight," "Ten percent off everything." I felt the hollow throb of hunger in my stomach, so I stopped at a streetside fruit stand and plunked down three quarters for a carton of shriveled, overripe strawberries.

On West Tenth, I saw the sign for an obviously gay bar called Ninth Circle. Three rough-looking boys gathered in front, lingering under a streetlight as if it were warming them, and they glanced up when I passed. I downed more strawberries and pretended not to notice. Their crotch-forward stances and their sneers made me think, *Hustlers, no doubt.* They were dressed alike—simple white T-shirts, jeans—and I was dressed like them.

A homeless man, one eye as inert as a dead flounder's, stopped me and asked if he could "have one or two cherries." I felt the group of boys staring. I handed the berries to the homeless man, which gave me a strange sort of martyrdom high.

Then I discovered I was being watched by someone else. A fortyish guy approached, the kind with a three-piece suit and briefcase, the kind that blends into whatever crowd he happens to be hurrying through. "Hi," he said when our eyes met. I said "Hi" back. Three minutes later, I was following him home, eager to smash the glass window of my recent celibacy.

The guy was a lawyer, and he'd piled his apartment's bookshelves with dictionary-size books on law. An American flag covered an entire bedroom wall. I saluted it. He took my hand away from my forehead and pulled me toward him. His eyes flashed in the darkness. I tossed my clothes into a corner; he folded and stacked his. His dopey basset hound padded in to sit beside the bed, attempting to lick my toes whenever my foot dangled over the edge.

The lawyer talked a lot during sex—standard, impersonal porno chatter I still loved. He unrolled a condom onto my dick, then maneuvered his body into a hands-and-knees position. He looked over his shoulder, and I slipped myself into him. For fun, I imagined what he might be thinking: It's sheer ecstasy having a teenager inside me; If only I were twenty years younger, I could be this boy's lover and not some freak fuck.

He came, I came, the regular shtick. His face got frantic. "You will stay, won't you?" He pushed himself from the bed, calmed his fanatical dog, started searching his pants pockets. I began to explain how I couldn't stay unless I called my roommate first. Then I stopped. The guy had turned around, was holding out a few bills.

Those *had* been hustlers on West Tenth. And the lawyer assumed me one of them. I took his money. "Sure, I'll stay," I said.

I thought: If this isn't fate, what is?

After the autumn equinox, New York grew dark faster. Around eight o'clock, the streets would curd with a cool and smoky air. The city smelled like fire, like an odor from some voodoo ritual. Machinelike people scurried here and there, no one looking at anyone else.

If my first New York sexual encounter had earned me fifty dollars, then perhaps the job search I'd been dreading could temporarily wait. Besides, I told myself, I've got to know this place first. I continued walking the streets. I sometimes returned to West Tenth, where the same cluster of boys stared without speaking. But no more men picked me up. Evenings, I'd arrive home before Wendy, usually with a moronic gift (old "Witching Hour" comic books; more earrings for her collection; roasted cashews from a street vendor) to tranquilize the guilt I felt for shacking up without paying. "I'm becoming a true New Yorker," I told her. "I don't miss Kansas one teeny weeny bit."

But I did miss it; no denying that. After my trick with the lawyer, I'd stretched back on his bed's doughy pillow as he curled his arm around me, my mind drifting. Before I fell asleep I remembered how Kansas had appeared from the airplane. As the 747 lifted from the Wichita Airport's runway, I'd leaned back in seat 17A, a slumbering woman and her young daughter beside me, and peeked out the window. Thousands of feet below, the earth became a patchwork of greens and yellows and browns, marked here and there with shiny barn roofs and silos, rivers that twisted like sapphire arteries, and yes, an uncountable number of baseball diamonds. On one kelly-colored outfield, antlike players jogged toward their dugout as the inning ended. An urge crept up on me, and I softly announced, "End of inning. Coming to bat in the top of the fifth. . . ." I imagined how Sun Center would look from the sky. That made me remember Eric, and I visualized my friend and my mom as I'd last seen them, standing at the boarding gate, hands waving in synch. The airplane entered a fluffy cumulus, and Kansas disappeared.

One day, after my legs grew weary, I walked back to Avenue B. Two queens bickered outside the corner deli. "I want *names*," one hissed at the other, and I swallowed away

a laugh. Beside them, pumpkins were stacked into a pyramid, anticipating Halloween. They looked foolish in the
middle of the city: pathetic, nothing like midwestern pumpkins, each no bigger than a dimwit's brain. They wouldn't
do justice to the upcoming holiday. I scrutinized them, tried
to decide which would look best in our apartment window,
bought the fattest.

"Jackpot," I said to the mailbox: a letter from Eric and a
postcard from Mom. The latter showed a cyclone demolishing a town. KANSAS TORNADO, the caption said. I read the
opposite side as I climbed the stairs to the fifth floor. Mom
had scribbled some quick lines about the freezers conking
out at the grocery, the weather turning cooler, the house not
being the same without me. "I miss you. Hourly."

I sat on the apartment floor and tore open Eric's letter.
It was dated three weeks back; he'd only recently sent it.
The letter consisted of eight handwritten notebook pages,
which I recognized as torn from the half–poetry journal,
half–secret diary I'd sometimes spied him carrying. Pages
one and two rattled on about his grandparents and echoed
Mom's Kansas weather report. Then, somewhere around
page three, things got interesting:

> Here's the main reason for this letter. Four days ago I met
> this guy. It's weird but I've spent tons of time with him
> ever since, all four days as a matter of fact. No, it's not
> what you think, we're not fucking. I don't even think he's
> queer. I can't see him ever having sex with anyone, actu-
> ally. Anyway, he's just started school at the stupid college.
> He's from this totally tiny nearby town called Little River,
> and I went there yesterday and it looks artificial, like it's
> only a dream of a town, its buildings and churches and
> trees like a movie set's cardboard cutouts, ready to topple
> at the slightest kick. That sounds stupid but it's true. His

name's Brian. He's blond, awkward-looking, glasses, zits, etc. So here's the story: he's obsessed with you. No, I'm not kidding. I caught him hanging out in front of your house, a while after you'd left. When I spied him, he asked, "Are you N. McCormick?" I freaked. I told him no. Turns out he used to play on your Little League team—well, he only played for a couple of games or whatever. He was squad's worst player, etc. Now take a deep breath, make sure you're sitting down for this, all that. Yesterday, after hem-hawing and beating around the bush, he basically told me that although he's not exactly sure, he thinks that when you and he were kids, you were abducted by a UFO and examined by space aliens. He was completely serious, and believe me I could tell from the look in his eyes. He blabbed on and on, sort of baring his soul about this woman friend of his who's been abducted, been on nationwide TV, etc., and telling me about these dreams he's had where you and he are inside a blue room and these extraterrestrials are reaching out to you, touching you all over, communicating with you in this weird sort of ESP way (and of course that last little detail really drew me in, considering my interest in ESP stuff). Anyway when he'd finished telling me all this he just looked me straight in the eye and said, "But actually I'm beginning to realize something else really happened, and all this is crap." (When he said "something else," it was as if the words were italicized, and when he said "crap" it was like he'd never sworn before.) So what's the story on this? Do you remember Brian or what? And WERE YOU ABDUCTED BY A UFO? If so, why haven't you told me about it etc? Weird.

Eric's letter continued, but at that point I stopped reading. At first I answered no, I couldn't remember anyone named Brian from my past; I couldn't even recall a Brian from my Hutchinson junior high days. The part about the UFOs twisted my face into a foolish smile, the kind that forms whenever I hear something astounding and irresistible. I felt as though someone had whispered the world's juiciest gossip, tickling me all the while.

Then I stopped smiling and really considered Eric's words. The kid named Brian, my Little League team, the part about "something else" actually happening—it seemed both familiar and unpleasantly intimate, so much so I felt embarrassed. Brian? I shut my eyes, thinking. Brian.

Instead of the boy, my closed eyes and concentration gave me a substitute image. Coach. The glitter in his eyes, the rough sand-colored mustache, his muscles' ripples and curves—all there, crystallized within a precious cranny of my brain. He was still part of me.

It was love, I told myself. Coach had loved me. But there had been others, boys whose faces I'd seen smiling from his photo albums. And I could remember three separate times when he'd brought other boys home to join in, to add fuel to the forbidden. Had one of the three been Brian? These boys' faces stayed vague, beyond surfacing. Perhaps Coach's emotions for them had caused me to feel jealous, inadequate, or damaged; whatever the reason, I had dislocated my memories of them. And their names were as incapable of being conjured as the names of men I'd tricked with from Carey Park, from Rudy's, from anywhere. When it came to names, I remembered *Coach* and nothing more.

"I'm beginning to realize something else really happened." I could hear Brian, whoever he was, saying that to Eric. Perhaps the UFO story amounted to nothing but bullshit. Perhaps he'd already told Eric about Coach, and they'd agreed to pull my leg all the way from Kansas, to see what I'd say. Perhaps, and perhaps not. I didn't want to think about it.

I considered telephoning Eric, but I couldn't. Only one other person knew about Coach—Wendy—and even she didn't fully understand the story. She couldn't know the privacy and the bliss I felt when he held me, and yes, the *love*. Coach existed in my past, my most special and unblemished memory. Eric could never know about him; Mom could never know. Whatever recollections Eric's new friend held, I couldn't allow them to interfere with mine.

But even as I thought this—as I fell back on the floor and tossed aside Eric's letter—I had the weird idea that I *knew* Brian, or at least understood him, as if I'd been burdened with the sort of ESP that Eric could only fantasize having. It was a confident knowledge, and it scared me.

Money dwindled fast. There one day, gone the next. Evenings, I wasted time with Wendy and her friends, drinking in smoky East Village bars. We alternated between straight and queer hangouts. I slept around; sex was nothing spectacular, nothing too different from what I'd had in Kansas. I wanted something more.

One night, in a place with the ingenious name of The Bar, a bartender asked where I hailed from. I told him; he smiled, thought a minute, and said, "You're not in Kansas anymore." He hadn't been the first to say that. Everyone thought the Oz references hilarious—bartenders, Wendy's pals, and an old dude whose eyes flashed with the leery optimism that yes, I was his for the night.

After the bartender said the line, I turned to Wendy, my face blazing with drunkenness and anger. "I hate Dorothy and Toto," I said. We ferreted our way around the place and sat on a bench beside the pool table. White ball collided with blue, knocking it into a corner pocket.

Wendy removed the rubber band from the ponytail that trailed in a long strip down her head's median. Her dyed-scarlet hair tumbled everywhere, so gorgeous I had to plunge my face and hands into it. It smelled like flowers—honeysuckle, I guessed. "Braid it," Wendy said.

I didn't know how. She shrugged and combed her hand through her hair. "It's like tying knots in rope, only with three ropes instead of two." I started tying, making a mess of it, until finished.

When Wendy got up to check her hair in the bathroom mirror, I headed over for another beer. The bartender was engaged in a hushed conversation with a friend, and he wiggled one finger to signal he'd be right with me. I heard the words "hustler bar." *What?* I leaned forward, inconspicuously trying to catch as much as possible about Ninth Circle. But the bartender and his friend weren't discussing the West Village. They whispered about a place on the Upper East Side, a bar called Rounds (What a stupid fucking name, I remember thinking). I couldn't hear everything—something about how the bartender and another friend had gone "as a joke" to Rounds, how the friend had caught a recent ex hustling there.

I couldn't have cared less about this melodrama; I just wanted to know where, when, and how. I shuffled over and ordered a beer, giving the bartender my best crooked smile. "Oh yeah, I've been to that place," I said. He appeared miffed that I'd heard his supposed secret, but I continued. "What street is that again?"

Before Wendy returned, the bartender had told me all I needed to know, vindicating himself of his earlier Oz remark. I learned that Rounds was located on East Fifty-third off Second Avenue, stayed open seven nights a week, sometimes enforced a vague dress code—no hats or tennis shoes, the bartender explained.

Wendy and I returned to our bench. She had brushed a wet hand over her knotted strip of hair, and water beads gleamed red on the closely cropped bristles at the sides of her head. She jerked her thumb to the right to indicate the bar. "More Kansas jokes?"

"No," I said. "He was just getting friendly." I handed her the beer. She tipped it, swallowing in heavy gulps until it was gone.

That following Friday, 8 P.M., Wendy hurried out to meet her friends for a speed-metal concert. I parted my hair on the side, combed back my bangs, replaced my shirt with a white button-down, and slipped on the ten-dollar pair of wing tips I'd bargained from a First Avenue thrift store. I snuffed the candle from the hollowed carcass of Wendy's jack-o'-lantern. "Here I go," I said, and stuck my tongue into its toothless grin. On the way to the subway, I checked my reflection in nearly every window I passed.

As I strode the avenues toward Rounds, I contemplated Eric's letter. The UFO bunk still confused me, but by now I'd cemented my certainty that this "Brian" was another kid from Coach's history, a boy he'd selected from the Little League lineup. If that were indeed true, then I'd had some form of prepubescent sex with him—a tidbit he'd either (a) disremembered, or (b) hadn't chosen to tell Eric. The three separate occasions when Coach suckered another kid into our afternoons still floated around in my head somewhere. I could remember Coach's voice, hissing instructions. "Suck his dick, Neil." "Put your hand farther inside me." I tried to imagine Coach saying something to the effect of "Let him fuck you, Brian." His voice remained, as lucid as crystal, as crisp as the five-dollar bills he'd hand to me and anyone else after we'd satiated him. In my head I envisioned a Forty-second Street marquee, strobes pulsing with NEIL AND BRIAN MEET THE LITTLE LEAGUE COACH. Yes, it was entirely possible.

I reached the doorway to Rounds, and I tucked these

thoughts away. After all, how could I successfully hustle wearing a face distorted with complicated memory? "I'll think about it later."

Chilly, carpeted, low-lit: the place's appearance seemed as far from the East Village bars as, say, a funeral parlor from an amusement park. Piano music tinkled through the air; an octogenarian blond woman sat before the keys, crooning a song called "Love for Sale." Fat queens huddled beside her, some mouthing the lyrics, periodically dropping bills into a glass vase on the piano. I stared at the singer, then looked around me. The distinctions between hustlers and johns were embarrassingly obvious. Everyone stood around, watching one another. The hustlers sipped at mugs of beer; the johns, fruity drinks with floating wedges of lime, lemon, or toothpick-speared olives. I took my place against the wall, one in a line of other teenaged or early-twentyish guys, most of whom didn't seem all that attractive. I stuffed thumbs in pockets and tried to force my features into whatever innocent expression it kept among its ranks.

The johns stared, stared, stared. Their eyes were the beady, slothful eyes of anteaters or vultures. *Neil McCormick, the new commodity.* I thought: I have them all in my grubby little hands, and I'm going to pierce them with pins, like butterflies.

After a five-dollar beer and some horrendous, nonprofit small talk with two johns, a guy approached who didn't look half-bad. "What's your name?" he asked, his tongue pink in the gap between his teeth. I told him, and he repeated it. "You're kidding, because my name's Neil, too." I mocked astonishment. The singer broke into "Just a Gigolo," her head bobbing, her eye winking lewdly at the surrounding johns.

The following minutes filled with standard john/hustler

dialogue. "Can I buy you a drink?" "Sure." "What do you like to do?" "Just about anything, as long as it's safe." "I usually pay a hundred and twenty." (I tried to suppress a gasp; still, as I'd soon discover, he'd quoted an average price.) "That sounds good." "Whenever you're ready to go, just say the word." "How about now?"

Neil-the-john lived in Texas and visited the city on business. His hotel smelled poisonous, hospitallike. I might have sneezed if not straining to appear as healthy and attractive as possible. When the door shut behind us, he took hold of my belt buckle and tugged me forward. "Happy Halloween, my little boy." I'd forgotten the date. I closed my eyes, conjured up a mental picture of a witch steering her broomstick across a bloated orange moon, and waited for the hour to end.

For the umpteenth time, I skimmed Eric's letter for specific sentences and words: extraterrestrials . . . abducted and examined . . . Little League . . . totally tiny nearby town. I stared at one word in particular, the name of the place where Brian lived. Yes, I remembered. I had been to Little River. Once, long ago. That summer.

The Panthers' game had been called due to a sudden rainstorm. One player remained standing in the dugout. His parents hadn't arrived to retrieve him. *Brian.* Coach had comforted him. "I'll drive you," he said. He opened the station wagon's backseat door, and Brian crawled in. But Coach hadn't taken him straight home. He had detoured to his own house; had invited us inside. The usual stuff followed.

Afterward, Coach had driven the station wagon to a munchkin town north of Hutchinson. *Little River.* I could remember the storm, the thunder, the windshield lined with tendrils of rain. I could remember the sweaty exhilaration that had always fizzed in my body after Coach had loved me. I could remember Coach beside me, one hand on the wheel, one hand on my knee. And I could remember Brian—yes, at last I thought I understood his piece in my past—as he'd sat in the station wagon's backseat, arms held stiff at his sides, his baseball glove still on. The car sped toward Little River, and as the town approached I kept turning to look at Brian, the black pinpricks of his eyes all blurry and blazing, as if trying to focus on something special that once was there, but was there no longer.

Zeke came from L.A., part of the "just in town on business" contingent of Rounds johns. He wore the expression of a female sword swallower I'd seen years ago at the Kansas State Fair—the face she'd made after the sword had slid in to the hilt. That wasn't the least bit attractive; still, Zeke approached me before anyone else did, and I wanted to finish for the night, needed the six twenties in my back pocket. He stood beside me, habitually touching himself here and there—for example, brushing his fingers against a shoulder, reaching down to scratch an ankle. It reminded me of baseball; the signals coaches give from the third base line as their players step to the plate. With Coach, knee touched to elbow had meant "don't hit the first pitch"; a rubbed nose, "bunt."

"Let's go," Zeke said. I followed him out, grabbing my jacket from the coat check booth. Rounds's doorman, chummy with me by then, glanced at Zeke's unsightly appearance. He raised an eyebrow, perhaps flabbergasted I'd chosen someone so ugly. I didn't care. The money was more important. Besides, I liked his name.

Our taxi took us to a midtown hotel. Lights from the street's various theater marquees made everything pulsate. Doormen, desk staff, and room service were decked out in two-piece black suits. They looked like snooty penguins, their eyes on Zeke and me as we stepped into the lobby. I put my nose in the air and boarded the elevator.

The hotel's rooms were small, warm, meticulously designed. An oversize reproduction hung from the wall above the bed, a detail from a Flemish painting I recalled studying during a high school art class. In it, a blurry milkmaid hovered over her pitcher. A window's ghostly sunbeam caught the glint of her jewels, the white of the milk. The picture made me want to cry or, better yet, leave.

Zeke saw me staring. "Vermeer," he said. "Well, sort of." He reached out, unbuttoned my shirt's top button.

In seconds I was naked, more myself than I'd been when dolled up in the silly dress clothes. But Zeke hadn't removed a stitch. He fell on the bed, rested his head on the pillow, and sighed. "I suppose it's my turn."

I watched as he undressed. His clothes were a few sizes too big; their bulk on the floor made me want to giggle. But there was nothing funny about Zeke's body. I searched for a description. "Skinny" and "slim" missed the mark. "Emaciated" was better. His knees were square bulbs, floating in his legs. His ribs made me recollect a section of abandoned railroad I'd once seen pushing from the cracked earth after the Cottonwood River's flood waters had receded.

But worse than the knees and the ribs was Zeke's skin. It seemed as white as the milk in the Vermeer pitcher. Purplish brown lesions scattered across his stomach and chest, angry blemishes that looked ready to burst. More marks disfigured his shoulder, an ankle, his knee's knobby vicinity. He was a compressed landscape, a relief map.

"I hope these don't disturb you," Zeke said. "They keep popping up in the most unexpected places. Don't worry, this is the safest encounter you'll ever have, I assure you that."

He turned over, presenting me with his boxy ass, more outlines of ribs, his hard backbone. He spoke into the pillow.
"Just rub my back for a while. I need"—I thought he would
say "you," which would have horrified me—"this." I couldn't
see his face, but he seemed on the verge of tears. If he cries,
I thought, I will sprint home. He patted the bed. "Make me
happy, if only for a while. You'll get your cash."

I sat on his ass and placed my palms on his back. I
wasn't hard, and my dick drooped against his ass crack. My
thumb touched another lesion, this one just a small purple
blotch. It appeared as harmless as a mole. *I have to make
him happy*, I thought. It was my duty. I was locked here, in
this new place where KS no longer meant the abbreviation
for Kansas, but something altogether different. I pressed
my thumb into the lesion, wondering if it hurt. I began to
massage his back, and as I did, his head relaxed into the
pillow. It appeared artificial, something I could untwist
and remove and hurl across the room like a basketball.
Above me, the milkmaid continued in her frozen moment
of pouring the milk for someone she loved. It was a beautiful day. Her cheeks were flushed, her mouth curved into a
smile that displayed her joy in performing such a pure
task. I watched her face and pushed harder, kneading the
flesh beneath my hands.

Zeke grunted softly. On a simple black table beside us,
his wallet was stuffed full with credit cards and cash, the
edges of bills clearly visible in the lamplight.

Afterward, I needed to be with Wendy; it was time to
come clean about hustling. The cab driver passed a corner
grocery. "Stop here," I yelled. I bought Wendy a bundle of
flowers: roses, carnations, and other varieties I'd only
glimpsed in encyclopedias or a foreign film I watched once

during a particularly spectacular acid trip. I walked the remainder of the way to the small coffee shop and café where she worked.

South American Blend sat two avenues and five streets from our apartment. With the sudden cold weather onslaught, the store's business had begun picking up, and Wendy had volunteered to work overtime. She had been staying past midnight, serving desserts, cappuccinos, and hot chocolates to pretentious people who occupied entire tables to "read" French literature or books about philosophical bullshit. When I stepped inside, I smelled the swirl of French roast, Irish mocha, hazelnut cream. The smell, infinitely more exotic than Mom's instant Maxwell House, still reminded me of her somehow.

Wendy greeted me at the counter, stirring a tea strainer through a teapot's steaming water. I held out the flowers, and she put her hand to her mouth. "For me? You shouldn't have."

After she'd placed them in a bowl, I leaned over the counter, my mouth to her ear. "Please say you've got a minute," I whispered. "We have to talk."

Wendy's boss had left for the night, and the customers looked sated for the time being. She followed me to the table nearest the counter and pushed me into a chair. "What did you do now?" Her tone of voice hadn't changed since she'd lectured me years ago, when I'd first started hustling in Carey Park.

My mouth opened twice, but nothing came out. On the third try, I said, "I've been at Rounds. It's a hustler bar on the Upper East. I've been hustling."

Wendy's expression looked like a special effect. Anger registered somewhere within it. She checked the counter, saw no customers, turned back to me. "Do you think I haven't figured out what you've been doing? Where you've been at night, dressed like a goddamn teenage executive, or where you've been getting money for beer? It's been part of you for years, did you think I'd believe you'd stop now? Especially now, in a city where you can make thousands doing it? No, I'm not that stupid, whether you think so or not."

"I don't think you're stupid."

"Maybe not, but I'm beginning to think you are." She paused, took a breath, looked me in the eye. "Do I want to hear this? Okay, fire away."

I started to pretend I'd been hurt by her comment; decided it was no use. "I've been making money," I said, "and things have been cool, actually. Nothing unsafe at all, nothing that could bother me. You always said during the Carey Park stuff that whenever something bothered me, I should stop."

Wendy swabbed her thumb over the table's semicircular coffee stain. "And tonight something's bothered you."

I told her the whole story. I described the cab ride, the hotel, the room, his body, his skin. "After the massage, all I did was stand at the side of the room, jerking off. That's what he wanted. There it was, this surreal mixture of the hotel's decor and this guy's obvious disease. He just sprawled out on the bed, watching me, jerking off until he came." I refrained from detailing the dainty pattern of white come/purple blotches on Zeke's chest.

Wendy's foot touched mine. "You just jerked off. That's all?"

"That's all." Her foot moved away, then came back and stayed. I could tell she wanted to touch and soothe me with her hand—a typical sympathetic Wendy Peterson gesture in this situation—but her overriding anger only allowed me the comfort of her foot. "You're mad at me," I said.

"Maybe. You just have to be so, so careful," Wendy said.

"You have to know that things are different for you now. This isn't Kansas." I'd heard that line so many times, but never from her.

The blue trapezoid shapes on the table's Formica surface resembled ugly, swollen purplish brown blotches. I wanted to say something more. I could tell Wendy about Brian, but that seemed too complicated, beyond any explanation my confused state could offer. "For the first time in my life," I told her, "I'm bothered by it. Sex. After tonight, everything just feels fucked up."

A postcard from Eric arrived the first week of December. Not a postcard, exactly, but an old paperback book's ripped cover—a romance titled *Gay Deceiver*, which I knew he'd stolen from United Methodist Thrift. On the other side was his trademark scrawl.

Neil:

Hope all is swell in New York. Hope you're making enough money, having a good time, etc. Life here is the same as always. Brian and I are trying to kill the boredom. Your mom took us watermelon hunting. She actually chased a raccoon. She claims she's got pickles ready for me. She's so cool. She says she's sending your plane ticket. Can't wait to see you over Christmas, birth date of baby Jesus ha ha ha. And Brian's dying to meet you. He says you have a lot to talk about. That's an understatement from what I can guess. If you wrote back sometime it would be earth-shattering. Anyway I'll see you at the end of the month—

Eric

"Brian," I said aloud. "Damn." The idea of him meeting my mom seemed appalling. I wondered again what he truly knew about me, about Coach. Whatever he'd remembered, I hoped he hadn't blabbed to Eric, or, god forbid, Mom. Why was this happening now?

Wendy had taped a calendar to the refrigerator. I stared at it, counting the days until my flight, until Kansas, until Brian. "Thirteen, fourteen, fifteen."

After Zeke, I avoided East Fifty-third. I sat in the apartment, watching TV, numbed by boredom. But that couldn't continue. Two days before Christmas, I contemplated the return trip to Kansas, my flight the following morning. I hadn't the foggiest what to buy for Christmas gifts; besides, I didn't have the dough. *One hundred and twenty dollars can be yours tonight,* I announced in a game show host's bray. Wendy was at work, oblivious to my combed and slicked hair, my ironed shirt, my shoes that shone under the bathroom light. "This just isn't me," I said. Oh well. I had to go back.

The piano chanteuse remained as bawdy as ever, substituting nasty lyrics into Christmas standbys. "Jingle Bells" became "Jingle Balls." "Chet's nuts," not "chestnuts," were roasting on her open fire. I shouldered my way through the crowd, which consisted of three times as many hustlers as johns. The hustlers avoided one another: we were all competition.

"Merry Christmas." I turned to see a kid named Stan, one of the few hustlers I'd chosen to befriend. His sense of humor made him my favorite, and I'd often chatted with him before getting down to business. He reminded me of Eric, thanks to his skinniness and dyed hair. When he spoke, he sounded truly prissy, enunciating vowels for utmost effect. He'd fabricated nicknames for some of the regular johns. My favorites: Special Friend (who got his name due to a line he apparently always used), Snooty Tooty (a man who wore headbands, brooches, and garish, flouncy clothes), and Funnel of Love (a troll notorious for lying on the floor, popping a funnel between his lips, and asking tricks to piss into it).

I listened to Stan until he strolled toward a john who'd been ogling him. Minutes passed. I downed a beer, then another. No one seemed interested. As I finished a third, Stan stepped back to my corner and pulled me aside.

"No luck?" I asked. The singer wailed away, abandoning her sleazy carols for a tune from *Gypsy* or *Guys and Dolls* or some other musical. When I moved my head to hear Stan better, the dizzy feeling proved I was swimming toward drunkenness.

"This guy wants a three-way," Stan said. "He's been watching you. He thinks you're ideal for fucking him while he sucks me off, all that. He's willing to give us seventy-five each."

"No way," I said. I didn't even think about it. My answer just popped out. And the reason I'd said no wasn't because the seventy-five bucks was less than my usual hundred twenty. I said no because the three-way possibility reminded me of Brian. This person I didn't know, this boy I'd shared with Coach, had managed to infect me somehow, to ruin my once-beautiful memories. I realized this now, as I stood in my hustler's stance in Rounds, both drunk and unwanted. I turned away, swallowed the last of the beer, headed for the door.

The walk from Second Avenue to Third felt more like a run. After a while I noticed a red car behind me, slowly following. Before I reached the subway stop, the car inched forward to idle at curbside. The passenger window slid down. A Kewpie doll face hovered inside the shadows. The face leaned forward into the light; I saw the driver wasn't a doll at all, but a man sporting a buzz haircut and a pink polo shirt. "Hop in," he said.

I half-remembered Stan lecturing me about trolls who preyed outside Rounds, men waiting for hustlers who hadn't snagged a trick for the night, attempting to get reduced rates. Stan had explained how a typical cheapskate john would drive toward the river, park in this or that discreet shadow, unzip, push the hustler's head toward a stubby dick, and hand over two or three twenties. Stan apparently had done this once and regretted it. "It's not worth it." I hadn't asked why. But now, I didn't care. I didn't bother setting terms or getting acquainted first. I opened the door and crawled in.

"Mind going home with me?" the man asked. "No names. No bullshit. I'll pay." His baritone came in brief, hiccuped sentences, as if someone were regulating his speech through a control panel, one overzealous thumb pushing a button. I nodded, and his car tore downtown.

He looked fortyish, straight, slightly criminal. At that point it didn't matter. We didn't speak; I put my ear against the cold window. The sounds around us seemed slowed down, far away. Rev, zoom, honk-honk. The radio's song droned on, a sugary voice repeating, "I guess I'll have to love you in my favorite dream." For some reason that sounded pretty. I dozed off at one point, due to the narcotic effects of the car heater and the beer.

I opened my eyes. The car was nearing my neighborhood, and I thought of Wendy. *Sweet dreams,* I almost said. We zoomed onto Delancey Street, then crossed the Williamsburg Bridge into Brooklyn. Things got incredibly quiet. Lights, brownstones, and storefronts blurred past. "Where are you taking me?"

"Brighton Beach," he said. I'd seen those words on subway maps, and I knew Brighton Beach was miles from Manhattan. I opened my mouth to protest. "No more questions," he spat. Surprise must have registered on my face, because he smirked and added a much calmer "I hope you're horny."

"Yeah, whatever." I wanted to blurt, One hundred and twenty dollars horny, but it didn't seem the time or place. My eyes closed again, and Zzzz.

When I woke, he was shutting off the ignition. He had parked beside an apartment complex. The world had hushed. I looked around, saw trees, residential houses, even a picket fence across the street. Only the orangy light from the nearby subway station remotely resembled New York. I wanted to be on that now, riding home. But I had work to do. He led the way into a claustrophobic elevator. His calloused finger touched the seven button. I noticed a black crescent on his thumbnail, a dark scar like a half-lidded eye. "Accident with a hammer?" I asked, my words slurring together. He didn't answer.

We entered his apartment, number 703. He shuffled around, turning on lights, then dimming them. I fell into a couch as if it were a pool of warm water. Somewhere, romantic music was playing. Minutes passed. I fought the urge to close my eyes. When he entered the room, I sat up and took a good look at his face. He seemed emotionless, regular, the sort of average joe that crafty policemen might stick into a criminal line-up to help a victim identify a guilty felon. "The bedroom's this way," he said.

More dimmed lights. I saw a bed, a bookshelf without books, and a single poster on the wall advertising a jazz festival, its *J* shaped like a saxophone. The guy opened a drawer. His hands moved toward my face. One held a miniature plastic spoon, its yellow and red handle molded into the shape of Ronald McDonald's grinning head. The other cupped a hill of white powder. "Snort this." I didn't want to, but I was already fucked up, and the coke looked cute, like glistening grains of sugar. I brought some to a nostril and breathed in. "Again," he said. Again.

He snorted the rest. Then he began tearing off his clothes and throwing them, arms flailing. Buttons popped; fabric stretched and ripped. He was evidently emulating scenes from various butch pornos. The polo shirt sailed past my head like a pastel pterodactyl. "Strip," he commanded. His dick had already hardened. It looked massive, an image from a joke's unfunny punchline, and it curved upward like a giant accusing finger. "Go down there, boy."

I figured I'd been lucky, considering most of the johns I'd tricked with had been older milquetoast types who hadn't forced me to suck or get fucked. A few had simply held me in wrinkly arms, whispering crap like "You're daddy's little boy" or something equally embarrassing. Now, with me drunk and god-only-knew-how-many subway stops from home, those elementary acts had slipped away. I fell to my knees and took his dick in my mouth.

"You like that, don't you?" he said. He fucked my face. "Swallow it deep. Moan for me, let me know how good it is." That seemed sickening for some reason. He thrust it farther, its head tearing at the back of my throat. It choked me, and I winced. I let up a little, pulling my head back, and as his dick slid out I felt him spit on me. I heard the distinct pull of the phlegm from deep in his throat, the pause, and finally the cartoony "phew" as the spit hailed from his mouth. A thumb-sized blob hit my cheek.

I stood. For the first time, I was scared. For the first time, I was fathoms away from my usual helm of control.

He shoved me onto his waterbed, the sloshing as sudden and loud as if I'd been tossed into an ocean. He placed a knee on the bed, grabbed his dick, and slapped my face with it. It hit the blob of spit, and a tiny puddle splashed into my eye. "You're not finished, slut," he said, then slammed back into my mouth. I was drunk; this wasn't supposed to be happening. I imagined corkscrewing his dick from his body and tossing it through the window, into his Brighton Beach garden, seven floors below. That image should have been funny, but it wasn't.

His arm wrapped around my chest. He flipped me over in one motion, as if my body had been hollowed out. Slosh, slosh. "I'm going to give the slut what he needs." His thumb wriggled around in my ass crack, then punctured the hole.

I pictured the black scar on his thumbnail, now fishing around in the place where only one other person had been, so many years before. I briefly drifted back there. "Tell me you like it, Neil, tell Coach how much you like it." I'd told him so. Had that been truth, or just a stream of gibberish? "Tell me."

"No," I said. "It's going too far." My head reeled, and I hoped he could understand the garble. "This is what I don't do." I managed to squirm off the bed, my arm held out to keep him away. He lifted his knee and stood before me, eyes flashing.

The room grew quiet. In the outside hallway, I could hear footsteps, a walk breaking into a run. "You were at that place," he said. "I know what you were there for. You'll do what I tell you. That's what a slut does."

"I don't know why I was there," I said. "I really don't." The door to the adjoining room was cracked slightly, and when I peeked around his shoulder I could see a bathtub's porcelain edge. "Just wait a minute," I told him. "Let me piss. Then . . . I'll be back in a second."

I expected his meaty arm to shoot out and grab me, but it didn't. I brushed past him, made it to the bathroom, slammed the door. It had one of those old-fashioned locks, a little hook-shaped latch that fit into a silver eyehole. I fastened it and sat on the tub's edge, breathing. The drug's grains exploded through my brain. In a matter of hours, I would land in Kansas again. Calm down, I told myself. Calm *him* down. Be careful, finish, get the money.

Then I heard him, trying to get in. I looked at the door. The john had wedged the end of a butter knife into the crack, and he wiggled it higher, toward the space where the latch connected door with frame. I actually felt my body tremble. The knife pushed higher, meddling closer to the latch until their silvers struck. The latch came loose, clicking back against the door. A second of silence passed. Then the door flew open, and the john came thundering in.

He's going to kill me, I thought. I imagined the thin, pliable shape of the butter knife thudding against my skin over and over, at last breaking through to razor my heart. I held up one hand to stop him. But he wasn't going to stab. Instead, he tossed the knife into the air. It made a half-revolution, and he caught it again, stepped toward me, and raised the thick handle. It smacked against my forehead. *Snap.*

I fell backward. The room spun in a blurry maelstrom, the naked john its center. I landed in the bathtub. My face was turned away from him, toward the gold circle of the drain. I saw stray beads of water, a soap bubble, a black pubic hair. "You're getting fucked whether you want it or not," his voice said, and in the cold space of the bathroom it echoed like a barbarous god's. "And I know you want it."

For a second I thought of Zeke, sprawled on his hotel bed, disease dotting his skin. This trick was much worse. I felt my legs being pulled up, slabs of meat a butcher hoists toward the gleaming hook. He maneuvered me into a failed headstand, and the side of my face slammed against the tub's bottom. Something made the sound of a walnut cracking.

The thumb pushed back into my ass. Another. Then, unmistakably, I felt him twiddling his thumbs inside me, that classic bored gesture I suddenly knew I'd never make again. The twiddling sent a warm throb deep into my stomach, and I groaned. He took that as his cue to pull my body toward his. My ass became his bull's-eye. His dick slammed against the hole, holding there, teasing it, and then my tight bud of skin gave way to it. He was inside me. "Gonna show you what that hole was made for." I tried to move my head, tried to focus on him, only saw the horrible bright white of porcelain and his head's shadow. The bathroom light crowned him with an enormous halo.

I felt skewered. His body pistoned back and forth as it had when he'd fucked my face. I moved my arm, attempting to stop even some fraction of his motion. In my position, I couldn't reach back to touch him. My hand smacked a faucet, and cold water began dribbling from the shower head, seasoning our bodies. My eyes closed. When I reopened them, I saw blood swirling toward the drain.

The shower of water enraged him, a rage I could feel shooting into my own body. "Slut," he screamed. From the corner of my eye I saw him reach toward the tub's edge; close his hand around a shampoo bottle. His arm raised, briefly obliterating the bathroom light. Then his arm came down, curving at full speed and force through the air. The bottle bashed against my head. The arm rose again. The bottle struck again. Blood squirted a red poppy onto the porcelain. Another swing. I thought, *It isn't breaking. It's shatterproof.* His dick stayed massive inside me. The bottle pummeled my head a fourth and fifth time. The noise it made—and I could hear it so clearly, a perfect sound rebounding through my head—was a hollow, almost soft *bup*.

The words *please stop* took form inside my mouth, but I couldn't say them. The shampoo bottle battered my cheekbone, my chin, my eye. More water needled down. He drilled farther through me, dismantling my guts, his dick seeming to lacerate whatever internal walls my body still supported. *Bup.* Pause. *Bup bup bup.* He beat me, matching his arm with the rhythm of his fucking. The bottle dropped, still not shattering, and landed next to my head. I read its label: BABY SHAMPOO. Below that, written inside a pink teardrop, NO MORE TEARS.

"God, you want it. Take that cock all the way inside there." His words blended into a moan, a yell, a kind of cough. I felt hot and gluey spurts bulleting deep inside me, bursts of wet heat, arrows aimed for the pit of my stomach. The spurts ricocheted off my body's ruined walls, staining me everywhere with their deadly graffiti, and if I opened my mouth I knew they would spew out. But my mouth was open. I was trying to scream.

I still strained to bat him away. It was too late; he had finished. He pulled his dick out and dropped my legs back into the tub.

Water streamed beside my face. My blood, a granular swirl of soap, and a stray bullet of his sperm blended into it and zoomed toward the drain. I found I could move at last, and I looked up at him. He walked out, swatting the light switch. The darkness wasn't what I needed, but it was close.

When I woke, the darkness remained. "I'm sober," I said, and my voice cracked on both words. I lay on the front lawn of the john's apartment complex. I couldn't remember dressing or leaving. Beneath me, blades of grass felt like ice picks. In the mulch beneath a dying bush, I saw a close-up view of pebbles, a screw, coils of tangerine peel, tangled ribbon from a gutted cassette tape, a torn section from a *Times* obituary . . . darkness ruffled everything beyond that.

I sat up and raised my head, counting the apartment's

ascending windows toward the seventh floor. He lived beyond one of those windows. He remained there, perhaps cleaning my blood from his porcelain tub, perhaps washing come from his pubic hair with a handful of baby shampoo.

Blocks away, the lights from the subway station gleamed their sickly orange. I was an hour's trip from home, but at least I knew how to get back. What would I tell Wendy? I pushed myself from the ground, and my head throbbed. Pain shot through my stomach, into my chest. My tongue snagged on the razorlike edge from a chipped front tooth.

To forget the pain, I thought about what the night had done. Everything had been hurled out of balance, a sudden and sickening displacement I could feel even as I walked toward the subway, as I lumbered and tripped like a hopeless drunk, like the person my mom had been when she'd barely survived her worst drinking days. "Mom," I said aloud. I almost put "I want my" in front of it.

This is what has happened, I thought.

The empty subway car shed light on my abraded knuckles, the dribbles of blood on my shirt. I started to count the stops on the way back, but I lost count after fifteen.

I remembered a detail from the days I'd first had sex for money. Then, when I arrived home from my Carey Park tricks, I'd scarf down whatever food I could find to rid my mouth of their anonymous tongues' residues. My duty done, I'd ease back into my little life. Those days were a fairy tale now. I spat on the subway car's floor to hopefully obliterate any smidgeon of virus he might have deposited there. If only I could use some similar gesture for my ass. I was filled with the queasy urge to shit, but I fought it back. I never wanted to touch my ass again. It felt as though something were jammed inside it still, something small yet full of hazard and horror, like TNT or a scorpion.

When I arrived home, the kitchen clock read 4:45. My

plane would leave La Guardia Airport in five hours. Wendy's bedroom door was closed. I peeked inside, saw her hair jutting from the blanket like a rooster's crest. This time I deserved the lecture she'd give. I stepped into the bathroom, leaving the light off, taking care to avoid the mirror. As I stripped, each movement made me wince.

I pulled down the lip of my boxers and stared at my dick. It was repulsive. I hated it. The boxers dropped to the floor, landing beside a green-and-yellow striped shirt I'd worn that afternoon. I sat, picked it up, held it to my face. I breathed the scent of how I was before. Outside, in the street, a woman screamed so loudly it might have been a machine. The screaming continued for two minutes, three, then stopped. In the seconds that followed, the entire world grew incredibly quiet, and I cried.

fifteen

DEBORAH LACKEY

When I arrived home, the only face that greeted me was the one on the television screen. There, the slobbering teenage girl from *The Exorcist* experienced the height of demonic possession. Brian lazed on the floor watching her, barefoot, his back to me. Another kid sat next to him, hair spiking in precarious angles from his head. A silver necklace, thick as a bicycle chain, sparkled under the stranger's haircut.

"You're sitting too close," I told them. "You'll go blind."

Brian rushed to the doorway to take my bags. "We didn't expect you this early," he said. I explained how Breeze, my ride from the airport, had risked my life by speeding the entire route to Little River. When I glanced at the sofa where our mother usually sat, Brian said, "She's still at work."

Brian's friend introduced himself. "Eric." His eyes, smeared with makeup, stared at my skirt's tie-dyed pattern. He offered his hand, its middle finger bisected by a ring that showed a grinning skull, silver crossbones, and the letters *R.I.P.* "Happy holidays," Eric said. "I feel I know you already."

I'd heard about him too, via different telephone descriptions. From Brian, Eric was "a friend of someone I'm trying to get in contact with"; from my mother, he was both "Brian's diversion from studying" and "a tad bit messed up, but well meaning." I shook his clammy hand and sat beside him; on TV, the green demon snarled at the priest. "If I remember right, this is just starting to get good," I said. "Worry about my bags later."

We watched the movie's remainder. There was something deranged and distinctly midwestern about a station that programmed *The Exorcist* three days prior to Christmas. I'd viewed the original at a horror movie festival in San Francisco, but this was the edited-for-television version. Scenes of violence and sex had been scissored into tameness. One line I distinctly recalled wincing at—the demon's guttural "Your mother sucks cocks in hell"—had altered, and the replacement voice-over growled "Your mother wears socks that smell." Maybe this change was for the better, considering what Brian had told me about Eric's parents.

The demon's face filled the screen, her cankered skin glowing. Brian grinned at me. "She looks like you did, that Halloween," he said. "Remember? The year you were the witch." Yes, I remembered.

Then Brian turned to Eric. "You know what I mean. That night. In the woods. The second time it happened." Eric nodded, and their eyes revisited the TV.

At one point I moved to see my brother better. During the scene where the priest and a friend sneak into the possessed kid's freezing bedroom, Brian upped the volume. The characters lifted the sleeping girl's dress to shine a flashlight on her skin, which by now had bleached to an otherworldly bluish hue. Brian's eyes stayed glued to this scene, entranced, as if they recognized something. The flashlight lingered as a pair of words blossomed on the blue flesh. HELP ME.

• • •

After the credits had rolled and the eerie tinkling piano soundtrack had faded, I climbed the stairs to my room. I began unpacking, layering clothes into my dresser drawers, mixing the smells of my California apartment with the indelible, almost spicy smell of home. A door slammed outside. Through the window's glass I saw my mother, decked out in her officer's uniform, rushing from her new Mustang into the house. Seconds later she stood in my room's doorway.

"I've missed you," I said. I hugged her, and we sat on the bed.

As usual when I returned home, my mother and I chatted about the same humdrum things. I answered her questions about the flight, the ride from the airport with Breeze. I assured her everything was fine with my apartment, my retail job, my night class on weaving and looming. She told me she was overdue for another raise at work; she had briefly worried about money when my father's child support checks stopped coming and Brian had entered college, but all was still manageable. "And I see you've met Eric," she said. "He's like the new son around here these days." I guessed by her tone she didn't mind.

"Things got a little strange during the summer," my mother continued. "But Brian's calmed down now. Maybe that's due to Eric, preposterous as that sounds." My mother's letters and phone conversations had enigmatically referred to these summer "problems," but I'd never received a direct answer about what any of it meant. I remembered half-jokingly asking things like "Has Brian joined a religious cult?" and "Is he having a nervous breakdown?" only to receive the standard "No, honey, it's nothing to worry over." Even now, I could tell, she would promptly change the subject before I inquired. "As we speak," she said, "Brian and Eric are downstairs, heating up dinner for us."

They'd not only cooked dinner, but had draped the table with a checkerboard cloth and lit clove-scented candles. The setup overlooked the window's wintery view of our empty field, the neighbor family's barren peach orchard, and, beyond that, the stark grays and blacks of the Little River cemetery. I took my place at the table; Brian sat at my left elbow, and Eric, my right. The last time I could recall all four sides being occupied, my father had been here.

Brian ladled potato soup from a tin pot. Since I'd last seen him one Christmas previous, he'd cut his hair shorter, lost about ten pounds, and begun wearing things I attributed to Eric's influence—a dark, bulky sweater, ripped denims, black Converse high-tops. These clothes didn't make my brother "tough" or "punk" or whatever else he might have been striving for. They just lent Brian an even goofier look. And he'd developed an odd habit—he occasionally blinked forcefully, a random nervous tic, as if attempting to dislodge dust from his eyes.

The meal shifted from soup to main course. I'd swallowed five or six mouthfuls before I noticed my mother's guns on the kitchen counter: three of them, as well as a leather holster and belt, a scattering of bullets, and handcuffs that shone in the kitchen light. One month earlier, my mother had called San Francisco to describe a disastrous escape attempt from KSIR. Although she hadn't been there for the mayhem, she was nevertheless disturbed by what had transpired. The inmates had held two co-workers hostage; prior to capture, their kingpin had buried a hammer's claw end into one hostage's skull. My mother had told me how she planned to buy extra weapons. I remembered trying to explain how bizarre that sounded—guns in Little River, a town of less than a thousand people, a town where the most criminal act to occur in the last two decades had been the theft of ten gallons of gas at the local Texaco.

"That's just all your San Francisco peace and love speaking," she'd said. "If you could see what I've seen. . . ."

My mother saw me staring at the guns. "Do those have to be out in the open?" I asked.

To appease me, she stashed the weapons in a cupboard and returned to the table. Her voice took on a mock serious- ness. "The way I see it is this. Now, if anyone tries to hurt you or Brian, they'll have to deal with me."

When she said that, Brian whispered a question to Eric. "Then where was she ten years ago?" My mother didn't hear, and I assumed I wasn't supposed to either. His words elicited a discomfited shrug from Eric. I didn't ask what he meant.

I woke during the night and thought of how, as a little girl, I would sometimes sneak across the hall to Brian's room. I'd kneel beside his bed, still woozy within my own somnolence, and imagine myself a world-renowned sleep researcher or a girl with superhuman powers who could enter the mind of anyone she wanted. I'd whisper words into the shell of his ear, words I honestly believed would reshape Brian's dream scenarios to make him happy.

Three-thirty, according to the bedside clock. Pinkish white clouds bloomed in the night sky outside my window, the kind that glow through the darkness. I hoped they sig- naled snow. Lines from "White Christmas" lilted through my head as I stood from bed. I tiptoed. Now, as an adult, spying on Brian felt criminal, but I opened his door anyway.

Brian had left his blankets strewn this way and that, one's fleecy corner spilling over the mattress to touch the floor. He wasn't there, and I prepared to trudge back to my own warm bed. Then I noticed how Brian's room had changed. His books were missing, as well as the posters he'd tacked up long ago, the advertisements for sci-fi films, the colorful monsters and aliens and astronauts that had held reign over his room for so many years. Gone, too, were the mobiles he'd hung in the corners, those ships and planes I remembered twirling from his ceiling on even the previous Christmas, the last time I'd come home.

Now, only one thing remained on Brian's wall, a small memento he'd taped to the space next to his bed. I stepped closer. It looked like a photograph. I could see a group of petite boys, standing and kneeling in two rows, staring out from the picture. They wore uniforms; some held baseballs and bats. I scanned their faces, their eerie smiles and eyes, before recognizing one of the boys as Brian. That had been so long ago.

I looked around me, at Brian's barren, strangely meticulous room. It had never been so clean, and something about it made me feel lonesome. I began to shiver, so I tiptoed back to my own room.

My friend Breeze telephoned the next morning. She and her husband planned to spend December twenty-third visiting friends in Garden City, and she needed a baby-sitter to watch her two children. I had nothing better to do. "Wonderful," I said. Then, as I hung up: "How typical."

The living room television was playing, sound off. A cartoon cast its vibrant greens and oranges over Brian's and Eric's faces. They lay sleeping on the floor, arms and legs splayed, as if frozen in a complicated dance. A pair of pillows from my mother's bed sat next to their heads, and Eric cuddled one against his ear. I assumed she had placed them there before she'd departed for work. She could keep three, four, even a thousand guns in the house, and it still wouldn't fool me: she'd always be her same worried, tame, overprotective self.

When I'd met Eric, his exaggerated seriousness and

shadowy, downcast eyes terrified me. It would have been easy to imagine him sprawled on the floor in some icy bathroom, his slit wrists gushing blood across the tiles. But now, there on the floor with Brian, he looked harmless, even angelic. He smiled in his sleep. I didn't want to wake him, but Breeze would be arriving soon with the kids, so I had to.

"Ahem." No response. I opened a window, letting the frigid air curl into the room, and slammed it shut. At the sound, Eric's eyes fluttered open. "Shit" was his first word. His hair looked like overgrown thistledown, garlanded with a ball of carpet fuzz. He looked toward the television, where a cartoon cat's eyes crossed as a mouse bashed its head with a sledgehammer. The cartoon blended into a commercial; Eric turned, seeing me. "Oh, hi."

"Good morning," I said. "Hate to wake you two, but an old friend's coming over to drop off her kids. How does helping me baby-sit sound?"

Eric yawned and placed a hand on Brian's shoulder: it was a motherly gesture, strange and feminine. He nudged Brian, rousing him. "Kids," Eric said. "How old are they?"

"Michael is about four, I guess. The little one's still in diapers." He gave me a horrified look. Brian, on the other hand, seemed confused, glancing from Eric to the television to me. "Breeze is on her way over," I told him. "We get to baby-sit the kids for the day."

While Brian dawdled in the shower, Eric assisted me in picking up around the house. He seemed to know better than I where things were located; he returned from the kitchen holding a can of furniture polish and a rag I recognized as torn from one of my father's old shirts. A lemony spray sizzled forth; Eric glossed the rag over the coffee table, the TV, the rocking chair's knucklebones. We didn't speak, but kept catching each other's eye: I watched him, he watched me.

Breeze arrived, clutching the baby in one arm, a wrapped package in the other. A suitcase sat at her feet. When I met her at the front door, I noticed her husband waving to me from their car. "We'd stay a bit, but we're in a hurry," Breeze said. Her breath clouded the air. The older boy, Michael, whirlwinded past me to perch beside the television. Breeze stared at him. "TV should keep him occupied." I took the baby from her arms, and she positioned the suitcase and package inside the door. "Diapers, food, all the necessities. The gift is just some fruit," she said. "Better eat it quick or it will spoil." She dug into her pocket and handed me a matchbook with a telephone number written on it. "We'll be at this number. We'll return before dark. I hope everything goes okay. Good-bye, Michael." She kissed the baby's head. "Good-bye, David."

Brian walked in, scrubbing a towel across wet hair. Eric pointed across the room toward Michael, who hadn't taken his eyes from the cartoon. The cat gulped a birthday cake which, unbeknownst to the animal, was crammed with dynamite; its stomach exploded, and the cat became a blackened shadow with shocked white eyes. Michael rocked to and fro, still wearing his coat, giggling along with the cartoon mouse.

Brian saw my armful of David, and he placed his fingers against the baby's face. "Wow." I pushed David forward a little, and one tiny hand reached out, as if beckoning Brian to hold him. "He won't cry, will he?" I shrugged and delivered him into Brian's arms.

"He feels like a gigantic sponge," Brian said into David's face. His voice altered, becoming thinner, inching up half an octave. "And somebody's squeezed the water from the sponge, but there's still a little bit left in there, just enough to keep the sponge damp." He thumbed David's nose. Eric looked at me, one eyebrow raised.

In the following hour, Brian and Eric helped me feed the baby, took turns trying to burp him, and clumsily assisted when I changed his diaper. They waited for him to fall asleep, gently smoothing creases on his shirt. David nodded off at last, and while he snoozed on the living room floor, Brian and Eric headed for the kitchen. They made lunch: peanut butter sandwiches, formed into shapes from Christmas cookie cutters. Mine was a star; Brian and Eric got bells; and Michael, a fat Santa Claus, toy-filled sack slung on his back. Michael licked a dot of peanut butter from his upper lip. "Mommy always lets me have dessert," he said.

Eric remembered the fruit and fetched Breeze's gift from its spot at the doorway. I let Michael rip through the paper. Inside a basket, behind see-through green cellophane, were pears, oranges, apples, bananas. "Some Xmas present," Eric said.

Michael stared awhile, deciding. He was a ferocious-looking child, with a pug nose and hair the color of copper. His forehead sprouted a cowlick, the skin beneath it revealing a vein's blue squiggle. He selected a pear and put it to his lips. His mouth punched a miniature hole into its yellow skin. "Yuck." He handed the pear to Eric, who stood and began juggling the pear, an orange, and an apple. He tossed them into various configurations, hands snagging them from the air like a magician's. Michael watched, fascinated.

Brian selected three paring knives from the kitchen. He lined a red Delicious, a yellow, and a green Granny Smith side by side, forming a stoplight pattern on the floor. He told Eric and me to take our pick. "We'll show you how to make apple-head dolls," he said to Michael. Brian and I had done this once when we were little. We'd skinned apples and carved faces, then arranged them in a window to harden and degenerate. Over a period of weeks, the apples took shape, wrinkling into amber-colored "heads" that looked like shrewd, prehistoric people. We'd jammed pencils into the heads and dressed them in doll clothes.

Michael gawked as we began peeling and carving. I whittled slits for eyes, nostrils, a frown; my apple took on the countenance of an evil crone. Eric changed the round shape of his face completely, giving it sunken cheeks, a square jawline, even meticulously shaping rows of square teeth.

Brian couldn't decide what to carve. Eric and I displayed our dolls as we completed each feature, but after Brian finished peeling, he passed his smooth apple from palm to palm, indecisive. "Mine's a skull," Eric told him, "so how about your trademark alien?"

Brian looked disgusted for a second. "I knew you'd say that." He adjusted his glasses, thumbprinting one lens with apple juice. "I told you to shut up about it. It's history." Eric fidgeted, and I concentrated harder on my knife's placement in my doll. Brian stabbed the knifepoint into the apple and curved it, hollowing out an almond-shaped eye. Another. The rest of his face was easy: two pinpricks for nostrils, a feeble cut for a mouth. He rubbed his thumbs into the apple-head's eyes, as if polishing them. "There," he told Eric. "Satisfied?"

When finished, we displayed the apples for Michael. "Normally," Brian instructed, "you'd wait for these heads to dry. But we don't have to do that." He grinned at Eric, apparently no longer angry. He searched the house for pencils and returned with three, fashioning bodies for the apple dolls.

The telephone rang, and I ran to the kitchen. It was my mother, calling from work to check up. I told her about baby-sitting, how Brian and Eric had helped me through the day. "Is everything okay with Brian?" she asked. When I said I guessed so, she seemed relieved. "He's been acting funny lately. More and more as Christmas approaches, though I can't tell why. Maybe I'm imagining things. But he was awake before I left this morning, and that was unnatural. Just staring out the window, all nervous."

"I don't know." I peeked into the front room, where Eric and Brian, now ventriloquists, performed a demented apple puppet show for Michael. Eric gripped the pencil bodies of the skull and alien apples and skipped them toward Michael. The little boy screamed. Brian quickly grabbed the alien doll from Eric's hand and pushed it aside.

My mother was still talking, and I tried to assimilate her words with those between Eric and Brian. Their conversation, while hushed, seemed more interesting. Eric asked "What's wrong?" but I didn't catch my brother's answer. Eric mentioned something about "one more day, then you'll calm down."

I heard an intercom page my mother's name on the other end. *"Sergeant Lackey, line one."* She paused. "You kids know I love you," she said. Another pause. "You will tell Brian I love him, won't you?"

"Yes." In the next room, Michael giggled. "Stop worrying," I heard Eric say. I looked in; he was speaking to Brian, not Michael. "Everything's going to be okay."

I didn't think about what my mother had said until that evening, when Breeze returned for her children. Michael rushed for the door, and Brian lifted David from the floor as if his skin were glass. He surrendered the baby into Breeze's arms. It immediately began crying; for an alarming second its cranky and swollen face resembled one of the carved apples. Breeze thanked us, and Brian swallowed a breath and gripped her shoulder. "Please take good care of them," he told her. "Keep both eyes on them, no matter what." I wondered what that meant. I looked to see if Eric mirrored my slight embarrassment, but he was watching the floor.

My mother's words echoed in my head again later, after Eric had driven back to Hutchinson. I stood at the sink finishing dishes. From the window I saw Brian, bundled in his coat, tramping through the blustery wind on the hillside. He crouched down, burrowing in the dirt with his fingers. He placed something in the little grave he'd dug. Then he stood again and began stomping his feet on the mound of dirt, as if throwing a tantrum he'd been waiting to throw for years. I instantly thought of the night our father had left, and the mindless dance Brian had reeled through, there in that very spot.

I wadded the dish towel; retrieved my coat from the living room. That afternoon, Eric had placed the crone, the skull, and the alien on the windowsill to dry; now, however, the alien was missing. I didn't need to hurry outside. At that moment I knew what Brian had buried in the dirt, knew what he'd stomped into the earth. But I didn't know why.

In my half-sleep, I heard my bedroom door click open. Brian padded in. Darkness almost camouflaged him, thanks to the black shirt and sweatpants he'd probably mimicked from Eric's wardrobe. He lurked in the shadows at the threshold of my room, his breathing's constancy like the steady ticking of a clock. Could he tell my eyes were open? At last he stepped forward, the side of his face and neck exposed by the moonlight's cold shelf. His skin looked clearer than ever, and I could see one eye, deep blue and dreamy, like a marble held to light.

"Deb," he whispered. He made the nervous blinking gesture.

I snaked a leg from under the blanket, and he stepped back. "It's okay," I said. "I'm awake."

Brian sat on the bed's creaky edge. Moonlight cast its diagonal across him, striping a banner on his chest. "I'm sorry," he said. "It's late." I toed his elbow, a gesture to signal it didn't matter.

He wanted to talk. He needed someone to listen; without speaking, I nodded, urging him on. "Tomorrow"—he looked at the bedside clock—"well, actually today, I'll meet this guy named Neil. It's really important. You don't know what I'm talking about, do you?"

I didn't. "What's happening? What's going on with you?"

"I don't know where to start. It's about all the things that used to happen to me. I used to pee the bed, I was always blacking out. You remember. All of that, everything, was stemming from something else. Whatever it was, it fucked me up. And I think I know what it was. I know, but I don't know. It's all fucked up." Brian's sentences didn't quite connect; they were like fragments gouged from various conversations. And I'd rarely heard my brother swear. But rather than making him seem tougher or more seasoned, these words did the opposite. They lent him a curious innocence.

"Go on," I said. I was whispering; at that second it seemed the only way to speak. "Be more specific."

"This guy named Neil. Whatever happened to me, happened to him too. But he remembers better than I do. I'm sure he knows what happened the night you found me in the space beneath the house. He might even know what happened that Halloween, in the woods, when I blacked out." Brian made a hiccuping sound, then quickly spat out the next sentences. "It wasn't a UFO. It was our coach. And Neil knows. He's going to be here soon. He's going to tell me. To confirm things. I've been waiting for him for years."

His words confused me. I opened my mouth to form questions; Brian must have anticipated this because he stopped me. "No," he said. At that moment he inched forward, leaning his head beside me, brushing closer until his ear touched my left shoulder. I moved my right arm and cradled his face in my hand, gently closing his eyelids with my fingers. His breathing grazed my skin, as delicate and even as a glassblower's.

The questions remained, but I couldn't ask them. I couldn't speak at all. I simply held my little brother as night dammed the room around us, until, at last, we fell asleep.

sixteen

ERIC PRESTON

A merman starred in my afternoon nap's dream. He lifted himself from the water, twisting his half-human, half-barracuda body onto a sea-splashed rock. His tail's scales glittered green, then gold, then green again. He brushed away starfish and anemones, sighed, and craned his neck to face the sky. His flawless mouth opened and he sang, mournfully lamenting the ordinary love of a mortal . . .

. . . his voice blended into my grandma's. "Eric, sweetie, you've got a guest." So much for dreaming. I hauled myself back to reality and remembered it was the night of Neil's scheduled return. But Neil wasn't the guest Grandma spoke about. "I believe it's your friend Brian," she said. Right—Mrs. McCormick had invited us for dessert, a Christmas Eve welcome-home party for Neil.

Brian appeared in the doorway. His looks had altered, his hair now brushed and parted, his skin scrubbed and shining, touches of pink zit cream daubed here and there. He grinned, but the expression seemed false. Was that expression due to Neil?

"Welcome," I said. "And happy holidays. Xmas Eve greetings, all that." My two-foot-by-two-foot window verified I'd snoozed too long, because dusk had begun to settle over the neighbors' mobile home. I could hear a woman's angry drawl: "Junior, move your ass right on in here for dinner."

Brian jangled his car keys. "Let's go for a drive before the McCormicks'. And bundle up. I think it might snow."

I slipped on an extra pair of socks and beelined to the bathroom. *Tonight's the night,* I told myself. Four months had passed since I'd met Brian, four months of listening to his obsessions and preoccupations alter and equivocate. Whether Brian referred to his memories of UFOs or, as he'd recently called it, "something altogether different, more real-life," one variable didn't change. And that was Neil. Neil had been the subject of the first sentence Brian spoke to me, and tonight Brian hoped Neil would provide the final piece to whatever puzzle he'd been linking together.

I splashed my face with water, brushed my teeth, and gargled with my grandpa's denture mouthwash. Grandma had taped a Christmas card to the bathroom mirror, on which a valiant reindeer led Santa through a starless night. I fingernailed the tape and pried open the card. "Dear Harry and Esther, Merry Christmas and Happy New Year, and a much-belated Sympathy for what happened last year. Sincerely, The Johnsons." I thought for a minute, couldn't remember the Johnsons, didn't care.

I hadn't seen Neil in months, and I wanted him to notice some smidgeon of change in my appearance. He'd expect my trademark "depressed," so I opted for "spry" and "carefree." I stripped off the black and shrugged myself into Grandpa's white cardigan. Back to the mirror. Did I look good enough to kiss? Brian pounded the door, yelling to hurry up.

We threw ourselves into Brian's car. Slam, slam. He blasted the heater, then the stereo. The music was from a tape I'd loaned him, a tape I'd originally borrowed from Neil. In the space between our seats, Brian had sandwiched the photograph from his Little League days—to show Neil, I presumed—and, beside it, a spiral notebook that resembled my journal. I didn't ask. Instead, I questioned him about our agenda prior to dessert at the McCormicks'. Brian answered with a brief "You'll see." I fantasized he'd gone off the deep end, stolen one of his mother's guns, and would force me to sidekick on a Christmas Eve terrorist spree. Well, maybe not.

Nearly every Hutchinson house had been done up for the holidays. Festive lights flashed from rooftops, windows, evergreens. A massive star strobed from the pinnacle of a water tower. An entire boulevard's elm branches had been tied with thousands of ribbons. Brian seemed entranced by it all, and he paused at the Chamber of Commerce to inspect their lawn's nativity scene. Electric candles illuminated the faces of Mary, Joseph, wise men, a donkey, a lamb, and a long-lashed heifer. Someone had stolen the baby Jesus. In its place was a red ceramic lobster, its claw hooking over the side of the manger to reach toward the world.

The car yielded at Main. A teenage girl crossed, gripping leashes on which two Chihuahuas trotted. She peered at us through glasses shaped like the infinity symbol. Her mouth formed the word "faggots." Brian didn't seem to care. I sent the girl a message: *May your dogs get carried off by owls.*

Low-hanging clouds had gathered, perching in tree branches and church steeples like chunks of meat on shish kebab skewers. "Not that weathermen are foolproof," I said, "but the guy on channel ten predicted snow, and it appears he's right." Brian nodded and whistled softly to the music: a vain attempt to make me believe he wasn't nervous. When he stopped whistling, I switched my attention from the clouds to the place he'd parked. The Toyota was idling behind the dugout of a small baseball diamond.

The field looked as though players hadn't competed on it in years. It was a far cry from Sun Center's fanciness. The outfield's brown grass had crept inward, a rash, to surround the spaces where bases should have been. Littering the infield was a flotsam of dead leaves, empty beer cans and tobacco pouches, Styrofoam cups, crumpled pages from the *Hutchinson News*. The field looked as conspicuous as a shipwreck. "Where are we?" I asked.

"This is the Little League diamond," Brian said. "It's where the Panthers, where Neil and I, used to play." At that, he left the car, stepped toward the dugout, and began climbing the fence. A sign beside him said REPORT ALL ACTS OF VANDALISM; the telephone number it gave was identical to the McCormicks' except for one digit. As the wind blew, the sign shook, clicking like a Geiger counter.

"I'm staying here," I yelled. "Too cold." Brian stood at the plate, staring forward, as if a spectral pitcher were preparing to lob him a home run ball. He began running the base paths; after second base, he seemed to lose himself in the amorphous border of the outfield, and he headed for the fence and its battered scoreboard.

With Brian minutes away from the car, I saw my chance. I wriggled the spiral notebook free from the crevice between the seats. On the cover, in blue ink, were drawings of moons, stars, clouds, and a swarm of orbiting spaceships. Black ink had x-ed everything out. I didn't want to snoop, really, but I reasoned it necessary. "I'll feel guilty later."

At first I touched the notebook's pages as tenderly as I'd touch a Ouija board after inquiring about my death. Then I plunged in. It didn't take long to realize it was Brian's dream log. Yes, I'd heard him mention this once or twice, during up-all-night blabathons when he'd expanded on his UFO stories. But that had been weeks ago. I skimmed through random entries, glancing up every few sentences to make certain Brian still paraded through the outfield. There he was, leaning against the far fence, head tilted upward. So I shuffled to the last pages. *Perhaps he's dreamed about me*, I thought.

As I came to the final dreams Brian had logged, I slowed my tempo. His handwriting was atrocious in spots, but I trudged through it. The dreams were dated over a month ago; I didn't see my name, but I did notice Neil's. I read.

11/10/91—
Last night, following my father's disastrous phone call, the dream I suppose I've been dreading all these months. This time, I see Neil McCormick incredibly clearly—he's there in the blue room, his rubber cleated shoes, pizza and panther on his shirt, black line of sunblock under his dark eyes—and then I see the shoes on the floor, the shirt, a white towel smudging away the sunblock. Neil's lips, warm and fluttery against my ear—saying It's okay, don't worry. Then a door creaks open and the figure is there, four wide strides and he's next to us, one hand on Neil's shoulder, one hand on mine. "Neil, get his clothes off." Neil's pile of clothes thickens, the little hill grows as my Panthers shirt, my socks, my pants are thrown onto it. In the dream I can't look into the figure's face, I can only stare into his bare chest—and at first I see the mysterious blue-gray skin again, the same skin from other nightmares, and slowly, slowly, slowly it starts to change—the change takes forever, it goes from blue-gray to just gray, then from gray to grayish white, all the while sprouting little blond hairs. At last its color is white with a hint of pink, proof that it's alive and blood is jetting beneath it, it's no longer the skin of an alien, but the skin of a human being. A human arm, wide and hairy and freckled, and it wraps around me—and beside me Neil McCormick says here we go—

11/22/91—
Back among the trees, Halloween, and the figure's there, his
mouth spitting out I sure liked you Brian, I always hoped I
would see you again—but this time the mouth isn't the alien's
skinny slit, it's a human mouth, full lips, blond mustache—
the mouth moves toward me, nibbles at my own lips, just as
they'd done two years before in the blue room with Neil—and
I know who it is. It's no alien, I'm thinking—my eyes are open
and I'm not eight anymore, I'm not ten anymore, I'm nine-
teen, and now I know what's happened to me, and I know
they aren't dreams. They're memories.

I looked up from the dream description. *Just as they'd*
done two years before in the blue room with Neil. Inexplic-
ably, the voices from the bizarre tape I'd played in Neil's
room rang inside my head, the burping and swearing tenor
of the little boy paired with the instigating bass of the adult.
My mind's warped lens focused back to a glossy spread I'd
seen in Neil's pedophilic porno magazine, but superimposed
over the preteen's head was first Neil's face, then Brian's.
The effect was more abhorrent than hilarious. "Oh, Jesus," I
said, as if that would remedy something. Then I thought
about the picture Brian had drawn from weeks back: the
shoes, the number ninety-nine on the glove, the baseball
scrawled with the word *Coach.* "Jesus," I said again. I pulled
out Brian's Little League photograph and paused first at
Brian, then Neil—his jersey, number ninety-nine—and,
finally, their baseball coach.

At last I understood. The clues had been here all the
time. I should have known months ago.

Brian was coming back, galloping toward the car, and
somehow his face looked different. It wasn't his clothes, not
the clean skin and hair, not the makeup that covered each
pimple. The change lurked somewhere inside him, sim-

mered through his blood and bone, and only now could I
see it.

He scaled the fence and opened the driver's side door.
Wind vacuumed the car's warm air, making me shiver. For a
second Brian appeared happy, eager to meet Neil, no longer
nervous. Then he turned his head, his gaze dropping from
my face to my hands. I still held the dream journal in my
left, the photograph in my right.

I couldn't fathom what to say first. "It's not a secret anymore" is what came out. "Now there's no more being cryptic
with me."

Brian took his things; jammed them back between the
seats. "I would have told you eventually," he blurted. "I really
would have." His glasses gradually fogged, and he rubbed
them on the knee of his jeans. I stared there, ashamed, as he
continued. "Right now, not all of it's come back to me. I still
need Neil. He has to tell me what he knows."

We sat, silent. The fence's sign banged and clattered. In
a nearby house, a door slammed, shutting someone out. A
gust of wind lifted a newspaper page into the air, and it
sailed across the car's windshield. I tried to read a headline;
no luck.

"You're such a snoop," Brian said. "I would have told
you." I wanted to apologize, but those words couldn't blanket all the things I was sorry for. All this time, I'd longed to
bring Brian and Neil together; instead, I felt like the subject
of a conspiracy. "Sooner or later you would have figured it
out anyway," he said. "I'm surprised you hadn't. Based on
what you know about Neil, plus the clues I've probably
given you here and there. You're not stupid." He started the
car. "It's amazing what people know. They just never say
anything, they deny it because they don't want to believe."
Yes, I thought, that was true. "Maybe Neil's mother even

knew what was going on, maybe she didn't want to believe that whatever was happening was really happening. Maybe *my* father, maybe *my* mother."

Brian shoved the dream journal back into my lap. "Turn to the last pages." I returned to the 11/22 entry. "No, snoop, the very end."

Flip, flip, flip. These pages stuck together, and when I pried them apart I saw reddish brown stains. "Your Rorschach test?"

"No," he said. "My blood." Brian glanced at his watch and backed the car from the baseball field. "The past few weeks, ever since I've been figuring things out, I've been getting nosebleeds. Haven't had them since I was a kid. Back then, the slightest pressure would burst capillaries." He touched his nose.

"I kept remembering something Avalyn said," he continued. "She talked about proof, about leaving remnants of yourself to prove something happened." At a red traffic light, he looked at me, and I placed my hand on the notebook's brittle pages. "My nose bled that night, the night of the missing five hours. Now that I know what happened, it's bleeding again. Strange, hmm? It's like my body's remembering, too." Brian's hand left the steering wheel. His fingers met mine on the dried smears and dots of blood. "This is my proof," he said.

I didn't have to give Brian directions. After he parked in the driveway, he simply sat, letting the car settle, as darkness lowered its canopy over Hutchinson's west side.

We stepped to the porch. In the McCormicks' bay window, blue and green lights winked from a tree garlanded with popcorn strings and candy canes. Tinsel speared from its branches like miniature javelins. A tin ornament was shaped like a gingerbread man, its eyes, smile, bow tie, and buttons chiseled into the surface by an amateur's hand, quite possibly Neil's as a child. I wondered if he'd made the ornament before or after that summer.

When I'd visited Neil in the past, his mom's excitement would overflow: the door would swing open, and she'd tug me inside as avidly as Hansel and Gretel's witch. Tonight her movements had slowed. "Good to see you both again," she said. "I apologize, though. Something happened. Neil's not well. Perhaps that's the best way to put it." Her voice sounded biblical: tired, wounded, meaningful. "He's had an accident. He's asleep now."

Mrs. McCormick pointed. On the kitchen table, two pies lounged beneath a divinity snowman, its raisin eyes and cinnamon stick arms guarding them. "But you can still stay. I've baked a peanut butter-peach, and a good old-fashioned apple."

Brian seemed lost. He eased into a chair, I took another, and Mrs. McCormick searched a drawer for a knife. Her searching knocked a wine bottle cork to the floor, and it bounced into a corner. I hunted for something to say. My gaze was preoccupied with pie number one's mosaic of peaches, peanut butter dollops, and crumbled graham crackers, and I didn't notice when the shadowy figure shuffled into the room.

"You're awake," his mom said.

Neil stood in the kitchen's doorway. His eyes looked drugged, slightly incongruous, and I saw that it wasn't a shadow beneath his right eye, but the gray crescent of a developing bruise. Another bruise curled across his cheekbone. His mouth wore a raspberryish sore. His earring was missing, the lobe swollen, infected. Below it, a cut had been Mercurochromed so thickly it glowed orange.

"Stop staring, Preston," Neil said. Then he stepped

toward Brian. "So you're the man." On "you're," his mouth widened to display his newly chipped tooth.

"Little League teammates," Mrs. McCormick said. She aimed the knife at a pie. "Neil never would have remembered a friend from that long ago. How neat that you managed to. How long since you two last saw each other?"

Neil touched the cut on his neck. "Not as long as it seems, I guess."

"Ten years," Brian said. "And five months, seven days."

I assisted Neil's mom by ordering the table with a quartet of forks and plates. "I'll have peanut butter-peach," she said. "How about you guys?" I chose the same, and Brian picked apple.

"One of both," Neil said. The bruise made his eye appear locked in a perpetual wink. I still loved him.

We ate, barely speaking beyond the standard "Mmm"s and "this is really great"s. Mrs. McCormick was the first to ease the tension. "This isn't the way Neil normally looks, Brian. He's a tough one, all right, but he's learning the hard way not to assert that toughness in just any old place. Hutchinson is one thing, New York is another." I saw him roll his eyes, mouth a silent, Oh, Mom. "By chance you ever go there, god forbid, take warning. If toughs on the street want something of yours, by all means give it to them, or else expect a scuffle." Brian nodded, but I didn't believe that's what had happened to Neil. I doubted Mrs. McCormick believed it, either.

After we finished, Neil gathered plates and forks, deposited them in the sink, and rubbed his mom's shoulders. "We're going to cruise around for a while," he told her. "There's something I need to show Brian."

"I imagine so," she said. "I guess you have some catching up to do." She saw us to the door; as we stepped out she gave us each a pat on the back. Then she stood there, waving.

•   •   •

Brian drove. Neil stammered directions. I sat in the back, but by then I could have sat on another continent and it wouldn't have mattered. They had crossed to another place. I floated away, inessential.

The Toyota turned onto Main. Ahead, beside the street, were the Kansas State Fairgrounds, the wreckage from the previous autumn's twelve-day carnival still remaining. Briefly I thought Neil would steer Brian there, but he indicated the opposite way. Brian swerved to a narrow street. "This is it up here," Neil said. "But you probably know that." Brian parked alongside the curb, shut the ignition, and folded his arms.

They got out, neither speaking. Brian fished the baseball photograph from between the seats. He stepped around the car and leaned against the passenger side door. Neil took his place beside him, wincing as he pushed himself onto the hood, and both he and Brian stared at the boxy, completely mundane house where we'd parked. When I joined them, the glassiness in their eyes looked foreign to me. I understood this as the place their coach had lived. The house sat back from a row of knee-high shrubs, a gravel path leading toward it. A two-door garage linked to the house's east side, its doors closed, a green garden hose snaking from its wall to the shrubs. Neighbors' homes were lit up, flashing their greetings and noels to the night street, but here, in this home from their memories, there was only darkness. No Christmas lights braceleted its exterior, no tree blinked its varicolored eyes from the front window. The only beacons were the illuminated doorbell's tiny rectangular beam and the porch light, the globe of which shone a curious blue instead of white.

"Blue," Brian said, seeing it.

Down the block, a group of carolers trudged through the cold, pausing before each house to warble their songs to neighborhood families. I listened awhile, not knowing what to do or say. No matter what the carolers sang about—the infant Jesus, enchanted snowmen, nightfall over an ancient village—their words seemed the same. A security underlied their voices, a knowledge that they'd soon be home in bed, a log snapping sparks in the fireplace, mom and dad snoozing in the next room.

"Merry Christmas," the carolers yelled at a doorstep.

"Merry Christmas," I said to Neil and Brian. They still stared at the house, stared beyond its glass and wood and aluminum siding, stared at what had happened inside, years ago. Neil's face was anxious, heartbreaking in its bruised and swollen state. Brian's face had leached of color.

I wasn't part of this. Where else did I have to go but away?

I could have said "I have to leave now," could have explained "it's better if you two are alone," but I didn't say a word. I raised my hand, fingers scratching the air in good-bye, and spun around. I stood there, my back to them, these two people I'd united at last. Then I began walking. The air made brittle stabs at my face, and I swallowed icy mouth-fuls.

I tried telepathy one final time. I didn't care about its foolishness. I zeroed my mind on theirs, hoping Neil and Brian would hear, just this once. *I love you both.*

A long-haired boy bent over the sidewalk at a neighboring house, his zebra-striped mittens sprinkling salt pebbles onto the cement in rhythm with the Christmas carol down the block. The boy seemed around my age. Neil's age. Brian's age. I wondered if he'd lived on this street ten years ago; if he'd known Coach. And then I wondered how many others there had been—where they lived now, the diversity of ways they'd chosen to remember. The boy stopped shaking the salt and hurried toward his house. I kept my head down, staring at the gravel lane, as if immersed in a book, a series of soothing and beautiful words spelled out across the roadside to lead me home.

seventeen

BRIAN LACKEY

The nervousness subsided, and my limbs grew numb. For the first time, Neil and I were alone, and we stood beside the house's battered garage to watch Eric's shadow trail farther away, each successive streetlight flashing him in and out of vision until his grandpa's white sweater was nothing but a speck.

I turned and stared at the house. "Blue," I said again.

There it was, the precise blue from countless nightmares, flooding the air around us as we moved toward the front door. The color came from the porch light, and it radiated a fuzzy semicircle over the yard. That same blue had shone through the windows on that long-ago evening, the rainy night Neil and I had been together inside this house.

Neil followed the gravel walkway toward the cement porch. He paused under the blue light, poised one knuckle against the door, and rapped gently. He waited, then moved his bruised eye to the door's rectangular window to peer inside. Breath steamed the glass. "No one's home." He rattled the doorknob. Locked. "Let's try the back," he said, jumping from the porch.

We skulked around the garage, and Neil lifted the latch on a chain-link fence. The backyard was a jungle of tangled, skeletal weeds; their frozen vines and stems crackled beneath our shoes as we walked. Stabbed into the earth were plastic sunflowers, the kind that pinwheel in the wind. Neil kicked one, splintering three of its petals. A cardinal regarded him from a circle of dirt, a female, her feathers a rustic caramel color. Instead of flying south, she had chosen to remain here, in this overgrown garden where I imagined marigolds and morning glories and bachelor's buttons would bloom in a warmer season.

Neil tried the back door; it was locked as well. He spied an overturned lawn chair, brushed away its layer of sand, and unfolded it under a window. He stepped onto it carefully, his body clutched by pain; still, there was a certain level of fused skill and grace in the way he moved. "You were a great baseball player, weren't you," I said. It was the first reference I'd made to the conversation I knew we'd imminently have. "I used to watch you from the bench."

"I was the best," Neil said. "He told me so."

Neil cupped a hand over his brow and peered into the window. "It's changed, but it's the same place." He stepped down, one foot on the ground, one on the chair. "What do you think? I say we go in."

Down the block, closer now, the carolers segued from "The First Noel" to another song I didn't recognize. Their voices wavered, as if each kid were shivering. The cardinal lifted into the air, flitting back and forth between two trees as deftly as a badminton birdie. Neil scanned the ground, and I followed his gaze. Beside a beehive-shaped snarl of weeds were glass shards, broken bricks, a rusting tin top from a cat food can, and children's toys: rubber pony, plastic shovel, foot-size fire engine. Neil kicked a brick. "Should I do the honors, or should you?"

"You'd better," I said. I bent to pick up a square brick chunk, then changed my mind. My hand closed around the fire engine. I relayed it to Neil, and he remounted the lawn chair.

He made a curious sound in his throat, a noise like a microphone's static. "Bottom of the ninth inning, and the score is tied," he said. "Bases loaded, two outs, the count full. McCormick rares back." Neil swung the fire engine behind him. "And here's the pitch." I held my breath, and he hurled the toy at the window. The glass shattered, the crash surprisingly quiet. "Strike three," Neil said.

Three more bashes of the fire engine's front end knocked the rest of the glass away. Neil tossed the toy back to the ground, and it clattered against a brick. He positioned his hands on the window frame and squirmed into the gaping wound. I hurried forward, gripped his shoes, and nudged him farther. The house swallowed him.

My climb was more difficult. I rolled up the Little League photograph, wedged it into my pocket, and stretched myself from the lawn chair. I would have to chance accident by stepping onto the chair's back and quickly thrusting my head and shoulders through the window. "Three, two, one, BLAST OFF," Neil said. It worked. I leaned into the house, and Neil's hands coupled with mine. I stared as our fingers intertwined; saw a triangular scar on Neil's knuckle. Neil pulled me through, and I tumbled to the floor.

Neil and I scanned our surroundings. My eyes adjusted to the drapery of shadows, and the room asserted itself: lamp carved from driftwood, mirrored dresser scattered with paperback gothic romances and makeup, paintings of a stormy beach scene and a cabin in a forest clearing. It must have been the family's master bedroom, considering the unmade double bed, the walk-in closet with sliding glass doors. "Not much for interior decoration, are they?" Neil asked.

I turned to him then, and for the first time that night I truly stared. Neil was my approximate height. His hair and eyes were pitch black, his eyebrows so thick they seemed mascaraed across his forehead. He had hardly changed from the boy in my pocket's photograph, that Little Leaguer's face a bud that had blossomed into the face before me. He was Neil McCormick, number ninety-nine. Seeing him after all these months, all these years, dried me up. I felt like a shell, with a mouthful of grist and an ice cube heart.

A pair of cats puttered forth from the hallway's darkness, noses in the air. The first was stocky and gray, white fur like a bib beneath her chin. The second had long, almost silvery hair, which pieced onto the floor as she rubbed against Neil's foot. "Awww," Neil said, and the jaw he'd been clenching for the past half hour instantly relaxed. He bent to scratch her head, and the cat's topaz eyes examined him. She begged for food, making a feeble and wee noise, more a wounded crackle than a meow, the sound of a dollhouse door, creaking open.

"Coach didn't use this room much," Neil said. "He kept baseball equipment here, other crap, odds and ends." He moved into the hall, and the cats and I followed.

We gave ourselves a tour. The house oozed a baby odor, a sugary combination of perfumy talcums and lotions and diapers, a smell surprisingly like roasted sweet potatoes. But something else lurked beneath that, and when I inhaled I got a whiff of the house itself, the smell that had attended its rooms for years, a smell as familiar as the blue light.

"Here's the hallway, the bathroom, the linen closet. And this"—Neil slapped a half-open door—"was his bedroom."

Neil went in, but I stayed in the doorway. He flicked the light switch, and I squinted. "They've made it a nursery," he said. On the wallpaper, elephants and clowns juggled polka-dotted balls. Figureheads decorated the bassinet's posts.

Cornflower blue jumpers, bibs, and socks had been layered across the floor, awaiting use. Neil switched off the light and stretched beside the baby's clothes, the movement causing him obvious pain. He stared upward. "He's here no longer, and the bed's here no longer. But that's the same ceiling." I looked. "All the little ridges and whirls and speckly-sparkly things. I used to get lost in its pictures, after we'd finished." He sat up. "You know what I mean by that, don't you."

"I know what you mean," I said.

Back to the hallway. There were two more rooms: a spacious kitchen to our left, the living room to our right. Neil tiptoed into the kitchen; the cats scampered about his ankles, expecting dinner. But I began walking slowly into the main room, my skin gradually translating, deepening to the translucent blue with each step as I moved toward the picture window, into the glow of the outside porch light. The world's silence swelled until I could hear my heartbeat. I stopped in the room's center. Here I was, at last, in the room from my dreams.

Behind me, Neil opened and slammed the kitchen's cupboard doors. "What's up with these people? He used to keep these things *stocked*." I turned to watch him prop a cookie jar between elbow and ribs like a football. He opened the lid, reached inside, and gobbled something I couldn't see. "That's better."

He noticed me staring. Whatever face I was making, its horror or solemnity stopped Neil in his tracks. He moved toward me and posted his hand on my shoulder. "Yes," he said. "This was the place, wasn't it?"

I reached up, grabbed his hand, and led him to a couch. Purple lilacs filigreed its upholstery. I sat on one flower, and he took another. The silvery white cat wandered in, upturned her implacable face, and creaked at us.

"Why now?" Neil asked. "Why do you need this now? Why did you search me out?"

"I'm tired of it," I said. "I want to dream about something else for a change."

Neil leaned against the cushions. Blue outlined his cheeks and chin, sapphiring his pupils, lending the medicine stain an eerie fluorescence. I was still holding his hand. The numbness persisted, and I waited for it to melt, waited to feel something new. Neil watched the frozen world outside the room's window for what seemed hours. Finally he turned his head to look at me.

"It's time," I said. "Speak." The forbidden moment had come; Neil would have to tell his story. Before he even opened his wounded mouth I knew what he would say. I knew it as conclusively as I knew my family, my self, and as he spoke it seemed as though his story had already ended, I was already tucked away in some warm and secure place, I was already remembering his words.

eighteen

NEIL MCCORMICK

"Look down from the sky . . . and stay by my cradle 'til morning is nigh." Or so sang the carolers. By the sound of their voices, they huddled together only a few houses from Coach's doorstep. I scanned the room, thoughts rocketing through my mind so quickly I couldn't catalog them: there's the spot where he kept his stack of video games. . . . Right about there, he first took my picture. . . . The same window where he'd drawn the blinds before he carried me to bed. . . .

I knew I had to talk now. Brian waited, eyes blinking behind his glasses, resembling a kid inside his first chamber of horrors. Holding his hand seemed preposterous, so I let go. If we were stars in the latest Hollywood blockbuster, then I would have embraced him, my hands patting his shoulderblades, violins and cellos billowing on the soundtrack as tears streamed down our faces. But Hollywood would never make a movie about us.

"It took a while to remember you," I told him. "Eric's letter mentioned you, and something seemed familiar. But really. I've never seen a UFO, let alone stepped inside one. If a little green man had examined me, I doubt I'd forget it." Brian smiled, his mouth an awkward arc. In the darkness he appeared almost handsome. "So I knew there was some-

283

thing more to your story. And then it hit me, who you were."

Brian stuffed hands in pockets and unrolled a photograph. "Look at this." Although the dark loosened its particulars, I could still make out the picture of the Panthers. "That one's me," Brian said, circling his face with his finger. His expression in the photo seemed lost, hopeless. "And that's you." I almost laughed at my pushed-forth chest, the black sunblock bisecting my face. Brian pointed to the figure next to me, but this time he didn't say a word. It was Coach. Even in shadow, I could distinguish the baseball cap, the steady and rehearsed grin, the mustache.

"I feel like he's watching us," I said. "But as for where he is now, I haven't the slightest. He coached some summers after the Panthers, but his teams were made up of older kids. I've always guessed someone complained, and the Little League people assigned him boys he couldn't handle in the ways he wanted. So I think he moved after that. I really can't say. For all I know, he could have suffered a stroke or a brain aneurysm, right here in this room. Maybe his ghost is watching us as we speak."

Brian seemed to ponder that idea, his eyes examining the room's china cabinet, its ottoman, stopping at its rocking chair. "He came back for me," he said. "It was an accident. It was Halloween, and I think some of the older Little League boys were with him. He saw me, he knew it was me. He followed me into some dark trees. It's the only time I'd seen him, and I haven't seen him since." Outside, a car slid past, headlights sneaking into the window to highlight Brian's face. "Maybe I'll never, ever remember the rest about that night. The reason is because I was alone with him. But the first time it happened was different. You were there. I'm relying on you now."

The photograph dropped to the carpet and curled like a scroll. I considered the best way to begin. I felt stranded, as though delivering a speech to a stadium filled with listeners. "This is crazy, but inside here are things I've never told." I traced an *X* across my heart with my fist. "Eric doesn't know, Mom doesn't know. I don't think anyone can understand, really. And this will sound odd, but when it first started happening, the feeling I felt more than anything else was honored." Brian looked at the floor, nodding. "He had chosen me, you know? Out of all the boys on the team, he'd picked me. Like I'd been blessed or something. He taught me things no other boy on the team or at school could know. I was his."

The cats stretched out to lounge at our feet. I resumed my story, gradually leading to the point in the plot where Brian appeared. "I guess he suckered me in. He was there at the right time, Mom was with Alfred, I was learning things early." Brian nodded still. "Are you following me?"

"Just go on. Don't stop."

"Coach took me to movies, told me I was his star player. He stuffed me full of candy and let me win a trillion video games. And then he was there, on top of me on the kitchen floor, rubbing his dick against my bare belly." I could still feel the scratch of the coarse platinum hairs on Coach's arms. I glanced to my left; to the kitchen's features that hadn't changed: the lemony color of the cabinets, paint spattered at the window's corners, the chandelier's green glass teardrops. I had watched those dangling above me, catching the light, on that summer afternoon, the floor beneath me carpeted with cereal. *Here we go.*

"After that, there was no turning back. From then on, I'd do anything he wanted. It lasted that whole summer. We were . . . in love." Those words were no longer accurate. I tried to spit out a laugh when I said them, possibly because I'd never said them aloud, had only kept them silent, for years, inside my head. But my throat had no laughter left in it. "I guess I sound like I'm preaching, like there's a moral here, that I should start bawling and scream 'my childhood was taken from me.' But I don't believe that."

There was so much more I could tell him, but everything seemed irrelevant. "We were in love," I'd said, and I wanted to take that back, wanted Brian to speak. I placed my tongue against the inside of my cheek, tasting the steely bud of my wound, soothing the place where the shampoo bottle had smashed my face. I know you want it, the john had said. Had that only been last night? New York seemed lifetimes away.

"The game had started," Brian said. "I sat on the bench, as usual. I wasn't good at baseball like you. And then everyone looked up at the rain, sprinkles at first, then torrents, drenching everything. The umpire called the game."

"Yes," I said. "I remember that. But no one was there to pick you up."

"My mother was working, she had planned to leave early to take me home after the game. But she didn't plan on a rain-out. My father had better things to do. I just stood there, as everyone drove off with their parents. And then you came over, you were beside me in the dugout. 'We'll drive you home,' you said."

Another car's high beams lit up the room, briefly illuminating the trio of people in the wall's framed portrait: a spectacled, orange-sweatered mom, a dad with an overbite and necktie, a baby in blue frills between them. The light stunned Brian. He must have thought the owners had returned, because he shot from the couch, then sat back down. "Sorry. I'm jumpy." He proceeded to explain that I had to continue the story from here. He called the rest "a blur," saying it was all part of five hours he'd forgotten.

"You sat in the back of Coach's station wagon." I could see him there. *I'll take you home, Brian,* Coach had yelled to the backseat, *but first we'll go to my house.* "He drove to his place. I led you around. But he didn't want you in the bedroom. That was our special place, I guess, reserved for just us two." I wanted to believe that. "He was in the mood for something different. He wanted both of us right here, in this very room."

I paused again, but Brian objected. "Keep going. Don't stop again until you've finished."

"The routine was the same whenever Coach invited someone else over," I said. "He used me as the prop to pull you in. I stretched out on his couch, which"—I patted the space between our seats—"was a hell of a lot more comfortable than this. And he took off my clothes. I wasn't even conscious of being naked; it's like God or whoever had created me to be that way. And I oohed and aahed to give the impression that what he was doing to me was the greatest thing I'd ever known." In a way, I thought, it was. Or it had been, at one time, now only part of memory. "That way, you'd be there, on the other side of the room, hopefully wanting Coach to do to you what he was doing to me. He had planned it all.

"In the game he played, I had to do things to you first, like a warm-up. I'd kiss you a little, preparing you, slipping my tongue inside to get your mouth all wet and shiny before he shoved his big soft lips and that thick mustache over your face and nearly ate you alive."

"I think I remember that part," Brian said. His voice was a spider's, hidden away in some far corner's web. "It came to me with Avalyn. I knew it wasn't the first time I'd been kissed." I didn't know what he meant, but when I started to ask he stopped me. "I'll shut up. Go on."

"Coach and I got your clothes off, touched and massaged you all over. I guess you whimpered, made sounds a deaf-mute would make. Coach loved that. His favorite thing was laying his tongue inside a kid's mouth, so I presume he sucked around at your tongue awhile. Then things progressed. There was this little game I loved, where Coach would open his mouth as wide as a fist and circle me with it. I mean my dick, my balls, everything." I expected Brian to blush here, but if he did I couldn't tell. I only saw his face, limned by the porch light's deep blue. "He did that to me, and then I tried to do it to you. To show you everything was A-OK. But my mouth was nothing like his. I was just a boy. So he went down on you, sucked and sucked. I watched, amazed and jealous and ten thousand other emotions. You kept your eyes closed mostly, but when they fluttered open they were glassy, far away."

Brian moved closer to me. I could see his hands shaking, and he bunched them in his lap. Then he took a deep breath, and as he exhaled he made a soft moaning sound. I realized he was trying not to cry. If I had a spirit, I felt it fly out of me then. And if Brian had a spirit, it flew hand in hand with mine, lifting above the couch, passing through the roof, hovering in the black and measureless air that blanketed the house where Coach once lived.

"Then the other game began. The five-dollar game." The carolers stood next door now, their voices harmonizing in the December chill. *Yet in the dark street shineth, the everlasting light.* "Coach would make me do things, crazy sex things, and if I could do them I'd get a five-dollar bill. Usually I'd get it even if I couldn't do them, just seeing my effort was enough for him. And he must have had an extra five bucks that night, because he wanted you in on things, too."

I waited. I could almost see Coach, standing over us, one hand on my shoulder, one on Brian's. *Go ahead, Neil.*

"We had to fist him. Do you know what that means?" Brian nodded, but by then his face seemed so dazed he would have made the necessary gesture at anyone. "I went first, of course. To show you. He stood over us, we looked up at him. That always got him off, I guess, seeing those surprised kid faces staring up like that. Or so I gathered, considering all the pictures in his photo album. On that night, the five-dollar bill was mine if I could reach inside him, ram my little fist inside his ass, then wring it all the way to the elbow. And goddamn, I did it. The way it felt— like plunging my arm into a tight, tight sleeve, its insides covered with wet sponges, and then the suction of his ass, squeezing my elbow—it was like his body wanted me inside it, it wanted to devour me whole. I can't forget that."

"And then it was my turn," Brian said. He snarled his words, his voice almost angry. "I did it, too. I know, because I felt the inside of the calf." His hand—no, his entire body— was trembling.

"Yes, you did it. Coach there, his ass jutting out, his face sort of erased and this blissed-out look replacing it. And you kneeling on the floor, your arm disappeared, gone, the fist and wrist and forearm swallowed up by his body." I could remember Brian perfectly now, that lost look in his eyes, eight years old. And I'd been right beside him.

And I could remember Coach, as well, perhaps better now than ever before. But something had changed. "Love"—that was what I'd always termed the emotion I carried for Coach. Now it was different, an emotion I had no adequate word for.

I couldn't go on. "And we put our clothes on, we got in the station wagon, drove you back to Little River, and dropped you off in your driveway. The end."

"And I had a nosebleed. Don't forget the nosebleed. It wasn't from aliens and their tracking devices. It was something else. I want to know how it happened."

I was sinking into the couch, it was suffocating me. I

stood and stepped across the room to the window. "You were so dazed you couldn't stand up straight. It was like he'd ripped something free from you, whatever controlled your balance, and when your arm pulled out of him you fell. Weird. You fell face first into my knee, and when we twisted you up onto the couch your nose was shooting this geyser of blood."

"Like this?" His voice lifted, excited, almost shrieking. "Like this?"

I turned from the window. The blue still shone off Brian's face, but he had removed his glasses, and his eyes had altered. They glittered and flashed like a puppy's. And below them, dribbling from one nostril, a stream of blood. It glistened, almost black. As I stared, its flow grew heavier, trickling down Brian's upper lip, his lower lip, his chin. "Like this?" he asked a third time, and he knocked his knuckle against his nose. The blood spurted then, a gush of it staining his jacket, his shirt, a lilac on the couch's cushion.

I bounded back to him. "Stop," I said. I pulled his hand from his face and propped his head into my lap, his nose in the air. I had to stop the bleeding. I swiped my fingers across his face, and his blood made an inky flourish on my hand.

Brian closed his eyes, blood trailing down his cheek and matting his hair. I felt it, damp and warm, seeping through my pant leg. It was Brian's blood, and for some reason I knew it was pure. No other man I'd held in my arms—and now, not even I—had blood this pure.

His eyes reopened, and he looked up at me. "Tell me, Neil," he said. "Tell me more."

I could hear the carolers' footsteps, their hushed giggles. They approached Coach's house. We had to leave soon. "One more thing," I said. "You were so erased that when Coach gave you the five bucks, you just let the bill drop to the floor. I saw the money lying there, and I picked it up. It was mine." Brian tried to exhale from his nose, and a bubble of blood widened and popped. "So I owe you, Brian. I've owed you that, all these years." I lifted his head a little, patted my ass for my wallet, found a five-dollar bill.

The carolers clomped toward the porch, arguing over what carols they still hadn't sung. "No one's even home," one said. "Let's yell Trick or Treat," said another. If I were in my regular mood, I'd stand at the door, smile through one or two songs, then hurl a fistful of dimes and nickels at them with all the strength I could muster. As I thought this, I heard a loud "Shhh." Brian and I froze, waiting. "Someone's home," a boy insisted, and when I looked to the window I saw a face peering in at us, a head with a red-balled stocking cap, gaping mouth, spying eyes made blue by the never-ending porch light. I tried to picture the scene he saw: two boys in the dark, sprawled together on the couch, holding hands; one battered and bruised, the other bleeding from the nose.

They began singing "Silent Night," which had always been my favorite as a little boy. They finished the first line, and Brian sat up from the couch. The blood's flow was subsiding. He pinched the five-dollar bill in both hands, looked at me, and ripped it in half. Again. He began tearing it then, ripping the halves into more halves, until the bill was torn into hundreds of pieces. He cupped the pieces in his palm and threw them, green shreds of money showering across the floor.

Brian leaned his head back into my lap. "It's over," he said.

"Silent Night" paused, and a caroler giggled. I stroked Brian's hair with my stained fingers. I wanted to tell him not to worry, that everything would be fine, but I couldn't speak. I just kept holding him, touching his hair and his face, letting him know I was sorry.

In the middle of that quiet I heard a soft clicking noise. At first the sound puzzled me; then I recognized it as that of a key in a lock. Brian panicked, standing from the couch, pulling me up with him as we attempted to make our break. But it was too late. The house's door clattered open, and the room's light flickered on.

A woman gasped. Through the open door I could see a sliver of carolers, some faces peering inside at the scattered tatters of money, some faces turned to the sky and the snow, now beginning to fall. And there, in front of them, in the room with us, stood the family, their outlines barely visible within the weight of the room's light. It was a light that shone over our faces, our wounds and scars. It was a light so brilliant and white it could have been beamed from heaven, and Brian and I could have been angels, basking in it. But it wasn't, and we weren't.